THEY'RE
SCHEMI...
DAZZLING PL...

TAVA: She was born to a world of wealth and luxury. But love was something she had to discover the hard way—on her own . . .

BUDDY: Texas rich and Dallas dangerous, he would betray his own father to get what he wanted—and what he wanted was the only thing Tava had held back . . .

GRACE: Twisted with drugs and alcohol, there was only one person she hated more than herself—her own daughter . . .

MICHAEL: Caught between a sex-crazed kidnapper and the most ruthless magnates in America, he found the courage to fight for the woman he loved . . .

THOMAS: America's top corporate raider, he did more than swim with the sharks—he fed on them . . .

HANK: His rival's wealth wasn't enough for him. He wanted his women too . . .

MONTANA HEAT

VALERIE GREY

POCKET BOOKS

New York   London   Toronto   Sydney   Tokyo   Singapore

This book is a work of fiction. Names, characters, places and incidents are either the product of the author's imagination or are used fictitiously. Any resemblance to actual events or locales or persons, living or dead, is entirely coincidental.

An *Original* Publication of POCKET BOOKS

 POCKET BOOKS, a division of Simon & Schuster
1230 Avenue of the Americas, New York, NY 10020

ISBN: 0-671-72728-1

First Pocket Books printing January 1991

10 9 8 7 6 5 4 3 2 1

POCKET and colophon are registered trademarks of
Simon & Schuster.

Printed in the U.S.A.

Montana Heat is for Katie, Libby, Kristin, Becky, Valerie and Carolyn. Their insightful comments encouraged and challenged me through three revisions.

And to my parents, Carolyn and Ken, for loving my first efforts and helping me believe that someday, if I worked hard enough, I could get published.

1

"I hope it's going to be peaceful," she whispered and smiled. Tava Blackhurst tried to hold her small, soft hands together in her lap. She was too excited to keep herself still.

The private jet pushed its way through the billowy white clouds over Wyoming toward Montana. The blue sky shimmered with an uncontrollable excitement.

"How're you doing, Tava?" a deep voice called over the speaker, filling the small cabin.

Tava picked up the receiver and said, "I'm fine, Mark. It's such a beautiful day, isn't it?"

"You should see up here. I'm watching the Grand Tetons. They're beautiful. You want to come up?"

"I think I'll stay put. Thanks anyway."

"You used to love sitting up here when you were little," Mark chuckled. "I guess college graduates aren't interested in this stuff."

Tava laughed out loud. "I swear, Mark, no one lays it on thicker than you."

"It comes naturally."

"Graduating from college is not a big deal. I don't know what the hell I'm going to do with the rest of my life."

"Don't worry about it, Tava. Just relax and let life happen."

"Easy for you to say."

"You worry too much."

"Sometimes."

"Well, hang in there, kiddo."

"Thanks." She replaced the receiver gently and turned her attention to the mountains twelve thousand feet below.

A warm, calm energy spilled through her young body and she shivered. She was almost home. Within the hour she would be walking through the front door of Blackhurst Manor. She had been waiting for this moment since September. All year long she had known that she would return to her family's summer home. It was here, in the shadows of the mountains, nestled on the outskirts of Sultan Valley, that Tava was going to decide what to do with her life. Nothing had prepared her for life outside of school and she was scared. Feeling off balance, she was hurrying home to sort her thoughts out. Blackhurst Manor was where she felt safest.

At twenty-one Tava Blackhurst was a graduate of William and Mary with a degree in English literature. She was a cultured, beautiful, bright young woman with her life ahead of her. She met challenges with a strong sense of determination and was eager to take the next step in her life, but she did not know what that was. Unlike her father, Thomas Blackhurst, she was not driven by an unerring passion. He loved buying and selling companies and it filled his every waking moment; it consumed him. But Tava craved inspiration. Though she wanted to be told what to do, she knew the decision was all hers. How she hated the independence that was being thrust upon her! It was a new experience and she was having trouble adjusting.

As Tava sat there filled with self-doubt, she was struck with a memory. Her mind drifted back six months to Christmas morning.

The snow was silently pelting the huge Georgian windows. Central Park was dusted with a white blanket of fresh December snow. From the penthouse the world seemed like a fairy tale. It was six in the morning and the streets far below were empty. Tava was sitting near the blazing fire, dressed in a white cotton nightgown and flannel robe, watching her father open his gifts.

It was just the two of them. It did not seem strange without her mother. She was in Spain, traveling with a close friend. Grace Blackhurst was not much for holidays. So much the better, Tava thought, more time to spend with Daddy.

Thomas ripped the wrapping paper away with a flourish. He paused dramatically, eyes closed, feeling for the contents.

"Come on, Daddy."

"Got to keep the mystery alive, honey."

"Oh, please." Tava was waiting expectantly. She was holding her breath. The anticipation was too much for her. This was a gift Thomas had been hunting down for almost two years. It had taken tremendous energy to find it. "Be careful, Daddy. It's old."

"Old?" A questioning look came to his face. "Really." He was teasing her now. He knew how to get her going and loved to get her riled. He loved these quiet moments with her. These special times were the moments he cherished and clung to. Tava was his only child and he cared for her deeply.

"Come on, Daddy. I can't stand it."

"All right already." He opened his eyes and gaped in amazement. He was holding a thick, leather-bound copy of the Bible. Its cover was gold edged and the leather was musty with the worn markings of a very rare edition.

As Thomas gingerly leafed through its thick, ancient pages he was overcome with gratitude. "Where did you find this?"

Tava was beaming. She knew how much he wanted this for his collection. "A friend at school. Her father trades books in Germany. He helped me."

"My God, Tava, do you have any idea how happy this makes me?"

"It is the one you were looking for, right?"

"Absolutely. It fills my collection. I didn't think I was ever going to find it."

"You just have to know where to look." She slapped at his leg playfully. "My turn."

"You? What do you want a gift for?"

"Come on, Dad."

He pulled a small box from his pocket. The box was wrapped in a colorful, floral chintz. It was small and beautiful. "Here. I hope you like it."

Tava accepted it quietly. Her father was always too extravagant and this little box promised amazing things. She almost didn't want to open it. She eased the top open and sat back heavily. It was a delicate 18-karat ring with a tiny band of diamonds. It caught the flickering of the fire and gleamed in the warm, half darkness of the living room.

Tava, with tears in her eyes, slipped the delicate piece out and placed it on her right pinkie. It was deliberately small and exquisitely crafted. She didn't know what to say.

"Beats socks, huh?"

Tava shook her head yes and leaned over to hug her father. She managed to squeeze out "Thank you, Daddy," before crying again.

The ring was her great-grandmother's. Great-grandmother Isabell was the first to make the trek from Europe a century ago. This ring was the symbol of the hard work that urged Isabell on in her early years. She commissioned it for herself at seventy-five and wore it till the day she died. In her will she decreed it be handed down to the family member destined to keep the flame alive. And Tava, just past twenty-one, and five months away from a college graduation, was being handed the most important Blackhurst family heirloom.

"Daddy, you can't give me this."

"Why not?"

"I haven't done anything yet. I'm nobody."

Thomas chuckled. "Well, Ms. Nobody, it's yours. Your great-grandmother started from nothing and look where we are now."

"You and I know that Great-grandma had nothing to do with where we are now. All of this is because of you and your hard work. You were the one who made our fortune."

Thomas was embarrassed. "Yes, well, that's beside the point. The ring is all yours and she wanted you to have it."

"Wearing it makes me nervous. I don't think I deserve it."

"Trust me, you do. There are big things in store for you, honey. I know it."

"I hope so 'cause I have no idea what I want to do with my life."

"Graduate and then you can figure it out." The ring looked perfect on her finger. It looked like it'd been made for her. "You look very beautiful." He cupped her chin in his strong hand. "I love you, Tava. You deserve that and a lot more. You make me very proud."

A tiny pocket of air jolted the private jet and shook Tava from her memory. She felt like crying. She loved her father and only wished she could spend more time with him. She knew he was an exceptionally busy man and did not begrudge him his work. It filled him with joy and she was content with sharing what free time he did have.

Tava began to feel the plane descending. It reminded her that her mother would be waiting at the airport and that thought filled her with a sense of nervousness. Tava approached each new situation with her mother carefully. They rarely agreed on anything and Tava knew from experience that Grace could be emotional. Her mother seemed to be predisposed to anger. Tava desperately wanted the summer to go smoothly.

"Promise me you won't step on her toes," Tava whispered to herself. "Just smile and be pretty and don't make any waves." She had a funny way of talking to herself when she was thinking about her mother. She was almost coaching herself through their impending meeting. Tava was not scared, but more anxious. It had been quite some time since they last saw each other and Tava knew her mother would be on edge.

The more she thought about her relationship with Grace, the more she was confused. All of her friends at school seemed to get along with their mothers. She wondered if it was just herself. She spent hours analyzing the situation and finally reached the conclusion that Grace did not like her. That was a hard pill to take but it helped her understand the situation. Tava was determined to get around this roadblock, though, and find a way to get through to her mother. She was tired of feeling she had to walk lightly whenever Grace was around. It upset her, and Tava decided to try and make things better.

The Fasten Seat Belt sign lit up and Mark's soothing voice came on, "Tava, we're starting our descent. We should be landing in about ten minutes." He clicked off.

She pulled her seat belt on and cinched it tightly across her lap. The one last thought she turned her attention to was Michael Petersen. Tava knew he was down there, working at the Sultan Valley Resort. She had invited him to the annual Blackhurst Ball and had five days to unwind till then. She decided to give herself those days and then see him at the party. Tava had to force herself to stay away from him because she felt it was important.

Their relationship started last summer and blossomed. They tried to continue the romance through the year but both found it difficult. She was on the east coast and he was on the west. This summer was going to be the final test. If their feelings were still the same, then there was a chance that it would last. Tava knew she was fixating on him and only hoped that he felt the same way. But with great resolve she held back and decided their first meeting should be at the party. It would be safer that way and easier to cover the hurt if his feelings had changed.

With that decision behind her she leaned back in her seat and closed her eyes. The images of her father, mother, and Michael filled her imagination and began to blend together. She did not try and separate them as they danced inside her head in a colorful collage of light and sound.

As the plane lost altitude Tava began to feel the pressure building in her ears. It was not painful but irritating. She gripped the arms of the leather seat and held them tightly, waiting for the airplane tires to touch firmly on the ground.

2

The plane was late. The busy airport, nestled at the foot of a mountain range, teemed with people. Summer was arriving in Sultan Valley and the air was warm and smelled wonderfully sweet. Only a few white clouds dotted the sky as the mountain winds swirled gently in the small valley.

Planes landed every few minutes and taxied to their private hangars. Grace lounged in the bar, watching with the detached air of a drunken woman. The dark interior enveloped her as she slumped over the counter adjusting her diamond earrings and ordering another martini. Running long fingers through her silver hair, she sighed heavily and waited for her third drink.

She was tired and upset. Tava was not supposed to come this summer.

The drink was placed on the bar and she tossed down two

dollars. She sipped the dry liquid quickly, feeling silly and lonely. Her short hair harshly framed her thin face. Her eyelids were held in place with several wipes of mascara. She used it heavily to accentuate her green eyes. A tiny nose hung over full painted red lips. Her face was like a tired mask.

Grace shook her head slowly from side to side. She was sinking farther into depression. Gulping her last few sips, she clunked the glass on the counter. She was feeling sick now and quick movements made her unsteady.

A voice came over the intercom, "Grace Blackhurst. Grace Blackhurst. Proceed to hangar nineteen. Your party has arrived."

Tava was here.

Grace let the tingling sensation subside. Grabbing her purse, she left the bar and staggered outside to the walkway. The heat caught her by surprise and forced her to lean against the wall for support. She pulled a tissue from her sleeve and dabbed it against her forehead. In the distance she watched the Learjet taxi to the family hangar. She found it ugly.

Regaining her composure, Grace made her way to the low slung building. The gangway lowered hydraulically and the captain stepped off. He was a good-looking man in his late thirties. Gray was creeping handsomely in around his temples and Grace found it appealing. Captain Mark Young was going on his sixth year with Blackhurst Industries. He tipped his hat toward her.

"Good afternoon, Mrs. Blackhurst. How are you?" He smiled a perfect smile.

"Mark," she grinned and brushed her hair back. "I'm a little unsteady. This damn heat always gets to me."

"I love this weather." He breathed deeply, taking in as much of the clean mountain air as his lungs could hold. "It was humid in New York."

"I miss the city. Did you see my husband?"

"He'll be coming in a few days." Mark was anxious to move on. Grace was dangerous. The woman was known for her volatile personality.

"Coming to the ball?"

Mark shook his head no. "I'm going to be out of town. I'm sorry."

Grace winked at him. "Too bad," she almost purred. "I was so hoping."

Mark shrugged, a little embarrassed. "Tava will be out in a moment. I'll see you later." He moved off toward the parking lot.

Grace was not a mother's mother. She was more detached. She was a disinterested observer in her daughter's life. Tava, to Grace, was another trophy to be dusted off for special occasions.

Grace discovered early on that she had no interest in raising her daughter. She treated Tava as an unplanned mistake and while Thomas forbade her from ever telling Tava, it boiled quietly underneath her cool exterior. Grace had not wanted children but Thomas had pleaded with her to carry his daughter to term. She agreed, but when Tava was born, she immediately had her tubes tied. Grace did not want another child and felt victorious in guaranteeing the mistake would not happen again.

Grace felt old next to Tava and it gnawed at her. From the beginning she had felt challenged by her daughter and it was this jealousy that Grace found hard to hide.

Tava's upbringing was relegated to a nanny, and Grace was happy to be rid of the responsibility. Thomas had to stop her from sending Tava to boarding school but Grace succeeded in sending her off to summer camps. It was because of these episodes that she began to feel estranged from Thomas. Grace was too proud to fight against it and secretly blamed her daughter. It was a nagging problem that would not go away.

"Tava!" Grace snarled. The heat was making her itch. She wore a short-sleeved, cotton Vanderbilt, and the sun was burning her arms.

"I'll be out in a minute," yelled Tava from inside. "You can wait in the car if you want." She sounded happy. There was a grating bounce in her voice aggravating Grace's headache.

"Hurry up!" She wiped at the perspiration beading along her hairline. The sun was hurting her eyes.

And suddenly Tava was there at the door. She was beautiful with long dusty blond hair tied loosely in a braid down her back. Her bangs were short and fell around her graceful forehead in a pleasing mess. She was five feet seven and perfectly proportioned. Her features were square and firm like her father's. Her deep blue eyes danced with a sprightly fire that mimicked her mother's when she was younger. She radiated strength and soaked in energy from the bright, warm day.

She smiled brilliantly. Dressed in a loose, billowy blue summer dress and sneakers she bounced down the steps and over to her anxious mother.

"Mother, how was Spain?"

"You know how Spain was. I told you over the phone." Grace accepted a kiss on the cheek. "What are those in your ears?"

"Some earrings I picked up in Greenwich Village. You like them?" Tava could hear a tone creeping into her mother's voice that she hated.

"Take them off." Grace was not pleased with the dangling ornaments. They consisted of large silver hoops with small bells suspended in the middle of each.

"Don't be ridiculous, Mother. They're just earrings. They're just for fun. What's the big deal?"

"I am never ridiculous, my dear. You look like a clown. I've got friends who would not understand my 'hip' daughter. We do have an image to uphold in this town in case you've forgotten. Take those damn things off and get in the car or I'll yank them out myself."

"It's summer, Mother. I'm home. We haven't seen each other in a long time and all you can talk about is a stupid pair of earrings?"

"I'm waiting."

"I can't believe this." Tava could see Grace was serious. She fumed inside. This was not a scene she wanted or was looking forward to. Like so many times before, Tava made the conscious decision to back down. She did not want a fight. Tava wanted to avoid a scene at all cost, so she methodically pulled each earring off and slipped them into her shoulder bag. She did not break eye contact with her mother, and when she was done she swept past Grace without speaking. With the bag dangling from her left shoulder she headed for the black stretch limousine. Grace trailed behind with a self-satisfied grin.

The door was standing open for Tava and she jumped in. She pushed herself into the far corner and tried to block her mother's face from her mind. Her feelings were hurt but she was not about to let her mother know.

Grace stepped inside the car. The driver, a muscular Swede named Hans, closed the door and slid behind the wheel. Gunning the engine, he pulled away from the curb. He nosed the long car out of the parking lot and onto the two-lane road. Driving north, he noticed Tava watching the firs pass by in a blur. The mountains towered above them, their craggy rocks jutting straight up in the clear sky.

The rolling field of trees and the quick sudden glimpses of squirrels made her smile. The images rolled pleasingly through her mind. Sultan Valley made her feel content. She liked this home the best. In New York she stayed either in the penthouse or on the farm upstate. Here, she felt free and uninhibited. Since the age of seven she had run among the huge trees, splashed through the ponds, fished in the streams, and played with summer friends. Sultan Valley was the only place, far away from the world, where she felt safe and completely happy. She couldn't wait to finally fall into her own bed and watched with mounting anticipation as they approached the estate's entrance.

Passing between two stone pillars underneath the Blackhurst Manor sign, Tava felt a sudden peace. Her body loosened and she sank farther into the leather seat. The car moved slowly along the driveway. Begonias, daffodils, poppies, and ferns lined the entrance like a color guard at attention. Huge pine trees created an arbor over the long driveway.

At the end of the long road they emerged into a circular clearing in front of the enormous mansion. The home was a single-level building with several wings radiating from the center. Done in rich gray with white trim it was reminiscent of the mansions in Newport, Paris, and Beverly Hills. The flowers around the house were in bright bloom and exploding with colorful brilliance. Tava smiled to herself.

The long, sleek car pulled up and stopped. Hans stepped out and opened Grace's door. She handed him her empty glass as she stepped out. "You were driving too fast. Don't let that happen again."

"Yes, ma'am." This was Hans's fourth year with the Blackhursts. As their personal chauffeur, he was assigned to Tava's father, when he traveled. Thomas Blackhurst found him washing windows at Blackhurst Tower, the New York City complex in the heart of Manhattan. Thomas liked and trusted him quickly. The Swede possessed an element of strength and a calm fortitude which went beyond definition.

Hans was well built. He needed to be; besides being their chauffeur he also acted as their bodyguard. His dusty blond hair, kept at a military length, complemented his ice-blue eyes. He had gladly accepted Thomas's offer for work and was privately trained in Germany. His driving skills were impeccable. He held a sixth degree black belt in karate and was now an expert with small handguns. He learned quickly and well. He treated his stay at Sultan Valley, driving for Grace, as a vacation.

He extended his long, tanned fingers inside the car, and Tava took them. He closed his strong hand around hers and gently helped her out. Their eyes met quickly, twinkled and passed. Grace was watching and Tava cared too much for Hans to jeopardize his position. She flashed quickly on a warm memory four years ago . . .

Dressed in gray sweats, sandals, and a loose cotton T-shirt, Tava slipped out the front door and closed it quietly behind her. She ran-walked along the gravel driveway past the beautiful Sultan Valley flowers. Ducking around the far corner, she made her way past the stables to the garage. The air was warm and sweet like the smell of honey. The stars overhead shimmered with a soft brilliance.

She found the stairs and moved quietly up them. She was very nervous but determined. She only hoped Grace did not hear her.

Tava peered into the small window expectantly. Hans, their new chauffeur, was doing sit-ups on an incline. Tensing his compact muscled body, he pulled himself up, touched elbow to knee and eased himself back down; each stomach muscle defined and glistening, quivering with a powerful strength. He was gorgeous and Tava gulped hard. She desired him like a forbidden fruit. This was her last summer before college and she was eager, determined, to start as a woman. Her virginity annoyed her. It made her feel too young. Grace kept her under lock and key but college promised many new ideas. Tava was longing to taste the world outside the Blackhurst's fortress walls.

She knocked once. Hans rolled off the sit-up board and padded over to the door in his bare feet. He opened it and smiled. He was not surprised but more amused. He had been aware of the way she was always watching him. He was intelligent and understood her yearning.

Tava pulled her gaze from his nylon shorts and found his face with her roving eyes. "Hi," she said demurely, her heart fluttering.

"Hello, Miss Blackhurst." His voice was deep and rumbly. They stared at each other for a moment. The silence was broken by a yell from the driveway.

"Tava!" It was Grace bellowing in a drunken stupor. "Where are you?"

Tava went white with fear. Hans swiftly pulled Tava inside, turning the lights off at the same time. He drew the curtains closed.

"There." He was smiling, his thick, pleasing accent willing her to relax. "The old cow won't find you." He grinned sheepishly this time.

Tava panicked for a moment. "I shouldn't have come."

"But you did," was his simple reply. "And I am happy." He kept a steady watch on her. She was so naturally beautiful. "What is it that I can do for you, Miss Blackhurst?"

"Well . . ." she stammered. She felt embarrassed and silly. "I like you."

"I like you too." There was a glimmer in his eye. He knew what she wanted but was not going to push the issue.

Tava suddenly lost any courage she had and started to walk out. "I shouldn't have come. I'm sorry. I'm being very stupid."

Hans gently pulled her back from the door. "I know why you have come, Miss Blackhurst. I appreciate the situation you're in but let me be honest," he began softly. "There will only be tonight. Too much is at stake for you and for me. I respect your father too much to abuse his kindness. And I respect your maturity and desires. Therefore, tonight is for you, but only tonight." He did not wait for her to answer. He touched her lips with his index finger and left it lingering there. He held her pretty face with his strong gaze and finally, gently, kissed her with such intensity that she went light-headed and stumbled back. He caught her easily and lowered her onto the fur rug. Kneeling down beside her, he delicately ran his hand under her shirt until it came to rest on her soft, supple breast. Tava watched him with expectant desires.

He touched her gently and Tava responded instinctively. Her mind raced with the excited rush of young love. She smiled and then wanted to laugh. She urged him down next to her and bravely reached up to kiss him. She drank in the sweet taste of his lips. He gave in to her and together they swayed in the half darkness of the small apartment.

Tava was exhilarated. She was so excited, she found herself short of breath when this man touched her. He made her feel so feminine and pretty. When he held her she gave into his strong, masculine touch and tingled with the thrill of love. This was so much more than she had hoped for that she was practically crying.

Hans took his shorts off. Tava was riveted. She had never seen a man like this before and was both frightened and ecstatic. He was hard and compelling, like the rest of his tight, rigid body. She almost fainted with delight. He knelt and slipped her out of her sweatshirt. She had dressed for this evening in the most expensive lingerie she could find. A French silk bra just covered her erect pink nipples. He was enjoying this, she noted, with satisfaction. And when he removed her sweat pants, he grew harder at the sight of her creamy pink panties. Trimmed seductively in lace, the high-cut bikini accentuated her strong, lithe body and invited him to explore further. Her legs were long, strong, and graceful. With her thin waist, perfect breasts, and long neck Tava's body flowed like a Greek statue. She felt truly beautiful for the first time under his gaze.

He removed her panties and began touching her delicately along the inside of her upper thigh. He teased her with his touch, just brushing her hair. Playing between her legs, he made her wet and she shivered from the bolts of pleasure shooting through her young body. Her hand found him and stroked until he moaned with pleasure. It felt strange, foreign, but wonderfully new to her. She responded to him and finally gave in to the mounting excitement between them.

They caressed each other until they could not stop. Tava explored him all over and was almost mad from the emotions swirling inside her. She felt tipsy and in a heated rush pulled him onto her. The movements were instinctual. She guided him into her with a spreading joy she had never experienced. It felt odd but wonderful. She was expecting it to hurt but it did not. He was too gentle and caring. His strong body moved with hers and together they exploded in a rapturous symphony of sparkling light and sound.

"Will there be anything else, Mrs. Blackhurst?" Hans asked professionally. Grace waved him off rudely. He turned to Tava. "Ms. Blackhurst?"

Tava smiled, "No, thank you, Hans. How've you been?"

"Fine, thank you, miss."

"Let's go, Tava, there are things to do." Grace whirled in a huff and waited at the door.

Hans tipped his cap, closed the door behind them, and got back in. He roared the limousine to life and pulled down the gravel road to the garage.

"Why do you have to be so mean to the workers?" Tava asked.

"Who do you think you're talking to?" Grace asked in a rush. Her bloodshot eyes swam in a furious rage.

"I asked you . . ."

Grace slapped Tava as hard as she could across the face. The force of the blow knocked the bag from Tava's hands and sent her reeling. She landed hard on the gravel driveway, her hands cutting against the rocks. She was stunned and tears of anger began welling in her pretty eyes.

"What's that for! What's the matter with you?" Tava yelled. At first she was stunned by the blow. It was the first time in her life that Grace had hit her. In all of their fights, over all of those years Grace had never laid a hand on her. She never had to. Grace was far too good with a cutting word or a hurtful demand. Grace was far too manipulative to resort to violence and this was why Tava was stunned.

"Don't make a big scene for God's sake. Just get inside."

"Mother! What's your problem?"

"I don't have a problem and if I did I sure wouldn't tell you." Grace whirled inside and left Tava gaping in disbelief.

Tava shook the pain away, cursed her mother, and picked herself up. "Damn it! I don't want this!" She knew her mother was uncontrollable until the liquor eased up.

With her face still stinging she moved slowly through the doorway and stood for a moment in the entry hall. The wide marble expanse was a round twenty-foot circle. It rose thirty feet in the air and was covered with a glass roof. Directly below, a fountain gurgled gently in an octagonal pond.

Tava turned left and moved down a long hallway. To her left a glass wall overlooked the driveway. To her right, polished, pale blond wood covered the expanse. Her reflection slid down the hall casting a shadow on the paintings. The sun filled the hallway, making it seem like an overexposed picture. The house was seductively quiet now. Its halls lay empty, expectantly waiting for life to fill them. Tava noted with pleasure the flower baskets brimming over.

The paintings, each an expensive collector's item, were tastefully mounted along the hallway. Some were very rare and hung in encased glass. Tava loved these and as a little girl spent hours studying them. She knew them by heart and felt a part of them somehow. Tava breathed in deeply and closed her eyes for a moment. She treasured the sense of warmth and security she felt here.

She passed through tall French doors into her wing of the huge house. Her room was set apart from the other bedrooms. Closing her large doors, she locked them and turned around. Soft, pink, and feminine, her room welcomed her back. Tava crossed to the enormous bed and climbed onto it. She pulled the feather comforter around her. She found the control buttons in the headboard and pressed the left one, watching with a lazy delight as the curtains swung back automatically. Beyond was a bright green, freshly cut lawn sweeping down dramatically to a gushing river. Several trees dotted the huge expanse and invited her down. She shrugged off the sensation and sank further into the bed. She stripped and fell asleep on top of the comforter. With her cheek still on fire, she dreamed fitfully of Grace and prayed for a peaceful summer.

3

The morning woke to bluebirds chirping outside Tava's window. The sun was just cresting above the rocky hills beyond the river. Its rays were starting to creep down the jagged hillside, shedding its blanket of light over the violet wildflowers. Blackhurst Manor was just coming to life.

Tava rolled over and opened her heavy eyes. To her surprise she discovered she slept the whole night through. The air was so warm, she wriggled out from underneath the comforter during the night. She brushed her hair from her eyes. The birds caught her attention and gently reminded her she was in the mountains. Unlike New York with all of its fast paced, fast living, here she heard the birds singing. With the pleasing sound in the background she pulled herself into a sitting position and kicked her clothes on the floor.

She held back the urge to run to the phone. Michael wasn't expecting her until the Blackhurst Ball but she wanted to see him so badly. She wanted to touch him and be touched. She missed him but she knew she had to be good.

He was working at Sultan Valley Resort. It was a sprawling complex with golf courses, tennis courts, restaurants, hotel rooms, and bungalows. Thomas Blackhurst owned a large portion of it and this was where Tava and Michael met last summer. He was not expecting to see her until the end of the week and Tava decided to keep it that way. It was selfish of her to bother him while he worked.

"Just wait till I see you, Mikey." She smiled broadly at the thought of him. She found him so handsome, it took her breath away. She wondered how she was going to deprive herself for four days.

Tava padded softly across the plush carpet into her

bathroom. The recessed lighting sensed she was there and came on automatically. The beautiful room was huge. To her left a large alcove stood waiting with her summer clothes; on the right a closet for shoes. Further down, double marble sinks and enormous etched mirrors. At the end of the carpeted room a bidet, toilet, and sunken shower. The shower brought a smile to her pretty, angular face. Polished pink Italian marble and brass fixtures accented the step-down cubicle.

A shower was what she needed and she headed directly for it. She reached down and turned the shower on. Six hot streams of water hit her from all sides. It was an extra feature her father built during the remodeling. He had surprised her with it on her nineteenth birthday.

Tava let the water revive her. The jets washed away the night's murky dreams and filled her with renewed energy.

She toweled off quickly and moved into the dressing alcove. She chose a light blue jumpsuit and sandals. She decided against makeup and left her hair falling naturally around her strong, graceful shoulders. Alert now and eager she crossed into the bedroom and was surprised to find the maid sitting on her bed.

"And what is that?" Annie teased in a thick Irish accent. She was pointing at Tava's pile of clothes, her fat fingers practically dancing. She was a small, heavy woman with laugh lines and graying hair. At sixty-three she was the oldest servant on the Blackhurst staff and Tava's nanny since childhood.

"Annie," Tava brightened, "I've missed you." She ran over and gave the woman a big hug. "Don't worry about the clothes."

"And who do you think is going to pick them up?"

Tava rolled her eyes in mock anger. "Me." She winked at Annie and kicked the dirty pile into the clothes hamper.

"Much better, you little terror."

Tava turned back toward her trusted confidante. "Someone ought to take that extra key away from you. Why are you bothering me so early?" Tava teased.

"You slept all day yesterday, you lazy thing. Goodness, I should think someone had to come to fetch you. Listen, little missy, I've been sent to collect you. The queen bee is waiting for you in the breakfast room."

"She's holding breakfast for me?" Tava let out a hoot of disbelief.

Annie laughed out loud. "When have you ever known that woman to wait for anybody? She's out there sucking up all the food she can lay her hands on." Annie and Tava shared an understanding about Grace. Grace would have gotten rid of her years ago except that Thomas liked her. Annie made him laugh and he appreciated it.

Tava beamed conspiratorially. Annie was right about Grace. She always was. "Annie, is Daddy going to let you stay all summer?"

Like Hans, Annie was on loan from the penthouse in New York. "He better or I'll quit. And he knows there's no one like me to put up with his stuff. I can only take so much of that city before I need my sanity back. I'm not made of stone, you know. No, thank you, missy. It's Sultan Valley for my old bones or nothing." She almost pouted and then let a grin slip out. "Get on with you. She'll be screamin' her head off if you're not out there soon."

"All right, I'm going." Tava left Annie with a wave and wandered down the wide hallway. This early in the morning the hallway was cast in long deep shadows. A hazy blue penetrated this side of the house.

As Tava walked through the huge house she felt with wonder the exciting sensation of mornings in the mountains; the sun cresting the ridges, the anticipation of long, hot days, swimming, shopping, and eating on rocky terraces of outdoor cafés. She could not wait to get into town. The tiny village of Sultan Valley was always bustling this time of year.

She was now in the entry hall; its double-story ceiling vaulted upward. The gurgling fountain reminded Tava of the time she was caught playing in the water. She was made to sit there for three hours as punishment by an angry Grace. Afterward she caught a cold and spent the next week in bed. Tava felt the urge to splash her hands through the crystal clear water but held back.

She crossed through the rounded archway opposite the front door. To her left was the enormous game room with a pool table, wide-screen Sony television, VCR, computer, CD player, and many other gadgets. The room looked like an electronic showroom. In the center were two enormous wooden horses salvaged from a merry-go-round. They were restored and repainted by hand and stood on display. They were beautiful with their pretty heads tossed back in frenzied laughs.

Across from the game room was the living room. It was rarely used but was dusted daily. Done in rich mauves the matching couches looked like sleeping sentinels. A huge stone fireplace lay waiting for a blazing fire. Tava felt an emptiness about this room. She was never allowed in it as a child and that still bothered her.

She knew why of course. Grace used this room to entertain all of her socialite friends from Sultan Valley. This was her mother's room first and foremost. Most of the early parties were held here and because of this Tava was always kept out. She felt an unfulfilled desire to be allowed in. The living room was still off limits to her curious mind as she tried to shrug off the memories.

Continuing on, she passed through the stainless steel kitchen. She spotted her mother lounging at the round glass breakfast table. She was sitting alone in the glass extension as the sun streamed in around her. She almost looked happy. Tava took a deep breath and pushed on. She tried to wear a smile.

The view was spectacular from inside the huge glass palace. Like Tava's room the lawn flowed down to the rushing river. Sculpted gardens spread out through the grounds. A series of red brick walkways wound their way down to a pink gazebo. Far to the right, rows of fruit trees stood in perfect lines waiting to be picked. The rose garden was in bloom nearby. Tava's favorite sculpted hedges done in the shape of fairy-tale characters stood to the right of the rose garden. It was magical to Tava, as if the whole area was glowing with a special, soft aura.

Blackhurst Manor was maintained by a full-time crew of fifteen. It was a showplace of tasteful opulence. It was built in the 1920s by a world-renowned artist. Thomas Blackhurst discovered it fifteen years earlier in disrepair and fell in love with it. He restored it, enlarging the rooms, remodeling the facilities, and building the pool. Even the river was redirected. It was now one of the most expensive homes in America. With a thousand acres of wilderness, guest homes, servants' quarters, stables, gardens, and the ten-bedroom central mansion, Blackhurst Manor was valued at twenty-five million dollars.

This never seemed to impress Grace. She sat at the table, bleary-eyed and annoyed. She was still recovering from her hangover. She was in a white satin robe and slippers. She was drinking tomato juice straight and smacking her large lips loudly when she swallowed.

"You want one of these?" Her voice was harsh and scratchy.

Tava sat at the opposite side of the table. "No, thank you."

Grace rolled her eyes. "You're not still upset over yesterday, are you? Are you?" Her voice was almost accusatory.

"I'm not happy about it, but I'm not going to let it worry me. You wanted to see me?"

Grace nodded her head. "How're you and this Michael person doing." She bit off a piece of toast and ate it slowly.

"Why?" Tava was suspicious.

"Why? Well, my darling daughter, because I'm not pleased that you invited him to my party, but you have and so I'm curious. I don't necessarily think he's the best choice for you."

"And who do you think is a good choice for me, Mother?"

"I haven't decided."

"Don't waste your time. Michael and I are happy."

"Well, I don't see how. You only had a summer fling."

Tava began to simmer. "What we had . . . I don't want to get into this with you. My relationship with Michael is my own affair."

"If you are going to see him, I hope he keeps you busy. I'm not terribly interested in seeing a lot of you this summer." She paused to let that sink in. Grace was very protective of her time here at Blackhurst Manor and did not want that jeopardized by Tava. A strange thought suddenly came to her. "Are you still a virgin?"

Tava turned red despite herself. "Why do you still amaze me?"

Grace smiled broadly. "How precious. You're embarrassed. Which means either you have lost it and you're being coy or you still haven't done it yet. Well, if you haven't, hurry up. It might take your edge off." She felt very satisfied with herself as she swigged her tomato juice. "How old are you now anyway?"

Tava felt like strangling her mother but said instead, "Twenty-one." Grace was becoming more abusive as the years went by and Tava was not sure how to handle it.

"Twenty-one? That makes me . . . I don't want to think about it." She was trying to make a joke and it fell flat. Instead she took another drink and put the empty glass down on the table. She seemed to make up her mind about something and nodded her head. Interlocking her fingers underneath her chin she began slowly, "Tava, you're not a child anymore so let me be honest. Frankly, I'm getting tired of the whole idea of this annual ball and I don't want to worry about it. So, for that reason, I'm glad you're here. I want you to take care of the rest of the arrangements."

Tava looked surprised and a little pleased. She'd been attending the summer parties since she was ten. She liked the idea of taking command. "What do you want me to do?"

"Everything. Christ, we've been doing this thing for so many years, it basically runs itself. All the invitations are printed and mailed so all you have to do is oversee the setup and coordinate with the caterers. Do you think you can handle that?" There was a tone to her voice suggesting a lack of trust.

Unfortunately for Grace this was just the kind of thing Tava was looking for. Since her graduation in early June she was floating, not really able to sink her energy into anything meaningful. The Blackhurst Ball was perfect.

"Well?"

"I'd love to do it." Tava was excited.

"You would?"

"Yes. Everybody's been contacted, right?"

"Uh-huh."

"Good. I'll let them know this afternoon I'll be coordinating the whole thing. You won't have to worry about a thing, Mother. Thank you."

"I'm trying something different this year. It's going to be a costume ball. It was getting so boring, we had to do something. I've ordered the costumes, and Lawrence will be out to fit us. The servants will all be matching and I've taken the liberty of choosing for you and your father."

"What am I wearing?"

Grace leaned back in her chair. "Be surprised." She had a little treat in store for her daughter and she did not want to give it away. She spoke evasively, in a monotone, and Tava let it be. "That's all," Grace said offhandedly. She was through with Tava and wanted her to go.

Tava was glad to leave. She decided she would have lunch in town. "I'll see you later." She got up and Grace stopped her.

"Tava?"

"Yes?"

"I mean it when I say I don't want to see you much this summer. I've got my own plans and my own friends. The last thing I want is to see a bunch of late-night parties with your little giggling friends."

Tava felt a wave of sadness fill her. For a moment she wondered what it would be like to share a loving relationship with this woman. All of her young life she wished for a companionship she could rely on. She dreamed of sharing her secrets with a mother who cared about her. She wanted more than anything else to be able to confide in her. Tava could not rely on Grace for anything and it hurt her very deeply. "That's fine, Mother. I didn't count on doing anything with you anyway, and I'll make sure my giggling friends and I play somewhere else. Good enough for you?"

Grace considered this for a moment. "I don't like your tone, young lady. This is my house. Don't you forget it. And Tava, don't fuck up this party. The locals count on us every year."

"I won't."

"You better not." Grace waved her away with a brush of her hand.

4

Blackhurst Tower was a monumental skyscraper in the heart of Manhattan just east of Central Park on Madison Avenue. Shunning the typical Wall Street milieu, Thomas Blackhurst moved uptown early in his career and shaped one of the country's largest venture capitalist firms. With his single-minded energy he forged a large conglomeration, stockpiling companies, buying and selling them like toys. These expensive playthings were like his children and besides Tava, the only joy he had in his life.

Thomas Blackhurst was fifty-nine. He possessed the body of a thirty-year-old and the mind of a genius. With workouts three times a week he kept himself in shape with blinding ambition. Like a king he employed a staff of fifty all moving to his direction. Nothing they did was without his approval. Thomas stayed in control. It was this factor that kept him going. Without his business he was nothing. His entire identity was locked up in the walls of Blackhurst Tower.

The Blackhurst Venture Group occupied the top floor of the gleaming skyscraper. It was built ten years ago with Thomas's money. Having quadrupled in price with the rest of Manhattan real estate, the building was now worth over 650 million dollars. From his executive suite he could see all of Madison Avenue. Central Park lay spread out like a green blanket. To his left the World Trade towers loomed in the far distance. It was here that Thomas formulated his strategies and planned his takeovers. This was his center of control.

He was impeccably dressed in a silver-gray wool suit. Privately designed and tailored in Paris, it fit him like a second skin. A muted red silk tie and leather wing tip shoes finished the ensemble. Thomas strived for simple elegance in his life. With his suits, his homes, and his cars he demanded the best in subtle ways. It was Thomas's style to pounce only after making friends. He sneaked up on his enemies with a big smile and a firm handshake. No one trusted Thomas Blackhurst but found it hard to deny him anything. He had an inner glow of confidence his competitors found hard to combat.

Leaning far back in his large leather chair, he played with his diamond wedding ring. He rolled it around his third finger again and again. On the other end of the telephone was Thomas's latest interest. He was talking to the president and CEO of Nicholls Development, an oil exploration company based in Houston. Hank Nicholls was a huge man with a deep laugh that shook him when it exploded. He was laughing now on the other end of the line.

"You want to what?"

"I want to buy your company."

"It ain't for sale, my friend. There is no way on God's green earth that I would ever let my baby go. I appreciate the interest but it ain't for sale. Now scram. I've got people to see."

Thomas was expecting this to be an easy deal but Hank was holding tough.

"Mr. Nicholls, I know I don't have to tell you that yours is a public company. Your shareholders have a right to at least look at my offer. If it's the money, you know that is always negotiable."

"I don't want your money. I don't need it. My company is not for sale. Understand?"

"What are you trying to do, ruin my day?" Thomas joked.

"What do you know about oil?" The question was tinged with irritation.

"I see potential, Hank, lots of it. I want to make you a rich man."

"Already am rich. You're barking up the wrong tree."

"I won't take no for an answer."

"Gonna have to. I ain't budging." Hank sounded like he was going to hang up.

Thomas rolled his eyes and drummed his graceful, manicured fingers on his oak desk and got an idea.

"Do this for me. I'm having a little party to kick off the summer. I want you to come. We can't do business over the damn phone. Let's sit down, talk this thing over and if you still say no, fine. At least you'll get a great party."

Hank's voice hesitated. "I don't like New York, Blackhurst. Never have. Makes me nervous. There're always people like you swimming around trying to eat up people like me."

"Jesus, Hank, I don't want to eat you up. I only want to talk to you. Plus the party isn't in town. It's at my place in Sultan Valley. Montana!"

"Montana. I haven't been to Montana for fifteen years. Got any horses?"

"Twenty-five of them. The whole damn town is turning out for this. We do it every year. What do you say?"

"You got me interested. I suppose there's an airport?"

"There better be. I built it."

There was a long pause on the other end of the line. Hank covered the mouthpiece and was whispering to someone in the distance. He came back on. "Yeah. All right. I need the weekend off. I'll see you then."

Thomas interjected before Hank could hang up. "Why don't you bring your boy along. What's his name?"

"Buddy. How'd you know I had a son?"

"I like to do my homework, Hank. No sense being stuffy about this."

"It's just me and the boy."

"I know."

"I suppose you would. I don't know. Hell, why not? It'd be good for him."

"Fine. We'll be expecting you."

"Don't think you're going to change my mind. 'Cause y're not."

Thomas hung up, pleased with himself. He buzzed for his secretary.

"Linda, get me Buddy Nicholls on the line. You'll find him at the Cattlemen Club, downtown Houston." He clicked off and leaned way back. Swiveling his huge chair around, he watched the other buildings. He saw strangers scurrying along hallways and sitting in their glass offices. All these people, he thought, living their lives. Thomas was a very happy man, specially when he was on the hunt. It was the game he loved more than anything else and he felt very

25

good about Nicholls Development. His phone rang and Thomas picked it up.

"Hello? Buddy? Guess who I just got off the phone with?"

"What's my daddy up to?" Buddy's young, weak voice whined over the phone.

"Your daddy doesn't seem to want to sell."

"Told ya, didn't I? I said you'd need my help. Nicholls is everything to my daddy. It's gonna take a lot to blast him out of there."

"It looks like I'm going to need a little help on this one. You could be a very rich man."

"I know, Mr. Blackhurst, I know. I'll get working on it."

"I appreciate that. Listen, I've invited your father for the weekend and told him to invite you. He's flying out to my summer place. Who knows what will happen."

"Yes, sir. That's fine. I look forward to meeting the great Thomas Blackhurst."

Thomas detected a strange note in Buddy's voice. He did not trust the boy, but knew he could be of some use in pressuring Hank. Thomas guessed correctly that Buddy Nicholls was the weak link in the organization and easily pried out by greed. Thomas knew what that kind of ambition could do and was very careful around young people, like Buddy, who possessed it. They were useful but unpredictable. It was always a dangerous line.

"Fine. See you then."

"Yes, sir."

They hung up. Thomas drummed the table, sensing victory. He seldom lost and was zeroing in on the kill. He buzzed for Linda.

"Linda, would you please have Kim come see me." He waited patiently, going over both calls in his mind. Presently Kim knocked and a moment later entered, closing the door behind her. She discreetly locked it.

Kim Marren was a tall, athletic woman in her mid-thirties. Her short black hair was swept straight back close to her head. She was striking. Her skin was deep black and creamy smooth. Her shoulders were broad but delicate. She had large, shapely breasts accentuated by a sheer silk blouse draping from her strong shoulders. Her pants were pleated and matched the blouse. She stood close to six feet in her red pumps.

She confidently crossed over to the wet bar. With practiced ease she poured two scotch and waters and carried them over to Thomas. She sat on the desk and handed one to him. Thomas accepted and sipped with vigor. She drank hers slowly, watching him with an amused smile. She was Thomas's personal assistant and his closest confidante. Kim was a fiercely intelligent, self-made woman from Brooklyn, educated at NYU, and recruited out of graduate school. After seven years with Thomas she could read his moods and right now he was very happy.

"It feels good, Kim. I'm this close to catching them. I can almost taste that company."

"How much are you going to offer?"

"Three hundred and seventy-five million dollars. That's high and they should take it. We might have to go a little higher. After we break it up it'll be worth more. Who cares about the money anyway? We've done this too many times for it to be the money. It's the adventure, honey." He laid his hand on her knee and kept it there. She nodded slightly and leaned back. Finding a series of buttons on the far right of the huge desk, she pushed one and the curtains automatically brushed closed. Lights suddenly slipped on and music emanated from the wall.

"You better watch that hand, sweetie," she teased in a soft, silky voice.

He winked at her. They understood one another. Kim had no delusions that these afternoons would ever lead to anything more serious. She was comfortable and happy with her situation. She was not Thomas's mistress but more his partner. They shared one another's company for the pure pleasure of it. Thomas never abused his position with her. He trusted her completely and shared with her all of his business secrets. He paid her extremely well and regarded her with the respect he would any executive. These afternoons simply were uninhibited fun, for the two of them. The thing Thomas loved about her was her complete independence. He found it refreshing.

"I think you're doing what comes naturally. Thomas, you bad thing. You ought to be ashamed of yourself." She was flirting now, enjoying the game they had made up together. She knew he loved it. She pulled away and inched her way on top of his desk. Kneeling in front of him, she slowly undid her blouse. Purring, she unbuttoned each button with a little sigh. Thomas sat back and watched. To her enjoyment she noticed him getting hard and dragged the striptease out longer.

The blouse fell around her. Her white camisole followed closely behind. Thomas noticed her glistening black skin with wonder and grew even harder as he watched her undo her lace bra. It fell away easily and he clapped his hands in delight. Rolling closer, he grabbed her around the waist and gently took her left breast in his mouth. He voraciously tasted until Kim gently pushed him away.

She undid his tie and shirt. They came off together and were followed by his shoes, socks, and pants. He was standing in striped boxers and she stuck her index fingers inside the elastic band encircling his waist. She pulled the front open and peeked inside.

"My goodness, Mr. Blackhurst. Somebody is certainly awake."

Thomas grabbed her and pulled her off the desk. He unzipped her pants and helped her step out. He held her bottom and pressed his quivering body next to hers. They kissed savagely and pulled apart. She rolled her nylons off quickly and danced away from him.

Standing in the middle of the room, she started to bump and grind to the music. To really arouse him she started to touch herself seductively. She ran her hand inside her panties and winked at him.

Thomas, out of his mind, rounded the corner and grabbed her in a big hug. He kissed her again, all over. She stood there with her eyes tightly closed as he roved up and down her body, exploring her with his lips and tongue. She ran her fingers through his hair and moaned softly.

Suddenly she was in his arms and being carried to the sofa. He laid her at one end and slipped out of his shorts. She moved over to him and took him in her mouth. She rubbed the back of his legs up and down and ran her hands over his bottom. She played delicately with his testicles, pressing just hard enough to arouse him.

Kim almost brought him to explosion and then backed off. They drew the moment out, neither wanting it to be over. He knelt and they kissed, their tongues playing wildly. Almost out of his mind, practically sick with pleasure, he grabbed her by the hand and pulled her to her feet. He swung her over the arm of the couch, front first. She squealed with pleasure and laughed when he entered her from behind. Together they rolled with the waves that hit them and finally ended up in each other's arms on the floor. They laughed, Thomas propped against the couch, and Kim leaning against his hairy chest.

5

Blackhurst Manor was alive with activity. Three different companies were transforming the beautiful grounds into a fantasyland. Like clockwork, strings of glittering white lights were laced through the trees. Long lines of suspended decorations were hung across the huge lawn. The bushes were wrapped with pink and yellow bows.

A hundred round tables were being placed around the huge pool and down around the gazebo. Six hundred chairs were unloaded and unfolded. Each table was dressed with a pale pink tablecloth and a centerpiece of roses. In the middle of each was a huge white candle.

To the far left of the pool, close to Tava's room, the caterers were busy setting up the serving lines. Beautiful rose-printed china, a thousand pieces of silverware, and hundreds of glasses were being placed in perfect order on the many rows of long, covered tables. A small, wiry man named Eric was deep in conversation with his assistant. They were solving minor problems plaguing the huge event. Where were the warmers? Was the wine chilling? Was there enough manpower? Eric attacked each question with cool professionalism and soon the assistant was sent off to coordinate with the dessert crew. Tava caught Eric's attention and waved to him.

"How's it going, Eric?" Tava was acting as a very capable supervisor in the midst of all the chaos.

"We're still deciding about the wineglasses. Chilled or not?"

"What did we do last year?"

"We chilled them."

"Let's chill them again."

"You've got it." Eric jotted this down in his notebook. "I've checked with the restaurants and everything is going fine." All the food was prepared for the evening by the three biggest restaurants in Sultan Valley. The food was going to be brought in from town in rented vans.

"I trust you, Eric. You always do a great job."

Eric blushed. He enjoyed the compliments but they made him embarrassed. He was a graduate of the Cordon Bleu in Paris. Cooking was his joy and it took him many years to strike out on his own. His specialty was high-ticket events like the Blackhurst Ball. His reputation was untarnished and as a result he spent most of the year flying from continent to continent, city to city, supervising the catering of important events. From heads of state, royalty, and presidents, to captains of industry, Eric May was the consummate chef.

Tava ran over the menu again. Besides the assortment of fruit flown in from Hawaii, the main dishes were going to be a selection of pheasant, king salmon from Alaska, and the choicest beef raised exclusively on Blackhurst farms. The wines were selected from the most impressive private cellars in the country.

Tava patted his arm and left him. Moving to the other side of the pool, she approached the artist, Salina. She was an exotic woman, raised and educated in Brazil. She made her reputation as a sculptress and was in the midst of creating two masterpieces from huge blocks of ice. With the help of two young female assistants, she chiseled and carved a gorgeously intricate pair of swans, a male and female. The birds' necks were curving delicately around each other in a love dance. Salina planned on floating the birds on a flowered platform in the middle of the pool.

Tava clapped her hands in amazement. "Those are beautiful!"

Salina smiled and nodded her head. "I'm glad you like." Their eyes met for a moment and Tava looked deep into hers, trying to learn from this woman the secrets of her success. Tava, like all recent graduates, was starting to feel the strain of aimlessness. Where would she go? What would she do with her life? Whom would she spend it with? All these questions whirled in her mind as she tried to sift through the conflicting answers. She gave up in desperation. Tava knew she did not have the talent to create works of art.

Tava was good with people. She wondered if she would like public relations. The one thing she did know about was her determination to make it on her own. She knew she could have her pick of jobs in her father's organization but she fought the temptation. She was not going to accept an offer from him. Success was going to be on her terms. She needed to prove to herself that she did not need her father's help. It was pride that kept her from her father's offer and it was a streak that ran very deep in the Blackhurst family.

She shoved thoughts of the future from her mind and concentrated on the present. She nodded approval and turned from Salina. She m de a mental checklist and walked across the lawn down to the decorators. They were busy dressing the gazebo. Speakers were being hidden around the ground to keep music piping through the evening. Tava wanted to make sure everybody felt joyous at this costume ball.

Tava approached Laura Cates, a well-dressed black woman in her early thirties. She was instructing her crew on placement. She smiled brightly at Tava.

"Honey, this is my favorite party of the year. You couldn't keep me away from this even if you tried."

"You're the only one we always call."

"You're too nice to me." She spoke to one of the young gentlemen wiring a speaker. "Make sure that's hanging out of the way, honey. We don't want it dropping off on the pretty guests." She gave him a big wink and he laughed.

"Yes, ma'am."

"I love it when they call me ma'am," Laura whispered.

"I wish I could get that kind of respect around here," Tava joked.

"Tava!" Annie yelled down from the house. "The costume man is here. He wants to fit you."

"Excuse me." Tava walked back up the gentle incline and met Annie by the pool.

"What's up?"

"That thing is here with your costume. He wants to fit you."

"Lawrence is not a thing, Annie."

"Well, I don't like the way he flaunts himself." Annie was a prude. She was lovable but unbending. Lawrence was gay and proud of it. Tava did not care, she liked him. Annie did not and Tava found it impossible to change her mind.

"Annie, don't be so closed minded."

"Don't tell me what to do, missy." She readjusted her huge bosom with a regal sweep. "And I better warn you. Your mother's done the ordering."

Tava looked nervous. "What's that supposed to mean?"

"Go see for yourself."

Tava felt a cold shock run through her. What had her mother done? She prepared herself for the worst.

"Where?"

"In her room." Tava left Annie and moved easily through the huge house. She was heading for her parents' wing. She cut through the kitchen and down the back hallway. More art hung on the walls. The carpeted expanse was done in dusty rose. Plants filled this side of the house. Tava passed the gym, sauna, and her father's "nerve center." This room was his office when he was away from New York. A fax machine, two computers, and three phones filled the masculine room. Her father's gigantic oak desk, an antique from the Civil War, was a polished monument to the man's brilliant abilities. Tava was only allowed in the room when her father invited her and that was rare. Still she peeked in.

Farther down the hall through a large archway, Grace passed by. She was moving from the dressing room into her sitting room.

The suite was a series of interconnecting rooms done in cold blues. The sitting area, like the eating atrium, was glassed in and looked over the south end of the estate. Wooded, with a series of lighted paths, at night it looked like the forest was alive. A stone fireplace lay to the right of the glass wall. A love seat and two stuffed armchairs were placed in a square facing the fireplace. Books lined the wall but were only decoration; Grace rarely read. She preferred to gossip with her circle of friends. Her world consisted of society affairs and rumors concerning who slept with whom, who was in and who was out.

Power was the word she cherished. Power was measured in money, and her influence was the mightiest. There were very few things Grace could not manipulate. With her husband's money behind her there were no challengers to her throne. Grace was the undisputed queen of society in New York City. In Sultan Valley she was simply the richest woman and commanded the envy of everybody.

The sitting room could be entered from three sides: the hallway where Tava now stood, a large archway to the right of the fireplace, and the opening into her bathroom. Like Tava's, Grace's bathroom was enormous. She loved bathtubs and hers was an oversized claw foot Victorian, refitted with jets. It was here that she talked on the phone to her friends. Even though she spent the summers on the estate she talked at least two hours a day to New York.

Tava followed her mother into the sitting room. Outside she could see the workers furiously preparing the grounds for the evening's event. Lawrence was helping Grace up on a footstool. He had several pins in his mouth. When he saw Tava he removed the pins, smiling brightly, and briefly left Grace to give her a hug and hold her tightly.

"How are you?" He had a soft, electric voice. He twirled Tava and nodded approvingly. "You look like a little doll, honey. Ooh, I could eat you up! Look at that tush!" Tava laughed. She had known Lawrence for three years. He was a local and made his living designing exclusive dresses for the richest women in town. He was noted extensively for his silk creations and his name was spreading quickly. The costumes he was doing for Grace were for fun. "You're gonna love what I did for you."

Grace sighed audibly, sounding excruciatingly bored. "Lawrence, please. Don't fawn over the girl. Pin this thing up and let's get on with it."

"Just shush." Lawrence winked at Tava.

"Don't you tell me to shush. Tava, yours is in my dressing room. Lawrence wants to fix these while he's here. The jackass isn't staying for the party tonight."

Lawrence laughed merrily and whirled on Grace. "You know I can't stay. I've got a date."

"With who?" Tava asked.

"None of your business. He's rich though." With that he knelt and started to pin the bottom of Grace's costume. She was going as Cleopatra. The headdress was still in its box. The dress looked wonderfully Egyptian and sparkled with flecks of gold. It clung to Grace's long, bony body like a tailored sack. She looked very dramatic. Lawrence knew his craft well and with some effort had pulled off a beautiful costume for Grace. She was appreciative and immediately commissioned two party dresses to wear in New York during the coming fall season. At five thousand dollars each they were going to be utterly original and envied by the New York elite.

Tava forgot Annie's ominous words and wandered through Grace's bedroom to the dressing room. She thought again, as she had done so many times before, how strange it seemed for her father and mother to sleep apart. Thomas's rooms were in the same wing but down the hall. She never learned the reason and resigned herself to never knowing. They had been sleeping like this for years.

She entered the all-mirrored room. The closet was a huge cavern at least four times the size of Tava's. The room was climate controlled to protect Grace's stunning collection of priceless clothing. Tava's costume hung at the end on a yellow lace hanger.

She went white and swallowed hard several times.

She suddenly felt queasy, as if someone had punched her in the stomach. She blinked her eyes hoping the costume would somehow change.

"I don't believe this," Tava groaned to herself.

Tava was planning on wowing Michael at the party and this costume was going to ruin everything.

She was afraid to touch it. The thing made her sick and she blushed uncontrollably. She wanted to strangle Grace more than ever.

"Tava?" Grace called into the dressing room. Tava could hear the tone in her voice and decided not to give her mother any satisfaction from this.

"Yes?" Tava did her best to sound cheery.

"What do you think?" Grace was holding her breath. She did not like Michael and was angry with Tava for inviting him. She had watched with growing displeasure as Tava's relationship with the boy flourished. To Grace, Michael was not up to standards and she took it as an insult that Tava did not get rid of him. It was even more embarrassing to her that Tava had met Michael at the Sultan Valley Resort. He had been working as a bellhop and still was this summer. Grace found this continually humiliating and said so to her daughter. Tava was acting very childishly and Grace decided to point this out with the costume.

Tava's costume was a baby girl's party dress.

All soft and pink, the dress was drenched in lace and looked like a huge, opened umbrella. The high neckline was embroidered while the short sleeves ballooned ridiculously at the shoulders. Stiff white petticoats kept the full skirt standing at attention and a large floppy bow, tied off in back, kept the high waist cinched just below the chest. The soft silk fell many inches above the knee. Tava was flushed with anxiety and feeling pressured.

"Oh, my God! I'm going to look so stupid. Mike's going to hate this!" she fumed. "What the hell am I going to do?" She racked her brain for answers. Tava knew there was no time to make a new costume. There was nothing workable in her closet. She prayed for an inspiration and was struck with an ingenious answer.

"Fine. If this is how you want to play, Mother, I'll be happy to comply." With her plan still formulating she stripped and pulled the dress on.

Behind the baby dress on a smaller hanger Tava discovered white panties decorated with pink lace across the bottom. Hanging with it was a matching bonnet, with ruffled lace and a floppy bow. On the floor below the dress sat black patent leather shoes and lace socks. She rolled her eyes and pulled the entire outfit on. "You really think you've done it, Mother, don't you?"

Tava felt ridiculous and was surprised when she started thinking about herself as a mother. Deep, intuitive emotions swirled inside her and warmed her imagination. Someday, with the right man, she looked forward to making a baby. The miracle would be hers but not until the right moment. There were still too many things to explore. Tava had too many questions about herself and her life to commit to any kind of long-term relationship. The most she could do was love Michael and that was enough for right now. She missed him terribly.

Tava turned to catch her reflection from all sides. The lace jiggled. The fabric fell with the whooshing sound of crinoline as Tava headed for the sitting room. She knew her mother would have to see.

"You look so cute!" Lawrence yelled. He was so excited. "Ooh, I do great work. Look at her, Grace!"

Grace was smiling maliciously. She was gloating and not hiding it. "What do you think?" She was expecting her daughter to scream.

Tava played it straight. If Grace was going to play dirty, Tava was more than happy to play along. "I love it. Lawrence, this looks perfect."

"You were right, Grace. She does like it! You look so beautiful."

"Thank you, Lawrence. Good choice, Mother."

"Let me see your bottom." He was beaming. He was ecstatic.

Tava dutifully lifted the full skirt and showed off her lacy panties. Lawrence clapped his hands.

"Yes! I knew those would work. That," he said pointing at Tava's bottom, "is one tight little tush."

Grace was not happy. "You really like that?"

Lawrence brushed the question aside and helped Grace down. "Why wouldn't she like it? Go change, Grace. She looks great and you're sounding like a doting mother." He urged her into the bedroom. "Be careful with those pins!"

Grace left the room, mumbling to herself, furious that her little plan was backfiring. She comforted herself with, "She looks ridiculous. Wait till they see her."

Tava waited until Grace was gone, then rushed over to Lawrence. She whispered seriously, "Now, Lawrence, we've got to talk."

6

Buddy swigged from a huge can of Budweiser. The helicopter he was riding in swerved suddenly as it swept low over the towering pine trees. They had been in the air for forty minutes. Their trip took them first from Houston to Denver. And now they were en route to Blackhurst Manor. Buddy wanted to fly directly into the small Sultan Valley airport but Hank decided a helicopter would be better. The trip from Denver was taking longer than he expected and Buddy hated flying. He was nervous they were going to miss the party and it was making him upset. He wanted to make a good impression.

Hank sat farther toward the front. The helicopter was the most advanced of its kind. Sleek and black, it slid through the air like a torpedo through the water. Powerful and fast it skimmed along at four hundred miles an hour. Appointed in rich supple Italian leather it was equipped with a bar, a five-thousand-dollar German sound system, and an executive washroom. The machine was big enough for eight passengers but only carried Hank, his son, and the pilot.

Hank was an enormous man. At six feet six inches and two hundred and fifty pounds he was a giant. He made his fortune in the oil fields and now owned the largest oil exploration company in the country. With oil becoming scarce his services were in great demand around the world. His talent was extraordinary and his success rate uncanny. Smart and gregarious, he knew himself and his talent and enjoyed the power he held.

He did not wear his weight well. His enormous stomach matched his ego and spilled over his jeans. He preferred loose shirts, unbuttoned down his chest and exposing two gold chains. He only wore Wrangler jeans and cowboy boots. He spoke in a heavy Texas twang and wore a huge ten-gallon hat. Hank did all he could to appear like the big Texan everybody thought he was. Very few people knew he had been raised in poverty in the poor section of Boston.

Buddy was over six feet tall like his father but not as heavyset. He tended toward the bony side. His hair was black and cut short. He kept it parted to one side. It lacked style but he kept it sprayed perfectly in place. His eyes were very strong and piercing but tended to dart furtively as he spoke. Buddy was a young man who cared about the way he looked. Appearances were very important to him. What he did not realize was that he made others uneasy. People instinctively steered clear of this young man. He was twenty-seven, ambitious, and those around him could feel that he was on the prowl to make his own mark in life. Buddy did not instill confidence; he instilled uneasiness.

His clothes were neat and well pressed. He kept away from his father's insistence on the cowboy look and tended more to the tailored, fitted look of creased wool slacks, button-down shirts, and leather loafers. He was actually the antithesis of his father and that pleased him.

There were many things about Hank that Buddy was not impressed with. One of them was the way he felt his father bluffed his way through life. To Buddy, Hank was never serious. And yet his father was extremely successful and Buddy was smart enough to know he could learn from his father.

Buddy planned on inheriting his father's company one day but there were still several hurdles to get over. One was the Board of Directors at Nicholls Development. He knew they did not trust him. The other was his father. Hank was hesitant in giving Buddy too much power and was constantly measuring his son's decisions. Buddy was not sure his father would ever hand over control.

Hank was not honestly sure his son was the right man for it. Buddy was a loner and only confided his secrets to himself. This made Hank nervous and angry. He felt his son slipping away and did not know how to bring him back.

Buddy was a genius with numbers and his organizational skills were impeccable. He was a meticulous planner and his powers of concentration were incomparable. He was a huge asset, but Hank continued to hold him back. He purposefully kept his son in tow, hoping to prepare him for the future.

Buddy understood his father more than his father understood himself. He read his father perfectly and played the older Nicholls for his own use. Hank's only weak spot was his son. Buddy knew it. Hank did not. So Buddy endured his father, aware one day he would have his chance to take control.

The helicopter swooped straight up and Buddy's stomach fell through the floor. The beer he was nursing decided it would not stay down and Buddy scrambled for a bag to vomit in.

Hank was happy the boy missed the expensive leather. After retching severely, Buddy fell back in his seat sweaty and run-down. He looked even whiter than before.

"Jesus, Buddy," Hank complained, "you're a disgrace, boy."

"Sorry, Daddy." Buddy wiped his mouth. "I don't like helicopters."

"Well, I guess they don't like you either." Hank shook his head in disgust and picked up the phone. He dialed Houston and spoke to his secretary. Watching the mountains sweep by underneath him, he found it hard to concentrate. This area of the country was so beautiful. Unlike Houston, which was flat and full of oil fields, Montana was a mountainous paradise. Hank started to feel drawn to this land much the way he felt drawn to Texas. He trusted this feeling deep inside him and decided to check into property.

". . . so, I told him you'd be gone the whole weekend."

Hank yelled at the woman. "That's not what I told you to say, doll! If you can't do the job, then get someone who can. Jesus Almighty, I wish I could get someone who could think!"

"I'm sorry, Mr. Nicholls, I thought that's what you meant."

"Well, it wasn't! It wasn't! I want you to call that jackass back up and tell him I want to see him in my office Monday morning. If he isn't there, he can pick up his check. I'm through fuckin' around with you people down there. Understand?"

She was quaking. "Yes, sir."

"Are you sure?" he snarled.

"Yes, sir. I'll call him right away. I'm sorry, sir."

"Call him now! What are you waiting for?" His voice was dripping in sarcasm.

"Yes, sir! Right away."

Hank slammed the phone down and brooded for several moments. His company was run with an iron fist and he hated it when people screwed things up. After a few more minutes he turned his attention back to his son.

Buddy was trying to sleep but Hank barked out, "I told you not to drink, didn't I? Why don't you listen to me?"

Buddy opened one eye. "I can't stand flying, Daddy. I drink to get me through."

"Uh-huh. And how do you feel now?"

"I feel terrible."

"That'll show you." Hank tapped his fingers against the seat. He was fired up and needed to fill his active mind. "You got the report on Blackhurst?"

Buddy nodded yes and pointed at his father's briefcase. Hank pulled the dossier on Blackhurst from the attaché case and studied it. Thomas was a formidable player. If they decided to go hostile, Hank was going to need an ace. He had several ideas but needed a little time to sift through them. "Buddy? We need strategy, son. This Blackhurst fella is tough. He means business. I can feel it. I got the feeling he ain't gonna take my no for an answer."

"I know, Daddy," Buddy groaned. "I can feel it too."

"I'm counting on your help, boy. I don't think this Blackhurst fella is going to give up without a fight." Hank had only accepted Thomas's invitation to buy himself more time. He needed a couple extra days to stop Thomas's plans. He was privately hoping the weekend would present new possibilities. Hank knew Thomas could go hostile and it worried him profoundly. It was a pattern he could follow in Buddy's report on Blackhurst's history. Hank was big, but not big enough to stop Thomas Blackhurst, legally.

Hank was not above getting down and dirty to keep what was his. He had done many things over the past years to cement his place in the industry. He was not proud of some of his efforts but they worked, and that was all that counted. Hank Nicholls had an uncanny ability to find the weak spot in a man and exploit it. It was a talent that few people had and he was looking forward to finding Thomas's.

7

Lawrence worked in another part of the house, altering his costumes for the big evening while Tava made one last check of the grounds and staff. Everything was humming and right on schedule. The costumes had just arrived for the workers, and Tava gave Annie the responsibility to get everybody dressed in time. Grace was in her room getting made up.

She was stewing.

Grace felt awkward and out of place. A drink was in her hand and she sipped it continually to calm herself. She checked the time. Thomas had called earlier, telling her to expect Hank and Buddy. There was still no sign of them. Thomas was due in shortly. She dreaded entertaining business associates. She normally steered clear of her husband's activities. They bored her.

The sun was just beginning its slow drop below the mountain ridge. The party was starting at nine when the sky would be glowing red with the dying flames of daylight. Grace was eager to see Thomas. She had seen him three weeks ago in New York and had spoken twice on the phone since then. She missed him. Grace wanted to feel his strong touch again. She felt like mending fences with him. They never made love anymore and if they were ever going to, it would be here at Blackhurst Manor. The country air did strange and wonderful things to people.

How long had it been since they had last made love? The question gnawed at her incessantly. She felt unwhole. The questions continued to plague her even when she was trying hardest to forget them. They followed her and she knew them all. Why had she let her marriage fall into such disrepair? Why had she let Thomas get away? What had happened to their love? They used to be so close when they were younger.

It was the questions that were driving her crazy. Even with all of the drinking she could not escape the horrible truth that her marriage was in shambles, but it hadn't always been like this. Grace could still remember the days when they were broke and living in an apartment the size of a closet on the lower East Side. They had had nothing when they first arrived in New York. Thomas had dreams of working on Wall Street, and Grace wanted to act. They supported each other's dreams, praying for success, and knew that with enough perseverance they would succeed.

New York City in the early years was not kind to either of them. It was where they learned their harshest lessons and where they reached their greatest triumphs. Grace never drank in those days. Thomas filled her hours and together they strived for success. Grace was lucky enough to hit it first. Initially she landed small roles Off-Broadway and those led to better parts. The theater filled her passion back then and she missed those times more than anything else. She finally made it to Broadway the third year they were there. During the first week of that run, in a play Grace still held close to her heart, Thomas broke into the business that would catapult him into the life-style that would change their lives forever.

By that time he was working as a low-level analyst in one of the bigger firms on Wall Street. He was quick and people liked him but he kept mostly to himself. Even then he was a driven man. While others pursued hobbies outside of work, Thomas pursued knowledge of the business world. His greatest love, he discovered, was tracking the movements of companies. He found he had a knack for tracking just when a company was going to collapse. He reasoned that these companies, while still worth money, could be purchased cheaply and resold, either in parts or as a whole.

The day finally came and Thomas was convinced he had found the right company. He gingerly approached a wealthy investor-friend and discussed his plan. The investor was so moved by Thomas's argument that he backed the young man. And so while Grace was debuting on Broadway,

Thomas was buying his first company. From then on success fell on both of them like rain.

Within two years Thomas was a millionaire and had his own company. The tide of success flowed so quickly that both of them were caught up in its wake. They enjoyed it and played with it and allowed themselves to be pulled along. It was at this point in their lives that Grace left the theater. She told herself that it was only temporary. With Thomas's success came major responsibilities and together they became the hottest young couple on the whole island. The parties filled their nights; Thomas was kept busy all day and Grace was overwhelmed with benefits, fund-raisers, concerts, and social clubs. The life-style began to consume them. Grace discovered she loved it and rarely thought of the theater world.

The problems began so slowly that neither of them felt it coming. They still loved each other but weren't able to spend as much time together; neither of their schedules allowed it. It was the pressure that began pulling them apart and they did not know it. By this time Grace was drinking socially and enjoyed the high she was getting from it. As far as she knew, everything was all right.

And then she found out she was pregnant.

It was like a heart attack. She was too protective of her own time and the time she shared with Thomas to accept another person into her tidy, organized world. She had given up the theater but was not willing to give up her privacy. Grace was not a woman intuitively called to motherhood. She did not know this about herself and it came as a surprise. So when Thomas encouraged her to have the baby, the final wedge was driven between them.

She carried Tava to term and immediately left her in the arms of a nanny. She threw herself back into her social life and Thomas worked, and they continued to degenerate slowly and irrevocably.

Grace would sometimes look at her daughter and feel revulsion. It made her feel guilty but she did try to find the likable qualities in her Tava. She perceived that even as a baby Tava naturally leaned toward her father for protection and guidance. Grace felt left out, not out of spite, but out of necessity. She discovered early on she was not prepared to share her love. She had no interest. Things like changing her little daughter's diapers were inconceivable. Tava was brought up in Annie's capable hands and as a result mother and daughter grew apart at an early age, and never found a path back together.

Grace felt jealous watching her husband dote on her daughter. She read it as Thomas's excuse to spend less time with her. It all became too much and Grace pulled farther into her own world where she was safe. Her one mistake was in never talking to Thomas about it. They had lost the capacity to communicate and now existed superficially. It was sad but she felt helpless to solve it.

Thomas recognized a problem but never had time to put his finger on it. Grace pretended life was normal and he was forced to believe her. Something was lost in his marriage but he did not know what it was. He had a beautiful daughter that he loved, his wife still filled him with joy, and his professional life was making him one of the most wealthy men in the country. Life was good but certainly not like it was when they first moved to New York.

The young makeup artist finished pinning Grace's silver hair back. Grace was going to wear a long black wig with her costume and was determined to look perfect. Her thoughts were wandering though and she could not take her troubled mind off Tava.

Why was she so impudent? Why couldn't she just behave and act like a decent young woman? She was twenty-one now, a college graduate, and should be spending her time looking for the right man. Tava had refused a coming-out party and that embarrassment set Grace back several months.

The more Grace thought about Tava, the more upset she got. She read Tava's lack of interest as betrayal. Grace had given the responsibility of preparing for the gala to Tava hoping she would fail. Secretly she hoped Tava would come to her with questions or ask her for help. And yet Tava took control and flew. The party was well in hand. Tava actually was guiding the huge affair with a confident, self-assured flair. This made Grace even angrier. She had forced the job on Tava and then felt angry when she was not included.

Grace took another swig from her whisky. She was getting very drunk now. The room was starting to sway. She wiped her mouth with the back of her sleeve. The rage boiling inside her finally exploded and she yelled at the woman.

"Get out! I'll finish this myself!" She brushed the makeup woman away from her hair. Grace stared at herself, sure now that Tava was deliberately being obstinate. She gnashed her teeth unconsciously and pulled her dressing gown over one arm. She felt an unyielding need to confront Tava now, before the party, to settle their differences once and for all.

She staggered through the large house. She ran down the long hallways stumbling into the walls. She finally found Tava's bedroom and barged in.

"Tava!" The room was empty. She whirled on her heels and moved shakily down the hall to the rear of the house. She spotted her daughter down by the gazebo. Grace paused only to take another drink. Several of the workers watched her and quietly nudged each other. Grace looked like an actress backstage after a show with her makeup still on. A warm, gentle breeze made her robe rustle around her long legs. She was naked beneath the soft wrap and did not bother keeping her robe closed. She offered quick glimpses of herself. She almost felt a sense of freedom exposing her breasts to these people. It gave her a vicarious thrill in her intoxicated state. She sensed their stares and actually loosened her gown a little more. With a deep breath she caught Tava in her sights and yelled down the lawn to her.

"Tava!" Her voice was shrill. Everyone within earshot stopped for a moment to see what the excitement was.

Tava looked around quickly. She was supervising the decoration of the gazebo and was standing with three burly men. They continued to work. Tava motioned her mother to come down.

If Grace had any calm feelings, they evaporated at this moment. She stormed down the path with her long rose-colored robe fluttering behind her. She was barefoot and the brick path hurt her as she moved down.

As she got closer, the workers snickered to themselves. Some leered behind her back. Others were turned on by the middle-aged woman. Grace was skinny but carried herself well. She stopped at the foot of the stairs, arms folded across her chest, breathing fire.

Her voice erupted. "Goddammit, when I call you, answer!"

The force of Grace's voice whipped Tava around. She was frightened when she saw the look in her mother's eyes. "What are you talking about?" Tava felt embarrassed in front of the men and tried to ease the tension.

"You've been doing your little high-and-mighty number since you got here," Grace sneered grotesquely.

"Doing what?" Tava was completely confused. "Mother, keep your voice down. Everybody can hear you."

"Everybody can fuck themselves if they want!"

The three men made quick excuses and hopped over the railing. They did not want to be caught in the middle of this. Grace was advancing now. She was so livid, her face was beet-red. Her voice was carrying all over the back lawn.

"You know what I'm talking about. You've been prancing around here like you own the place. I don't know what your problem is, sweetie, but if you're gonna keep it up, you're gonna be sorry." Her voice was slurring. She was ranting with so much passion, her face was horribly contorted. The veins in her neck were straining from the pressure. "I can't stand this little attitude you're putting on. I know what you're up to!" She poked her daughter with her finger and pushed Tava back against the railing. "You can't treat me like this."

Grace could hear a tiny voice of reason echoing inside her. It was trying to yell out, "Stop this, Grace. It's not her fault." But she pushed the nagging thought aside. The events were too much for her. She could sense Tava ridiculing her. The whole party was turning into a competition in Grace's mind. She could not stand the fact that Tava was handling the affair so well. It galled her to see her daughter being treated with respect by the workers, respect they didn't seem to extend to her.

If Grace listened to herself, she would have known she was also jealous. The real reason she was angry was because she perceived her daughter pulling Thomas away from her. She had been carrying the sense of abandonment for a long time, and all of the elements leading up to the party were finally taking her over the edge. She was an angry woman for many reasons and she was taking out all of her own frustrations on her child. Tava was left totally stunned and completely unaware.

Everybody was staring now. Tava was mortified and

started to get angry herself. She hissed through her teeth, "Keep it down!"

"Let 'em watch!" Grace laughed hard. "I don't care. I'm paying their fucking salaries!"

"Mother, please," Tava pleaded. Her preparations were going so well. The party was starting in three hours and Grace was making a fool out of both of them. "I don't know what you're talking about. So just shut up. Please."

Grace was stunned for a moment. "Shut up? You're telling me to shut up? You ungrateful little bitch!" Grace staggered back and gulped down her last shot of whisky.

Tava was devastated. She tried to move around her but Grace blocked the way. "I didn't say you could leave." The glass slipped from her hand and shattered across the floor and down the steps. Moving forward, she stumbled through the shards and cut her feet. This enraged her and she flew at Tava like a mad cat.

She grabbed Tava's hair and slapped her as hard as she could. Tava reeled backward, hitting the railing and knocking some of the decorations off. Tava struggled to stay on her feet but the pain was blinding her.

Grace jumped again and Tava threw up her arms in self-defense. She caught her mother in the mouth and Grace was knocked aside. The blow drew blood.

"Mother, stop this! Stop this!"

Tava tried to run for the stairs again but Grace caught her by the blouse and ripped it down to her waist. Tava kicked at Grace's legs and knocked her to the ground, giving herself enough time to reach the top stair. Grace regained her balance and in one ugly lunge caught her daughter by the foot. Tava went tumbling face first down the stairs and into the broken glass. She crumpled in a ball at the bottom. The tears were delayed but the pain was immediate and deep. Tava went into shock.

Grace looked horrified when she saw her daughter's torn blouse, bloody face, and trembling body. She was petrified. Quick glances around her saw the workers beginning to close in on them. She panicked, but only momentarily.

She rushed over to Tava and hovered there. A loose circle of people formed around the mother and daughter, and Grace took her cue. "She tripped. Did you all see that? My baby tripped." Her voice was quick and short of breath. She was drained from the encounter but determined to slide the blame onto something else.

She knelt by Tava, not really comprehending the pain she had inflicted, and roughly nudged her shoulder. Tava only curled up into a tighter ball and Grace said, "Baby, are you okay? You tripped, honey. You tripped!" She looked imploringly at the faces around her. She was convinced they all thought she was lying. "What're you all staring at? Don't you have better things to do! What the hell am I paying for? It's sure as hell not to have you loaf around, for God's sake. Get back to work!"

No one moved for a few seconds. They were nervously trying to see if Tava was all right.

"I said, get back to work! Now!" Grace stood up quickly and rushed the crowd. She could not stand to have them staring at her, accusing her of Tava's fall. "My daughter tripped, all right? You've all had your fun, now give her some breathing space!

"Honey? Mama's gonna help you inside now. Don't try to talk, baby. Mommy's going to take you to the doctor. It's okay, sweetie. Shh. Everything's going to be okay." This was all show for the crowd as they slowly gave in and began to back away. They were not happy with the situation but Grace was not a woman to tangle with right now. She was acting crazy and no one was interested in taking her on.

8

At thirty-five thousand feet the sky was hauntingly quiet. Thomas watched as the clouds moved slowly beneath him. A tiny smile blew across his sculptured lips as he recalled the flowing curves of his assistant. He had so much fun with her, it was hard to pull away for the vacation. He did not look forward to seeing Grace.

The summer ball was his wife's idea. Every June it was their welcome to the community. Grace felt a need to enter with a big splash. She loved the show of huge events and from the very beginning the Blackhurst Ball was the premiere event of the summer. It attracted only the most cultured element in Sultan Valley, and like most jewels quickly became the hot ticket.

Early on Thomas foresaw the potential for Sultan Valley and now quietly owned sixty percent of the good land in the area. He was partnered in the biggest resort and was head of the town council. Sultan Valley was his crowning glory. Like Tava, he truly relaxed in the rugged mountain air. Sultan Valley was the only place he allowed himself the luxury of dreaming.

Thomas conceived some of his most outrageous business ventures fishing in the rivers bordering his estate. Years ago Sultan Valley was run-down, a leftover mining town. Today it rivaled the best summer and winter resorts. Unlike the overrun tourist traps in other mountain resorts, Sultan Valley was a planned community, well thought out from the beginning. Thomas knew he would retire to this mountain paradise and wanted a community he felt comfortable in. He was shaping the world he most enjoyed living in.

Thomas glowed with satisfaction. He was a hardworking man constantly driving himself to do better. It was rare when he paused in his busy life to congratulate himself on his success. But with Sultan Valley he allowed himself the freedom.

He straightened his Brooks Brothers trousers and used the phone to speak with the pilot. "Gary, what are we doing?"

"About four hundred and twenty miles an hour. We'll be landing in half an hour. Smooth sailing all the way."

"That's what I like to hear. Do me a favor. Call ahead and make sure my daughter is there."

"Yes, sir." Gary clicked off.

Thomas leaned back into the sumptuous seat and closed his eyes. He began to reminisce about his little girl. He counted his blessings. He knew several men whose children had developed drug habits, dropped out of society, and sometimes ended up wasted on the street. Thomas did not know why Tava had escaped those temptations. He hoped it had to do with him. He had always tried to be a good father. He worried that his schedule kept him separated from her but he tried to compensate. He knew he loved her.

Next to him in an oak cabinet a fax machine buzzed. He ripped off the single page and scanned it quickly. He slapped the piece of paper with pleasure.

He was reading the Nicholls Development financial statement. What he saw was a company worth more than its shares. Hank's company was primed for takeover and all he wanted was Hank's blessing. It was just too good a deal to pass up. He checked his Rolex and eagerly awaited landing.

Like Tava's plane the week before, Thomas's landed and taxied to the family hangar. The engines were shut down and Gary lowered the stairs for him. Hans stood at the bottom and took Thomas's briefcase. They shook hands and Thomas followed Hans to the shining limousine. The night was beginning to grow dark and the airport lights danced across the glossy paint of the car like a million fireflies.

Hans held the door for Thomas and then climbed in behind the wheel.

"Where's Tava?"

Hans spoke over his shoulder as he pulled away from the curb. "There's been a little accident."

Thomas's heart stopped for a fleeting moment. "What?"

"Tava fell, sir. I'm taking you to the clinic."

"What happened? Is she all right?"

"Yes, sir. She's going to be fine. I'll let Mrs. Blackhurst explain." Hans was a diplomat and very careful with the internal politics of the Blackhurst family. He felt the situation would speak for itself. He wanted to see Grace squirm out of this one.

"Where's Grace?"

"At the clinic. She asked that I take you there immediately."

"Step on it!"

"Yes, sir."

The clinic was a small facility on the edge of the Sultan Valley Resort. It serviced the guests and was well equipped to care for Tava.

A female nurse in her late twenties worked diligently to

remove the glass from Tava's face. It looked much worse than it really was. Tava had apparently absorbed most of the fall with her hands but could not avoid the glass entirely.

The nurse, a friendly woman named Gwen, first washed the dirt, sweat, and blood from the wounds. Tava grimaced when she moved across the cuts. They were not deep but hurt terribly. Next, with the help of a magnifying glass she removed the tinier pieces from around the eyes. Luckily they did not leave noticeable marks and some of the bigger scars were hidden by her eyebrows.

Gwen moved up the forehead. One cut left a scar above Tava's left eyebrow and curved along the same crease. It looked like a permanent frown line and only added to Tava's features. The only real mark was on her right temple. Several pieces of the glass lodged along the cheekbone and left a line about half an inch long. Gwen stitched it up and gave Tava a clean bill of health. She was relieved to see Tava smiling.

Thomas burst through the front door of the clinic.

"Where is she?" Thomas was panicked.

Grace intercepted her worried husband. She grabbed his arms and they exchanged a long, frightened hug.

"What happened?" he asked.

Grace was white. Tears welled in her bloodshot eyes and she looked pathetic. Thomas kissed her out of sympathy. She began haltingly, "I . . . don't . . . know." She broke down. "Our little girl, Thomas . . ." She could not continue and reached out to him for support. He took her and comforted her. She tried again. "She stumbled by the gazebo, into glass. They say she's going to be all right."

His touch soothed her. She felt a certain release with his strong arms around her. It was like the old days, she thought to herself. She found herself beginning to believe her own lies about Tava. She was even more frightened now of Thomas finding out. This episode would surely ruin anything they had left. Little Tava was her father's pride and joy and if he found out the truth it would devastate their relationship. Grace felt like crying now. She felt defenseless. She knew she had painted herself into this corner. Her blind rage betrayed her and she was fearful of having to pay the price. This was not how she wanted her marriage to end. She was petrified and clung to Thomas in utter desperation.

"Thank God she's okay." For an instant he was overflowing with love for Grace. He remembered her twenty-one years ago, fresh, full of life, and gorgeous. He had not felt this kind of uninhibited nostalgia for a long time. He felt terrible seeing her sad face. She must have been crying a long time, he thought to himself. "I'm going to go in and see her. Are you all right?"

Grace nodded yes and he left her in the waiting room. The worried look stayed on her face. She needed this deception to continue although she was dreading the worst. Tava was refusing to speak to her.

"Honey?" Thomas called from behind the curtain.

"Daddy? Come in." She smiled when she saw him. She felt safer with him there.

"How are you, sweetie?" He took her hand and held it firmly. It hurt him to see her like this. Her face was still red from the cleaning. The cut along her right temple looked painful. Thankfully nothing seemed to be disfigured. "What happened?"

Tava held her breath. A thousand thoughts ran through her mind. She wanted to scream at Grace and make sure this never happened again. But the only thing to come out was, "Please call Mother in here." She felt a peaceful calm overtaking her. She was relying on her instincts to say the right thing. Grace had gone too far this time. Tava knew her mother was petrified. The one thing Grace had no control over was Thomas and she feared that more than anything else. His money was her key to happiness.

Grace was still struggling to appear worried instead of drunk. She was feeling queasy and felt like vomiting. It was all she could do to stay on her feet. She reached for Thomas's hand to steady herself. She managed a very weak smile in Tava's direction.

"Feeling better, baby?" Her voice was barely above a whisper. She was quaking and sinking quickly into a delirious terror. What would Thomas do when he found out?

"I'm okay, Mother. Daddy asked what happened and I thought you would like to hear." Tava was very purposeful now. Finally this was her chance to corner Grace and force her hand.

Grace was near fainting and determined to call Tava a liar if it came to that. Pictures of a divorce flew through her mind. How could she let this happen? Why did she let this little girl get to her? At times like this she hated herself because of Tava. To think that all this boiled down to competition. Grace denied it in herself, shoved it deep inside her, and blamed Tava for her own inadequacies.

Tava took her time and let the fear seep into her mother's bones. She wanted Grace to remember this moment. For her own sanity and for a little revenge she was enjoying these few seconds. Coolly she said, "I tripped."

Grace fell backward and Thomas eased her into a chair. He smiled and managed a laugh, "You've got to be more careful, Tava."

"Don't I know it," Tava replied. "Can you believe it, Mom? Me, tripping?"

A nervous smile appeared on Grace's face. It stayed there, frozen and unmovable as she tried to come up with a response. She knew a statement was expected of her but she did not know how to get it out. Her daughter had pulled off the only coup that could make Grace feel worse. She had lost in a more frightening way than she could have imagined. Tava, in one short moment, had surpassed her and taken control. Grace was surprised, wary, and a little impressed with her daughter. This was not the Tava she was used to and she was going to have to be very careful from now on.

"You've always been a little klutzy," Grace said softly, the words catching in her throat.

9

Michael Petersen was being coveted by a drop-dead beauty queen from Anaheim, California. Her name was Charlotte Teal and she was spending the summer at the Sultan Valley Resort cleaning rooms. Like Michael, she was working her way through school. She was heading for a bachelor's degree in physical education at Cal State, Long Beach.

The moment Charlotte saw Michael she wanted him. She was five feet eight with a model's healthy glow. She was a provocative nineteen-year-old with bleach-blond hair, a round jaw, piercing green eyes, large, voluptuous breasts, and a tight, shapely bottom. On her free hours she kept her tan a deep inviting brown. Her beauty brought her attention, which she wanted, but her thoughts were only on Michael.

He was six feet tall with dark brown hair. He possessed a lithe, graceful athlete's body. His eyes were hazel with a strong, steady weight to them. Michael lifted weights to exercise his body while classes exercised his mind. He carried himself confidently like a man at peace with himself. There was a gravity to him that people responded to. People looked to Michael as a natural leader.

He was driving Charlotte crazy. The more he avoided her, the more she found him attractive. She detected a well-grounded masculinity in him and it turned her on. While he was very comfortable around women, he still grew embarrassed with Charlotte on his trail. He did not want to hurt her but did not know how to tell her to stay away. Only Tava filled his thoughts and desires.

After three weeks on his path Charlotte hatched a plot and was waiting for him in his room. She used her maid's key to gain entry, stripped down to a silky green teddy, and crawled onto his bed. She timed it perfectly and smiled innocently when Michael flipped on the light. He did a double take and then grew extremely red.

Charlotte knew the effect her body had on men and used it often to get the things she wanted. She wanted Michael. She greeted him with a little nod of her head, conveying her desire.

"Charlotte, what are you doing?"

She giggled coquettishly and slowly pulled herself off his bed. Instead of dressing she lit a candle and turned off the lights. Michael was caught, fascinated, and unable to breathe. All he could do was stand there in the flickering yellow light of the candle and watch Charlotte turn her head slightly to catch his eye. She held him in her gaze.

"Charlotte, please . . ."

She cut him off by touching his lips with an index finger and whispering, "Shhh."

She placed the candle on the floor by the bed. Crawling onto the mattress like a cat, she arched her back, licking her full red lips. She slowly pulled herself onto her knees and presented her back view to Michael. She leaned on the wall, her forehead touching the cool cement, and thrust her ass in his direction.

Michael was swimming in a heated, turbulent sea of confusion. He felt unsteady as pictures of Tava slipped through his mind. Charlotte's taut, glistening body was calling him. Still leaning against the wall, she reached down and undid the snaps between her legs. At that point, with the soft teddy loose around her body, she rolled off the bed and unzipped Michael's pants. She tried to burrow in and was frustrated when Michael started backing away. He zipped his pants back up.

"Sorry, Charlotte. I can't do this."

"Everybody cheats."

"Not everybody." He was cooling now. The shock had worn off and he was becoming annoyed with her.

"Are you crazy? Every boy at this resort wants to sleep with me."

"I don't want what everybody can get."

"What's that supposed to mean? Are you gay?"

"No. Get dressed and leave, please." He was beginning to get angry. Charlotte's attitude bothered him. "You're a very pretty girl but I'm not interested."

Charlotte stood there like a confused child. She did not know whether to scream, get angry, yell, or cry. Emotions she never felt were coursing through her at incredible speeds. She absentmindedly pulled on her jeans. "I can't believe it. You can't get it up. Is that it?"

"Charlotte, I'm getting tired of this. You are not God's gift to love."

"What's that supposed to mean?" She found her shirt and pulled it on.

"Just because I don't want to sleep with you doesn't mean there's anything wrong with me."

"I think it does. You're an idiot not to want this." She pointed at her body. "I'm the best fucking lay on the West Coast. You're a real asshole."

"Get out of here. You might see things more clearly if you stopped thinking with your crotch."

She glared at him. "You're going to be sorry for this, Michael. No one does this to Charlotte Teal and gets away with it. No one." She collected her purse and slammed out of the room. Michael watched her go and sat heavily on the bed. He checked his watch with a sigh of relief and realized he was not late for the Blackhurst Ball. He thought about Tava for a moment. He knew she was in town and found it endearing that she wanted to hold off their reunion until the party. He knew she was a busy woman and respected it but he still could not wait to see her. He was like a little boy in his excitement.

10

As the helicopter sped through the darkening night Buddy thought of several ways to get his father's company out of its predicament. Partnership. Privatization. Poison pills. All of these strategies he kept to himself. Thomas Blackhurst's interest in the company was just the opportunity Buddy was looking for. He decided to see how far he could play it. He leaned farther back in his seat and daydreamed of wealth, power, and women.

The younger Nicholls never had luck with the opposite sex. He was introverted with women and lacked confidence. Buddy could conceive of the perfect relationship but reality never matched up. His one experience was with an Asian prostitute hired by Hank for Buddy's sixteenth birthday. The gesture was a friendly welcome-to-manhood gift.

The woman's name was Ariel. She was tall and shapely with makeup splashed across her face. His knees shook and his teeth chattered when she approached him. She knew it was his first time and saw the terror in his young eyes. She knew she was being paid for more than just sex and gently led the boy through the paces.

She stroked him, saw the flicker of excitement in his eyes when he grew hard, and guided his young, inexperienced hand over the mysterious parts of her little body. Buddy liked this. Chills caught him as he imagined again that first sensation of touching the warm, quivering body of a woman. He explored her by touch; she the leader, he the student. Silently she lowered herself on him. He practically cried with joy and fright. The moment was more than he'd ever dreamed it would be. To be that close to a woman and to experience her lusting desires proved to be too much for the boy and he exploded prematurely, pulling himself from her in embarrassment. She dressed slowly, laughing at the frightened little thing on the bed.

He did not say good-bye that night. He simply pulled the covers up around himself and slept. His memory of her filled him with one of his few happy memories. All of his dreams were filled with her. All he could bring himself to do now was stimulate himself with Ariel in his mind. The thought of approaching a woman terrified him. His shyness consumed him. He kept his distance from women out of fear while his desires burned inside. He knew one day this split, the desire and the fear, would ignite and carry him over some brink. He secretly hoped one day to meet a woman as kind as Ariel to lead him again into the innocence of love.

The helicopter was still forty minutes away from Blackhurst Manor.

11

Michael couldn't keep himself still. He cinched his waist-band and stepped back to admire himself in the mirror. He looked dashing as a swordsman. The costume was thrown together but very effective with a flowing white cotton shirt, a black patch over his left eye, shining silk pants, and knee-high black leather boots. He wanted to look perfect. He wanted to surprise and impress Tava. He was hoping to sweep her off her feet tonight. He was going as Zorro and wanted to be dashing and suave. He was craving her and counted the minutes to seeing her.

It had been too long this time. She was consuming his thoughts. During the last few weeks it was almost impossible to keep his mind on his studies. Everywhere he turned, something reminded him of Tava. Their time together last year, during the long, lazy summer months was like a dream now. His memories were taking on the hazy glow of recollection. He knew the fire was still ignited in him but he needed to reaffirm his love for her. The long-distance relationship was such a strain and yet they had persevered. It was amazing they had made it the entire year.

He was confident that Tava cared for him. Above all else he had to hold her. He dreamed of her body; her gorgeously shaped breasts, her strong happy face, her tight bottom, and long, smooth legs. It was more than he could handle and he had to tear himself away from these thoughts. It was like torture to think them without her.

Their schedules never coincided during the year. He at UCLA and she at William and Mary. They wrote, and talked on the phone. They only saw each other three times during the entire year. She flew out to see him on each occasion. Michael did not have enough money to fly out to see her. Each time they only had a weekend together.

The long times apart were painful. Being without her touch hurt him. He lay awake at night picturing the two of them, quietly in love under a moon, she nestled close to him sharing his warmth. All he could think about was holding her. All his memories were like a jumble of emotions running through his head. Last summer had been such a wild, heart-pounding time of discovery for both of them. This year apart only proved one thing to him. He could not live without her.

At twenty-six he was preparing for his final year in philosophy. Many things crowded his thoughts: the future, his thesis, his life. The one recurring thought was a hope to spend the rest of his years with Tava. That alone was the only thing keeping him going through the painful, lonely hours apart. L.A. was like a prison without her.

Michael was hoping tonight he could share all his thoughts with her. He did not want to scare her. Making it too serious might jeopardize everything and he wanted to avoid that. Even marriage was creeping into his thoughts. He feared the tender part of him, the part that needed to be held. He did not trust himself to say the right things to her. Michael was a complicated young man who, until Tava, had never felt the soft brush of love across his heart. Women were something to be pursued, conquered, and at all cost kept at a distance.

Tava ignited in him the fiery emotions of true love for the first time. These new feelings frightened him but he knew they were honest and understood the risks might lead to a happy future. He hoped so anyway. He loved her, he discovered, and could not wait to tell her.

12

The Blackhurst family arrived home an hour before the start of the party. They needed to move quickly. Hans unloaded Thomas's bags and carried them to his suite. Annie greeted Thomas with a funny indifference. She cracked a joke about his suit. Thomas replied by assuring her she would be fired if she kept up with this impudence. Annie snorted in disapproval and said, "That'll be the day, Mr. Blackhurst." At this point she took Tava by the hand and whisked her away down the hall. Time was growing very short and Tava needed to be cleaned up for the party. Annie made sure to give Grace a cold stare before she left.

Thomas watched his daughter disappear down the hall. "Thank God she's all right."

"She's a tough little girl," Grace reassured him. She took his hand and held it. The feelings stirring inside her at the hospital had not gone away.

"She's not so little anymore."

"That's the truth." She tried to keep the bitterness out of her voice. She did not trust Tava now. Grace knew she had lost control and it bothered her. Grace despised sharing power, and in one swift motion Tava had snatched it from her.

Grace turned her attention to her husband. He was tall and very handsome. Tava's strong jaw came from him. His eyes were magnetic. She wondered why they had stopped loving each other. Both were in a comfortable rut. They shared the same last name, attended parties together, but did not talk to each other anymore. Their marriage was now one of convenience. Thomas lived alone in his world of money. Grace felt lost in hers. The years pressed down on their emotions and dulled them to a point where they were embarrassed to remember they had once shared the same bed and the same passionate intimacies.

Tonight in the entrance hall, with the afterglow of a drunken stupor, Grace wanted to undress him. The force of this surprised her but she responded to it immediately. She moved into him and hugged him tightly. She nestled her face into him and was elated when he put his arms around her.

"It's okay," he whispered and squeezed her tighter.

She thrilled to his deep, commanding voice and gently rubbed against him. She vaguely remembered he enjoyed being touched, secretly, in public. As young lovers they explored their sexual frontiers and learned what fantasies the other liked. She surprised herself with the memory and smiled deliciously. As her heart beat faster she inched her hand down his front and tried to play with him.

Thomas was caught off guard. He was confused by Grace's advances. The last thing he wanted now was sex. Grace's advances suddenly forced the realization that the woman holding him was a complete stranger. Their lives were in a set pattern now and did not include love. They tolerated each other. Thomas wondered if they even liked each other anymore.

Grace's drinking upset him. He could not stand undisciplined, ungrateful behavior. Thomas made his money on the foundation of hard work. Grace supported that for many years but became lazy. Money was her drug. Her circle of friends thinned through the years and now only included very rich, ungrateful, unhappy women. They did not value the work it took to place them in such privileged positions. At this level life was taken for granted.

All of this came together in the moment she touched him and was so bewildering, he hugged her and said, "It's all right," just to give him time to think. He was in no mood to hurt her. Thomas respected the woman she once was and hoped could be again. It hit him he was at fault for not trying harder. He should insist on a treatment program. He wished they were young again, poor, in love, and full of passionate energy. How was he going to explain this to her now?

She was pushing her breasts close against him while her right hand rubbed his crotch and her left held him tightly around the waist. They were locked together and Grace was growing hotter. She wanted to feel more fire. The flames of excitement were intoxicating.

Thomas summoned the strength and held her from him. He kissed her on the forehead and smiled. "Grace," he began, "isn't this party starting soon?"

"There's time."

"Darling, I don't even know what I'm wearing."

She instantly withdrew. The fire died and turned to familiar hate. She saw him in a different light now. This was the same old thing all over again. He was getting his rocks off with some little tramp. She suspected it and blamed him for her drinking, and the vicious cycle began again.

She shrugged off the passionate embers and came back to reality. Tava was still a little schemer, Thomas was still her estranged, uncaring husband, and she was the oppressed, misunderstood mother and wife. All of these pictures made Grace feel whole. They were her protection from her hidden truths.

"You're going as the court fool," Grace bit out. "That's fitting, don't you think? You're always so full of jokes, Tom. Like the one about how you love me." She sounded bitter and wanted to. No one refused her like this without feeling her wrath.

Thomas took it in stride. He was used to these outbursts and they bored him. They reminded him of why their relationship was in the state it was. He tried to let her down gently. He made up his mind to get her help and maybe they could try over. "Honey, we'll talk later. I promise."

"Then you'll be talking to yourself. I don't have anything to say to you, Thomas Blackhurst. I really don't care. If you'll excuse me, I hear a drink calling."

"We need to talk, Grace."

"Don't pretend you care, Tom." She brushed past him. "Don't bother, sweetie. I know where your excitement comes from these days." She disappeared down the hallway to finish preparing for the party. The guests were going to start arriving shortly and she needed to be ready.

Thomas was empty. The six-hour flight was draining. The excitement with Tava left him keyed up but with no way to alleviate the tension. And now with Grace he felt depressed. He decided to give himself the luxury of a quick workout. He needed to ease the stress. The party would begin without him. Thomas made his way to the gym.

Arriving, he closed the door behind him and stripped. Crossing to the closet, he pulled out a pair of shorts and a towel. Putting these on, he found a phone and dialed New York. Kim's sleepy voice answered.

"Hello?"

"Kim. This is Thomas."

"Christ, it's late. What's wrong?"

"Nothing. I just wanted to let you know I'm here okay."

"Great. Can I go back to sleep?"

"Listen. How would you like to fly out here? I need help on this end. I think I may take an extended vacation and run the office here. What do you think?"

"I don't know. What about Grace? I don't want to fuck up a good thing. I like you, Thomas. You're a great lover and a great boss. I'm not sure I like the sound of this. You know what I mean?" The question was not meant to be answered. Thomas understood exactly. This is what he loved about her. She was a street-smart young woman, completely confident and self-assured. She did not want her good thing to go away. "Thomas, are you there?"

"Fly out. I've got the feeling things are going to be changing around here and I want you near me."

"Listen, baby, I don't want to rush this thing. You know and I know what we have. I don't want to let it break apart too fast. It's fragile, Tommy. We've got to be sure. You've got to be sure." Kim knew him and when he said something he meant it. She wanted to trust him to do the right thing but she was leery. "Well, what do you think?"

"I like you, Kim, and I can't make this thing run without you. I think it's time to let us grow a little bit."

"You positive?"

"Yes."

"All right then. I hope you know what you're doing. You want me to hop a commercial flight?"

"That's fine. Get here as soon as you can. Call when you get in. Hans will pick you up." Thomas was ready to hang up but hesitated for a moment. Right now he was acting on instinct, not quite sure what he was doing. He felt intoxicated by Kim. Her voice calmed him. He needed her. Grace's advances had made that even clearer. "Indulge me."

"I always do."

"What're you wearing?" he asked, closing his eyes as he imagined her lying in bed, her eyes sleepy and her short hair tousled. He pictured her loft in the Village, her bed. He knew she was sleeping on pink-flowered sheets.

"You bad boy. Who wants to know?"

"I do."

"I'm naked, Thomas. And I miss you."

After a short workout he showered and toweled off. With Kim on his mind he made his way to his rooms. Unlike Grace's blue-carpeted suite, Thomas's was more introspective. His rooms were decorated in rich hardwoods. The floors were polished to a shine and forest-green throw rugs dotted the huge area. The walls were paneled and lined with books. Thomas was an avid reader and filled most of his free moments immersed in the explorations of history, philosophy, and religion. He was thoughtful, very well-spoken, and quietly intense. He was comfortable with himself and appreciated the advantage that gave him. In business he was politely ruthless; in private, a warm and adoring lover and friend. His rooms matched his personality and radiated a manly strength.

He moved through the rooms easily. His dressing room was mirrored and carpeted in forest-green. He dropped his towel. His body was taut and did not exhibit any flabbiness. His chest, arms, and back were muscular and well-defined. His legs were strong and powerful. Years of exercise had turned Thomas into an agile, quick athlete. He was strong and graceful and his movements exhibited tremendous confidence. He flexed his arm and admired the bulging muscle. Not bad, he thought to himself, not bad at all for an old man. He grinned.

Everything seemed to be going so well. Tava was all right. Fresh out of college, her whole life was before her. Grace, although unsteady, could be made happy with the right treatment. With Kim's help that would be one of his first orders of business. It was becoming increasingly important to Thomas that Grace be made comfortable. He had neglected her for too long but still felt there was time to help her. Kim was a delightful question mark and he waited with mounting anticipation to see where things between them might lead.

Hank Nicholls and Nicholls Development were the two things making his blood rush. Showering and shaving, he fixated on his political maneuvering. Hank's son Buddy fell very quickly, much to Thomas's pleasure. He saw traces of himself in this skinny Texan. Ambition can be very frightening in the wrong hands. Thomas smelled it all over Buddy and was using it masterfully. A little money dangled just in front of the young Texan's nose and Thomas had him jumping through hoops. This was a thrill for Thomas. He had jumped through enough in his day to understand exactly the emotions in young Buddy Nicholls's veins.

Thomas finished shaving and rinsed his face. Time was growing short and he could hear the sounds of the first arriving guests. He found his favorite after-shave, Polo, and splashed it on. This evening was going to be liberating. He loved this summer event and intended to have a tremendous time.

Naked, he walked back into his bedroom and found his costume. He was not surprised to find a brightly colored court jester outfit. Its three-pronged hat, multicolored jacket, pants, and slippers all added to the festive air. He knew why Grace had ordered this but it didn't bother him. He found it fitting. In Shakespeare, he knew, the jester was usually the smartest character in the play.

13

Lawrence was in Tava's room finishing the last seam on her dress. "Hon, I'm gonna tell you this only once. Your momma is gonna scream when she sees this. If she knew what I was doing, she would absolutely flip. Promise me you'll tell her this was your idea, please."

"Of course I'll tell her. You're a doll for helping me." Tava sat at her makeup table doing herself up. She was outlining her eyes in black and lengthening her lashes with mascara.

"I guess you know what you're doing." He bit off the last piece of thread and fluffed the dress out in front of him. "Done. If you made me late for my date, I'm gonna kill you." He packed his bag. "Hope you have a real nice time. Sounds like this party's gonna blow 'em all away. Give your momma a kiss for me and tell her I'll call in a couple of days." He zipped his bag and stood up. He crossed over to Tava and gave her a quick kiss on the top of her head. "You look great. And don't do pigtails. It's so predictable. You better tease it up, honey. Don't think I don't know what you're going for. I guess the whole virgin motif is shot to hell. *C'est la vie,* as they say. Stay out of trouble, sweetie."

Tava touched his hand and winked at him in the mirror. "Thanks for your help, Lawrence. You're the best."

"Don't I know it. Wish me luck. I think I may fall in love tonight. This guy's eyes just about steal my heart." He sighed and whirled. "See ya." He walked to the door just as Annie walked in. He smiled broadly and moved around her. He knew she could not stand him. "Good night, Annie. Love your outfit." He disappeared.

"He wears his pants too tight," Annie said.

"Oh, please, Annie. How do I look?" She turned her pretty face toward her nanny and smiled.

"You look like an angel. I can't even see the scar. You want me to do the bow?"

"Please."

Tava teased her hair into a wild mess on top of her head and let Annie spray it into place. The look was both provocative and sexy. Her hair was like a lion's mane. Her eyes sparkled. Tava applied her base and blushed her cheeks. She was going for a very adult look.

"Now," Tava said mysteriously, "look what I've got." She slipped her robe off and crossed to the costume.

Annie looked disapprovingly. "How many times do I have to tell you not to walk naked in front of the window? The guests are arriving. Someone might see you."

"I don't care tonight, Annie. I really don't."

The older woman still closed the curtains tight. Tava stepped into her lacy panties. Annie frowned.

"Those look silly. Men will get the wrong idea."

"Good."

"Too many dirty thoughts in your head tonight, Missy. I don't like it."

Tava winked at her. "Wait till you see this." She grabbed the dress and ran in the dressing room. Annie tapped her foot impatiently and pulled a strand of gray hair away from her face. She was done up as an Elizabethan serving wench. Her ample chest spilled over her bodice.

"You should hurry up. You're already late."

"Relax," Tava called out.

"Relax? You relax. I've got a busy night ahead of me."

"Are your eyes closed?"

"No. Just come out here and let's go."

"You're no fun." Annie sprayed on some of Tava's perfume. She liked the smell and it reminded her of the many times she had found little Tava sneaking her mother's perfume and stinking up the house. Tava used to scream at the baths Annie put her through to scrub off the scent. "Are you ready?" Tava yelled again.

"Just hurry up."

Tava, beaming, held her breath and made her entrance.

14

Hank and Buddy were changing in the helicopter. They were twenty minutes away and starting to feel the excitement. The blades from the helicopter whirred feverishly and Hank swigged from a glass of bourbon.

"That goes down nice." He watched his tall son struggle into a Mafia costume. The muted 1930's-style suit and matching wide-brimmed hat made him look sinister. To this he added a cigar. "What are you, the Godfather?"

"I like the Mafia, Daddy," he drawled in his mild Texas accent.

"Why?"

"'Cause of the power. I like the way they got things done."

"So you want to show off as a crook?"

Buddy was sick of his father's nagging. "I have a respect for the way they handle their affairs. I'm not saying it's right, but it works."

Hank grinned quietly. "Sometimes you're a chip off the old block."

"What're you wearing?" Buddy diverted the conversation to his father. He hated being compared to Hank.

"What I've got on. I brought my best hat. That should suit these people. They'll think I came as a cowboy. I'm gonna pretend to be Mr. Roy Rogers. What do you think?"

"Real great, Daddy." He turned away from his father and stared out at the tiny bright lights below them. Sultan Valley was shimmering in the distance. He wanted to land quickly. He was starting to feel sick again.

15

The guests continued to pour into Blackhurst Manor. The grounds were alive with excitement. Bunches of brightly colored balloons lined the long driveway and added a very happy air to the evening. It was getting dark but the sun's light was still ablaze in lavender hues. A white cloud hung low in relief above the hills.

Invitations were checked at the entrance before the expensive cars were allowed through. Black limousines, Mercedes, Rolls Royces, and Italian sports cars lined the two-lane road in both directions. Six hundred guests were expected this evening.

Security was there to control parking. The drivers lined up dutifully after they discharged their passengers. The guests were let out at the front entrance and ushered through the house to the back lawn. The evening was warm and the mood was electric.

The workers were dressed as English servants in white wigs, silk overcoats, stockings, and buckled shoes. The ladies were dressed as milkmaids.

The scene was extravagantly lush. The guests continued to stream in, done up in brilliant colors and costumes. Young and old and cultured, this group was an international set; an exotic mix of politicians, well-placed locals, movie stars, and businessmen. All of these people were friends to Thomas and Grace. Although Grace was in decline, tonight she was at her social best. This was her element and she came alive in it.

She stood by the pool and greeted each guest by name. She was brilliantly gifted in the social arts. Each person shaking her hand felt honored and pleased to be included in her elite circle of guests. This party was a barometer to success. You knew you had made it if the Blackhursts invited you.

The music played with the guests' emotions. It wooed them into a hypnotic dance that whirled them away into the Blackhurst fantasy. The sounds mingled with the noise of the arriving guests and caused an air of electricity to descend on the ecstatic crowd.

The costumes were incredible. The women came as goddesses, angels, movie stars, clowns, and dancers. The back lawn began to fill with a multitude of color. Like a huge crazy quilt the colors mixed and mingled. A certain amount of ego came with them and everybody wanted to look and be the best. Grace was careful to stay away from competition. She intended everybody to feel their best. Secretly, of course, she wanted to outclass all of them with her Cleopatra. She looked stunning in full regalia: long straight black hair, striking makeup, arm and finger jewelry. Her gold lamé dress, close to her body, was sequined and beaded with thin lines of black thread. The dress was stunning and made Grace glow. She easily outshone the others in the crowd.

She was all smiles as she stood there greeting each guest. Her detached air of superiority seemed lost tonight. She was bright, clear-eyed, and engaging. She reached out to her guests with complete confidence. It was in this kind of event she came to life. She was happy at this moment, totally in control, far away from the push of the real world. This time, more than any other, fantasy filled her senses and she lived without the hesitant scent of doubt.

Mark Young, Tava's pilot, approached Grace in the receiving line.

"Good evening, Mrs. Blackhurst. You look beautiful." He could not believe his eyes. Usually she looked tired and run-down.

"Mark, you said you weren't coming. Welcome." She kissed him on the cheek and let her lips linger a little longer than normal.

"Change of plans, you know. Did Mr. Blackhurst make it?"

"He's circulating. You can't miss him. He's playing court jester tonight." She tried to find her husband in the crowd but could not see him.

"I'll keep an eye out for him." He was at a loss for words. "Tava out yet?"

"I don't think she's made it. You know young girls." With

a lingering hope she still counted on hurting Tava. The hope was keeping her spirits up. Grace attributed Tava's late appearance to embarrassment.

The volume of noise was high and getting higher. As the guests spilled in, the area grew more and more crowded. A band, set up in the gazebo, struck up a lively tune and caused the huge crowd to start dancing. It was turning into a wonderful evening. The beautiful women danced as their billowy costumes swirled in graceful arcs around them. It was as if the night had become frenetic with excited bodies moving in time with each other.

Annie was scandalized.

She was so caught off guard, she had to lean against the door. "What have you done to that dress?" was all she could get out. What was initially shock was turning very quickly into humor, and the laughter started to spill out like a raging waterfall. She doubled up in laughter and practically limped to the bed. She sat heavily, shaking her head.

Tava stood there as if nothing were wrong. Lawrence had spent the majority of the day altering the baby dress to meet Tava's demanding specifications. She was determined to surprise her mother. She was furious with Grace and this was her way of getting back. Tava twirled around, thoroughly pleased with the creation.

"Can you believe this? Isn't Lawrence amazing? This should cause quite a stir, don't you think?" She allowed herself a little smile. "Would you stop laughing and talk to me. What do you think?"

"I think your mother is going to have a fit. You're an embarrassment and I cannot wait to be there. Give me five minutes to work my way out to the reception line. I don't want to miss this." She stood up quickly and moved toward the door. "Do you know what you're doing?"

"Absolutely. Mother deserves this after her little stunt today. Do you know if Michael's arrived yet?" There was an expectancy in her voice she could not hide. She had been counting the minutes since her arrival in Sultan Valley. She wanted tonight to be magical and wanted to surprise him.

"No. I'll keep an eye out. If I see him I'll send him down to the gazebo to wait for you. All right?"

This pleased Tava and she let Annie go without another

word. She turned to her mirror. Everything had to be perfect. She began to consider this as her "coming out" party.

Grace was smiling broadly. She was enjoying the attention her costume was causing. She preened under the watchful stares of her guests. It pleased her. She caught Thomas's eye across the throng and called him over.

He excused himself from a circle of business associates and sauntered through the crowd to his wife. On occasions like this he was, like his wife, the consummate actor. They moved almost unconsciously through the evening, greeting, chatting, and laughing with their guests. They both learned the art of entertainment and practiced it with incredible ease. To them this evening was as much a job as sitting behind a desk. To the outside world Grace and Thomas were madly in love with each other and reveled in the sheer joy of celebrating with friends.

Thomas moved around the line and pecked Grace on the cheek. He smiled at a woman in her mid-thirties dressed as a 1920's aviator. Her name was Heather Downing and she was heir to one of the largest landowners in the adjoining valley. Her name was at the top of Thomas's memory and he greeted her warmly.

"Hello, Heather. Thank you for coming this evening. Your costume is wonderful. You must be Amelia Earhart. Am I right?"

"Of course you're right, Thomas. I was just telling Grace how wonderful she looked. And you . . . where did you get that funny outfit?"

He looked very serious and then broke into a smile, "I stole this from Grace. I was going to go as Cleopatra. It's a very long story." He laughed deeply and Heather was enchanted. She accepted a kiss and moved on. There was a brief break in the line, and Grace took the moment to whisper in his ear.

"She's a little young for you, Thomas."

"Shut up, Grace."

"Where are your associates?"

"I don't know. I've been expecting them."

"I think I'll mingle."

"Fine. I'll watch the line." He sipped from his glass of champagne.

Grace signaled a waiter and was given a martini. She drank deeply from it and then floated off. She was halfway down the steps when she called back, "Where's Tava?" Thomas shrugged his shoulders as he greeted new guests.

Michael was driving north toward Blackhurst Manor. The evening was crystal clear. The stars were shimmering like sparkling diamonds. The sky was crammed with them. It was nights like this that made him never want to leave.

The line of cars waiting to enter Blackhurst Manor was long. Michael had to slow his little VW and finally stop. His excitement was growing and he could feel the blood rushing through his veins. He heard the music from the live band floating through the warm summer evening. He caught the faraway sounds of laughter. The party was evidently huge, as usual, and already teeming with excitement. He felt a wave flowing over him. He suddenly knew that Tava was waiting for him. He could feel her excitement and understood she was as anxious to see him as he was to see her. He smiled sheepishly to himself, convinced that he was making all of this up but secretly hoped it really was true. He hoped when two people were in love they could feel each other's moods and emotions.

Hans was directing the flow of traffic and commanding the small platoon of parking attendants. The hundreds of cars were moved through smoothly. Each chauffeur rounded the circular driveway, let their owners out, and then moved off to be parked in the east field. The horses had been stabled for the evening in order to make room for the cars. For those who chose to drive themselves, an attendant took the car for them and parked it. This evening was meant to whisk the participants into a fantasy world, where all wishes could come true. The Blackhursts had outdone themselves this year.

Tava had decided on a few touches of her own. She added colored lights along the entrance way to enhance the feeling of entering a wonderland. All the beautiful flowers were accented with a shot of light. The entrance was a tunnel of color. In addition she hung several ferns from the overhang in the front. Each was draped in creamy pink silk that fell dramatically toward the ground.

Grace was moving among the guests down on the lawn, laughing and carrying on the chitchat that made her infamous in New York. It was a mild amusement to her that she could keep up on all the scandals in Sultan Valley and still be completely versed on the social scene back home. Rumors were her delight and she collected them like fine jewelry. She seemed to need them. In one quick survey of the grounds she saw Thomas still greeting the new arrivals, Annie moving among the guests serving drinks, the throngs of costumed people milling with each other, and quite suddenly a flash in the night sky.

The sound came seconds later. It was the high-speed flapping of helicopter wings. Hank and Buddy Nicholls were descending.

From the helicopter the estate looked like a funny machine with hundreds of moving parts. Hank instructed the pilot to circle twice before setting down. He viewed the main house, the garages, and guest buildings with a certain envy. Even from the air Blackhurst Manor was perfect. Its fenced areas looked manicured and inviting. The rough outer fields were perfect for horse riding. Even the ring of high hills called to him. Like an instant friend the feeling of comfort was seeping its way into his Texas heart and wooing him. He was realizing the powerful lure of Sultan Valley.

"Go lower," he called up to the pilot. "I want to make an impression."

The pilot understood his boss's command and dropped the machine twenty feet. He switched on the exterior lights and the helicopter lit up like an ominous black monolith. It made its last circle over the estate and then returned to the grassy back lawn. It hovered there for a few moments and then began to descend.

The guests were both unnerved and exhilarated. They thought this was one of the Blackhurst surprises and readily cleared the area to allow the huge machine to land. The wind practically blew several of them over but they laughed anyway, eager to keep up appearances and not to offend their hosts.

Hank looked down below and laughed long and hard. This was exactly the entrance he wanted. He was surprised by the number of people but was only happier to show off.

Buddy broke the silence. "I can't believe you're doing this, Daddy. What're these people gonna think?"

"That I'm important, son."

The wheels touched ground and the engine whined down to a halt. The crowd waited in suspended animation until the hatch was released and the stairs extended down.

Thomas seized the moment and signaled the band to start playing again. He walked confidently down to the aircraft and waited for Hank to appear. He knew who it was, of course, realizing it when the helicopter made its first approach. He found the stunt inappropriate but was willing to let it pass. He knew many things about this oilman and was eager to shake his hand.

Buddy appeared first. He looked dapper and commanding. There was no sign of his troubles in the air. There was an eager sense about him. Thomas was surprised by the young man's height and his gawky appearance. He took Buddy's hand vigorously and welcomed him anyway.

"Glad to finally meet you, Buddy."

"Mr. Blackhurst? Nice to meet you, sir. My father will be out in a moment. I'm sorry for the landing." Buddy was embarrassed by the stunt.

"No harm done, son. I like a little spice in my parties. That's why I invited you. There's drinks up by the pool. We'll talk later." Thomas knew the boy was trying very hard to make a good impression. He dismissed him and waited for the father.

Hank finally appeared in all his Texan splendor. He had donned a cowboy's riding jacket and descended the stairs with the biggest Texas grin he could muster. He chomped on a cigar he had lit especially for the occasion. Before he hit the first step he stopped and took off his hat. Then in a deep, resonant voice he bellowed, "Howdy, folks. Hank Nicholls!" With that done he descended the stairs and shook Thomas's hand.

"Nice place, Mr. Blackhurst."

"Nice helicopter, Mr. Nicholls."

"Oh, hell, call me Hank." The big man slapped Thomas on the back and laughed.

"Please call me Thomas. Long flight?"

"Hell, long enough, Tom. Where's the drinks? This ain't no dry state, is it? I brought my own stash if it is."

"Up by the pool." Thomas motioned up toward Buddy. "I see your son has already found it."

"Leave it to Buddy. Listen, Tom, you want this baby flown out of here?"

"Tell you what. Why don't we just leave it there and fly it to the airport in the morning? We'll set you up in one of the guest houses."

"Great."

"While it's here, mind if the guests wander inside?" Thomas was testing Hank. He knew he had him in an awkward situation and enjoyed it. If Hank hesitated, he did not show it. "Hell, yes, partner. It'll be like Disneyland!" With that he moved quickly up toward the booze. All the flying had made him thirsty.

Michael was just coming through the hallway. He saw the helicopter blades winding to a halt and watched Buddy grab the first bottle of beer he could find. He found him strange and disconcerting. It was Buddy's eyes that warned him first. They sent chills running through Michael's taut body. He rarely felt immediate revulsion for anyone and was surprised to feel it now. He decided to forget it and turned his attention to finding Tava. He needed to see her. Now. Finding it hard to concentrate, he moved quickly to the back door and started scanning the crowd for her. What he saw was Grace storming over the lawn to her husband.

"What the hell is this all about?" she demanded. She was having trouble gauging the effect Hank's little prank had played on her guests. The majority seemed to be treating it lightly, as if it were part of a game.

"I don't know, darling. I had no idea he was going to land in the middle of the party. Just play along. Business as usual, honey. Never let the competition see you sweat." He smiled conspiratorially and brushed her cheek with his lips.

Grace was tired of playing these business games and did not feel like playing along. She found it disgusting and decided she had had enough. She took a deep breath and headed directly for Hank.

She crossed the distance quickly. Hank was gorging on honey-dipped chicken wings. Buddy was off by himself staring at the ice sculptures in the pool.

"Mr. Nicholls . . ."

Hank turned slowly with such a commanding air that it stopped Grace from finishing her sentence. "Yes, ma'am?" he drawled sweetly. "You must be Mrs. Blackhurst." He took her delicate hand in his and kissed it. "You look beautiful. Thomas did not do you justice when he spoke about you on the phone. He promised me I would be meeting his wife. He did not say I would be meeting his beauty queen."

Grace was stunned and suddenly short of breath. No one ever spoke to her like that. Even Thomas never uttered those kinds of words. She felt nineteen again and the thrill made her lose her balance. All of her animosity for this huge Texan fell by the wayside. She lapsed into her social persona and hid behind it while she collected herself.

"I was saying, Mr. Nicholls, what a pleasure it is to meet you. You have such a nice airplane." She hung on the last word, making it sound almost racy.

"That, my dear woman, is a helicopter. I hope I didn't give you a start."

"Of course not. I like a man with a little flair."

"Like your husband?"

"Among others."

Their eyes were locked in a match of wills. The sparks were already flying. Grace was meeting her match. Her head felt hazy and she reached for a drink to steady herself.

Hank was pleased. "You feeling all right?"

"Just a little queasy, Mr. Nicholls. Nothing a little drink won't take care of."

"Maybe you should sit?" He found a chair for her and urged her into it. His attention was drawn to loud voices by the entrance. He could not make out the cause of the commotion until the crowd parted.

Tava was making her entrance.

It took Grace several moments to comprehend the situation. What she saw was her daughter greeting the guests. Most of them had known her since childhood and she was now greeting them with the ease of a Blackhurst. Joking, caressing, shaking hands, and kissing, she had learned something from her mother.

It galled Grace to see her in the costume. Nothing had gone right about that and all she wanted to do was to rip it off her. Not only was Tava not embarrassed, but she was receiving compliments. Grace's last hope was that Michael would find the dress ridiculous.

Buddy needed to swallow hard. Until Tava came in he was not paying attention to the party. And now he was riveted. She was glowing. Her makeup was delicate and lit her face like an angel; her lips were brushed in dusty red and her beautiful long hair was sprayed, tussled, and provocatively piled up on her head; her long nails were painted blood-red. She was so graceful and refined. To Buddy all sound ceased and he only heard his own heart beating. His palms were sweating.

Grace choked when Tava turned. Suddenly Tava's plans were all too evident. Grace's little joke had been turned on her and Tava was throwing it back in her face. She had turned her little girl costume into a mockery. She had deliberately manipulated the dress to come off as sexy. Grace could see the effect Tava was having on the men. She grew embarrassed and incensed that Tava would do this to her. She felt betrayed and angry. Mostly she felt upstaged and that burned her more than anything.

The dress was now far more than when it started. With clever cutting the entire back of the dress was removed down to the base of her spine. Her shapely, feminine back was open and accessible; sexy and calculating. A pink bow was placed pertly at the bottom of the opening, suggestively calling attention to her backside. The short skirt flared out now like a ballerina's. Tava also had Lawrence raise the hem in the back so that now her lace panties were clearly showing. Her lacy bottom played with male emotions and she was drawing a tremendous amount of attention.

The front clung to her breasts. Lawrence had removed the front smock and replaced it with see-through netting. The open panel descended between her breasts down to the bow around her waist. Tava was going without a bra and abundantly filling the dress.

It was designed to show off her body and Tava was pleased with the end result. The sleeves were still puffy at the shoulders but the dress was something quite different. The effect was both provocative and very sexual. Tava suddenly seemed very grown-up and in command of her surroundings. She knew what she was doing and was aware of the reactions she was receiving. Tava's entrance was spreading quickly through the throng.

The reactions were more than Tava expected. Initially she felt silly and exposed in the daring dress. No longer a cute, little baby girl, she was now something much more. Men were flocking to her, carefully, of course, but she could feel their stares. She felt self-conscious until she caught her mother's blazing eyes. Then she felt victorious. Tava relaxed and decided to enjoy the attention. She searched the hordes of people for Michael.

Thomas was equally surprised, but not angry. He discovered almost sadly that his little girl was no longer one. She was very much grown-up. It was a little racy for him, almost uncomfortable, but he reassured himself that she knew what she was doing. He had to laugh when he saw the whole outfit.

Tava caught her father's eyes as she moved through the crowd. The push of the jovial crowd made it difficult for her to get to him quickly but Thomas remained where he was until she arrived.

"Hi, Dad," she said tentatively. She was unsure how he was going to react.

"That is some dress." He had to smile. "You're causing quite a stir."

"You think so?"

"Yes, I do." He twirled her. "My darling daughter, you are certainly full of surprises."

Tava smiled in appreciation. She needed his encouragement. "Got to keep up with the times, Dad."

"I suppose." He leaned down and whispered, "I guess my little girl's all grown-up."

She kissed him gently on the cheek. "I guess so."

"Well, God help the boys then." He had to laugh. It dawned on him he really shouldn't be surprised. Tava was as much a Blackhurst as he or Grace and that meant making an impression. Tava was certainly living up to that. "I'll see you later, toots." He winked at her. "Have fun." He shook his head in mock fatherly confusion and allowed himself to be pulled away by the crowd.

Tava was starting to feel antsy. She could not find Michael. It took her a half hour to make her way down to the gazebo. She was besieged by well-wishers. Tava nodded and smiled but did her best not to encourage. She found these society women too talkative. All she wanted to do was get to Michael and kiss him. He was the only thing on her mind.

Michael spotted her immediately. Tava did not see him. He was in the gazebo, sitting on the rail looking dashing. He noticed women staring at him. It was something that happened a lot and he liked it, although he kept it in perspective. He was a man in control of himself and understood there was only one person for him. Gratification came many different ways and Tava Blackhurst filled them all.

He was sipping from a tall, thin-necked glass of champagne and soaking in the atmosphere. These affairs were so foreign to him. At the resort he waited on these people all the time, but tonight it was different. He was now one of them and it made him feel strange. He wasn't sure he liked it. The thoughts disturbed him but it was not the idea of money, he told himself, it was the way people flaunted it. He decided he was not impressed with this extravagant show.

When he saw Tava he felt hot and short of breath. He wanted to rush over immediately but held himself back. He wanted Tava to discover him. It was a silly little game but he was so excited to see her, he wanted it to be perfect.

His hands were sweating and he felt his pulse quickening. A smile appeared on his lips and remained there. It had been so long and finally she was here! It was all he could do to keep himself put. He knew she had to greet everybody and waited impatiently. It was a slow torture but at least he could look at her.

So many things were whirling in his mind. She was so beautiful! He could not understand the effect she was having on him. Perhaps it was the pale pink of her dress or her gorgeous body on display for all to see. This outfit was naughty and racy. The billowy sleeves, the frizzy hair, her long shapely legs highlighted by the short little skirt, all of this added to his heightened craving for her. He was very hard and finding it difficult to hide it.

Tava was about to go mad and then spotted him. He looked so dashing! He was more than she remembered. She knew time played tricks and had been worried. She had had strange thoughts that maybe he might have changed but it was not true!

She never knew what swooning was until now. It was too much for her and she had to excuse herself from the latest chitchat and hurry down the path. Michael jumped off the banister and they met, half-running, and collapsed into each other's arms. Finally, after all the waiting, they were touching.

Michael hugged her tightly, pressing himself against her. He breathed her in and tingled with the excitement of holding her. "I missed you so much," he whispered in her ear.

"Oh, Michael," was all she could get out and then broke into tears. His touch transported her away from the noise. For a moment she was all alone in paradise with the man she loved. She felt his muscles underneath his clothes and responded to them. He was solid and dependable and daring and handsome and a million other words she smiled at. She looked deep into his eyes and laughed. Finally, after all the waiting, she was with him.

He dabbed the tears from her eyes and stroked her face. He held her face gently in his hands and just looked at her, drinking in her reflection.

She could not take her eyes off him. He looked so handsome. "How are you?" She was drying her eyes with the back of her hand.

"I'm fine." He smiled at her so tenderly, tears formed in his hazel eyes. "I've got so much to tell you, I don't even know where to begin."

"Same."

"I'm sorry I missed your graduation."

Tava smiled at him, "That's okay. Your flowers were beautiful." They were holding hands now. "You're wonderful to me."

"You deserve it and so much more. You're absolutely

gorgeous. That dress is something else. I wonder if you could show any more off."

"Michael, you're almost sounding jealous. It's a long story. I'll tell you later." She crinkled her nose. "What do you think, honestly? Pretty stupid, huh?"

The words were out of his mouth before he could stop them. "It makes me want to jump you right now."

Tava was delighted. "Michael," she admonished, "we can't."

"I can't wait to play," he whispered.

"Michael! Keep it down."

"How 'bout we sneak off for a little bit? What do you think?"

Tava giggled. She was finding it very hard to concentrate and started to think of ways to disappear for a little while. "Let me see what I can do," she whispered back. All this did was make Michael more excited than he thought imaginable. He could not get his mind off her beautiful body. He was hungry for her now.

Before they could make their escape Grace appeared with Hank and Buddy. She was all smiles. She was putting on an act and Tava read right through it.

Michael shook her hand. "Hello, Mrs. Blackhurst. Nice to see you again."

Grace ignored him and turned to her daughter. "Tava, I want you to meet Mr. Nicholls. He's one of your father's business associates."

Hank loomed above Tava and extended his huge hand. He took Tava's with a strange look in his eye. He held her hand for just a second too long. She watched his eyes roam up and down her body. She felt naked in the skimpy costume.

Hank turned to his son. "This is my boy, Buddy. Say hi to the pretty young thing."

Buddy felt unstable, as if he were flying in the helicopter again. He was never steady around women, and Tava was certainly no exception. He wiped his hand discreetly against his leggings before shaking her hand.

"It is a pleasure to meet you, Tava. You look great." Buddy tried to sound friendly but only ended up sounding uneasy.

Tava did not like the feel of Buddy's cold, clammy hand, and instantly knew she did not like either of the Nicholls.

Nevertheless she introduced Michael to both of them. Both men kept their attention on Tava.

"Your mama just got through telling me all about your graduation." Hank was pouring on his southern gentility. He found himself trying to impress the young woman.

"Well, Mr. Nicholls, Mother unfortunately missed a very nice ceremony. She just couldn't find the time to make it. She's a very busy woman."

"Now, Tava dear, you know I was tied up with business," Grace cooed.

"I know, Mother. I know."

"A woman's work is never done, Grace. My dear, departed wife was the prime example of that, God rest her soul." Hank turned his attention back to Tava. "You are just the prettiest little thing, all dolled up. Isn't she, Buddy?"

"Yes, sir, she is." Buddy was feeling awkward but entranced. Tava's sparkling blue eyes were working their magic on him.

"You're just as cute as a little button."

Grace was becoming uncomfortable with the men's response to her daughter and devised a way to drag them off. "Oh, there's someone I think you both should meet. His name is Patrick Thorn, Sultan Valley's new mayor." They were quickly spirited away, leaving Michael and Tava alone once more.

Michael did not say anything, and did not have to. He gently and firmly took Tava by the hand and moved around the crowd up toward the house. Tava was now aware of her own heightened senses. She gently tugged Michael away from her father as they neared the entrance.

She guided them to the right and down around the house, then cut back through the trees toward the river. To their right the guests continued to dance, drink, and talk. The evening was moving smoothly now and the moon hung high in the sky.

The young couple moved without speaking. Michael realized where they were going and took the lead. Rounding a dark corner, they were both surprised by an older drunk woman. She was sitting beneath one of the trees, a bottle in one hand and a napkin in the other. She smiled at them as they went by but did not say anything.

Michael led them down to the edge of the slow-moving

river and over a small footbridge. Careful to stay hidden they slipped along the riverbank opposite the pink gazebo. They crouched and for a moment watched the guests whirl like frantic ants. Tava saw her father. Hank and Grace were moving among the crowd like hectic ships in rough waters. Buddy was nowhere in sight.

One last look was all they needed before they disappeared into the underbrush. Strictly going by memory now, they moved through the trees. It took five minutes but finally they reached a small clearing encircled by dense underbrush and closely planted trees. The clearing was a secret hideaway the two lovers had discovered last summer. It was bathed in the soft warm glow of the evening moon. Here they would be safe.

Michael sat first and gently pulled Tava down next to him. He urged her closer and put his protective arm around her small, firm shoulders. Together they stared at the stars.

"I love you," he said. It surprised him but he immediately knew it was true. "I really love you and I want you to know that. I've spent the last three months thinking only about you."

Tava almost cried again with happiness. She felt alive and tingled with excitement because she was also in love. "I love you, too, Michael." She looked up at his strong jaw and brushed it with her graceful fingers. She let her hand trace down his neck and onto his chest. Slowly she moved underneath his shirt and played with his hair.

Michael eased back. He kept one hand tucked underneath his head and the other stroking Tava's exposed back.

She kept her hand encircling in small, gentle circles, inching down until she stopped above his waistband. She took the time to unbutton his shirt and kiss his nipples. She stroked him and followed with more kisses around his neck. She licked along his jawline while her hand burrowed down and played with his testicles. She noted with pleasure that his erect penis quivered with each brush of her hand. She stroked him until he moaned with pleasure.

She helped him out of his pants and took him in her mouth with a buoyant, teasing flair. She wanted to be near him, feeling his skin against hers. So many times she had fallen asleep dreaming of pressing herself against him, feeling the pressure of their two bodies in bed. She bit him playfully and laughed.

Michael was in heaven. He indulged himself, gorging on the sensations. And then, it was his turn.

He gently pulled Tava up and kissed her full red lips. Their tongues met in a sensuous moment and parted. Their lips danced together, pulsating with the rhythms of the night. He was inspired and took her in his strong arms. Cradling her, he laid her on her back. He leaned down and kissed her again. This time it was stronger. He stroked the strong line of her jaw. His hand descended and cupped her shapely breast through the silk. He toyed with her nipple and thrilled to Tava's moan of delight. He kissed down her neck and followed the path between her breasts. With an easy motion he lifted her petticoats and continued down between her legs. He licked delicately at the inside of her upper thighs. She shook with the thrill.

He played with her down there, driving her delightfully crazy, bringing her almost to the brink and then easing off. He was toying with her and loving every little twitch it caused.

They were on top of each other again, this time rolling over and over on the soft blanket of leaves. The warm earth beneath them urged them to new heights. The open air ignited an enormous hunger. They could not satisfy their thirst. He pulled her lace panties off, deftly parting her legs, and rolled on top of her.

In the darkness a branch crashed down. Tava stiffened and pulled her dress down. Michael turned around violently and peered into the distance. He was caught up in the moment and did not want it to pass. He was craving Tava and wanted her now.

"What was that?" Tava asked, unnerved. She urged Michael off her and sat up. She straightened her dress and pulled her panties back on while she scanned the dark woods. She caught a quick glimpse of something moving in the shadows. She couldn't quite make it out. "There. I saw something move."

"It was probably just a squirrel."

"I don't like this." She kept looking and suddenly saw them. Bright eyes, seemingly hanging in the air by themselves. They were big and frightened. "Get out of here!" Tava screamed. The eyes disappeared and they both heard the crashing sounds of someone running through the woods.

Michael was on his feet and plunging in after the intruder. His nakedness stopped him quickly. The branches bit at his body and forced him to turn back. A swatch of fabric caught his eye and he picked it off a sharp branch. He returned to their little clearing. Tava was up and pacing around. "I missed 'im."

"I hate that! How can someone spy like that? God, that makes me angry!" Tava paced back and forth. She felt violated and it upset her.

"I found this on a branch. Look familiar?"

Tava recognized it instantly. It was the color and texture from Buddy Nicholls's Mafia suit. She kept her discovery to herself. The last thing she needed was Michael beating up her father's business associates. Still it confirmed her instant dislike for the man. He was a Peeping Tom and it made her feel dirty. "Let's just forget it, okay? We'll find time later."

Michael reluctantly agreed. His fire was still aflame with desire but it would have to wait. "Goddammit it," he breathed.

Tava turned to him and smiled. She saw the anguished look on his face and sympathized. She wanted it, too, but not if the circumstances weren't right. It had to be perfect. "Don't look so hurt. We've got a long summer ahead of us."

Buddy plunged on through the woods. He was desperate to reach the party and terrified of being caught. He was angry with himself for being so clumsy and obvious. He ran like a madman and finally gained the little bridge. There he paused and listened. The silence convinced him he was not being followed.

"That was too close," he panted, trying to catch his breath. He pounded his fist into his open hand. "I'm so stupid!" Even as he was saying this his mind was filled with Tava's beautiful face. He was entranced by her unique beauty. Her gorgeous breasts! Her hair! Her eyes! Buddy wanted her now and was lost in the unfulfilled dreams of a frustrated young man. He wanted to make love to her and have her please him like she was pleasing Michael.

He hated Michael now. He was disgusted with the way Tava touched him and felt jealous because he wanted it too. Tava Blackhurst was going to please him, sooner or later, he vowed.

"I've got to have you," he hissed forcefully.

With that he ran across the bridge and made his way back to the party. His mind was already whirring with ideas.

It was getting late and the party was still raging. If the evening held to tradition, it would be two or three in the morning before the crowd started to disperse. The music continued to fill the night air, and the guests were still dancing with wild abandon.

Grace retired to a table by the pool and held court. She watched with an air of authority and boredom. She was tired now. Parties were so much work and they never seemed to match her expectations. She found most of these people boring.

"We don't need this prestige," she murmured to herself. "We took care of it years ago." To herself she allowed a moment of self-satisfaction. She and Thomas had built something special here, and even for Grace, Blackhurst Manor meant more than just a vacation home. Still, she longed for the social season in New York.

Hank found her and sat down heavily. "Hey, Grace," he drawled in his deep Texas twang, "I can't find my son. You seen him?"

"No," she answered.

Hank leaned on the table and stared at Grace. He lingered until the air became uncomfortable. "You're the best-looking thirty-year-old I've ever seen."

Grace blushed. "Don't be ridiculous. You've had a little too much of my champagne."

"I know what I'm saying. Ever since my wife died, I've had this lonely itch for some lovin'. You know what I mean?"

"No, I don't." She eyed him suspiciously. "I don't think you know what you're saying."

"Afraid I do, Mrs. Blackhurst. I've got a little problem I thought you might be able to help me with."

"And what would that be?" Grace took the time to light herself a cigarette, pretending Hank was making no impression on her at all. She was feeling a schoolgirl's crush. Hank was a handsome man. She had instantly noticed that when he stepped off the helicopter. He certainly had a commanding presence and Grace appreciated that in a man. She enjoyed the way he carried his masculinity.

"I can't seem to shake you out of my mind. Can you believe that?"

"There is much I find hard to believe about you, Mr. Nicholls." She took a long, deep drag on her cigarette and held it for several seconds. She let the smoke dissipate in front of her. For a moment Hank was obscured. "What are we talking about?"

"A few things, I think. Your great champagne. My son. And my wife."

"How did she die?"

"In a fire. It was very sad and very long ago. I don't like to think about it."

"And you never remarried?"

"When you've had the best, it spoils the rest."

"Is that how you feel about all women?"

Here he grinned. "No. Not pretty ladies."

"Have you seen my husband?"

"I think he's fallen in love with my helicopter. He keeps taking tours through."

"My husband loves gadgets."

"I love softer things." The tone of his voice was giving him away.

"I can see that."

"Can you?"

"Yes. I believe I can."

"And you? What do you love, Mrs. Blackhurst?"

"I think I'm the opposite from you. I love the harder side of life."

"Interesting way of putting it."

Grace was amusing herself. She did not, as a rule, have affairs with her husband's business partners. And yet this one seemed different. He was paying tremendous attention to her, something Thomas was unable to do. This might just show Thomas a few things, she thought to herself. Hank might just fit the bill.

"I don't know much about you, Hank."

"Not much to know. I'm my own man. I don't make many

demands. I only do the things I want to do and right now that includes our little chat."

"I'm honored."

"No need to be. I feel comfortable around you. You throw a great party and not many people know how to do that these days. So? You gonna give me a tour of the house or do I have to go chat with someone else?"

He's blunt if nothing else, she thought. His surety piqued her interest. It was the cockiness she found intriguing. "I don't like my guests to wander alone. Perhaps a tour would be the right thing to do. Ready?"

"Always."

Hank stood up and offered her his hand. She brushed it aside and stood by herself. Silently she moved around the pool and into the kitchen. Hank followed behind.

The helicopter door latched shut. Buddy locked it and turned his attention to his guest. Thomas sat easily in the plush seat and stirred the ice in his drink with a finger. He enjoyed Buddy's secrecy. The boy was eager and Thomas knew this played to his advantage.

Buddy moved quickly to his briefcase and withdrew a manila folder. He leafed through several sheets and pulled out a list of facts and figures, handing it to Thomas. As he accepted the sheet Buddy sat down quickly and leaned forward, kneading his hands and bouncing them on his bony knees.

"I just want to say how much this means to me, Mr. Blackhurst. You're a legend where I come from. Meeting you is a great honor."

Thomas kept the young man waiting for a few seconds and then said, "Why did you come to me?"

"Why?" The question caught Buddy off guard. He stammered a little and then began. "It's business. I see things that can be changed. My father doesn't." Buddy was awed in the presence of the great Thomas Blackhurst. He could not believe he was involved in a deal with him. He had so much to learn from this man. "It's important." He brushed the hair from his face while removing his large-brimmed hat. "I feel stupid in this outfit."

"Rule number one. Never let your surroundings dictate you. You dictate the surroundings."

"That's what I'm trying to do, sir."

Thomas smiled at the "sir." It amused him. "What is this sheet?" He pointed to the piece of paper.

"Well, if you read it, it's the numbers on the takeover."

"I don't want to read it. I want you to explain it to me. In your words."

"My words?" Buddy was sweating.

"Yes, your words. Now. I don't have all evening." He looked out the portal and saw the guests. The party was still raging. It was now 1:00 A.M.

Buddy cleared his throat. He was not prepared to speak. Normally he let his writing speak for him. "Well, if you notice on the sheet, I've done some analysis of the dissolution of Nicholls Development. I think, as you'll see, that the current break-up value is well above the market rate. I checked the stock exchange at closing yesterday and we were trading at forty-two. I think the real value of the share is much closer to seventy."

"That's not true." Thomas spoke in a low, powerful tone that meant he was serious. "Seventy is too high. You should know that."

Buddy froze. He was sure his calculations were correct but was not prepared to go against Thomas. Perhaps he should recalculate. His mind whirled and could not find his error. He tentatively said, "I am pretty sure, Mr. Blackhurst, that I have figured this correctly. If you take into account the research and on-site consulting branches of Nicholls, we really are worth much more than we are trading for." He was sure he was right.

Thomas scowled. He was testing. He needed to know how serious Buddy was. His cooperation in this deal meant that Buddy was prepared to work behind his father's back. That kind of ambition and greed was something Thomas could use. Buddy was proving his worth.

"Seventy? I have my doubts, but for the sake of argument, move on."

"Yes, sir. As you know, my father controls thirty percent of Nicholls stock. The other seventy is owned publicly. I think we can convince the stockholders that selling is to their advantage. We might even convince my father to sell his shares. The profit he stands to make is unbelievable."

"I don't think profit is all your father is about. He seems to treat this company like a child."

"Too much so in my opinion. Nicholls could be so much bigger. My father is holding back. He does not see the need for growth. I think he's missing a golden opportunity."

Thomas contemplated the young man before him. Clearly Buddy was passionate about this. He was willing to work against his father. What made a boy like this work? Thomas really was finding a part of himself in Buddy and was deciding he did not like it. But business was business and this was one of the more interesting prospects on the market. The profit potential was astounding. Buddy was right. Nicholls Development's research facilities alone, when split off and sold, would pay for the price of purchasing the company. The only sticking point was Hank. It was usually very difficult to convince stockholders to sell when the man in charge was identified so closely with the company. It was going to be an exciting fight.

"Why are you willing to fight your father on this?"

Buddy thought for a moment and then answered. "Because I don't like him very much. I think he deserves what's coming to him."

"Harsh."

"So is he. I am not bitter, Mr. Blackhurst. I simply want my chance. Things are not moving fast enough. You are my best bet. If you won't help me, I'm sure I can find someone who will. I have compiled several case histories showing my father's judgment to be less than brilliant. It should help us in the fight."

Thomas had to admit he was impressed with the boy's thoroughness. The homework was done. Still, he needed more. "This kind of fight is not won on the merit of judgment. The stockholders are happy. Your father is not an idiot."

"No. But he does have some embarrassing secrets that he may not want out." At this, Buddy grinned. This was his ace. He wanted to work for Blackhurst Industries so badly, he was willing to sell his father's deepest secrets to make it happen, and he felt good about it. "I have a number of things which you may find interesting."

"I think I am impressed." That was all he had to say. He

stood up. "I have a party to get to. We'll talk more. Enjoy yourself." Thomas started to move for the door.

"My father may decide to stay longer. He seems to find Sultan Valley pleasing."

"As do we all, my boy. As do we all."

The door was locked with a metallic finality. The drapes were closed and the lights dimmed. Grace brushed by Hank, letting her hand graze across the front of his pants. She felt free for several reasons. She was in her domain. She was aware of what she was doing. And she wanted to hurt Thomas. With all this in mind she toyed with Hank, eager to see where it might lead. She missed the touch of a man and if it was not going to be Thomas, it might as well be Hank. At least he showed interest in her.

Hank followed Grace down two steps into her plush bedroom. There was music playing softly in the background. Grace moved to a panel of buttons in the wall and pushed one. The ceiling silently pulled back and revealed a glass roof.

"I enjoy this under the stars."

Hank held his place. "I like the stars, Grace. And I like you."

"Sure you do." Her voice was gravelly. "You must be uncomfortable in all those things. Why don't you take some of them off?"

He shook his large head no. "Ladies first. Call me strange but it sets the mood. You don't mind indulging me, do you, honey?"

She did not. She found it amusing and first removed her wig. She pulled her silver hair from its bun and let it fall around her face. She ran her long fingers through it and fluffed it out. "Ta da! The real thing still interest you?"

"Yep." He leaned back against the wall and cocked his hat farther back on his head. "You look just fine."

She reached behind and undid the clasps on her dress. It slid down her body like water. She stepped out of it, keeping her eyes on him the whole time. "Imagine this body when it was twenty. It'll make you feel better."

"Darlin', everything's put in its place real fine." He was hot.

"You going to help me out of the rest of this?"

"I think that can be arranged." He took his hat off and placed it carefully on the chair facing the bed. "You like my hat, Grace?"

"Honey, I like everything about you," she purred.

He moved to her and held her by the shoulders. She moved willingly into him, finding his touch cathartic. She melted in his arms. He helped her out of her silky lingerie and laid her on top of the covers.

He laughed like a madman and undid his shirt. His whoops of pleasure blended with the noise outside. His pants came next and soon he was naked. Grace was exhilarated. He was more awake than she ever remembered Thomas being. It made her nervous but the thrill was enough to urge her on.

"What's all the excitement?" she teased coyly.

"I think you know, little darlin'. Why don't you slide over here and make old Hank feel welcome?" He knelt on the bed. Grace breathed heavily.

She reached over and stroked him. He groaned audibly and she did it harder. She kissed him. She rubbed between his legs, grabbing his testicles firmly in her hand; enough to hurt. He responded by massaging her breasts between his fingers.

Grace was too excited and felt herself peaking too soon. She eased off and leaned back against the pillows. "Hank, you're driving me crazy. I can't keep my hands off you."

"Likewise, little darlin'. Come here." He grabbed her by the legs and pulled her down to him. She tried to squirm away but he held her tight and spread her. He moved inside and then withdrew. "You're a good little girl, ain't you?"

"Oh, I hope not."

"Roll over."

She did. He ran his hands along the backside of her legs. He kneaded her and then lightly, but firmly, brought his open hand down on her bottom. The smack was loud and sounded more painful than it really was. Grace recoiled. She'd never been spanked before. He did it again. This time with more force. She responded to it by trying to get away but he pulled her back.

She realized quite suddenly she was enjoying it. Instead of trying to get away she found herself raising her bottom to provoke him. She squealed with mock cries. Hank, grinning wildly, gave her one last slap across her butt that left her stinging while he rolled her over onto her back.

"That should hold you for a while." He began sucking on her right nipple and reacted when she ran her fingers through his hair. He sucked harder and finally could take no more. He moved on top of her and together they heaved in unison. Grace clung to him with all of her strength to keep the sensations alive. They were out of their minds and finally came with the intense force of two hungry souls. Hank collapsed and rolled off her.

Grace was hungry for more. She felt liberated and could not stay still. She laughed and rubbed Hank knowingly. He smiled and patted her hand. She stayed with him until he fell asleep.

Naked, she pulled herself from the silk sheets and crossed over to the window. She leaned against the cool glass. She felt free. Her spirit was soaring as she watched the crowd sway back and forth to the muted music. The liquor was still flowing. Some guests were wandering in and out of the woods. Grace smiled, secretively, pleased with her husband for bringing Hank here.

16

Hank and Buddy were standing in the small town square. Behind them a rock fountain gurgled steadily. Surrounding them were large patches of grass and colorful beds of flowers. Flowerpots hung from every lamppost. The little park was ringed by shops and restaurants. The old architecture was maintained by a town fund. As a result, the effect was a little, vibrant town from the late 1800's. It was both quaint and beautiful.

Hank was feeling the need to be near his enemy. His evening with Grace had ended hours ago when he sneaked out to his own guest house. He was more determined now to keep Nicholls Development out of Thomas Blackhurst's hands.

The first thing he needed to do was find a base of operations. He pulled a realtor from the yellow pages and made an appointment. Now they crossed the cobblestone street and went into the posh real estate office of Heather Downing. Both men were greeted by an older gentleman dressed in a red polo sweater and green cords.

"You must be Mr. Nicholls." He extended his hand and shook Hank's with a firm resolve. He did the same for Buddy. "I'm Heather's husband. She wanted me to tell you she would be right out. Please have a seat."

"You know my name but I don't know yours," Hank said.

"John Downing. You may have detected a slight accent on my part." John was from England and spoke in the refined tones of a gentleman. "Don't let it alarm you. I'm from Britain. I just flew in this morning. Beautiful day, yes?"

"Makes me feel at home."

"And you, young man. What do you think of our Sultan Valley?"

Buddy kneaded his hands. "It's nice."

"Sounds like a ringing endorsement to me." John laughed good-naturedly. "Heather tells me you're interested in purchasing?"

"I'm thinking about it. I need a north satellite for my operations in Houston. This seems perfect."

Heather appeared from the back. "Sorry I'm late. I just finished showing some acreage to a gentleman from Saudi Arabia." She paused only to take a breath and then continued. "My name is Heather Downing. What a pleasure to meet you, Mr. Nicholls. And this must be your son?"

"That's right." Hank did not know what to think of the creature before him. She was flamboyant, forthright, and every inch a lady. Her fingernails were long and blood-red. They matched her tailored Karan suit and matching pumps. Her long, frosted hair was pulled back with a flowing scarf.

"Would you like to go now or have lunch first?" she asked.

"Let's get on with it. I have several people waiting on me."

Heather did not miss a beat. "Well then, shall we go?" She ushered them out the front door. "I thought we would start with my favorite. From what you said on the phone you're looking for something fairly big."

"I want something with flash. That's the only way we do it in Texas. I'm fallin' in love with your little Sultan Valley, Ms. Downing."

"We'll be pleased to have you as a neighbor."

The house was one block removed from the town square. It was an enormous Victorian, rising four floors above the street. Accented with turrets and gingerbread detailing it was the biggest in the little village of Sultan Valley. They toured the rooms without speaking. Hank just nodded his approval. They walked through it thoroughly and now were standing on the front lawn facing the huge mansion. It was all white with blue trim. The house was maintained impeccably and from the polished hardwood floors to the brand-new kitchen it was a showplace with no rivals in town.

Hank stood silently for several minutes. Heather did not interrupt.

"How much?" Hank asked.

Heather answered just as simply. "A million and a half."

Hank smiled and turned to Buddy, "Write her a check, son."

17

Grace watched Kim pull herself out of the pool. The sight of the woman infuriated her for two reasons. One, because Thomas had asked her out here. Two, because Thomas was going to stay awhile. Usually he came for a week and then left. Now, for some reason, he had decided to stay indefinitely. With his personal assistant with him he could run his business from the estate. She knew one thing for sure. She was not going to let Thomas get in the way of her affair with Hank.

She thought of nothing else. Like Buddy she, too, was fixated. Hank was so much more a man than Thomas. He was strong in his convictions. He demanded more of Grace than Thomas ever had and she liked that. He made her feel complete and this was a feeling she had lost with Thomas.

She watched Kim towel off. Grace was jealous of the taut, young body but did her best to ignore it. "He's probably sleeping with the bitch," she murmured angrily. She took a deep drag on her cigarette and let the ashes fall.

Tava was in her room. Flowers were on her dresser staring at her. They confused her and made her upset. The last thing she wanted was complications this summer. Her reunion with Michael was more than she had hoped for and now this.

The flowers were extravagant and ridiculously expensive. They took up most of the dresser. She read the note again and cringed. It read:

Dear Tava,
   I saw these and thought you might like them. We've decided to stay the summer in Sultan Valley. I hope I can see more of you.

                          Sincerely, Buddy Nicholls

"Good morning, Grace," Thomas said as he moved into the kitchen. He was dressed comfortably in white shorts and a striped short-sleeved sport shirt. His hair was still wet and combed straight back. He walked over to the counter and poured himself a glass of fresh squeezed orange juice. "Beautiful day, isn't it?

"I guess." Her voice sounded bored. "Why is she here?"

Thomas sighed. They had already been through this. "Grace . . . Kim is here because I need her. She's my right-hand person on this. Don't be jealous."

"I don't see why all of this can't be handled in New York."

"Because, dear, I want to try something new. I like it here. I don't need to be breathing New York City twenty-four hours a day."

"I have things set for this summer. They did not include you. Or for that matter Tava. Now I'm stuck with a full house. I really wanted my privacy this time. I really needed that." She was sounding manic.

Thomas looked at her with a concerned air. "Grace, are you happy?"

"What the fuck do I have to be happy for? You ignore me. You fool around behind my back and now apparently in my house. We don't know each other anymore, Tom. Maybe that doesn't bother you, but it does me." She sat heavily at the table.

Thomas remained where he was and sipped his orange juice. He was trying to keep himself calm. He found his wife so selfish. "Grace, don't blame me for your unhappiness. If we've drifted, I'm not the only one to blame."

"Oh? What did I do?" Grace spat out.

"You stopped caring."

"Hah! Tell me another one, Thomas. Go on, Mr. Rich Man." She pointed around herself. "You think any of this makes a damn bit of difference?"

"It didn't use to, my dear. And that's the problem. You're addicted to our life-style. I don't think you can imagine a life without this kind of luxury. I don't think you've driven a car since your college days. You're pampered, honey. You're acting like a spoiled brat."

"I don't have to take this." She threw her glass down. "You're sick, my friend."

"I'm sick? Grace, don't get me angry. I think we both know you're the one who needs the help."

"Help? Are you serious? I'm not crazy. And I'm not seeing a shrink."

"So what do you want?"

The question seemed so simple. Grace thought she had an answer for it, but was silent. Here was the man she had once loved, changed somehow and almost a stranger. She did not know what she wanted.

"Leave me alone, Thomas."

"You never spend any time with us. You ignore us. You only seem to live to please yourself. What do you expect if you're feeling a little left out?"

"You used to care about me, Thomas."

"I still do, Grace. I just think you need to talk to someone who can help."

All Grace needed now was Hank's touch. It was the only thing she felt close to. Somehow his fingers wiped away the present and everything became clear. Nothing mattered when she lay with him.

"I know you're sleeping with her, Thomas. You better not let me catch you at it. I swear to God I'll make your life a living hell if I do."

Thomas thought very carefully before he said anything. "You already are, my dear."

Tava was by the pool wearing a blue-and-green bikini. She felt the hot noonday sun beating down against her. The air was dry and still. She decided on a quick lap in the pool to revive her resolve. She dove in gracefully and made two laps. Her body skimmed through the water like a dolphin. She was graceful and powerful, and the combination made her beautiful to watch.

Pulling herself from the crystal blue water, she let the sun dry her as she made a call. The phone rang twice and then Hank picked it up.

"Hello?" His voice was loud and energetic. Tava remembered it from the party.

"Mr. Nicholls? This is Tava Blackhurst. May I speak to your son, please?"

"Tava? Well, darlin', it's good to hear your pretty little voice. How's the family?"

"Fine, thank you."

"Your mama? What's she up to today?"

"I think she went into town. Is Buddy in?"

"I think so. Listen, you probably heard we're staying the summer."

"Yes. I did."

"Come into town and see the new place. This is a nice old house and there's plenty of room."

Tava knew of the purchase. It was a beautiful house and she had always admired it. It was unfortunate that the Nichollses had bought it. "Yes, it is beautiful."

"You think you might come down and see us?"

"That would be nice."

"By the way, did I tell you how pretty you looked on Saturday?"

He made her wary. Hank was a big man with a wandering eye. "Thank you, Mr. Nicholls."

"Ah, hell, call me Hank."

"All right, Hank. Is Buddy there?"

"Well, let me check." Hank covered the mouthpiece and yelled for his son. "He'll be here in a sec'. Now I mean it, you come down here and see us."

"Thank you. I will." She had no intention of ever seeing him.

Buddy came on the line. "Hello?" Even his voice sounded sweaty.

"Buddy? It's Tava Blackhurst. I wanted to thank you for the flowers. They were very sweet."

Buddy stuttered. "Well . . . I just thought . . . you know . . . that you might like 'em."

"I do. Thank you. I've got them in my bedroom." She could have kicked herself for saying that. "Listen, I've got to go. Maybe I'll see you around."

"That'd be great. I'd like that."

"Good." She was trying to hang up the phone tactfully but Buddy was hanging on. He wanted something more but was too afraid to ask.

"Maybe we could go out sometime. You could show me the area?"

"Let me check with Michael and see if he can get some time off. We wouldn't mind showing you around. You met Michael, didn't you?"

"Yes . . . of course I did. You let me know. I'll talk to you later." He hung up quickly. Even the mention of his arch rival made him steam.

18

On Monday Thomas was pacing. Hank had not shown any interest in talking at the party and Thomas was anxious to force his hand. Nicholls Development was just too good a jewel to pass up. What he was about to do was designed to force Hank to sit down at the bargaining table. This could still be a peaceful, friendly deal. It just needed to happen quickly. Thomas was not a patient man.

Kim was at a computer and on the phone to the office in New York. She was in conference with the legal department and the buyers. The New York Stock Exchange ticker was flashing across her screen. Nicholls was trading moderately today and the time was right to make a splash.

"All right, gentlemen. Now is the time. I want *The New York Times* ad to run tomorrow. Martin, I expect you to have the shares bought within the next twenty minutes. Legal? Are you there?"

"Yeah, Kim. What's up?"

"Are we prepared with the SEC filing? We want to keep this legitimate. No screwups. Everybody is to be informed ahead of time. We don't want to give Mr. Nicholls a heart attack."

"We're ready on this end, Kim. Just say the word and we'll messenger out. They'll have it in fifteen minutes, just jolt him a little."

"Hang on. Thomas wants to say hi."

Thomas tapped into the phone from his desk. He was reviewing a computer printout. "Harry? I just wanted to double-check. We're okay with the banks? No margin for error?"

"No, sir. Everything is right on schedule. We've got the backing behind us and we're ready to go. As a matter of fact, we're all getting a little anxious. We're biting at the bits here. Just say the word, boss, and we'll throw this thing into action." Harry was head of the legal department at Blackhurst Investments and loved takeovers as much as Thomas. He had been with the company almost from its inception.

Thomas took a deep breath. This was the most exciting part of the game. "Ready, everybody?"

They all chimed in yes.

"Go."

The well-oiled Blackhurst machinery flew into action. The first move consisted of four different parts. The notice of takeover was filed with the Securities and Exchange Commission. A full-page ad in the *Wall Street Journal* and *The New York Times* let the public know what Blackhurst Industries wanted and was going to do. Individual letters were mailed to each shareholder explaining why the Blackhurst offer was the best for the company. And finally, the first fifteen percent of all Nicholls stock was purchased in one lump.

The feelers on Wall Street went crazy and the stock jumped five dollars before the bell rang to close the session. Before the day was out Thomas owned fifteen percent of Nicholls Development, and the world knew that he wanted the whole thing.

All he had to do now was sit back and wait for a call from Hank.

19

The house rang with Hank's thunderous voice. The call from Houston told him Blackhurst Industries now owned fifteen percent of Nicholls Development. Soon Thomas would demand a seat on the board and start making offers to buy the whole thing.

Hank was wounded. Thomas was serving notice that he was serious. There was no going back now and Hank was furious. The last thing Hank wanted was to drag his prized company through the turmoil of a takeover. He was white with fury and kicking through the house with an enormous anger he could not squelch.

He kicked over several chairs and pulled curtains down from the living room windows. He caught his reflection in the mirror and was so angry, he put his fist into it. The glass shattered like rainfall and covered the wood floor with tiny shards. The blood only infuriated him more and he yelled at the top of his lungs.

Buddy found his father on his rampage and wisely stayed out of his way. He climbed the stairs quickly and found the phone in his room. He had a suspicion and needed to confirm it.

He dialed Thomas's home and waited for an answer. Kim picked it up.

"Blackhurst Manor. May I help you?"

"This is Buddy Nicholls. Put Mr. Blackhurst on."

"One moment please." She covered the receiver and whispered over to Thomas, "Buddy is on the line."

Thomas smiled widely and picked up his phone. "Buddy, how are you?"

"What have you done?" Buddy kept his voice down for fear his father might hear him.

"What do you mean, what have I done?"

"Mr. Blackhurst, my father is yelling like a madman. He's tearing things down. Did you move on us?"

"Yes. I own fifteen percent. Think your father is in the mood to talk?"

"No way. Why didn't you let me know? I thought I was in on this with you." Buddy was hurt. He had expected to be included.

"I only own fifteen percent, my boy. You have to help me get the other eighty-five."

This eased the young man. "I would let things cool down. I know he'll formulate something and be in touch. He can get awfully angry."

"Sounds like I got his attention."

"Yes, sir, you did."

Buddy was fixated on Tava. He was lost in this predicament and all he could do was fantasize. It was unhealthy and he tried to break himself from the spell Tava unwittingly cast on him. He felt weak and out of control. Eating was becoming difficult and concentrating for long periods was impossible. Their time together at the party was so short that he was forgetting what she smelled like. Her picture was fading in his memory and all he could remember was a faint image of Michael on top of her in the forest.

He was growing anxious. He could not keep still around the house. Nothing interested him. It was as if the world had come to a screeching halt, waiting for some sign of recognition. What was it that drove Buddy to fixate on Tava? He tortured himself with that question. Why him? His life was on an exciting track that did not include women. And then she entered it and was diverting the course. He needed to be mentally strong over the next few weeks. He was about to help his father's rival steal the company and for that it was necessary to focus. Tava was keeping him from that. He grew resentful and started blaming her for his desires.

Hank found Buddy pacing in the second-floor study.

"What is it, boy?"

"What?" Buddy was startled. "Nothing."

"I don't want you being absentminded. I've got a few ideas on this that I want to bounce off you. I can feel

Blackhurst getting ready to pounce and it's bothering me. We need to make ourselves look unattractive. Maybe a poison pill. We need to make this company not look so good. You know what I mean?"

"That's going to be difficult. We've shown strong profits but our stock isn't valued at what it should be. I don't know how to fix that."

"I don't want to hear no. I want to hear good ideas. I have no intention of working for Thomas Blackhurst." Hank dug into his pocket. "Listen, go get this developed for me at that one-hour place on the square."

"What is it?"

"A roll of film."

"Of what?"

"Don't ask so many questions. Just go do it. I want it back tonight."

"It's kind of late, Daddy."

"That's what money is for, son. Spend as much as you need to get me what I want. Also tell him if he looks at them I'm gonna sue his ass off. This is private business. And tell him I'll be by to pick them up personally."

Buddy was suspicious. He desperately wanted to know what was in this roll of film but did not know how to find out. "And I don't get to know what's on this?"

"You got balls, boy, digging into my personal affairs. All I'm gonna tell you is this: what's good for me is good for you. So shut up and get moving."

Buddy left the house and let the door bang shut behind him. Hank was left there, giddy with the prospect of his pictures. He finally had what he needed to get himself clear of Thomas. "My ammunition is on that film, and even the great Thomas Blackhurst isn't going to be able to stop me." He smiled and began to rumble with laughter. "Goddamn, I'm good at this. I'm too good. Makes you wonder why I'm not president of the whole damn country." That thought made him erupt more as he moved into the kitchen to eat.

That evening, alone, Hank Nicholls spread his pictures out in front of him and gloated. They were better than he hoped for. The focus was crystal clear. There was no mistaking the subject and the expressions were beyond belief. He wondered to himself if he felt guilty and knew he didn't. This was perhaps his most ingenious and despicable ploy, and he was loving every minute of it.

One by one he touched each of the twenty-four photographs and piled them neatly into a pile. He carefully slipped them into their envelope and slid the packet into his breast pocket. He felt a calm sense of relief permeate his body and quietly whispered, "Now I'm safe." With the photos safely developed he began to make his plans to visit Grace Blackhurst.

20

It was just after lunch in Sultan Valley and the sun was beating down on the town square. Grace was still bitterly angry over her confrontation with Thomas the other day and unable to get Hank out of her mind. She needed to see him. On the pretense of giving him a housewarming gift, she bought an expensive bottle of wine and some flowers and sent Hans home.

Grace made her way to the old Victorian and mounted its graceful steps. She rapped on the huge front door. There was no sound inside. She wondered if anyone was home. She knocked again.

From inside Hank yelled to Buddy, "Get the fucking door!"

Grace held her ground. A little temper was something she was sure she could rectify.

The door was opened and Buddy did his best to smile. Grace smiled back pleasantly. She, like most people, felt uncomfortable around Buddy and wanted to spend as little time with him as possible. She held out her gifts. "These are for you and your father. Welcome to Sultan Valley."

"Thank you." Buddy accepted them and urged her inside. He ran ahead into the study and told Hank. Hank rose from behind his desk and greeted Grace warmly. He took a certain pleasure from having his enemy's wife in his domain.

"How nice of you to come." He saw the gifts in his son's hands. "Those are beautiful. I think this is the first time anyone has given me flowers. Buddy, go put 'em in water. Leave the wine here." Buddy did as he was told and disappeared quickly. "Have a seat. Where are my manners? What do you think of our little place?"

"It's the most beautiful house in town, Hank. Everyone is very jealous. You've made quite a stir in little Sultan Valley."

"Good."

"Hope you like red wine." She pointed to the bottle on his desk.

Hank picked it up and spun it in his hands. He read the label and knew it was very expensive. He tore the foil off and uncorked it. He found two glasses, poured for both of them and toasted. "To the most beautiful woman in Sultan Valley."

Grace clinked her glass with his and drank. The taste was dry and woody. It slid down her throat without the bitter aftertaste of cheaper wines. She inhaled the aroma and clung to the scent.

Hank appreciated the flavor and downed his immediately. He poured himself another glass. "I've got a little surprise for you."

"You do? Hank," she hung on his name, "I'm so happy you're spending the summer."

"Me too." He moved around his desk and opened his top drawer. He pulled out the packet of pictures and tapped them against his hand lightly. "Consider these a little souvenir."

Grace opened the packet and pulled out the twenty-four photographs. For a moment she did not know what she was looking at and then it started to dawn on her. Flipping through them faster and faster, she could not believe what she was looking at. She felt queasy and reached for her glass. She downed the wine, trying to dull the pain. Hank waited for her reaction.

When she finally spoke her voice was cold and directly to the point. "What do you want?"

The photos were of her and Hank together during the party. Somehow all of it had been captured on film, from the spanking to the lovemaking. She felt betrayed and utterly helpless. Still, she kept her wits and didn't panic.

"This is going to sound insensitive."

"Can't be worse than this." She threw the photos on the ground. They splayed across the floor around Hank's feet.

"First, you probably know your husband has moved against my company."

"No. When?"

"Monday. He now owns fifteen percent of what I have worked my whole life to build up. I do not appreciate his tactics or his motives. My company is not for sale."

"So?" She just wanted to know the terms. These photos were very dangerous to both her and Thomas.

"I want you to keep your vulture of a husband off me. I want you to stop him."

"I'm not sure I can do that."

"I'm sure you'll find a way." Hank was angry and feeling very vindictive. Grace was a small pawn in his elaborate game. She was his safety net. He knew he was not going to be able to stop Thomas legally and Grace was his perfect ploy. "One more request."

"Yes?"

"Your daughter. For one night."

Grace was confused. "What does that mean?"

Hank spoke slowly and with grave importance. "It would mean a great deal to me if I could spend one romantic night with your daughter."

"Why?"

"Because she's beautiful, Grace."

"I can't force her to do that. My God, she's just a child."

Hank laughed cruelly. "I think she dispelled that quite clearly at the party. She is tremendously pretty and I want to experience that kind of freshness before I enter into battle with your husband."

"You're sick."

"Not really. But it does give me a certain thrill to know I have slept with my enemy's two favorite women." He smiled broadly and gloated.

"No. Absolutely not." Grace was adamant. The emotions were too much to keep up with.

Hank sighed heavily. "You know, Grace, I know women like you. I know the kind of worlds you create for yourselves. Just imagine what would happen if these pictures were printed in something like the *New York Post*. What do you think your society friends would say to that?"

With one single question Hank snared her in his trap. There was no way she could let this get out. It was not just Thomas anymore. Her entire foundation was built on a reputation and to tarnish that would be committing suicide. She would be a complete outcast in the only world she understood.

"You can't do this."

"I *am* doing it, honey. You can blame your hubby if you like. And I hope you don't take this personal. You were good, darlin'. Real good. I haven't had that much fun in a long time. You're a little devil in the sack and I appreciate that. That's why I want a taste of your Tava. I bet she's a wildcat." He was rubbing it in now. He was bitter and angry. He knew he had her. Grace would have to accept. Something like this would devastate the only security she had ever known.

Grace was desperate. She felt like an animal trapped in a corner. There was no way out. She would have to do it. "All right." She hated herself for saying it. "All right. I'll see what I can do. I'll need one of those photos."

"Take your pick, and then clean up, won't you?" He moved over to the window and forced her to choose among the lurid photos. Grace picked one of the most embarrassing and put it in her purse. She begrudgingly piled the rest together and returned them to their envelope. She threw the evil packet on his desk.

"I'll let you know. You'll have to give me a couple of days. I don't know how she's going to take this. Talking to my husband is going to take a little longer."

"I trust you, honey. Tava first if you like."

"How did you get these?"

At this, Hank smirked. "Well, I tell ya. That, I believe, is my most clever part of all this. I've got myself a miniature little camera tucked away in my Stetson hat. So, all I've got to do is set it for automatic and every few minutes or so it takes a little picture. Course it didn't catch all of our fun but enough of it, don't you think?"

"You had a damn camera in your hat! That's why you were so careful about putting it on the chair. I can't believe it. You betrayed me, Hank."

"Darlin', I didn't betray anything that didn't want to be betrayed. You know that."

"You set me up."

"Yep. That's what I did. And I'm thankful of it. Now your weasel husband'll get off my back and leave me alone."

"Don't call him that."

"At this point I'm going to call him anything I want. Now why don't you run along home and get working on what I want. You know the way out."

Grace wanted to say more, try and talk him out of it, but she knew there was nothing else she could do. Even if she could steal this bunch, he had the negatives and could print as many as his sick little heart desired. She left quickly, slamming the door behind her.

Buddy found his father watching her leave. "What was that all about?"

"Just a little game of chess, son. You know, I'm sort of flattered. I think she's got a crush on me."

"What? Really?" Hank did not answer and Buddy could see his father was lost in thought.

Hank had not known what he wanted from those pictures until Grace walked in. He was just protecting himself against Thomas. He had never expected Thomas to move this quickly against him. He smiled. Sometimes he impressed himself. He was very good at planning ahead and this time it had paid off. It was a perverse little revenge. He wanted to hurt the Blackhurst family and now, armed with the pictures of Grace, he thought he had a fighting chance to escape Thomas's long reach. With memories of Tava at the costume ball, he grew pleased with his choice of revenge.

21

"Grace is having a problem with me being here," Kim said. She pushed away from her computer and put her feet on the desk. She felt uncomfortable in the house. Grace was avoiding her and refusing to speak. "Maybe I shouldn't have come."

"Don't be ridiculous. I need you here. My wife has nothing to do with that. What's the stock look like?" Thomas was upset. Nicholls Development was not making any official response to the takeover announcement. It was still too early to hear from the shareholders. Thomas did not like the silence. It made him wary. He was trying to flush Hank into a discussion. He did not want to go hostile in his attempt to get the company but was prepared to do it.

Kim watched Thomas concentrating. He was so distinguished in his demeanor. "Think I'll ever be invited to the dinner table?"

Thomas spoke without looking up from his writing. "Grace has the strangest idea that we've been sleeping together."

"We have been."

"Then you probably won't be invited to dinner. But don't take it personally."

They both laughed. They needed the release. The last few days had been grueling tests of strength. This was a cat-and-mouse game played with high stakes. As a team they were experts.

Thomas's problems with Grace persisted. She was more and more withdrawn and erratic. He noted her behavior growing worse since the takeover offer on Monday. Why this might bother her he could only guess. He attributed it to her general unhappiness and made a note to call his doctor for advice. He wondered if she was a manic-depressive. Certainly all of the drinking did not help the situation. He wondered to himself how, after all these years, they allowed themselves to fall into this kind of rut. It seemed unfair to gain so much materially and be so unhappy personally. He missed the woman he had first met all those years ago.

22

Michael was missing Tava. It was all he could do to keep his mind on work. Guests were flying in from all over and it seemed like he was responsible for getting them all to their rooms. He was filling in for a friend who had covered his shift the night of the Blackhurst Ball.

He was struggling with a pile of Gucci suitcases. A young couple from the Middle East, on their honeymoon, was following behind, holding hands.

He navigated them among the manicured paths. The resort was laid out like a lush, exclusive club. The atmosphere was very genteel. The grass was bright green and cut daily. The paths were red brick and crisscrossed in many directions. Each guest had a bungalow to themselves. The suites were grouped in sevens and surrounded a private pool and Jacuzzi.

Trees swayed gently in the warm wind and added to the dreamy quality. The resort was known for its attention to detail and the service was world-class. Michael led them to Bungalow 32 and opened the door for them. He let them enter first and then followed behind. The little house was gorgeous. Done in warm blues and roses the carpet looked like fresh fallen snow. The artwork was impeccable and lent itself to the sumptuous effect.

They entered past a well-appointed kitchen into the living room. Stepping down into the open area, the feeling was elegant and understated. The room flowed naturally down to French oak doors and to the pool beyond. Michael let them get situated and unloaded the bags into the bedroom. Once done, he entered back into the living room.

"I hope you find everything to your liking." He moved over to the kitchen. "You'll find everything you need here. If there is anything else you want, please call. The refrigerator is stocked with the food you requested and we will be happy to get you anything else you might want." He pointed to an overflowing fruit basket with wine. "This is for you with our compliments. Is there anything else I can do for you right now?"

The young man whispered something to his wife and she disappeared into the bedroom. He approached Michael with a small grin. "Two things, please." With this he pulled out a hundred-dollar bill. "Firstly, my wife and I would like to indulge in, shall we say, certain substances. Do you think you might arrange that for us?"

This was not a new request for Michael. Drugs were kept extremely quiet and Michael gave him a number to call. It was the part of the job he despised. "They will be able to handle your requests."

"Very good." The young man seemed pleased and pulled out another hundred-dollar bill. "And lastly, if there was a certain proclivity that I would like to indulge, how would that be accomplished?"

The resort had connections in this area. Michael did not need to ask what the man was into; the person at the other end of the line could help with that.

Michael gave it to him and gratefully accepted the generous tip. Working at the resort was quite lucrative with this clientele. Michael told the man to ask for him if there was anything more he needed.

He left quickly, closing the door behind him. The money would come to good use. He was planning on taking Tava to dinner over the weekend. He had Sunday evenings off and was eager to share them with her.

He started back up the walkway to the lobby. He knew there would be a steady stream of guests waiting to be helped. Rounding a corner he bumped into Charlotte. It was awkward. She was still fuming over his rejection.

"Hi, Michael." Her voice was hiding something.

"I thought you were supposed to be working the east complex today."

"Larry sent me over to get you."

"Why?" Larry was their supervisor and he rarely spoke to them.

"How should I know, Romeo. He wants to see you. Now." She was enjoying this.

"What do you know?" he asked.

"I don't know anything, Romeo. Maybe you broke a few too many hearts."

"What's that supposed to mean?"

"You'll find out soon enough. Say hi for me." With that she flounced off.

He moved quickly through the grounds and found the administrative building. It was a low-roofed little building painted in white. The support staff was run from this little office by Larry Hampton, an older man in his late sixties. A former Marine, he ran his staff like a drill sergeant. Michael was always uncomfortable in his office. He entered the small building and knocked on his boss's door.

"What do you want?" Larry yelled from behind the closed door.

"Michael, sir. You . . ."

"Get your butt in here!"

Michael opened the door quickly and closed it behind him. Like in the Army he had to stand at attention in front of the grizzled man's desk. He waited for what seemed an eternity while the man riffled through a stack of papers. Finally he was done and slammed his pen down on the empty desk.

"What've you got to say for yourself?"

"About what, sir?"

"At least have the decency to own up to it."

Michael struggled to stay calm. "I really have no idea what you're talking about, sir."

The older man stared at Michael with icy coldness. "I had a little talk with Charlotte about a half hour ago. She doesn't say many nice things about you."

"I don't think she would, sir."

"Why?"

"She thought she and I were going to be an item this summer. We're not."

"An *item*? Is that what you call it? I don't tolerate this kind of behavior in anybody, mister. She says you raped her."

Michael felt slugged in the stomach. His world began to spin and he found it difficult to keep his balance. He was completely caught off guard by the accusation and did not know how to respond.

"Well? What do you have to say for yourself?"

"I . . . don't know . . . what to say."

"Well, you better think of something quick 'cause you're about to be fired."

"Sir, I would never do that! I can't believe this. She came on to me, for God's sake. We didn't do anything!"

"Say what you will but you're out of here, my friend. Pack up your things. I should warn you, I've told her to go to the police with this. I refuse to keep your kind on my staff. Security's going to escort you off the premises. Move." His voice was very serious. Michael knew he was being framed but there was nothing he could say to this man to make him stop. Charlotte must have done one hell of a number on him. All Michael could do was stand there in disbelief and shake his head.

"You can't do this. Where's the proof?"

"I believe the girl and that's all the proof I need. Get the hell out of my office before I beat the shit out of you. You're a sick boy. You better get some help."

Michael stumbled out of the office. It was all happening too quickly. The security guards were waiting for him. They were big men and escorted him to his room, waited for him to pack his suitcase, and threw him off the grounds.

"Don't come back!" the guards threatened as they sauntered off.

He stood there for several moments and finally climbed in his beat-up VW and drove off in the direction of Blackhurst Manor. The only person he wanted to be with right now was Tava.

The room was dark. It was sandwiched in the back of a cabana filled with cleaning supplies. It was the safest place at the Sultan Valley Resort. The phone rang once and was picked up.

"Well?" said the male voice. The tone was eager and expectant.

"It worked." Charlotte said. "He's out. It was beautiful. The security guards threw him off the property. Larry almost killed him."

"Thank God. I wasn't sure you could handle it."

"Honey, I can handle anything. That jerk had it coming to him. Anyone could have done it but I'm sure glad you picked me."

Buddy was more than excited. He was elated. He wanted to yell with pleasure. This was working perfectly. First he wanted to get rid of Michael and then move in on Tava. He knew with Michael out of the way there would be no competition. He could feel Tava's interest in him. Buddy knew that under the right circumstances Tava would fall into his arms. He was convinced of it and doing everything within his power to get it done. His father was right. This was what money was for. "Your check is in the mail."

"The asshole deserved it."

"You've been a great help." He was gloating now. Buddy could picture himself with Tava, arm in arm, strolling down Sultan Valley's Main Street. He craved her touch. His need to be near her was overwhelming.

"So . . . you want to get together later?" Charlotte asked coyly. Buddy's money was very attractive.

"What? Don't be ridiculous."

"What's that supposed to mean?"

"You're a slut. Good-bye." He hung up the phone and forgot about Charlotte as he continued to daydream about Tava.

23

"You want me to what!"

Grace was fidgeting. The strain was overwhelming. She cornered Tava by the pool, making sure they could not be bothered, and was trying to explain the situation to Tava. "I don't know how else to ask you."

"This is the sickest joke yet. I don't believe this." Tava was so angry, she could barely hold herself back. What was Grace thinking? "Mother, you're crazy. There's no way I would let that man touch me."

Grace put her hand on her daughter's arm but Tava shook it off. "Darling, this is not an easy thing to ask. I have reasons, honey. Believe me, I know I've been bad to you. I'm sorry. I'm not feeling good. I take all the blame. But the problem still exists. Hank likes you. If you don't do it, it'll hurt Daddy very badly."

"How could you do this?"

"I'm only human, Tava. I needed a little warmth."

"Forget it."

"I'm sorry, Tava. Please forgive me." Grace was getting nowhere with Tava and finally produced the incriminating photo.

Tava never thought of her mother as a sexual person. She sometimes wondered if her mother saw men. But how could she do it with Hank Nicholls? He was so grotesque. He dripped with the fake swagger of someone who thinks he is important. Seeing her mother compromised in such a kinky act was almost laughable if it wasn't so terrifying.

She understood the complications. This was blackmail and would cause considerable embarrassment to her father. Tava was trapped. She did not want her father dragged through the mud because of her mother's stupidity. "Can't you just pay him off?"

"How can we do that? The man doesn't want money. He wants you. Can you imagine if these get published somewhere? Do you know what that would do to your father?"

"And if I do it?"

"Then the pictures will be destroyed. Do it. Please, Tava. Turn your mind off, go in there, let him do it, and then get out."

"I can't believe this." All Tava could do was picture Hank looming above her. It horrified her.

"He's trying to hurt us, Tava. We have a reputation to uphold. Imagine losing all of this." Her pleas were powerful. They scared Tava and made her uneasy. All she ever knew was wrapped up in the Blackhurst mystique. To ruin that would be devastating, terrifying. And the thought of hurting her father made her want to cry. She could not deny him the success he'd fought so long and hard for.

It was the most difficult decision she ever made. There, by the pool, in the hot, dry heat, the water lapping against the side in a rhythmic dance, she quietly and with great resolve accepted her fate.

"All right," she whispered.

Grace sat back heavily. "Thank God. I'll call and make the arrangements. You might as well get this over with as soon as possible. Your father must never know, Tava, *ever*. If he found out, it would kill him. All he needs to know is that I screwed up. I'll be the one to tell him. He'll stop the takeover for me, but he can't know about this part with you. I don't know what he's going to do to me." She lit a cigarette. The nicotine was not strong enough to calm her. She was spinning an intricate web, trying to keep herself above water and it was taking huge amounts of concentration.

"Don't worry, I'll keep it to myself." Tava did not want to be near Grace right now and stood up to leave. "Mother, how could you do this to me?"

Grace considered her answer carefully. She was perhaps in the lowest part of her life and her future seemed murky. All that came out of her mouth was, "I was lonely."

Tava turned to leave but stopped. "Mother?"

"Yes, Tava?"

Tava was steady and very sure of herself. This entire mess

made her feel as if she were trapped in a dream. "This is it. We do not know each other after this is over. You're dead as far as I'm concerned. I don't think I have ever known a more hateful person than you." She turned and walked inside.

Grace wanted to stop her and raised her hand to call Tava back. Something told her to leave her daughter alone and Grace watched as Tava disappeared inside. She knew she had gone too far. This really was a terrible thing to do to her, but she had no other choice. Grace was trapped and this was the only way to protect herself.

She lowered her hand as if all of its energy had seeped out. "This time, Tava, I agree. I'm sorry," she said sadly, her voice barely audible.

Michael parked near the garages. He was fuming. How could Charlotte be so vicious? She knew he needed the money for school. He was deeply depressed and intensely frustrated.

He clambered out of his Bug and cut around the back of the house. He wanted to avoid Grace. She didn't like him and he was not in the mood to tangle with her. He moved across the grass and sneaked around to the French doors. He peeked inside and saw Tava, facedown on her bed. He squinted through the glass and saw her body trembling.

He tried the door and it slid open. He squeezed inside and closed it quietly behind him. "Tava?" he whispered.

She was surprised. Her cheeks were tear-stained and she was trying to catch her breath. She gulped for air and was so overcome, her words were stuck in her mouth. She cried and Michael was scared for her. She shook like a little girl. Michael ran to her and held her in his strong arms.

"Honey, what is it?"

"I . . . can't . . ." she stumbled over her words. "Oh, Michael!" she wailed.

"What, baby?"

She shook her head and cried some more.

He comforted her and eventually she lay in his arms, spent, holding tightly to him for support.

"Why're you here?"

Michael told her.

Tava listened in rapt attention. She trusted Michael

completely and to see him accused of rape was disgusting. She kissed him. "I'm sorry, honey."

"Why are you crying?" he asked.

Tava froze. "I can't tell you, Michael." The realization brought more tears to her tired eyes. She fought them back with all her strength. "Trust me. Please," she pleaded.

"Are you sure?"

"Please," was all she could get out. From deep inside her she suddenly wanted Michael. She wanted to love him and be loved and by doing it, erase the horrible experience that lay before her. There were so many emotions swirling inside her confused head that she desperately needed the time to rest and rely on instinct instead of reason. With Michael she could do this.

She closed her eyes and began to caress him and when he tried to speak, she quieted him and encouraged him to softly explore her, helping her to forget what was to come.

24

"Well, that's fine. Just fine. I'll expect her around eight tomorrow night. I appreciate your help, Grace. I'll be good to her."

"Listen, you bastard, don't you hurt her." Grace was feeling guilty. She was on the phone to Hank arranging the evening and doing her best to keep this from Thomas as long as possible.

"What kind of man do you think I am? For God sakes, Grace, I think the world of your daughter. I'm not gonna abuse the relationship. I just figure you owe me this. I knew I could count on you." He took a deep breath and considered his next words. "What about the other thing we discussed? I know I don't have to remind you about our deal. I'm more than happy to burn my little picture album, but you've got to help me out on this."

Grace squeezed her eyes closed. She had no intention of telling Thomas. Tava was a smoke screen to buy her time. Grace had every intention of nailing Hank to the wall. She was not about to tell Thomas of her affair. She valued her life too much to change it. If she played it right, Tava would provide her with the time she needed to regroup and come out fighting. "These things take time. I've given you Tava. My husband isn't going to take this very well."

"That is probably an understatement, darling. What is today? Friday? All right. This is how it works. I see Tava tomorrow night. And your husband calls off his blood-hounds by Monday morning. That gives you three days to figure out some kind of lie. And I got a strong suspicion that's what you're gonna do. No excuses, Grace. I either get both things, when I want them, or your picture goes out all over the damn country."

"Don't threaten me, Hank. I don't see why you have to be so ugly about it."

"I'm not being ugly. Your husband started this. And he can stop it. Give Tava my best. Tell her I can't wait." He put the receiver down. The line went dead and Grace listened to the buzz. She finally replaced the receiver. She did not know how to get out of this one. Hank was holding all the cards.

Grace brushed her stringy hair from her face and smoothed out her skirt. She was angry. Kim walked by and triggered something in Grace. It was a hate that boiled over and Grace could no longer hold it in.

"I want to talk to you."

Kim was sunning herself in a brief bikini. Her body was long and hard. She was stunning. "Hello, Grace. You really have done a wonderful job with this place." Kim was hoping to stall the inevitable.

"How is this takeover thing coming?" Grace began.

This caught Kim by surprise. Grace was never interested in Thomas's business affairs.

"I'm not sure I know what you mean."

"Well, Thomas has offered to buy Hank's company, hasn't he?"

"Yes."

"Well, I don't think this is a very difficult question. How is it coming?"

Kim did not trust Grace. "Thomas is very hopeful that he will get it. Everything is on our side."

"So, it's a sure thing?"

"As sure as anything in this business can be. I didn't know you liked the stock market."

"I don't. I was just wondering what Thomas does for all those hours in there." The words hung thickly in the air. They both knew what Grace was talking about. "What is it *you* actually do, Kim?"

"I do several things, Grace. Your husband trusts my opinion."

"He does, does he? Well, you must like that an awful lot."

"I enjoy my job." This was becoming uncomfortable and Kim wished Thomas was out here.

"Does it come as a great shock to know I don't like you?"

Kim shot back, "No. I can understand that. I spend so much time with Thomas, you must feel jealous." This time she smiled with venom.

Grace understood the rules. Kim was protecting herself and Thomas. Grace sympathized with that. She intended to break her down quickly. "Have you slept with my husband?"

"I'm just sunning out here, Grace. Is there a problem with that?"

"It's a simple question."

The tension hung between them like a thick blanket. Neither one moved for several seconds.

Kim finally shifted in her seat to get a better angle. "Were you a virgin when you met your husband?"

"I don't see how the two mix."

"Sexuality is such a silly thing, don't you think? It always causes hormones to get excited."

"My hormones are fine."

"So are mine. My guess is we get them exercised in a lot of different ways. You still seem like a very active woman."

"I don't like your tone, Kim."

"Look, Grace, let's face facts, okay? Your husband is a very hardworking man, who sometimes needs a little relaxation. If he can't get it at home, my guess is he finds it somewhere else."

"I want you out of my house."

"I told Thomas you might feel this way but he told me it

wouldn't be a problem. I think you should talk to your husband."

Grace leaned down very near Kim and spat between her teeth. "If you touch him, I'll kill you."

Grace meant it.

25

Buddy was intoxicated. His mind was filled with a million pictures of Tava. He could not concentrate on anything else. Hank found him sullen and quiet. He noticed his son murmuring to himself and going out for long walks.

Buddy's desire for Tava was filled with fantasy. He ran chance meetings through his head so many times, he almost believed he actually saw her. He wandered the small downtown praying to bump into her. He dreamed of holding her hand and imagined the small, warm fingers intertwined with his. He fixated on her hands. He wanted to kiss them, stroke them, feel them rubbing through his hair and kneading his shoulders.

His nights were filled with long, flourishing dreams of the two of them on long walks on the beach. At times they were in each other's arms, kissing madly and holding each other as if there were no one else. Much to Buddy's shock he was falling in love with Tava and it hurt him. He was not able to see her. He hired a taxi to drive by the gates of Blackhurst Manor. He hung low in the seat, careful not to be seen. He imagined her at the party, dressed so sweetly, so beautifully. He wondered what her lips tasted like and imagined them to be soft, supple, and full of passion. He found her perfect.

Buddy was not interested in the takeover now except to wonder where he fit in Thomas's scheme. There was still much he could do to help. Even a public statement against his father would help fuel the fire in Thomas's favor. Buddy still considered himself a useful tool, someone with enough smarts to end up on top of the messy heap. But for now his thoughts were on Thomas's daughter.

He spent his waking hours dreaming up ways to meet her. In each case he lost heart. His ideas ultimately seemed too farfetched and ill conceived. He berated himself for falling for her. He resented her for causing this in him. But he loved the passion it caused and gave into it freely and with abandon. At last he decided to send her another dozen roses with a note confessing his feelings. He hoped by laying it all out, he could sway her. Honesty, he prayed, would be his savior.

He hoped Michael would be out of the picture. He smiled maliciously. It had been easy to find Charlotte. A simple lunch and a stroll around the grounds. A few careful questions told him all he needed. He understood people like Charlotte and had used her to get rid of Michael. He was sure Michael would now be forced to leave Sultan Valley.

The roses, he told himself, would do the trick. Every woman loves roses.

A phone rang in the distance. It took four more rings for Buddy to shake himself from his daze and pick up the phone.

"Hello? Buddy, is that you?"

"Mr. Blackhurst?"

"How are you, boy?"

Buddy was suddenly worried. "Mr. Blackhurst, you shouldn't call here. My father might hear you."

"Don't worry about it. He's eating out."

"I didn't hear him go."

"Trust me, Buddy. I've got eyes everywhere. It's safe. I need some feedback, son."

"About?"

"Christ, your father hasn't made a move. What's he doing?"

"I don't know. He doesn't seemed worried. I don't get it. Something's got to be wrong." Buddy's head was clearing and he was beginning to focus. It became clear to him Hank was taking a very relaxed stance to the takeover attempt and he couldn't figure out why. "It's strange. He's got to be up to something."

"You're damn right it's strange. We come out with a

multimillion-dollar offer and we don't hear anything from the CEO. What's he planning?"

"I wish I knew. He's keeping to himself a lot. But I can't get over his attitude. It's like he knows he's going to be okay."

"Well, that isn't true. You and I know that. Keep your eyes and ears open, Buddy. I'm counting on you."

"Yes, sir. I know that."

"You're one of the team, son."

"Yes, sir. I'll let you know. My guess is he won't make any move until Monday."

"All we can do is wait. I don't like this kind of game but I can play it."

"Yes, sir."

"Keep up the good work." Thomas rang off.

Buddy replaced the receiver and sat down near the phone. He was on the second-floor landing next to a huge stained-glass window. The sun was covering him with a reflected rainbow of light. It was a strange effect. He sat there silently, letting the heat wrap around him like a security blanket. His mind drifted back to Tava.

26

"I don't want him here."

"Shut up, mother. I don't want to hear it. He's staying in the guest house and you better be nice to him." Tava was in her mother's room.

"What do you see in him?"

"A lot more than in you."

"I don't need that. Are you ready for tonight?"

"How am I ever going to be ready?"

"I've spoken to Hans and he's going to drive you. Does your boyfriend know?"

"No, he doesn't and he better not. I think it's a good idea if you just stay away from him, Mother. I don't want you talking to him." Tava was changed now. Grace no longer intimidated her. "I have one condition."

"What? For God's sake, Tava, this is for your father."

"Have you told him yet?"

"Soon. I have to find the right time."

"I still have a demand. You're going to accept it."

"What is it?" Grace snarled.

"I want you to pay for the rest of Michael's education." Tava folded her arms defiantly over her chest and hung her weight on her left hip.

"And how am I supposed to do that?" Grace replied.

"Come off it. I know how much you've got stashed away. His tuition won't even make a dent."

"Tava, I can't . . ."

"Fine. I'll go tell Daddy." She turned and was nearly out the door before Grace called her back.

"Don't try to bluff me, dear."

"You can't take the chance, can you? I want the check made out before I leave tonight. Fifty thousand should cover it."

"I don't know."

"I do. Write the check or I tell Daddy. Period." This time she really left and walked all the way back to her room. She needed to be alone, collect her thoughts, and wait for the hours to pass. She felt like a convicted murderer facing the electric chair.

Hank scared her, both physically and mentally. How could a man demand this? The idea made her sick. She did her best to stay calm but her thoughts drifted back to Hank. He was just waiting there for her.

The evening rolled around slowly. The sun checked the hours in a slow arc toward the mountaintop. The air cooled slightly and the crickets began to chirp. Tava was pacing back and forth. Her palms were sweating and she found herself rubbing them against her pants. She was dressed in a large pullover sweater, blue jeans, and sneakers. She consciously dressed down to make herself seem less attractive. She wanted this over as soon as possible. Tava kept checking herself in the mirror. She had purposefully left her face free of makeup. She wanted to look plain in hopes Hank might change his mind.

She had felt dirty and showered for half an hour straight. Afterward she carefully gelled her diaphragm. She even sneaked one of Michael's condoms and carried it with her.

Tava kept talking to herself in a soft, nervous patter. She reassured herself she was all right and this would be over soon. She felt the need to keep her mind on her objective. Save her father, save the family. Hank was nothing to her but a faceless thing. She blanked him out as much as possible. She was not going to feel anything. She was going to turn off as many senses as she could.

Tava sent Michael away early in the evening. She told him to trust her and he did. He did not know what the big secret was but respected her enough to give her the privacy she wanted. He could see it was important to her and he understood that. The hour was drawing near and she gathered herself. She checked her pocket for the condom and her wallet. Opening it, she found she had one ten-dollar bill, some change, and lipstick. She left everything else behind. The less she took, the less she had to worry about.

She padded down the hallway aware of the sound her rubber soles made against the polished wood. She caught her reflection again in the windows and felt some relief in seeing how terrible she looked. "Please," she prayed, "don't let him go through with this."

Hans was waiting by the car.

"How are you?"

"I've been better," Tava replied and crawled in back. She felt lonely. Hans's door closed up front and the car came to life. Tava watched her house disappear behind her as they moved down the driveway toward the road. She closed her eyes and took a deep breath. She was terrified and could not turn her mind off.

"It doesn't matter," she whispered to herself. "It'll be over soon," she kept repeating to herself over and over.

Hank finished splashing on after-shave and pulled on cream-colored slacks, a fresh short-sleeved shirt, and dress boots. He wanted to make a good impression.

"Buddy!" he called.

"What?"

"Go see a movie or something, boy. I need the place to myself."

Buddy moved closer to the door. "You need what?"

"Someone's coming over. I want you to scram. I want some privacy."

"Now?"

"Yes, now. Move it."

Buddy stepped away from the door. When had Hank found time to meet a woman? Buddy had no interest in his father's personal affairs. He grabbed a sweater and left out the back door. There was a love story at the local theater. His flowers were going to be delivered tomorrow and he was getting up enough courage to call Tava again.

Hank finished in the bathroom and moved into his bedroom. He slept on a king-size mattress in an oak frame. The bed was huge. Tonight he made it perfect, turning on the nightstand light and dimming it low. He wanted the atmosphere to be inviting.

Next he moved downstairs into the living room and flipped the radio on to a country station. The lights were on and the house was sparkling. He took a seat and sipped at a scotch and water.

The Blackhurst limo entered the city limits. Tava had Hans stop at the corner. She was filled with terror and her body shook with fear. She felt cold. She felt like crying but would not allow that. This was too important, she told herself. She needed to conserve her energy. Concentration was the key. She needed to be aware of everything. Tava did not want anything going out of control.

Hans was watching her in the mirror. "What is it, Tava?"

She sighed heavily, trying to cover her fright. "Oh, Hans. Nothing. I'm just seeing Buddy Nicholls tonight."

"Uh-huh. What about your young man at the house?"

"Hans, I love Michael. This is just business. All right?"

"All right. You want me to wait?"

"Yes." Then she thought better of that. It might look

wrong. "No. I'll call you at home when I need to be picked up. This may take an hour or two."

"I'll be by the phone."

"Thank you. You can drive up now."

Hans pulled up in front of the huge Victorian. "Tava, you need any help, just call. That's what I'm here for."

"Thank you, Hans. I'll remember that." There was nothing she wanted more than to have him drive her away. But she couldn't run away, not while her father was in such a precarious position. She would do this for her father. "I'll be fine."

Hans climbed out and moved around the car. He opened Tava's door and helped her out. Her hand was like ice. He gave it a comforting squeeze and then let her go. This did not have a good feeling to it. He wondered what Grace had to do with it.

Tava watched the limo pull out of sight. She turned her attention toward the huge house. She climbed the stairs but before she knocked, the door opened and Hank was standing there, towering over her, smiling.

"Come on in." He sounded at ease and pleasant. He opened the screen door for her and let her enter in front of him. The door closed behind her with finality. "Why don't you just have a seat in the parlor? You want a drink?"

Tava was barely hearing him. Her body was on full alert but her mind was taken off guard by his gentility. He was speaking softly, almost in a caring voice. She reminded herself what she was here for. This man was despicable.

He poured a scotch and handed it to her. Tava thought it all seemed so planned. She was revolted by the entire thing. She sat on the couch, perched on the edge. This man was a stranger and she did not know what to say to him.

"How's your mama?"

"Fine. I guess. Where's Buddy?"

"A movie. I didn't think it'd be such a good idea to have him around." Hank sat calmly and continued to smile. "And your daddy?"

Tava was abrupt. "Look, I'm not here for small talk. You and I both know that. So let's just get to it, all right? This is repulsive enough. I'm here to keep up our side of the bargain."

"You're tough, aren't you?"

"I'm not anything. I just don't want to be around you any longer than I have to. I think you're a jerk and if you had any decency you'd let me go."

Hank shrugged his shoulders. "There's the door."

Tava's heart leapt. "You mean I can leave?"

"Sure. Just tell your daddy to keep his eye on the papers in the next couple of days. Your mama is a wildcat. I wonder if a nice glossy spread in *Playboy* would look good? What do you think?"

Tava sat back down. "Fine. If that's the kind of game we're going to play, let's get it over with. We gonna hump here?"

"Let's not be crude. You're here 'cause you want to be. You're a consenting adult, little darlin'."

"You're sick."

"No, no. I've just got a natural curiosity. I've always had a healthy imagination. I just want to see if it matches the real thing." He winked at her.

Tava shivered. "Can we please get this over with?"

"All right, darlin'. I like a little wildcat. Follow me." He carried his drink with him and left the living room. He moved through the dining room and into the kitchen. Tava trailed far behind. She expected him to jump her right there.

He pulled open a cupboard and grabbed a small bottle of vegetable oil. "You ever tried it with this?"

"Are we going to do it in here?"

Hank laughed and shook his head no.

Tava fought the urge to run out the back door.

Hank motioned her to follow him. He retraced his path and walked up the stairs. He gained the landing and turned left. Moving into his bedroom, he held the door open for her and waited for her to pass through. He closed it behind her. The click of the door latch was the most frightening sound she had ever heard.

Tava's heart was racing. She was frightened beyond her worst nightmare.

"Have a seat on the bed. Like the music?"

"What?" she asked distractedly.

"I asked if you liked the music." He did not wait for her answer and crossed over to his bureau. With his back to her he opened his top drawer and rummaged around his socks until his finger fell upon a button. He pushed it quietly and heard the gentle whir of a camcorder come to life. He turned to check her reaction. She did not notice. It was added ammunition in his arsenal against Thomas. He knew he had no intention of giving up until Thomas formally backed down.

"How're you feeling?"

"Sick."

"I'll make you feel better. Why don't we start with a back rub. That'll ease the tension." Hank began to strip.

She tried to avoid looking at his hulking body as he spilled out of his clothes. The more she looked, the more worried she became. He was huge. Standing over six feet, the man must have weighed three hundred pounds. His belly hung very low and his floppy nipples were more like breasts. The thought of his double chin against her face was disgusting.

He was down to his shorts now. With a little shrug they fell to his feet and he stepped out of them. He was still flaccid.

He climbed onto the bed stomach first. "Go ahead, darlin'. What're you waiting for? Take it easy on the oil. You don't need too much."

Tava reluctantly grabbed the oil from the dresser and walked over to the bed. She was opening the bottle when Hank said, "Take your clothes off, for God's sake." Her fingers froze. This was really happening and no matter how she pleaded she was going to have to go through with it. She hated Grace for this.

She placed the bottle on the floor and removed her sweater. Hank watched. He leered when she kicked out of her jeans. Tava began to remove her bra but he said, "Leave yer skivvies on. I like the way you look in 'em."

Tava, painfully red now, picked up the bottle and screwed the cap off. She poured some oil into her open hand and put the bottle on the floor. She moved closer to the bed and tentatively dabbed the liquid on Hank's fleshy back. He was hot and groaned a little when she rubbed harder.

"Go ahead, honey. Climb up on top of old Hank."

"Why?"

"I like the idea of you straddling me."

With grim resignation Tava stepped onto the bed and positioned herself over Hank's naked butt.

"There now, don't that feel better?"

Tava did not answer. She wanted to throw up. She stroked his back harder just to keep her mind occupied.

Twenty minutes passed without a word. Tava was tired. Her joints were aching and her arms hurt from the kneading. Hank stirred beneath her and groaned. "That was great. Stand up a minute, I got to roll over."

Tava quickly got off and crouched in one corner of the gigantic bed. With some effort Hank rolled over and Tava was sick to find him erect. She swallowed violently and Hank smiled lasciviously.

"Come here, gal. I want to kiss ya." He grabbed her by the arm and pulled her toward him. She allowed herself to be kissed. His breath was hot and smelled of booze.

"Take off your bra," he whispered.

She obeyed. The flimsy fabric fell away and her breasts were exposed. He moved down and took her left nipple in his mouth. He moaned with obvious pleasure.

Tava felt his mouth biting at her in a frenzy but couldn't really feel it. Feeling numb she kept her eyes staring at the wall. She was not there. She did her best to project her thoughts outside of her body. She was floating now above herself, watching a fat man suck her. In this way Tava kept her sanity. She allowed her body to go through the motions. Keeping herself detached was the only thing she could do.

He pulled away from her. He pawed her by running his stubby fingers up and down her body. "Take your panties off and kneel on the bed doggy style."

She did. She was frightened but kept herself steady. She promised herself the minute he was done she would pull on her clothes and run.

Hank pulled himself into a sitting position on the end of the bed. He regarded her smooth, young body as she pulled off her cotton bikini. He was close to orgasm now. He guided her into position. She flinched underneath his sweaty touch.

"You're beautiful." He got up on his knees and grabbed Tava around the waist. With both hands he pulled her closer to him and started to enter.

Suddenly there was a knock on the door and Buddy barged in.

"Daddy, I couldn't . . ."

"Get outta here!" Hank roared like an animal.

Buddy stumbled backward pulling himself from the room. He saw Tava's fearful eyes and suddenly knew his father was raping her! His body fell into automatic and with incredible speed Buddy was enraged.

He kicked the door completely open. It crashed against the dresser and splintered the wood. Buddy's eyes hunted for an object and his gloved hands fell on an iron table lamp. As if in slow motion, he ripped it off the dresser with one hand and yanked the cord from the wall with the other. Then, in one long, graceful arc he brought the heavy piece of metal straight down, smashing it against his father's up-turned face.

The sound was horrible. Bone splintered and was crushed beneath the heavy metal weight. Hank fell off the foot of the bed. His body tumbled in a heap on the carpet. Tava was yelling as she watched Buddy bring the lamp down five more times on Hank's quivering body. Each blow cracked out like a ball against a bat. She saw with horror the blood dripping from the base of the lamp and slowly began to make out Buddy's words.

"How could you? How could you? I love her!" He kept repeating it over and over until he threw the lamp aside. He stumbled backward against the dresser, spent. He was panting hard, gasping for breath. His eyes were like a child's, big and full of fear. He started shaking.

Tava, practically paralyzed, moved enough to grab her clothes around her. Both were so stunned, all they could do was stare at each other.

It seemed like an eternity.

Finally Buddy spoke. "Are you okay?" His voice shook.

Tava nodded her head.

Buddy, noticing her nudity for the first time, looked away. "Put your clothes on."

That brought Tava out of her reverie and forced her to scramble into her things. She stayed on the bed. Hank was not making any sounds.

"We've got to call the police."

"I came back. The movie had already started." He saw his father on the floor and winced as if someone had hit him. "He's not moving."

"Check to see if he's breathing."

"No." Buddy was too scared to go near the body.

Tava eased herself off the bed and crept around the end. She almost screamed when she saw the red mess. The left half of Hank's face was caved in. Nothing remained of it save for shards of bone. He was limp and obviously dead. Tava backed away instinctively. "He's dead. You killed him."

"I had to. I saw what he was doing to you. I couldn't let that happen. I couldn't stop myself." He spoke quickly. He was looking at her now. "You're okay, aren't you?"

"Yeah. I'm fine. We hadn't . . ."

"Good. He got you up here, right? He forced you up?"

"Yes. He did."

"He won't bother you now."

Tava noticed Buddy's eyes change. They went from scared to cold. There was a distance now; a strange half smile came to his face. A cool calm washed over him. It was like a snap in his brain and he was free. "I killed him."

Tava eased herself off the bed. She did not like the tone of his voice. She was just to the door when Buddy extended his long, thin arm and blocked her way.

"You're the only one who knows I killed him, Tava."

"It's all right, Buddy. You were protecting me."

He fixated on the word protect. "I was protecting you. You needed my help. Now . . . I need your help to protect me."

He was in shock. He was rambling on and not making sense. "You're protected," Tava reassured him. "The police are going to come and clear this up."

"They're not going to understand this. Look at him! If they see this, I'm dead. No one's going to trust me." He panicked. "They're gonna take the company away from me."

"Let me get the police, Buddy. It's okay."

"No, it isn't. Goddammit! Your father isn't going to hire me now. He's gonna think I blew it. I can't believe how stupid I am." His voice was rising and his face was growing red.

"Let me go, Buddy." She tried to get around him but he continued to block the door.

"No!" He grabbed her arm and squeezed it violently. She recoiled from the pain. She tried to pull away but he held her tighter. "No one is saying anything." He sat her down on the bed. "I don't know what to think. Just be quiet while I figure this out."

"Why don't we go downstairs, Buddy?"

"No!" He paced in front of her. "We've got to get rid of the body."

"You don't have to get rid of the body. You saved my life, Buddy."

"No one's going to believe that, Tava. Look at him. I've got too much riding on this. People aren't going to have any confidence in me."

"I'll tell them the truth."

"We've got to hide him. This whole thing's gonna blow over and they won't know." He was ranting now and started shaking again. He couldn't hold his thoughts together. "I don't know what to do."

"Let me help you," Tava pleaded. The stress was too much for him and she was worried. She spoke in soothing tones. "We don't have to go anywhere, okay? We're just gonna stay right here. Everything's going to be okay."

Buddy sat heavily next to her on the bed. His mind was cluttered. "I don't see any options."

Tava rose gently and inched toward the door.

"I was so close. Just a couple more days and we would have had the bastard. All of that power! Don't you understand?" His head swung right and he caught Tava trying to leave. The solution was so simple.

He bounded off the bed and grabbed her from behind. He caught her by the hair and dragged her back, stumbling over his father's body. Tava landed on top of him and rolled off. She was frantic now. Buddy was out of control and she needed to escape.

Buddy recovered first and climbed on top of her, clamping both hands around her throat. He squeezed down madly. Tava gagged and struggled against him. She was beginning to black out.

"Bud . . . don't . . . I . . . can't . . . breathe."

"Shut up!" he yelled at her. "Shut up!"

With one last push she summoned her energy and scratched at his eyes. He screamed in pain and released his hold. She was off the bed and stumbling for the door.

Buddy lunged for her. She ducked and her hand fell on the lamp. She scooped it up and hit him as hard as she could. It glanced off his shoulder and nicked him in the head. He faltered and fell to his knees, blocking the bedroom door. Tava was frantic to escape and ran for the only free door in the room.

She flung it open only to find a closet. She saw the video camera and realized it was still taping. She was too frantic to understand the full importance of it but she knew she needed the tape. Her body worked faster than her mind as she started reaching for it. She checked Buddy and saw him climbing to his feet. She fumbled with the ejection button. She was so scared, her fingers froze on the small buttons. She banged the camera against the wall and finally threw it on the ground. The machine shattered and she grabbed the video cassette.

Buddy hit her from behind. He tackled her with full force and they both collapsed inside the closet. Struggling to keep her grip on the cassette, she brought her elbow down on Buddy's back and knocked the air out of him. He fell back gasping for air and Tava grabbed her chance and ran for the door.

Buddy was desperate to stop her. She was the only person alive who knew what he was capable of. With her out of the way he could take control of the entire Nicholls empire. His eyes caught the camcorder lying in pieces on the ground and realized Tava had a tape. He struggled to his feet to stop her but was too dazed to move quickly. She had proof that would hurt him now!

Tava rounded the landing and headed for the stairs, sure that Buddy was right behind her. She made it halfway down the stairs and stumbled. Trying to grab for the railing, she twisted her ankle and tumbled down. Hitting the bottom of the stairs, she watched, horrified, as the tape flew from her hands, skidded across the floor, and dropped loudly down the living room heat vent. It made a hideous sound as it scraped to a stop at the bottom of the narrow shaft.

Tava tried to stand but the pain blinded her. She felt her ankle and thought it was sprained. The pain brought tears to her eyes and fatigue was beginning to overtake her. She crawled to the black hole near the baseboard. She was stopped cold by a bloodcurdling scream from the top of the stairs.

Buddy stood at the top, swaying uncontrollably, yelling with a ferocity that paralyzed Tava with chills.

"Come back here! Come back here, bitch!" he kept repeating. He tried to run down the stairs but collapsed instead, landing hard but still managing to remain conscious. He grabbed for Tava's receding foot as she bolted for the front door. He needed the tape but was losing consciousness. "Don't go home!" he screamed. "I'll find you and when I do I'm going to kill you, Tava! Do you hear me? You're not safe!

"Bring it back here! Bring it back here, Tava, or I'll kill you!" He pulled himself to his feet as he watched her run through the door.

The words sprang from Tava's mouth before she knew what she was saying. She knew she had to protect herself, and the tape was her only salvation. She needed Buddy to think she had it. "I've got the tape, Buddy! And it's going to show them everything!" she lied. She made it out the front door and ran through the night. She knew he was right behind her and was frantic for a safe place to hide.

She was too disoriented to find her way and stumbled into the central square. She was too far from the police station to run for help and did not know where to go. Her eyes frantically searched for help and fell on a Greyhound bus, its massive steel frame shaking from the vibrations of its huge motor. She could hear Buddy in the distance. His voice was getting stronger as he neared the square.

The bus was about to leave and the driver was helping the last few late-night passengers in. Tava was desperate and instinctively ran for it. Her mind was filled with the horror of blood, and all she desired was a dark hiding place.

She ran through the gardens. Her foot was in intense pain. The passenger door slid shut before she could get to it. An attendant was closing the baggage doors beneath the passengers. She circled around the bus and found one hatch still open. Without thinking, driven by desperate necessity, she clambered in and pushed her way to the back. She could hear the man pulling the hatch doors closed. From the darkness she spotted Buddy on the far side of the square. He was madly scanning the streets for her. Tava instinctively covered herself with the suitcases and pressed herself against the cold metal floor. She squeezed her eyelids closed and sobbed silently. Stuffing her sweatshirt into her mouth, her body was racked with wild convulsions of fright. Like a child she wished it all away. She huddled in the darkness, praying for the hatch to close. She could hear Buddy yelling her name. She saw him frantically searching the town square for her. And then she was plunged into blackness. The compartment was locked from the outside.

As the bus pulled out of Sultan Valley Tava erupted into uncontrollable sobs. Her body shook like a rag doll. It took two hours for the lurching beat of the engine to slowly lull her into a fitful sleep filled with the terrifying visions of Hank's blood and Buddy's gruesome assault.

27

"Mr. Blackhurst? Mr. Blackhurst?" Hans knocked on the bedroom door. He was worried. Tava had not called at all last night. Something was wrong. It was 7:00 A.M. and he was concerned.

"Hans?" came the voice from inside. "It's open." Hans let himself in and closed the door behind him. Thomas was pulling on his robe. "What is it?"

"I'm concerned, sir." Hans made it a point to ignore Kim. She was curled up underneath the blankets still asleep.

"What's the problem, Hans?" Thomas sat on the edge of the bed.

"Tava, sir. I've been waiting all night for her call. I thought you might know why."

"What do you mean? Where is she?"

"I thought you knew. I left her at the Nicholls's estate at 9:00 P.M. last night."

"Why'd you do that?" Thomas was confused. Why would Tava be visiting the Nichollses?

"Mrs. Blackhurst arranged for me to drive her."

Thomas made no comment. "What time again?"

"9:00 P.M., sir. Tava gave the impression she would be two hours. I thought you should know."

"I appreciate that."

"In light of your takeover attempt, sir, it seems odd."

"I'm aware of that, Hans. Let me talk to Grace. Stay close. I may need you."

After Hans left Thomas made his way down the hall to Grace's suite. She was still sleeping when he knocked. "Grace?" He opened the door and peeked in. The curtains were still drawn and the room was dark. A little light crept in around the edge of the curtains. He moved across the drawing room into the bedroom. Grace was in bed, perfectly still. He shook her leg lightly. "Grace. Wake up."

She roused herself groggily. Her speech was slurred and her mouth dry. "What . . .?"

"Why did you have Hans drive Tava to the Nicholls estate last night?"

Grace hid her surprise and answered slowly. "Tava had a date."

"Buddy?"

Grace nodded. "Right. She was going to show him a little of Sultan Valley. He sent her flowers, Thomas."

"He did?"

"I asked Hans to drive her over."

"How late was she staying out? Hans has been waiting all night."

Grace's heart skipped faster. "She hasn't called yet? That's strange." She was awake now. "I'm sure she's fine, Thomas. They probably stayed up to watch the sunrise."

"Did Michael go with her?"

"I don't think so, Thomas. Why don't you send Hans out to look for her if you're so worried."

"That's not really his place, Grace."

"Then why don't you call the Nichollses?"

There was a muffled knock and Kim's voice filtered through the rooms. "Thomas?"

"Yes. What is it?" he called out to her.

"There's a call for you."

"I'll call them back later. We're busy in here!"

"You better come, Thomas. It's the police."

Thomas left Grace immediately. Grace scrambled out of bed and dressed quickly. She was trembling with fright. All of this was going perfectly until Tava came into the picture. Grace berated herself for trusting her daughter.

"Goddammit it, what has that little bitch done now?" She could feel the wall of lies pushing in around her. She finished dressing and hurried after Thomas.

"What!" Thomas was on the phone in the kitchen. He was shaking with anger and yelling. His face was deep red. "I can't believe this. Where is she?" He waited for the response. "Fine. We'll be there in ten minutes!" He slammed the phone down. "Hans!" he yelled. "Get the car. We're going into town."

Grace burst into the kitchen. She gave Kim a cold stare. "What is it, Thomas?"

"The sheriff. He wants us down at the station." He was shaking his head. "I can't believe it."

"What is it?"

"Hank Nicholls is dead."

Grace's gasped. "Oh my God!"

"How did it happen?" Kim broke in.

"He wouldn't tell me. I've got to get dressed. We're leaving in five minutes."

"I don't want her coming, Thomas!" Grace yelled. "This is family business!"

"Grace!" Thomas barked. "Leave her alone."

"I don't want that whore coming with us!"

Kim waved Thomas off. "That's okay. I'll stay here."

"No, it is not okay! Grace, you better learn to live with Kim or I swear to God I'll make your life hell! I will not have my friends intimidated by your pathetic paranoias!"

"Screw you, Thomas! And screw your little bitch!"

Thomas was seething with anger. He was having tremendous difficulty holding himself back. Kim could see this and moved quickly to stop him. "I'm going to stay here. Now is not the time for this discussion. You both get in the car and go. I'll let you know if I hear from Tava." She was very convincing and calmed the tension. "Thomas, go. We can talk about this later."

Grace slammed out of the house. Thomas paused at the door and looked back at Kim. "Thank you. You're the only voice of reason in this whole damn place. Sometimes I think we're all going crazy." With that he swept out of the house.

28

"I don't know what happened. I missed the showing of the movie so I went home and heard my father yelling upstairs. I went up, I opened his door, and there she was. Tava was standing over him with this lamp in her hands beating him over the head. I tried to stop her but it was already too late." He took a long pause and wiped tears from his eyes. "She killed him." Buddy broke down again in uncontrollable sobs. He was sitting in the sheriff's office, looking haggard.

The sheriff, a large, burly man named Jack Stanton, brushed his walrus mustache with thick, pudgy hands and watched the boy. He was finding this hard to believe. "Little Tava Blackhurst killed your father?" Buddy nodded yes. "Correct me if I'm wrong but he's way over six feet, right? And probably three hundred pounds."

"She did it, Sheriff. And then she attacked me. Look at me for Christ's sakes!" Buddy's face was swollen with ugly black-and-blue marks. They were very convincing. He unbuttoned his shirt and showed Jack his bruised ribs. "I tried to pull her off my daddy and she turned on me. She caught me with that damn lamp and then ran for the stairs. I tackled her and we both went down the fucking steps. I blacked out and she was gone when I came to."

"Uh-huh."

"If I'm lying, where is she?"

Jack was anxious. Tava was gone and from his conversation with Thomas she was not home. There were only three patrol cars in the valley and all of them were on alert for

Tava. She couldn't be far. Jack had a hard time believing this skinny young man but right now there was nothing else to go on. He had a rich oilman dead in his morgue and the oilman's son beaten up badly.

The coroner was running the autopsy now. The lamp was being dusted for prints. The house was roped off and sealed. This was Sultan Valley's first murder and Jack knew it was going to blow through his little town like a tornado.

"That little bitch," Buddy spewed.

"Now hold on there, son. Until we get this all figured out I think you should keep your mouth shut. You're free to leave but don't go far. We're gonna need you handy." He let Buddy go with a wave of his hand. The bruises on the boy's body were real. Something terrible had happened in that house—that was plain to see. But Jack just couldn't believe that Tava had been involved. He knew her. He had seen her grow up in this town. He liked the family. He knew Grace was having problems but nothing any family doesn't go through. He was even at the Ball. He had seen Hank and Buddy land in the helicopter. To think that only a week ago the town was bathing in the glow of the beginning of the summer season and now this. This was going to hurt the town and it had to be solved quickly. "Shit. Just what I needed."

Jack just couldn't get over the picture of Tava, at the party, looking so sweet and innocent, caught up in this ugly affair.

Thomas and Grace were ushered into the police station. They were walked quickly to Jack's office where he greeted them like old friends.

"What the hell is going on, Jack?"

Jack spoke calmly. "We don't have much. We do know Hank Nicholls is lying dead in our morgue. We know his son, Buddy, is beaten up pretty badly and we know Tava is missing. Where is she, Thomas?"

"I don't know. She was left at the Nicholls place last night about nine o'clock. My driver left her there and was expecting her to call a couple of hours later. That's all we know. Hans came to me this morning when she didn't phone and then we heard from you. What is going on?"

Grace sat there silently.

"I know you're both upset. I'm just trying to get the whole picture here, so bear with me. Why was she at the Nicholls place?"

"Grace knows this better than I do."

"Well," she started, "as far as I know, Tava was going to show Buddy the nightlife."

"You're sure?"

"Of course I'm sure, Jack. All I know is that Tava came to me asking for the car. So I set it up with Hans. Where's my little girl?"

"We don't know. I'm going to be up-front with you folks. We have a lot of questions but right now Buddy Nicholls is saying . . . Tava killed Hank."

Thomas was the first to react. "You can't be serious! Who does this little shit think he is? My Tava could no more kill that man than kill me! Jesus, Jack, you know that!"

"I know, Thomas. We're checking into his story. The kid is beat-up pretty badly though. Something happened in that house and we want to find out what. Without Tava's side of this we're in the dark. I've got my people out looking for her. It's important to get her in here as soon as possible. Do I make myself clear?"

"Of course you do. We'll cooperate with everything."

"So what you're saying is that Buddy Nicholls is accusing my child of killing Hank?" Grace asked. "Why? That doesn't make sense." Grace knew that could not have happened. Hank had only wanted to sleep with Tava. But maybe he'd gotten too rough and Tava had had to protect herself. My God, she thought, what if Tava really did kill him?

"This whole thing is confusing. Buddy says he was coming back from a movie and walked in on them. Maybe Tava went to see Hank. Any reason why that would happen?" He was looking at Grace.

"I have no idea. All she did was come to me to see if she could borrow the car." Grace realized excitedly that with Hank dead, his threat had no power if she could get the photos back.

"What're you doing, Jack?" Thomas asked.

"Well, if we don't find her within the next few hours, I'll have to put out an alert. I hope it doesn't come to that. But if it does, it's as much for her protection as ours. We simply need her part of the story. Right now it doesn't look good because she isn't here. My guess is whatever happened she's scared and afraid to come in."

Thomas was speechless. He looked to Grace for support but was only greeted with confused, angry eyes. She was in her own world and he could not gauge her reaction.

It all seemed so unreal. Nothing like this ever happened to Tava. She was his perfect child. She was loving, warm, compassionate, and caring. She had never hurt anyone and now to have this confront him was maddening. By implication she was being accused of a heinous crime Thomas knew she did not commit. It was impossible and yet, until she was found, all this could do was grow. Thomas felt out of control and he hated it. There was nothing he could do but hope his daughter showed up quickly. The very real possibility existed that this situation could get out of control and he knew that could get dangerous. He decided quickly that if she did not show up soon, he would have to start searching for her himself.

29

Tava woke with the sound of rain pelting against the side of the bus. She was groggy and disoriented, and her body was aching all over. She spent the last few hours on her back twisted among suitcases. The cold metal floor felt damp and the rumbling of the engine echoed loudly through the small compartment. Tava pushed a case off of her and tried to sit up but there was not enough headroom. She could see dull morning light through the cracks of the hatch. She wondered where she was.

The first thing she needed to do was get to a phone. Her father needed to hear about Buddy and what he'd done. He would clear all of this up, she knew. She was too tired to start crying again but the pictures of Hank and what Buddy did to him filled her with terror. She felt abused. The picture of Hank lying dead continued to haunt her. She never saw a dead man before last night and the picture was one she would never forget.

Tava felt the bus gearing down. She tensed, worried now about sneaking out without getting caught. She feared the unknown. What would she say to the bus driver if he caught her?

The bus made a sharp turn to the right and Tava fought to keep her balance. The bus was stopping and she maneuvered herself up near the front. She was hoping to sneak out quickly while the attendant opened the other hatches.

The huge Greyhound lumbered to a stop and the engine shuttered off. Tava strained to hear voices. The bus driver's came through muffled, "Daltonville. We're not staying long, folks. You've got five minutes to stretch your legs."

Tava pressed her ear to the hatch and heard footsteps coming toward her. She pulled away, trying to press herself back into the shadows. She jumped when the compartment next to hers opened. Ten seconds later hers was thrown open and the driver turned away to talk to one of the passengers.

"Which is yours?"

An elderly woman peered in. "Well, now, I don't know. It's red."

"What's it look like, ma'am?"

"Big," she answered. She peered into the darkness until her eyes fell on it. "There it is. The one in the back."

"All right. Stand clear. I'll get it."

The driver climbed in. Crouching, he moved through the bags and grabbed the large case with his big hands. He yanked it up and over the other suitcases, pulling it behind him as he climbed out of the compartment. "Here it is."

"Thank you, dear."

"No problem." The driver hoisted it on a wheeled cart and pointed the woman toward the low hung bus station. He turned back to the compartment and leaned inside. "Get the hell out of there! Now." He stood back and folded his hairy arms across his chest.

Tava's heart sank. She was caught. Sweat beaded instantly across her forehead as she picked her way out of the mess.

Tava did not know what to say. She gulped and decided to let him speak first.

"What the hell are you doing in there?"

Tava kept silent.

"Have you been in there since Sultan Valley?"

"Yes, but I can explain. I was being chased and I needed a place to hide."

"Who was chasing you?"

"This man. He was trying to attack me."

"Well, you don't look too good."

Her sweatshirt and jeans were smudged and her face was still dirty. "I've never done anything like this before. I'm sorry. If I could just borrow a phone, I can get this all cleared up."

"Sultan Valley was three hundred miles ago. I can't believe this. Well, come on in. We'll get this figured out. How old're you?"

"Twenty-one."

"You look younger."

He took her by the arm and guided her into the station. It was a large room with a small grilled office off to one side. It was a prefab building and deserted at this time of morning. Tava checked the clock on the wall: 10:00 A.M.

He moved her into the office and sat her down. "Morning, Harriet. We've got a stowaway."

Harriet was a small, stubby woman in her late sixties. She was wearing khaki pants and an oversized green sweater. Her hair was pulled back in a tight bun. She looked severe and unfriendly and stared coldly at Tava. She eventually said, "I don't see why college kids can't just pay the damn fare." She sniffed and turned away.

The driver was on the phone. "Yeah, this is Louis down at the station. Listen, I got someone down here with a hell of a story. She spent all night in the baggage compartment. She looks kind of beat-up. I'll leave her here. I got to go. What? Fine. 'Bye." He hung up and turned to Tava. "You sit tight. Someone from the police station's gonna be down."

"Fine. Thanks."

"I've got to go. See you, Harriet."

Tava watched him leave. As soon as the police arrived, she told herself, this whole thing would get straightened out.

"Damn kids. Always monkeying around."

Tava did her best to ignore the woman. "May I borrow your phone?"

"No, you may not," Harriet said disgustedly. "There's a pay phone in the lobby."

Tava sighed and stood up. She walked out of the office and found the phone on the far side of the concrete room. She reached for her purse and realized she didn't have it. She checked her pockets and came up with a ten-dollar bill. She picked up the receiver and dialed collect.

"Hello?" Thomas picked it up first. He sounded strained on the other end of the line.

"Daddy?" The tears started to well this time. "Daddy, it's Tava."

"Thank God. Are you okay?"

"I'm fine. Just a little bruised up."

"Where are you, sweetie?"

"Daltonville. I fell asleep on a bus."

"Honey, the police want to see you. Stay put. We're going to come get you."

"I don't have any money."

"That's okay. Just stay where you are. I'm going to have Mark fly in and pick you up. Can you get to the airport?"

"I think so. Someone's coming down to talk to me from the police here. They can take me out. They may want to talk to you."

"That's fine. Honey," Thomas was careful, "what happened?"

Tava sobbed now. She couldn't block the horrible pictures. The blood kept haunting her. "I . . . can't . . . they . . ."

"Take it easy. I understand." He was soothing and used his deep voice to comfort her. "It's okay, honey."

Grace picked up on another phone. "Tava, honey, it's your mother. They're saying you killed Hank."

It was out before Thomas could stop her. "Grace!"

"What?" Tava was not sure what she heard. "Who's saying that?"

Thomas broke in. "Nothing, honey. We'll get this all cleared up when you get here. The plane will be there in an hour. Grace, why don't you hang up?"

"Thomas, she has a right to know and I want to know what happened."

"What're you talking about?"

"Grace, for God's sake, shut up!"

"Be quiet, Thomas. Tava dear, Buddy is saying he walked in and saw you kill Hank."

"I didn't kill him! Buddy did!" Tava began to panic.

"We need you back here to clear this up."

"I didn't kill anybody!" She only cried harder. "I did not kill Hank and I can prove it!" Suddenly the woman behind the counter seemed dangerous. Tava did not know what to trust. Her frame of reference was getting too confusing.

"Stay calm, baby." Thomas soothed. "How can you prove it?"

"I don't want to tell you over the phone!" She was embarrassed and still trying to protect her father from the truth. She was also realizing she could only trust herself now; it was safer that way.

The blaring whine of police sirens screamed through the early morning silence and broke her reverie. It shocked her so badly, she stumbled back against the wall in fright. "Daddy, the police are here. I don't know what to do." She was terrified.

"They're there to help you. Just stay calm!"

They were coming for her. She knew it completely and realized she needed to be free to save herself. No one could help her. Not if she was being framed for murder.

She quickly glanced at Harriet, who was busy with her early morning paperwork. There was no one else in the building. Through the window Tava watched two police cars screech to a halt. The sirens continued to blare and the lights revolved incessantly. The noise hurt her ears.

One young policeman withdrew a bullhorn from the car and yelled, "Tava Blackhurst! Don't move. You are under arrest! We're surrounding you so just stay where you are. We don't want anyone getting hurt!"

She watched the flashing lights shine in her eyes for a split second and then she ran. She left the phone dangling by its wire as she bolted out the back door. She plunged into the deep underbrush and kept running. She had to stay free, she told herself, until she cleared her name. It was the only option she had!

Two hours later, huddled near the town limits, Tava brushed herself off and crept into town. She was nervous. She knew the police were looking for her but she needed to eat. Her stomach was screaming for food. She felt terrible. The bruises on her body ached. She wiped the dirt from her face and pulled her hair back.

Tying it into a knot, she decided she needed to change her appearance. If her mother was right and she was being accused of Hank's murder, she couldn't allow herself to be caught. She was alone and frightened, terrified now of trusting anyone. She was scared to turn herself in for fear she would lose her evidence. The tape was her only key to safety. Without it she was lost and she feared Buddy would pull some legal stunt to keep her from getting it. She did not know how she was going to do it but she was going to steal the tape back.

"No telling what that asshole has said about me," she murmured under her breath. The thought of Buddy made her seethe with anger.

Tava's eyes fell on a two-pump gas station just off the main street. It was deserted. She crossed over to it, careful to watch for the police. She tried the bathroom door and found it locked. She got up her strength and found an attendant. He was a small man with a big beard. He scowled deeply and rubbed the sleep from his eyes when she came in.

"Hello. My name is . . ." she caught herself. She was going to have to watch that. *"Marty.* Would you mind if I use your bathroom?"

"Only for customers," he growled.

Tava wanted to yell at this little man. Still she found the patience to continue. "I won't be very long. I've been traveling all night."

"You look terrible."

Tava tried to smile. "I know."

The man eyed her for several seconds and then shrugged his shoulders. "All right. But don't mess the place up."

"I promise. You wouldn't have any scissors, would you?" She had an idea.

"Why?" He was suspicious. The last thing he needed was some teenager killing herself in his bathroom.

"Honestly? It's hot. I want to cut my hair."

He shook his head in disbelief. "Women. Yeah, sure, I guess. I've got 'em here somewhere." He dug in his desk and fished out a large pair. He handed them to her along with a key to the women's washroom. "I don't know how sharp they are."

Tava hurried around back and ducked inside. She was surprised by her reflection. The dirt on her face and the bags under her eyes made her feel ugly. She wanted to wash her face but realized it made a good disguise.

"Come on, Tava. Think. We've got to get through this," she warned herself. With uneasiness she grabbed a huge handful of hair and cut it. Seeing it fall in the sink made her sick.

When she was finished, the rough haircut looked more like a boy's. It was short on the sides and longer on top. She now looked more like a child of the streets. Her clothes were stained and torn. Her face was dirty and her hair had become a short, tangled mess.

Next she remembered her diaphragm and removed it. Throwing it away in the garbage can, she was thankful Hank had never penetrated her.

She looked at herself in the mirror. "At least they won't recognize me," she said to herself. She dropped the scissors in the sink and left the bathroom. She ducked behind the gas station and went back into the shrubs. She wanted to disappear again. She felt safer among the weeds.

Her clothes bothered her. It dawned on her that the police would have a description of what she was wearing. She needed a change of clothes. Tava dug into her jeans and fished out her ten-dollar bill. Hardly enough to buy new clothes on, she thought. As much as she hated to do it, she was going to have to steal them.

She was skirting along a row of houses. She followed a slow-running creek along the back and spotted clothes hanging out to dry in the warm morning air. She looked for something that might fit her. The only piece she saw was a sleeveless red floral-print dress.

"No one's going to recognize me in that." She got as close as she could to the laundry line and scanned the backyard for people. There was no one in sight so she ran up, grabbed it off the line, and ran back to the safety of the trees.

She held the dress out in front of her. "I can't believe this." It looked like a hand-me-down and fell above the knee. She shrugged her shoulders and stripped. Pulling the dress on over her head, she smoothed it out and then buried her other clothes. Without a mirror she wasn't sure how she looked, wanting only to blend in with the locals. She felt ridiculous but safe.

Farther down the creek she reached a road and was quickly in downtown. The small Main Street was busy. Tava spotted a diner and crossed the street. She felt awkward in the red summer dress and kept brushing back her new short hair. The warm air felt funny aginst her neck.

She walked into the busy diner and sat at the counter. She scanned the menu and decided on the biggest sandwich she could find.

"I'd like the Turkey Delight, please, with fries and a chocolate shake."

The waitress smiled. "You aren't hungry, are you?"

"Just a little." Tava spoke quietly, trying not to draw attention to herself.

"I'll get this up for you. New in town?"

"Just passing through. I'm getting my car looked at up the road."

"Well, welcome to Daltonville."

"Thanks."

The sandwich finally arrived and Tava devoured it. She paid less attention to the taste and more attention to the way it filled her stomach. She finally felt full and slurped up the last of the shake. She wasn't sure what to do next and decided she would have to hitchhike. The idea made her stomach turn. She was used to limousines and now to be reduced to this was criminal. She felt disoriented and unsure of herself.

She paid her bill and was left with four dollars and some change. She left the restaurant and started following the road outside of town. She passed in front of a barbershop and was just about to cross the street when she heard a voice behind her.

"Excuse me a minute!"

Tava did not know what to do. Should she run? Should

she stay and talk? The questions ran through her head. She took the chance and turned around. A well-built man in a policeman's uniform was standing on the sidewalk with his hat in his hands. He was holding the barbershop door open with his foot.

"What's your name?"

Tava tried to think. Her fake name escaped her and she stumbled over her words. "What do you mean?"

He smiled, "I mean, what is your name?"

"Um . . . Carol."

"Right. Carol, you new in town?"

"I'm just passing through. I'm getting my car looked at up the street," she lied again.

"Do I know you?"

Tava smiled sweetly. "No. I don't think so. Did you go to MSU?"

"No." The policeman let the door close and knelt down. "You dropped this"—he picked up two quarters—"when you went by."

Tava tossed off a silly grin and walked back. She extended her hand for the money. "Thanks."

"No problem. Listen, you don't know anything about a bus this morning, do you?"

"Should I?"

"Just wondering. Where'd you say you were going?"

"I didn't. I'm just traveling around."

"Okay. Have a good day." He started inside and then popped his head back out. "Tava?" he yelled after her.

She instinctively turned her head. "What?"

He grinned a huge smile and wagged his index finger at her. "I thought it was you. There's people looking for you." He started down the sidewalk toward her and Tava broke into a run. She hit full stride in four seconds and sprinted down the center of the street. It was all the policeman could do to keep up with her; she moved fast. "Tava!" he yelled. "Slow down. All I want to do is talk." They were drawing the interested stares of the townspeople now. Tava, a young woman in a worn dress, pursued by the town deputy down the middle of their Main Street.

Tava was petrified. Her fear propelled her on. She picked up speed and rounded a corner between the feed and hardware stores; he was just a few seconds behind her. He knew she was running into a dead end. He kicked himself for missing her at the bus station and could smell a victory. He wanted to be the one to catch a suspected killer. He doubled his efforts and sprinted into the alleyway.

He was standing at the end of the alley. Dusty red-brick walls towered three stories above him. There was no way out. He scanned the boxes and trash bin. He was sure he would see one of them move and give her away. He tried to quiet his own hard breathing in order to hear hers. Someone from the street called down the alley.

"What's up, Terry?"

"Go on back now. Keep away. This is police business."

"We'll get 'em, Sheriff. I'll keep a lookout out here."

He turned his attention back to the alley. "All right now. I know all about it. You're in some serious trouble and I don't want you to make it any worse for yourself. Resisting arrest is a serious offense. Now, I want you to just come on out and leave well enough alone. Come on, honey." He waited for an answer but all was silent. She definitely was in there, he just couldn't tell where.

He began to slowly move toward the green dumpster to his right. It was possible she was hiding in there. He drew his gun. She didn't look dangerous but she was wanted for murder. He eased up slowly to the side of the large, rusting trash bin and threw the top up.

Empty.

He felt his heart pumping. "Well, if you're not in there, then you've got to be over here." He leveled his gun at a pile of old boxes. "You got five seconds to come out of there." He made sure to cock the gun loudly. "One." He waited for her.

"Two." He stepped closer.

"Three. Come on out now. This is serious. I mean it. This is no joke, young lady.

"Four." He was sweating now. The tension was getting to him.

"Five. All right. I'm coming in." He moved toward the boxes.

He took two steps before Tava descended. She was hanging off the fire escape just above Terry's head. He moved underneath her and she dropped heavily. Her left foot hit his shoulder while her right crashed against the top of his head. They collapsed together in a heap. He groaned unconsciously beneath her. She knew she needed to move quickly. She checked him over to make sure he was not hurt and then rummaged in his coat for a pen. She grabbed a pad of paper from an outside pocket and scribbled a quick note:

I am innocent and can prove it. I did not kill Hank Nicholls!

Tava

She replaced the pen and left the pad on Terry's chest. She summoned her last reserve and bolted for the open street. She raced by an older man at the entrance. He yelled something at her but she couldn't hear him.

She ran for the open road. Main Street became the main road south and it was here she hoped to find a ride. She was running on instinct now. It was self-preservation fueling her run and she did not know when her energy would end. It scared her. She'd never been chased in her life.

She felt herself being confronted with concepts and ideas she never imagined she'd have to deal with. It was the most disconcerting feeling. She felt unsteady. Her life was out of balance and it was all she could do to maintain any sense of calm. She was being pursued by the police. She was being framed for the murder of Hank Nicholls and she'd been almost killed by Buddy.

Through all of this she heard herself calling out for Michael. She wanted to feel his sensitive touch. She wanted to be held and whispered to. She wanted to feel the reassuring brush of his lips against hers, telling her everything was going to be okay.

Tava was now fighting for her sanity. All of this was too much for her as she limped out of town. She felt the rage and confusion boiling over. She was about to explode. Tears began streaming down her angular cheeks but she refused to break down and sob. She needed to keep her wits about her. She needed a strength she never knew she had.

Terry was going to gain consciousness soon and come after her. What she needed was a ride and she needed it now. She felt foolish sticking her thumb out to strangers and felt terribly exposed. She was sure people knew who she was. Still she persevered. She had to.

It was still early and there weren't many cars driving through town. Tava spotted a semi gearing up and moving toward her. She brushed her hair away from her face and tried to smile. She hesitantly waved her thumb in the trucker's direction and felt a mixed sigh of relief and fear as the huge machine pulled off the side of the road. In the distance a crowd was gathering around the alley and Tava moved faster. Gulping, praying for safety, she ran up to the huge Kenworth and climbed up the tall cab. She heaved the door open and met the trucker's eyes. Tava discovered it was a woman. She was in her late forties, graying around the sides, and dressed in a plaid shirt and blue jeans. She smiled brightly and waved Tava in.

"Hey! Where you goin'?"

"I don't know . . . I'm just going West."

"That's fine. Me too. Close the door and let's go. I don't have all day." She revved the engine and threw it into the first of its eighteen gears.

Tava settled into the seat and pulled the large metal door shut. She leaned way back. Seeing the receding reflection of Daltonville in the background, Tava silently crossed her fingers and hoped they wouldn't follow. She knew it was a fruitless wish and just wanted enough time to lose herself among the crowd.

30

"It's a terrible thing . . . I appreciate your sympathies . . . God bless you . . . No . . . I'm going to have the funeral here . . . No . . . Daddy wouldn't have wanted to be flown all over the country."

"Now, Buddy," his aunt intoned, "I don't think that's what my brother would have wanted at all."

"Well, I tell you what, Aunt Mamie. If you want to come

out here and take the body back, fine. My plan is to do it here."

"You sound so cold, Buddy. This is your father. I'm sure he would have wanted a burial in Texas."

"Look, I've been through a lot with this murder and I'm gonna have it done here. We'll worry about a memorial service in Texas. Now, leave me alone." He hung up. He reminded himself to watch her. Nosy family members might be a problem.

Buddy leaned back in his desk chair. He was enjoying himself. Within a matter of hours everything was arranged. Hank was going to be buried in a beautiful plot underneath a fir in the middle of a mountain cemetery. Buddy had already hired a minister to say a few words. He did not expect anyone to be there. As a matter of fact, he was discouraging it. He wanted to play the lonely, grieving son. The picture would look better if he bore his torment alone with the minister.

Public reaction was decidedly confused. The investigation was continuing into the death of Hank, and people were overwhelmed with disbelief that Tava Blackhurst had anything to do with it. To them it was the most ridiculous story they'd ever heard. However, it was pointed out, the Blackhurst girl was nowhere to be found. She had disappeared among the heated accusations, and the rumors were starting to fly.

Buddy was keeping a low profile and letting the facts speak for themselves. There were just a few loose ends he needed to take care of. He crossed into the hallway and down to the living room. He moved inside the large expanse and paced in front of the unlit fireplace.

A man sat patiently waiting for him. He was dressed all in black with mirrored glasses on. His face was pockmarked and scarred. A deep gash, healed over, ran from under his right eye down the length of his nose and through his upper lip. It must have been a devastating wound, inflicted by a knife. He did not move. He seemed to have the stillness of a Buddha priest in meditation. His name was Z and he waited for Buddy to speak.

"Sorry to keep you waiting." Even though Buddy was growing in confidence, this man still unnerved him. He exuded danger. However, Buddy's money was good and, for now, bought one of the best killers in the industry.

"The only thing we have on her is a bus trip to Daltonville. The police tried to get her there but she got away. From there I'm afraid you're on your own." Buddy waited for the man to react. He wasn't sure the man had heard him. "I said . . ."

"I heard you." Z spoke softly with tremendous intensity. His voice was barely above a whisper, yet rang through his chest like a cannon. His broad shoulders lay still underneath his leather jacket. His muscles were compact and hard as stone. His body did not move when he spoke and his head remained still. "Tava Blackhurst. Daughter of investors Thomas and Grace Blackhurst. Wanted in connection with the murder of your father. You want her dead. Why?"

Buddy tried to laugh. "I thought you people didn't want to know the details."

"If I'm going to kill them, I want to know why. This is not an easy thing. I need a purpose."

"I just want it done!" Buddy was desperate. He was enjoying his newfound power and could not afford to have it ruined by Tava Blackhurst.

"You are a spoiled child. Good night." Z rose and moved to the door.

Buddy followed. "No, please. I'm sorry. I'll tell you why." Z remained standing. "You have five minutes, little boy."

"I need her dead because she's got a tape I want. It shows some very sensitive things being done to her."

"Sexual?"

"Yes." Among other things, he thought to himself. "If anyone sees it, I could be ruined and my father's memory would be dragged through the mud. I don't care how you do it to her, but I want that tape."

"You are a dangerous boy. I am quite sure I don't like you."

Buddy chafed under the label of "boy." "I am not a child and, as far as I know, you don't have to like me."

"Five hundred thousand." Z crossed his arms. He remained completely still.

Buddy choked. "Jesus, you're kidding."

"Good-bye, Mr. Nicholls." Z was out the door this time

157

before Buddy convinced him to come back. "My time is very valuable, little fool. What you want done is highly specialized. This is not a movie. This is not make-believe. You want me to take the life of another human being. I wonder if you understand what that means. Take it or leave it."

"Fine. I'll do it." Buddy would have to sell stock to get the money.

"In exactly twelve hours a man will call. He will provide you with an account number. At that point you will transfer five hundred thousand dollars. If it is there, I go to work. If it isn't, we will never see each other again. My time is valuable so be very sure. I am the best you will ever find. You can consider her dead, but only if I have my money. Is that understood?"

"Christ, that's a lot of money."

"Boy," he slipped out venomously, "that is cheap for what you are asking me to do. No discussion. Either it's there or not. Good night."

"I want that video back!" he called to Z's back. He watched the mysterious man disappear into the darkness. Buddy felt a cold chill run through him. He had too much to do. The money would not be easy but it was possible. But first things first.

He swept into action. First he phoned George Cove, the Nicholls's personal lawyer.

"George? Buddy Nicholls. How soon can we get the will read?"

"Well, son, soon. Couple of days."

"I want it read tomorrow. I'm flying in for two hours. Have it ready by two."

"You can't leave Sultan Valley, boy. There's a murder investigation going on."

"I know that, George. I'll be back tomorrow night and no one will know."

"Son, I don't know if . . ."

"George, things are changed. My father had a certain way of doing things and I have mine. If you value my business, you'll learn to adapt. Have it ready." He hung up and immediately dialed the Nicholls offices. A young female voice answered.

"Nicholls Development. How may I help you?"

"Dottie? This is Buddy. There's a few things I want you to do for me. One, clear out my daddy's office. Put all his personal things into boxes and get rid of the furniture. I'm moving in. Understand?"

"Yes, sir. But I think Mr. Poole was thinking of . . ."

"*I* am moving in. Do it or you won't have a job tomorrow. Also, call an emergency meeting of the board. I want them all there by two-thirty tomorrow. We have to solve this Blackhurst mess. Do you have all that?"

"Yes, sir." Her voice was nervous.

"That's good. I trust you, Dottie, don't forget that." He hung up. For the last call he used a small navy blue phone book he carried in his breast pocket. It was where he found the people that had found him Z. It was also where he knew his father kept his private banker.

Buddy dialed, and the phone was picked up immediately. "This is Buddy Nicholls. I need some money."

31

Thomas was in his study. The lines of worry were deep, and shadowed his normally vibrant face. His world was quickly falling down around him. His only child was alone and scared, running from a fear she could not understand, and he was impotent to help. All of his pent-up frustration was bottled up with nothing to shower its fury on. He was mortified with gruesome thoughts of Tava being brutalized out in the harsh world. He needed her safe and he needed her near him. He could only protect her if she was close. The best lawyers in the country were poised to fly in to her defense. No one believed the murder story, but until she came in the circumstantial evidence was mounting against her.

Thomas spent the entire morning with the state's district attorney trying in vain to keep Tava's name from the news and police stations. Not even his considerable influence could sway the legality of a wanted suspect. Tava was now one of the most-wanted women in the entire state. All police agencies were notified and a picture of her was being forwarded to every precinct. By the end of the day every policeman and policewoman in the state would know who she was and what she was wanted for.

Thomas tried to hold down his seething contempt. He brought his clenched fist down hard on his massive desk and it shook from the violent force.

"Goddammit!" The room echoed with the sound of his anguished cry and fell silent. Kim eased herself into the room and called from the door.

"Thomas?" Kim never saw him like this. It frightened her and made her want to hold him.

"Come in." He waved her to a seat in front of the desk. She took it and stared at him intently. Thomas tried to smile but the effort failed. "I want Tava back here. This is like some horrible joke. I just don't understand it."

She did her best to comfort him. "Thomas, you know she didn't do it. Until this is cleared up, we have to be strong."

"I know that, my dear. Believe me, I know that. But there's only so much I can do. I have all of this fucking money but none of it seems able to get my daughter back here safely. My God, she's already scared. What if she does something stupid and they try to shoot her? She's being listed as a murder suspect. They probably have her listed as dangerous, for God's sake!"

"So go find her." The statement was short and classically simple. Through all of this mess Thomas was searching for the one thing to make it all bearable. Until then he had felt completely impotent and now, thanks to Kim, he was given his chance.

"My God, that's beautiful. It's perfect." He was growing excited now. His face seemed relieved of some hidden pain. "Get Hans in here."

Kim left quickly and walked to the garages. She found Hans in his apartment. She knocked and he answered quickly. "Hey there. Thomas wants to see you."

"It's about time." Hans walked out in front of her without bothering to close the door. Kim tried to keep up with him. He found Thomas's office and entered after a light rap on the door. "Yes, sir?"

"Hans, I don't know how to ask you this. I wish it was something I could do myself but I would botch it up. I'm too old but you're trained. I would like it if you would find Tava for me."

"Yes, sir. Gladly."

"You have been much more than an employee to me, Hans. You have brought me security and peace of mind these past years and that is something I have not communicated to you."

"There is no need, Mr. Blackhurst. You and I have an understanding. There is much you have done for me and this is one way that I can begin to pay you back. Five years ago I was nothing. I was washing windows. And now, now I am better prepared. I will do this for you, gladly. Tava is dear to all of us." His accent was crisp and to the point. He was hiding inner feelings, mixed emotions, and was equally as happy as Thomas to be given the chance to do something. "I will leave immediately. I will fly to Daltonville and then go by car. Surely she has left that town by now. I will do my best to keep you informed. I will need provisions."

Thomas appreciated this man's Scandinavian coolness. He was pleasingly efficient and economical in his speech and his actions. He was a professional and Thomas recognized the inner strength in him. He walked to his safe and spun the dial until the door slipped open. He withdrew a large wad of thousand-dollar bills. "There is fifteen thousand dollars. Spend as much as you need. If you want more, let me know. I want her found, quickly."

Hans took the money and folded it inside his jacket. It was time to go. "The plane will be ready?"

"I'll phone now."

"I may not be able to call. Trust me to find her."

"You have all my trust in the world."

Annie was sitting in Tava's room. There was no more to tidy. She rearranged all of Tava's clothes three times and cleaned the room. She was trying to keep her hands busy.

Thinking too much of her little Tava, alone and running for her life, made her cry terribly. One of her few real joys in the world was Tava. She thought of Tava as her own daughter. Tava was her only real family and until the girl was found, she felt she could not breathe. She didn't trust the Nicholls boy. What had he done to make Tava run so far away?

Grace found Michael in the guest house. She entered without knocking and found him pacing the huge room. This particular guest home was designed as a huge, one-room enclosure. Kitchen, bedroom, and living area all flowing together.

"Michael?"

"Have they found her?" He was frantic.

"No, they haven't. The police are still looking." She dug in a pocket and pulled out a check. "Here. Tava wanted you to have this." She shoved it in his hands and backed away. She was as cold as ever. It frightened Michael to be around her. She was too unpredictable.

"What is this?"

"A check. For your education. Tava wanted you to have that."

"Why?" He'd never seen a check for so much money.

"Don't ask questions. It's a private matter between my daughter and me. You are fairly incidental in the whole thing." Bitterness crept into her voice and it was not lost on Michael. "I think it would be a good idea if you went home. You're not doing any good here."

Michael was taken aback by her blunt, unsympathetic tone. "I want to help."

"I don't see what you can do. Quite frankly, seeing you simply hurts me too much. I would like you to leave."

"I don't want to. I want to be where Tava can find me."

"I am not asking you, dear boy, I am telling you. Get out. I don't know what she sees in you anyway. Take your grubby money and go before I have you removed."

Michael was angry now. He tried to control his temper. "Listen, I don't know what you have against me but, for the love of God, can't you put it behind you? Why can't we all be pulling together for Tava? She would want us to be strong."

"I don't need a lecture from you."

"This may be difficult for you, Mrs. Blackhurst, but I love your daughter and I'm going to marry her."

Grace went white. Marriage was inconceivable with this boy. He was too common and too independent. Tava was going to marry when Grace thought it was time. "Dream on, Mike. You're not getting your hands on my daughter."

"Back off."

"Listen to me! This is my house and I want you out of here! You don't have any business with this family! We don't want you here! You've got ten minutes to leave or I'm calling the police!"

"You really are a bitch." His voice was bitter and angry. He spat his words out with a commanding surety. "I don't know why Tava puts up with you. But you better not cross me. I will not take your shit."

Grace began to laugh. "Oh, my little boy. You're getting all red. Better run home so Mama can change your diapers." She rolled with hilarity. "Gonna huff and puff and blow me down, Mike?"

Michael was overcome. She was taunting him and he knew that. This was not the time or place to fight and he had enough sense to pick up and get out. As soon as he saw Tava, this would all be cleared up. "Hey, bitch, this is what I think of your money." He ripped the check in half and threw it at her.

Grace stopped laughing as the paper hit her in the face. She glared silently at Michael as he threw his clothes into his duffel bag and stomped past her. With her back to him she called out, "You know, sport, if I was a little younger, I'd want to take a look inside those cute jeans of yours."

"You're sick, lady. You're a drunk and you're really twisted! And let me tell you something. You may think you can come in here, throw your money around, and get me out of your daughter's life, but you can't. I love your daughter and she loves me. Whether you like it or not we are going to be together. So stick it up your ass, Grace." He slammed out of the house, causing the windowpanes to shake.

Grace smiled. Michael was gone without her money and for the time being all she had to concentrate on was getting her photos back. Her mouth was dry and her heart was still pumping from the excitement. She found the wet bar and poured herself a double bourbon.

Hans prepared very little. He double-checked his gun, loaded extra bullets in his pocket, and made sure the money was safe. He was experiencing the early jitters of a hunt. The stakes were terribly high. His quarry was someone he cared for and that made him nervous. He needed his mind clear and unemotional for this. He could not afford to make any mistakes. He knew he might not just be competing with the police. Whoever killed Hank Nicholls would certainly want Tava Blackhurst dead also. Time was important and there was not much of it.

He was a fighter and a very skilled specialist. This was the sort of thing he was constantly preparing himself for. His body was in perfect shape, each muscle honed to perfection. His mind was now attuned to what lay ahead. It was important that all of his senses act as radar, searching for Tava and protecting her from harm. He felt electric. A rush of adrenaline ran through him. He checked himself in the mirror. The gun was hidden inside his windbreaker, hanging from a shoulder holster. The days and nights were now too hot to warrant a coat and carrying one would only slow him down. His aim was to blend in. Nothing about him should draw attention. He wanted to look like a normal tourist, enjoying the mountains.

Michael spotted Hans heading for the garage. "Have they told you anything?"

"No."

"Where're you going?"

"Away. And you?"

"I just had a run-in with Grace. She's kicking me out."

"Good luck." He realized how Michael must feel. "You care for her, don't you?"

"Yes. I love her."

"Well, perhaps you can keep my secret. I am going to find her."

"Where?"

"Wherever it takes. She must be protected. There are too many interests involved."

"Take me with you." Michael was desperate. He needed to help.

"Sorry. I know how you feel for her, but this is for professionals."

"Please, Hans. I have to go with you. I'm going to go crazy just sitting around."

"No." Hans's voice was resolute.

"I want to help. I can keep up with you. I promise."

"This may be dangerous."

Michael saw the man's mind was made-up. Still, he was desperate. Tava was out there and he could feel her fear. "I am going, with or without you. The last thing you want is me botching it up, running around by myself. Two sets of eyes and ears are better than one. Come on, Hans. I can be watching your back. Plus friends traveling together are going to look a lot less suspicious than one lone tourist. Take me with you."

The young man's energy was admirable. Hans looked him over and was impressed enough to realize he was in decent shape. His intensity was worthwhile. Still, a novice might provide problems. It was a gut feeling. There was something about the young man that made Hans trust him. "This could get very ugly."

"That doesn't matter. We have to get her back."

"All right. You follow my orders. You do everything I say, when I say it, or you're out. Is that understood?"

"Yes. Definitely."

"If you get in my way, I cannot guarantee your safety."

The sentence hung there in the hot air. Michael was caught in Hans's stare. He believed the man, absolutely. "Fine."

"Then we go." Together they climbed into an estate truck, gunned the engine to life, and headed for the airport.

32

The huge truck signaled and merged off the road into a huge gravel lot and glided to a stop. Tava woke from a fitful sleep with a start. "What was that?" Her legs were cramping and her back felt terrible. They had been driving steadily and Tava was getting very weak.

"I'm stopping to stretch and get something to eat. You want to come in?"

Tava was quiet. She knew she couldn't afford a full meal. She realized she was very hungry though. Food was something she was going to have to improvise. "I'm not hungry." She was too embarrassed to ask for food. Tava had never had to ask for anything in her life and this was the ultimate in humiliation. To be reduced to a beggar made her sad and upset.

"You are hungry, ain't ya?"

"No," Tava lied.

"Bull. Come on. I know when a girl is lying and you haven't had much practice. I'm buying." Helen climbed down from her rig and started for the restaurant. Tava clambered out behind her. She had to jog to catch up. She felt weak and disoriented.

"How long was I asleep?"

"About five hours." Helen cast a sideways glance at Tava. "What're you running from?"

"I'm not."

Helen smiled and backed off, "Don't look like that. I'm not going to bite yer head off." Her voice was cigarette raspy. She was full of warmth and smiles, and Tava began to ease slightly.

The door clanged open. The place was filled with truckers. Most of them were middle-aged men who recognized Helen.

"Hey, old girl!" one man yelled from the counter.

"Danny, you old fart, how did you get in here?" she kidded back. A chorus of laughter erupted from the man's friends.

"Who's the kid?" someone else asked.

"She's a friend and you keep your crummy little eyes off her, understand?" Helen smiled but was serious. The men accepted that and directed their questions to her.

"Where you been lately?"

Helen answered slowly. "I've been doin' a lot of Denver-Seattle runs. Don't ask me why, I guess the Lord decreed it. I can tell you these mountains get a little boring."

"What're you talking about? It's beautiful up here."

"You can keep it." Helen spotted a table. "Scuze us, boys. We've got to eat."

They laughed, and one old codger swatted her on the butt when she passed. She frowned at him, smiled, and then punched him in the shoulder. "My ass is my own, mister." She looked at Tava. "Men. Can you believe it?"

Tava was too embarrassed to answer. She followed Helen to the table and sat down quickly. She was still feeling awkward in her short, badly fitting dress. She hid behind her menu.

"Have whatever you want," Helen urged her. She knew the young girl was hungry. She wondered how many street kids she'd seen over the years. Too many, she thought. This one seemed different though. There was an air of mystery. "How come you were running back there?"

Tava put the menu down and looked out the window. The sun was bright and streamed in. She wanted to avoid the question but didn't know how. "I got into a little trouble."

"That's what I thought. Your folks?"

"Not really."

"Boyfriend?"

Tava grabbed at that. "Yeah, kinda. It's personal." She returned to the menu.

The waitress, in a manila uniform, ambled up. "What's it gonna be, ladies?"

"Gimme a burger, fries, and ice tea, please," Helen said. "Heavy on the onions, okay? You never give me enough onions."

"Look, Helen, don't bother us about the onions. We're always givin' you more onions than anyone else." The waitress scribbled the order down and then looked at Tava.

"Just give me the same." Tava hoped it would be enough to fill her aching stomach. The waitress left.

"Let me see your hands."

"Why?" Tava was suspicious. She was fearful of giving any of herself away. She did not want to let anyone in.

"Just give me your hands." Helen pushed the water aside and laid her hands down on the table. Tava hesitantly offered hers. Helen held them lightly. "You're cold, honey. It's burning up in here and you're freezing."

"Cold blood, I guess."

Helen turned Tava's hands over in her palms. "My God, you're a baby! What are you doing out on the road by yourself?"

"I don't know what you're talking about." Tava pulled her hands away.

"Those hands haven't seen a day of work in their lives. Oh, I hope you're being careful. It must be something big."

"I'm going to be fine." Tava was worried.

"Well, it's none of my business. You need any kind of help?"

"You're already helping me more than you know."

"Well, if that's the way you want it."

The food arrived. Before Tava attacked hers she said, "Thank you, Helen, I appreciate all of this."

"I haven't done anything." The older woman sat back and watched Tava dig in. She ate like a ravenous wolf and devoured her meal in minutes. Helen made a point of leaving her fries and offering them to Tava.

They ate their meals in silence. They finished and while Helen paid, Tava waited outside in the parking lot.

"Thank you." Tava wanted to hug the woman but didn't know how. She lingered by the truck, not knowing how to say good-bye.

"You sure you don't want to come with me?"

"Positive." Tava could not afford to go all the way to Seattle. She knew she had to stay close to Sultan Valley. Running from her problems was not going to solve them. She realized she needed to start working her way back somehow and then come up with a plan. She was still too shaken to think beyond that.

Helen hugged her. The look on Tava's face broke her heart. She knew she wasn't going to get Tava's story so only offered her support. "Take it easy, honey." She climbed into her cab and started the engine. "Be careful. Remember, you can't trust anybody around here."

Helen gave one last wave and pulled out. Her truck moved over to the highway, signaled right, and merged onto the road. Before the truck gunned its huge engines, Helen brought the huge machine to a lumbering stop. She climbed out of the cab and walked back to Tava.

"Somethin's not right about this." She was frowning.

Tava's heart leapt. "I can't ask you to help. It's too dangerous."

Helen heard her truck's engine rumbling behind her. "I've got things to do. I don't have time to be running myself into mysteries." She seemed put out. "But I also can't turn my back. Wouldn't be right. Listen, level with me. How bad is it?"

"Bad." Tava still vacillated. Should she tell? If she did, what would the consequences be? It was not fair to Helen. "I don't want you to get hurt."

"I can take care of myself. I haven't been driving trucks for ten years for nothing. It's stupid but I'm asking you to tell me."

Tava's answer was simple and direct. She trusted this older woman. "I'm being framed for murder."

"Oh boy." Harriet slapped her forehead.

Tava shrugged her shoulders. "The police want me."

"Shit. Well, get in the truck. Hurry. Christ, they're probably looking at us right now." Tava stood there dumbly. She didn't know what to do. Helen grabbed her by the hand and pulled her along. She shoved Tava into the cab and then climbed in herself. The engine revved to life and in ten seconds they were on the road west.

Silently a huge Harley-Davidson kick started to life. Its owner pulled the machine upright, palmed the machine into gear, and throttled out. He kept way back watching the semi through mirrored Ray Bans.

* * *

"That's a hell of a story. Sounds like the jackass got what he deserved."

Tava didn't like to think about it. The story just poured out uncontrollably like a steady stream and finished just as suddenly. She sat there, dazed, numb, and cold. The truck was cruising at seventy-five now and the cab was noisy and vibrating.

Helen shook her head. "The tape's your proof. You know that. You've got to go back and get it."

"How?"

"I don't know. He's probably got the place swarming. Maybe not though. He thinks you've got this video, right?"

"I'm almost positive."

"Well, if it's there, it's gonna stay there. No rush on that. I've got this load to drop off." She pulled at her lower lip, thinking. "You help me drop it off and I'll take you home. We'll forget Seattle for now."

"You would do that for me?"

"I like ya, kid. God knows why, but I like ya."

"But what about the police?"

"It sounds to me like they think you're on your own. They won't be looking for you in a big old truck with me. If anybody asks, you can be my daughter." Helen laughed at that. "Imagine me with a daughter. I can't get over it." She laughed harder. "Sound okay?"

"Sure. Please be careful though. You're taking a big risk."

"I'll keep that in mind."

The huge truck sped west. Helen was working her big rig up to State Highway 287. She planned on getting to Great Waters fast. She was delivering a huge load of firewood to a distribution site there and her plan was to get it unloaded as quickly as possible. They would reach the city by nightfall and with luck unload in the morning.

It was a strange, solitary life, Tava thought. She could read the years on Helen's face. What was it like to travel these lonely roads, day after day? "This may sound stupid."

"Shoot." Helen kept her eyes on the road. This little escapade was making her nervous. She kept feeling someone following them.

"Why do you drive?"

Helen's face went blank. Then she screwed it into a question. "What do you mean?"

"Why do you drive a truck?"

"Why not? It pays good. It's an honest living. I'm my own boss. You oughta think about it."

"I don't think I could do this."

"How come?"

"It's too big."

Helen laughed now. Her voice was deep and filled the cabin. Tava couldn't help but smile. "Honey, nothing's too big. You're not a baby. You can do what you want to do. This rig"—she patted the enormous steering wheel—"is just like a VW Bug once you get the hang of it. Trust me." She gave a sideways glance at Tava. She knew Tava was pampered. She wondered how protected. "Ever been pregnant?"

"No," Tava answered quickly.

"I didn't think so. I had a baby once. I lost her."

"She died?"

"No, honey. Drugs. Which is kind of like dying for the mama."

"Where is she?"

"I don't know." Helen was quiet for a moment. "I think she'd be about your age now. How old're you?"

"Twenty-one."

"There you go. Tell me the truth. How rich are you?"

"My father is rich."

"Which makes you rich."

"Helen, what does that matter?"

"I've got to know what I'm dealing with. I'm sticking my neck out for you. I think it's fair."

"Well, my father is . . . Thomas Blackhurst."

"Who?" The question was genuine and directly to the point. Helen had never heard the name before.

Tava was stunned. Everyone she knew had heard of her father. In strange situations it gave her immediate recognition. Like her mother, Tava had grown up comfortable with the automatic stature her name brought. "Thomas Blackhurst?" Tava found it funny and somehow refreshing. "He's an investor." This was all new ground for Tava and she was thrilled.

"What's he invest in?"

"Companies."

"He buys stocks?"

"Well," Tava said now, "he buys the companies."

"The whole thing?" Tava nodded yes. "Shit. So you're rolling in it." Helen just smiled and drummed the steering wheel with her palms. She took an opportune moment and gunned the huge rig past a station wagon. She waved at the smiling children and blew the air horn.

"I guess you could say we're well-off."

"No, honey. You could say you're rich!"

Finally they reached Great Waters. The road was windy and slowed the flow of traffic. It was dusk as they entered the old mining town. Tava found it hard to remember the small towns they went through. To her tired mind Darrington, Hardy, and Casual all blended together. Each little town looked the same to her. She noticed absently somewhere along the way Highway 287 had turned into Interstate 15. Great Waters was new for Tava, as was most of this country.

It was strange never visiting these places. Tava realized she had spent most of her time in specific places. Her entire existence was taken up with college, New York City, and Sultan Valley. The realization was not frightening but curious. She'd never seen the places in between. They didn't exist until now. This instant was a watershed. Whole new horizons shimmered into being. Tava understood finally how backward she felt. She decided she had been suffocating in her own small world. She realized all of her friends were the same way. It was pathetic, she decided. Her entire life was so sheltered from this. From real people.

The street lamps rolled by in repetitious, silent white glows. The light wiped across Tava's angular face as she remembered a phone call six months earlier.

"Michael?"

"Hi. What'cha doing?"

"Studying," she lied while her girlfriends looked on. They were making faces at her.

"I miss you," Michael said earnestly.

"Same." She did miss him but didn't want to show it in front of Tiffany, Marianne, and Pamela.

"Your voice sounds funny. Anybody there with you?"

"No. Listen, I've got to go, okay? I'll call you later."

"Tava, what's wrong?"

"Nothing. I'll call you tomorrow. I'm just busy. 'Bye." She hung up. She instantly felt terrible. She loved Michael and was repulsed by her behavior. But she felt trapped by these three.

"How was Michael?" Tiffany's voice was high-pitched and icky sweet. The put-down was very evident.

"I can't believe you're seeing him," Pamela intoned. "He's halfway around the world. Grow up. Don't you know long-distance relationships never work? God, T."

Tava hated to be called T. These three were Phi Beta Delta sorority sisters. They were interviewing Tava for membership. PBD was the most exclusive sorority on campus and Tava was considering joining them in her last year of college. She was lonely without Michael and wanted to fill the void.

"Is that him?" Pamela pointed her long, painted finger at Michael's picture. "Where does he go again?

"UCLA."

"Oh God, T. A West Coastie? I can't believe you'd stoop so low. Jesus, T, get with it."

Marianne jumped in. "Doesn't pay to mix, Tava. I've seen it time and time again. It's just not worth it."

Tava took a long hard look at these three. They all sat on the bed made-up with pearls, earrings and expensive clothes. Tava suddenly realized she was turned off. She thanked God she had enough sense to see through their games. "What're you talking about?"

Marianne's back straightened. She was PBD's lead recruiter. "I don't think I like that tone, T. PBD girls treat each other with respect."

Tava couldn't hold herself back. "I know for a fact, Marianne, that three years ago you dated a guy from UC Davis and he dropped you cold. Something about being frigid, I think. So don't talk to me about seeing Michael."

Pamela flapped her lips. "Wait a minute. You can't say that to her."

"PBD girls stick together, Tava Blackhurst," Tiffany chimed in.

"Yeah, like blood clots. Get the hell out of my room. I think you three are the most boring kind of people. Just look at you. Everything's just a pretty little picture, isn't it?

You're all locked up in your perfect little world playing make-believe."

Marianne sat stone-faced. "You just lost your chance, Tava dear. There's no way you're getting into my sorority."

"Big fucking deal. You only wanted me for my father's money anyway."

They all turned red.

"Get out of my room!" Tava was stern now and angry at herself. She needed to call Michael back and apologize. He was what she cared about. How could she let these girls make her feel bad about him? She felt stupid. "Get out now!"

They rose and filed out. Marianne was last. She tried to pause dramatically at the doorway. "I hope you know what you're giving up."

"Go suck Tri Delt dicks. And, Marianne, my daddy can buy yours a hundred times over. So get off it." Tava smiled as Marianne stomped out.

Tava remembered the call to Michael. She had apologized and explained what happened. They talked the night through. That was a happy memory and brought a smile to Tava's worn face.

The truck geared down for a stoplight. Great Waters was deserted. Tava looked up and down the empty streets. This city was completely depressed. Coal mines were drying up and the miners were moving away. Now Great Waters was just a medium-sized depressed burg with a few thousand sad inhabitants.

Tava was upset by the grimy, squat, brick buildings. She watched a bum leaning up against a painted Rexall wall. He was urinating and she turned away quickly. "It's so sad."

Helen overheard her. "Damn right it's sad."

Tava was discovering how truly isolated she was. These past few days were forcing her to confront her basic beliefs. She was being put into situations she would never choose herself. She stole for the first time in her life. She hitchhiked. She hit a man and knocked him unconscious. She was more terrified than she imagined she could ever be. All of these thoughts sent a cold shiver through her, and Tava wondered if she was going to survive.

Helen found her way through the small town easily. She made the Great Waters run four times a year and expected the closed sign as they pulled up to the front gate. She cut the engine and climbed down. She stretched her forty-two-year-old bones. "God, that feels good." She spoke to Tava. "Gonna sit there all night? Come on down. We're gonna leave the truck here and get a room across the way." She pointed across the street. The neon vacancy sign blinked in the window of the Traveler's Motel. "Don't forget to lock up." She didn't wait for Tava as she started across the deserted street.

Tava quickly joined Helen. She kept looking around for a sign of danger. She felt wary being in the open.

Together the two women walked into the tiny, wood-paneled office. The doorbell clanged noisily as the door closed. An old, grizzled fat man in a stained T-shirt pulled himself out of a recliner behind the counter and ambled over.

"Yeah?"

"We need a room," Helen said loudly. "How're you, Pops?"

He made a face. "Why do you keep coming back to Great Waters, woman?"

"To see your smiling face." Helen signed them in.

The door behind them burst open with a clash of bells. Tava whirled around and found a delivery boy dropping the newspapers on the faded couch. He left without speaking.

"You want your usual room?" Pops asked.

"Does it still have bugs?"

"My rooms don't have bugs."

"All right, I'll take it. Relax."

"Who's the little girl?" He squinted his eyes.

"That's my daughter. Say hi to Pops, honey."

Tava did not hear her. She was standing over the papers feeling as if there were no air. The front page was plastered with Hank's murder and her graduation picture.

"Honey, I said say hi to Pops."

Tava recovered only long enough to say, "Hi." Her eyes sought out Helen's. "I need a paper, Mom." She grabbed the top one and ran outside.

Helen joined her quickly. She pulled the paper from

Tava's cold grip and read the headline. She compared the two pictures. "Well, at least you look different with the short hair. We need to get you out of sight."

Helen found the room and quickly locked the door and closed the drapes. Tava sat heavily on the queen-sized green velour bedspread. She was in a daze now. The cover story hit her like a brick. It was true now. There was no longer any denying it. She was the prime suspect in the murder of Hank Nicholls and now everyone was going to see it. She was utterly lost.

Helen read the cover story. Pictures of Buddy were on the second page. He was quoted as saying, "I saw her do it. I tried to stop her but she ran out before I could do anything about it." Helen pondered the implications and looked at Tava. "My God, Tava! What have you gotten yourself into, honey?"

The motorcyclist cruised into town minutes behind Helen. He found the semi in front of the Todd Warehouses. He touched a calloused finger to the tail pipe, found it hot, and knew he had the right one. The motel was the natural choice. He didn't approach it immediately. First he cased it. In seconds he discovered which room Tava and Helen were in.

He decided not to move yet. He was biding his time. There was no escape. He watched, intently, not rushed but patient. He had all night. Tava was running. He knew that and it amused him. She was such a novice. It was embarrassing. He would wait and make his move in the morning.

He almost lost Tava's trail in Daltonville. It did not take long though. Tava's escapade with the police was his first clue. From there it was easy to trace Helen's semi truck.

He found it almost endearing the way Tava was hiding. The stolen dress and the cut hair were all the desperate devices of an amateur. It made him smile, his white teeth gleaming in the darkness.

He recoiled from the town's smell. It was old, dusty, and tinged with the thick smell of coal. He hated this country: the trees, the mountains, the fresh air. New York was his preferred city. There he maneuvered expertly, attuned to the rhythms of the huge crush of humanity. The seamy world he populated was a bizarre mix of corrupt businessmen, thieves, murderers, and junkies. His trade was a skilled one. He was good at what he did and his fee reflected it. A call to Switzerland had confirmed Buddy's money transfer. The young Nicholls was serious and that was when Z had swung into action.

Now he stood in Great Waters, casing the sleepy motel, unimpressed with the challenge. Getting the tape would be child's play. Snapping the girl's neck would be a simple matter. He debated about Helen. Her fate depended entirely on the moment. Killing was a necessary thing; needless killing was not. Too many deaths only caused confusion and Z liked to keep it neat and simple.

"We'll see," he said. His hands itched for activity. He held himself back from barging in. There was no challenge or art in that. Z demanded more from his assignments. This one he knew was going to drag on a little longer. He was teasing the situation and it amused him. He enjoyed stretching the anticipation out. Experience told him waiting yielded interesting and surprising opportunities. The possibilities were endless.

Helen emerged from the bathroom, a towel wrapped around her body. She felt clean again and refreshed after the long drive. She found Tava curled up on the bed, asleep. She checked her watch: 1:00 A.M. It was late and the warehouse was opening in six hours.

She clicked the TV off. The fuzzy reception died and the screen went black. Helen leaned against the dresser watching Tava. The newspaper article explained it all. This girl was heir to one of the largest fortunes in the country. If she had killed Hank, she was dead. No judge in the state would go leniently on her in order to prove to the public that justice worked. Helen also knew that intense wealth carried with it a whole different set of standards. She wondered if she was envious. She had her truck, some money, friends. No, she decided, that much money is a curse. This poor girl was running from a nightmare created by wealth. For Tava's sake, Helen hoped the videotape existed. Tava seemed so incapable of helping herself, Helen wondered how she was going to pull through. To be so rich, so young, and so unworldly. Money *was* a curse.

33

The morning came early. The clouds hung low and blocked the sun's rays. It was a gray day. The morning seemed black and the wind swept through the tiny streets of Great Waters. People stayed inside. Once the storm started it was going to last all day.

Helen peered out the window. The truck was all right. Her watch told her it was 6:00 A.M. She was anxious to unload the truck and get back on the road where she felt safe. In the night she had decided to get Tava back to Sultan Valley as soon as possible. There was nothing more she could do for the girl. She planned on leaving her with the police or her parents. They could do more than she could.

She nudged Tava awake. "Wake up, kiddo. Time to hit the road."

Tava's eyes flew open. She was frightened. Helen calmed her down.

"It's okay. Shhh. It's okay."

"Helen," she said sitting up, "I had this horrible nightmare."

"That doesn't surprise me. You've got time for a shower if you want. I'm gonna go over there, get them started on the truck and then be back. Okay?"

Tava did not want to be left alone. She liked Helen's company and was growing used to it. "What's the plan?"

"I'm taking you home. If we drive straight through, we should be there by ten or eleven tonight. You decide if you want to see the police or your parents. It doesn't make any difference to me. All I know is you can't handle this by yourself and there's not much I can do for you. Get it?" Tava nodded yes. "Good. Lock the door behind me and jump in the shower. I'll be gone about twenty minutes." Helen checked her watch again and then grabbed the room key.

She left and waited to hear the door lock behind her before crossing the parking lot to her truck.

The wind whipped at her short hair. She zipped up her jacket and started to feel the first drops of rain. Making her way across the two lanes, she noticed the first warehouse-man beginning to unlock the gates. She recognized him.

"Hey! Paul! How're you?"

"Helen! I can't complain. Is that your rig?" He pointed at her truck.

"I got to get it unloaded quick, okay? I'm in a rush today."

"No problem. The rest of the guys should be here soon." He waved and walked back in the office.

Helen crossed over to her truck, unlocked the driver door, and pulled herself into the cab. She closed the door and rubbed her hands together, blowing into them. It was cold for a summer morning.

She didn't see Z behind her. He quietly rose from the tiny sleeping space behind the seat and crept up on her. He was cool and patient. And then, as fast as a striking snake, he clamped his thumbs against both sides of her neck. She was too startled to struggle and lost consciousness as the blood stopped flowing to her brain. Z kept her alive though. He was in a good mood today.

He was fast and lethal. Helen was slumped forward in the seat. With some effort he dragged her back into the sleeping area, laying her down and smirking.

"Sweet dreams." He dug in her pockets and found the room key. He left the truck and locked the door behind him. He knew Helen would sleep for at least an hour. That was an eternity for what he needed to do.

He was across the street in fifteen seconds. The key slipped quietly into the lock and he inched the door open. He heard the shower pouring down and silently slipped inside. He closed the door behind him. Withdrawing his gun, he screwed the silencer on and checked for bullets. The black metal weapon was unneeded but he liked to keep it out for effect. As with Helen, he enjoyed using his hands for this kind of work. Z heard the water cut off and sat on the bed to wait.

Tava stepped out of the stall. She felt invigorated. She toweled her short hair dry and then her body. She was hungry and wanted breakfast. She threw the towel around her waist, tucked it in, and stared at herself in the mirror. The image surprised her. She thought she looked boyish in her short hair. There was no style and it lay disjointed across the top of her head. She did her best to fight it into something presentable. The bruises on her body were just discolored marks now. They only faintly hurt to the touch. She felt better, but still drained.

"Keep up the spirit, Tava. We're going to get through this," she said to herself. She walked into the bedroom.

Z's voice was low and threatening. "Do not scream or I will kill you now." He was surprised by her youthful beauty. Naked from the waist up, she was incredibly appealing. "What a waste," he remarked offhandedly.

Tava instinctively covered herself. Where was Helen? She screamed inside her head to stay calm. She waited for him to say something.

"In my work I meet many different people and I must say you have been the most intriguing." He paused to take a deep breath. "You are very pretty. Put your clothes on, please. We are leaving." He even smiled.

Tava did as she was told. She stepped into her things and soon was completely dressed. He watched her steadily, "Please don't think your friend's coming back. She isn't. That only happens in the movies. I am considering not killing you." At this he tapped the newspaper. "You are a surprisingly rich young lady. I underestimated that. By the way, where's the videotape?"

Buddy sent him! "What videotape?"

"I will break your fingers one by one if you try and be coy."

Tava felt like fainting. "I don't have it." She did not want to tell the truth but was desperate to stay alive.

"Really?" He saw the terror in her eyes and believed her. "Where?"

"I don't know! That bastard took it from me! Why do you think I'm running?" Tava was surprised by her little lie. She prayed he would buy it.

Z considered the possibilities. Buddy did seem adamant. Z did not think young Nicholls had it in him to be deceitful. Z knew Buddy was too stupid for that. Perhaps he was wrong. "You may be lying. We will determine that later. Do you have a coat?"

"No."

"You shall wear mine then." He slipped his black leather jacket off and handed it over. Tava shrugged it on. She swam inside it. "We have a long way to go and the weather is not good."

"What are you going to do?"

"I am undecided, Tava Blackhurst. It seems as if the rules have changed. Our friend Mr. Nicholls may have voided his contract with me. We'll see. Let's go." He urged her toward the door. As she passed by he grabbed her by the hair and pulled her to him. "I have been given a tremendous amount of money to kill you. If you try and run or in any way draw attention to us, I will." He pushed her out the door.

Together the two moved cautiously through the parking lot and across the road. Tava watched Helen's truck, hoping the older woman would appear. "You didn't hurt her, did you?"

Z had his big hand on her left arm and kept her moving past the truck and down the length of the chain-link fence. As they walked he bent down close to her ear and hissed, "Maybe she's dead, Tava Blackhurst. I wouldn't let it worry me though. You won't be seeing her again anyway." He increased the pressure on her arm and urged her on.

No one suspected them. Tava wanted to cry out but the streets were empty and she was too frightened to try and run. His grip warned her of his incredible strength. Tava easily understood the man was a professional from the way he held himself. This was his show and he was running it.

Her mouth was dry, her voice hoarse. Her tongue felt thick and unyielding. She felt like gagging in the summer wind. That same question haunted her over and over: what is he going to do with me?

"By the bike." He moved her over to the huge motorcycle and forced her to sit on the back. The bike slanted at a strange angle and it made it hard to sit up straight. "Give me your wrist." Tava offered it meekly and he clamped hand-cuffs around her left hand and the other end to a metal bar running along the bottom of the seat.

"What if I fall off?" Tava pleaded. "Please. Don't tie me to this thing." She hated motorcycles and the thought of being chained to one terrified her.

"Shut up. If you want to be safe, hold on to me." He

mounted the bike and heaved it into a standing position. He ignited the huge motor, and the low, guttural roar of the engine shook underneath them. Z slipped the bike into first gear and shot out of the dirty alley. They sped past Helen's truck and all Tava could do was watch helplessly as it disappeared into the distance.

The rain pelted them. The water drops stung as they hit Tava's face. She kept her eyes closed. The fierce winds buffeted them so violently, Tava was sure they were going to blow off the road. She gripped the handles on the seat and held on for dear life. This man, she thought, must be completely mad to drive through this kind of weather. What was he trying to prove?

And then the seed of a plan crept its way into her harried thoughts. At first she pushed it away. It scared her and she refused to acknowledge it. The potential for failure was too great. But, she reasoned, what did she have to lose? Her life? By now Tava had been through so much, she wondered what life was really all about. She reasoned there had to be more than this. Life was not being forced to ride a motorcycle in the middle of a summer storm with a lunatic at the controls. There had to be a better way than this.

She peeked through her half-closed eyelids and saw the empty road ahead of her. To her right a rock cliff rose straight up. Little rivers of muddy water were already trickling their way down in a hundred little streams. They were making their way across the two-lane road and down the steep embankment on Tava's left.

Tava peered down as best she could. The hillside was covered with trees and the storm was making it all very dark. She knew it was steep and the rocks were a very real threat.

What should she do?

"I can't go on like this," she said to herself. "There has to be a better way. I can't just wander through life and let these people push me around. I'm not a kid anymore, for Christ's sakes!" And with that she accepted her plan.

With her free hand she felt along the metal bar. She felt along frantically for any sign of freeing herself.

"Stop moving so damn much!" Z yelled. While he was an

expert on this motorcycle, the weather was causing him difficulty. Tava's movements were forcing him to concentrate his balance on the heavy machine. "Sit still now!" Z did not have patience for silly little women who didn't follow orders.

Tava realized she was being too obvious and that was going to get her in a lot of trouble if she was not careful. She did not stop. Keeping her body as still as possible, she kept her hand searching for her freedom. She inched along the cold, smooth metal and finally found the break she was looking for. The metal tubing bent down sharply at the end and was open on the bottom. Her heart jumped in elation.

With her cuffed hand she silently maneuvered the handcuffs off the end of the bar.

She was free!

Tava was running on instinct now. She had no idea what she was going to do but it was going to be soon. She hoped he was like other men. The kind that leered at her in New York. She did not like these men and understood deep inside her what they wanted. It repulsed her but she accepted it as a bizarre fact in society. Now she hoped to use it against Z.

With mounting danger, her heart pounding, she used what was supposed to be her only free hand and wrapped it around Z's stomach.

"Is that okay?"

"What?" Z did not appreciate his concentration being broken. Though he did enjoy the sensation of Tava's hand around him.

"Is it all right if I put my hand here?" she yelled over the wind.

He nodded yes without speaking.

Tava leaned into him, pleased that his large body broke the forceful push of the wind against her. From this position she planned her next move.

The motorcycle was going relatively slowly in this weather and Z slowed down even more around curves. Tava's plan was to jump. It was the only way she could think of to escape. She realized the longer she was with him, the harder it would be to get away. She needed to escape quickly. She had no idea where Z was taking her and did not want to find out. There was no telling what this man was capable of.

Tava dug deep inside her for the resolve and the courage to follow through. Nothing in her life had prepared her for this. She had no guideposts or helpful hands. She was alone for the first time in her life. This living nightmare was almost too much for her to cope with. Tava bit back the tears. There was no time for emotion now. These moments were far too precious to waste with tears. Tava realized in a sudden flash of fear that no one was going to save her but herself.

Tava did not want this independence. It was being forced on her by cruel circumstances. She needed Michael's warm soothing touch. Her father could help, she thought. Thomas Blackhurst always had all the answers.

"Not this time, Tava," she whispered into the wind.

Death flashed across her mind and almost blinded her. Tava had never thought about her death and now on this motorcycle, alone with a dangerous killer, she confronted it head-on. There was no time to put it all into perspective but she knew the possibility existed. She froze in her place and couldn't find the strength to move her body. Her body seemed to have a will of its own. Thoughts of blackness filled her head. What was beyond? Do I want to take the chance, she asked herself. What if I just stay here with this man and hope for the best? The questions raced at her with amazing speed. They forced her to reconsider but finally the only real truth she could find was based in reality. Death was as real as life and if her time was now then so be it. Now was the time to take charge. With monumental resolve she summoned the courage she needed and with an iron will confronted her worst fears and put them to rest. It was now or never.

Tava waited for the right moment. The road was very curvy as it wound up into the mountains. The lanes were very narrow and she knew her chance was at the corners. The motorcycle practically crawled around each turn and Tava was confident she could jump and disappear into the trees before Z recovered. The rain would help, she reassured herself. Tava knew that if she survived the jump, she was going to have to run like hell.

With three quick breaths she tensed and prepared herself for the next turn. It was a sharp one and she needed to go now before she lost her nerve. Maybe, she hoped, she could make it back to Great Waters before nightfall and find Helen.

She wasn't sure how she was going to jump but knew in the next few moments that her body would do what it had to do.

The motorcycle slowed and crept around the sharp turn. Tava, terrified, pushed herself away from Z and in one huge effort launched herself off the bike. She hit the hard tarmac and rolled five times. She kept her body in a ball as much as she could and finally came to a stop, splayed across the center line.

Z lost balance and fought with the bike to stay up. Tava's jump surprised him so much, he didn't have time to compensate. The huge machine veered toward the edge and then swerved back, shooting across the road into the embankment. Tava watched as Z rammed the dirt wall and the bike popped a wheelie, falling backward on him. She only waited long enough to make sure the road was empty before she scurried across it and threw herself over the edge, deep into the unknown forest.

34

Grace sat alone, puffy-eyed, fighting back the tears of frustration. She ran her fingers through her thin hair and brushed at the wrinkles in her blouse. She wanted a drink badly but Thomas had ruled that out. He was becoming uncontrollable and she knew it was all because of Kim.

"Goddammit, Tava! Why did you have to do this to me?" She spat the question out and wiped the spit from her lips. She was feeling the strain of sobriety. Her vision was blurred and she was visibly shaking. "Goddamn that girl." Grace pulled herself out of her chair and stumbled out of her suite, down the hall and into Thomas's study. He was there with Kim, going over some papers.

"I want a drink, Thomas."

"No. And that is final." Thomas seethed with contempt. He still blamed Grace for scaring Tava away during the first call. And now, no word from her for so long. "Would you just get off it, Grace? There are more important things to deal with." Thomas was losing his patience. At least Kim was calm. He wanted to hold her hand for reassurance. "What's the matter with you? She's out there, Grace, somewhere, alone and frightened. Jesus, can't you see that?"

"Of course I can see that, Tom! I'm not blind. This thing is tearing me up, too, you know! Christ, do you think you're cornering the market on hurt and pain? She's my daughter too!"

"Then show some sympathy. How 'bout some compassion? The way you're acting, you wouldn't care if she were dead or not."

"What!" Grace was livid. She crossed the carpeted floor quickly and leaned way over Thomas's desk to slap him. Thomas stopped her hand in midswing.

"I can't believe you're doing this. I just can't believe it." He threw her hand away. "If you can't help, then get the hell out. Kim and I will take care of this."

"What does this bimbo have to do with it?"

Kim broke in before Thomas could answer. "Grace, I am not here to cause trouble. I'm only helping Thomas. Now that the story has broken in the papers, it's getting very sticky in the business community. This is probably going to go national."

"Bullshit."

Kim continued calmly. "I don't think so, Mrs. Blackhurst. Thomas is one of the most famous raiders in the business. You are the queen of New York society. Unfortunately this is exactly the story the newspeople love. I think they're going to turn it into a huge circus and there's not much we can do. I don't have to tell you how damaging all of this is going to be. For you and Thomas."

Grace was not impressed. As far as she was concerned, Kim was just a cheap, black whore. "You think you're so damn smart," she snarled. "Go fuck yourself."

"Grace! That is enough!" Thomas ordered, furious with

his wife's behavior. "Go get your damn drink, for God's sake, but stay out of here. We've got too much work to do."

Grace smiled. "Does he ever brag about his dick, honey?" She laughed in Thomas's face and walked out of the room. She slammed the door behind her and found the liquor cabinet. She mixed herself a large double whisky and gulped the first swallow. As the liquor spread through her body she shivered from the warmth. Soon she relaxed as the buzz began to sink in. Common sense returned and with it the dreaded images of ruin.

The photos. The more Grace thought about them, the more she was consumed with fear. They were the only link between her and Hank. What if they were discovered? What if Buddy found them and used them against her? Why hadn't they been found yet? All of these questions were caught up inside Grace's mind and terrified her. She couldn't let those damn little photos ruin her now.

"I've got to get those back," she mumbled to herself. "I can't let anyone see them. Not after all I've done. That bastard is haunting me."

She wanted to call Buddy and offer him money. She wanted to lie to him and somehow convince him she'd forgotten the photos there the day she had visited. But she knew it was a lame story. She knew her options were slowly falling by the wayside. She was terrified. How was this all going to end?

"Grace, how could you let this happen to yourself?" She stirred her drink with her right index finger. She licked it dry as her thoughts turned to Tava. "She's the one to blame for all of this. If she'd just done what she was supposed to, the photos would be in my hands now and safely destroyed. But now," Grace said to herself, "I'm stuck with this over my head, and my stupid daughter is running from the police for a goddamn murder!" Grace threw her glass across the room and cringed when it shattered against the stone fireplace.

Grace was feeling desperate. There was no one to turn to and she knew it. Who was going to get her out of this? Who would ride in and make all of this go away? Grace wondered if she were losing her mind. She felt unsteady for a moment, as if the room were swaying back and forth. She stumbled to a seat as the walls started to close in around her. She fended off the nightmare images with her waving hands. This was too much. She was being driven mad, she realized, by those around her. "They're out to get me. Those goddamn parasites won't leave me alone. They're going to run this in the ground before I can fix it." The words spewed out of her mouth too quickly. She wiped her lips. Her head was spinning from the strain of concentration. She needed a plan immediately. "I've gone through too much to let this get me now. No one's going to ruin what I've worked so hard for. I refuse to let this happen!"

Annie arrived to see what the noise was. She found Grace huddled on the couch, practically collapsed in pain. She was unimpressed. To Annie, Grace's binges were becoming more and more typical. She found Grace deplorable and completely insensitive. She expected Grace to worry about her daughter and was continually shocked to find the woman thinking about herself. Annie loved Tava and was frantic to have her home safe. Grace was acting as if she didn't care.

Grace caught Annie staring at her and stiffened. "What do you want, you old hag?"

Annie's anger began to boil. She did not want to pick a fight with Grace. "Ma'am?" she said as neutrally as possible.

Grace leveled a withering eye at the older nanny. "I guess you think you've got a lock on the sympathy vote around here. Don't forget your place." Grace meant these words to hurt.

"I don't think I understand what you mean, Mrs. Blackhurst."

"I'm her mother, Annie! Not you! I am! Do you understand that?"

"Could a fooled me," she muttered to herself. "Yes, ma'am. I never doubted it for a moment."

"What's that supposed to mean?"

"Nothin'. I appreciate the hardship you're going through, Mrs. Blackhurst. I've been with this family long enough to know how heartbroken you must be about all of this. It must be tearin' you up inside, you poor thing."

"Thank God someone's noticed. Did you hear Tom! No one seems to think I care about Tava, for Christ's sakes. She's my little girl. I want her near me, Annie. I want to hold her and protect her from all of this. Why don't you all see that? Jesus!" Grace was making an enormous effort with this speech. The alcohol was making her wary of everybody.

"We understand how this must feel, you poor thing. Why don't you rest? I'll bring you some tea."

"Don't patronize me, Annie. I'll have your ass out of here so fast it'll make your head swim. I will not be addressed that way in my own house. Do I make myself clear?"

Annie nodded her head yes.

"What?"

"Yes, ma'am. You make yourself very clear."

"Don't think Thomas is going to stick up for you forever. One of these days, Annie, one of these days." Grace lurched to her feet and banged into the coffee table. Her leg started to bleed but she didn't notice. She stumbled past Annie toward the kitchen. "You goddamn people think so highly of yourselves it makes you start to wonder. I think we've been too nice to all of you over the years." Her voice trailed off and could be heard in short, muffled bursts as she rifled through the cupboards looking for a clean glass.

Annie was furious. She was doing her best to keep it inside but she could not hold it in any longer. She needed to express herself quickly before she found herself doing something terrible.

She made her way quickly down the hall to Thomas's office and knocked. For the first time in her life she did not wait for an answer. She was too preoccupied with Grace to wait. She walked in on Kim holding Thomas in her arms. He was sobbing uncontrollably. His body shook in its chair, and Kim was beside him, stroking his hair and whispering to him softly.

Annie's heart broke. The poor man was under so much strain. She understood the loss he was feeling. He must feel so helpless sitting there unable to find his daughter. God knows what was happening to her. Annie realized sadly Thomas could not buy what he needed: Tava's safety.

"Excuse me," she said quickly and tried to leave.

Thomas did his best to dry his eyes. He straightened in his chair and waved her back in. He kept Kim close to him and held her hand. "It's okay, Annie. Come in."

"You poor man. What you must be feeling." Annie shook her head. "Any word from Hans?"

"Not yet."

"I'm sure you'll hear soon."

"What can I do for you, Annie?"

"It seems so petty now. Well, it'll just have to come out. It's Mrs. Blackhurst, sir. I think she's . . . in need of some help."

"Meaning?"

"She's becomin' quite abusive, sir. And I don't mind. I know she can have her spells but it does get a little bothersome, sir. Specially now with the family in such an uproar. Far be it for me to cause more trouble but I'm afraid she might do something to herself or one of us." Annie gulped and pushed on. She felt very uncomfortable talking to him like this. "I don't mean to be disrespectful. You've been wonderful to me all these years and I don't want you to think I'm not grateful."

Thomas rose from his chair and crossed around the huge desk. He approached her and gave her an enormous hug. "Thank you for being honest, Annie. I have always respected your judgment. I know what you're saying about Grace is true. And I want you to know I am going to have her helped. Just bear with us a little longer. Come to me if she tries anything again. I know what you've done for Tava, and I want you to know I appreciate it. My daughter is a wonderful young woman and a lot of that is due to you. Trust me, Annie. Once all of this is done there are going to be a few changes." He held her arms and escorted her to the door. "We are all going to get through this, Annie, if it takes everything I have."

35

Tava stumbled through the trees, convinced that Z was following her. The forest sounds terrified her and propelled her on. She was absolutely exhausted now, completely depleted of any energy. Her only thought for the last hour was to escape Z's grip and get free.

"Home," she murmured to herself. "That's where I have to get to. I can't handle this. These people are out to kill me!" She stumbled and fell against a tree. From deep inside her the sobs of anger and fear exploded. She heaved with the sad convulsions of a frightened young woman. "I can't do this," she yelled at herself. The emotion was dangerous. She needed to stop but couldn't find the will to do it. The tears streamed down her dirty cheeks and dripped on her dress.

Through her blurry vision she looked at her hands for the first time since the fall and found blood. She looked closer, still crying, and found ugly red gashes across both her palms. Her hands took most of the impact from the fall. They hurt terribly and the pain was beginning to become unbearable. She was becoming aware of her body. The jump from the bike did more damage than she realized. Her whole frame was finally awaking to the pain.

The rain was reaching down to the forest floor and reminded Tava to keep moving. Z could still be behind her. She knew enough to know he wouldn't give up. He was terrifying. She pictured his eyes and shivered from the memory. He was an evil man. It was his solid, cold stare that frightened her the most. His cool, professional demeanor was unsettling. The way he so casually talked about killing and death. "How can people like that exist?" Tava asked herself. "Why do you want me dead, Buddy Nicholls?" Tava knew that answer. He was a psychopath and she realized he was going to do everything he could to destroy her. Tava was his only evidence about the killing. The young man was twisted just enough to think Tava was a threat.

She stood up with some effort and pushed on. She did not know where she was and only hoped she would find someone or some shelter soon. The wind was picking up and lightning was beginning to scar the sky.

Tava trudged on for another three hours. She was numb to the bone. Her body was beyond pain now. Tava was learning to live with the stabs of hurt racking her body. Her mind was blank. She only comprehended her next step. The towering trees above her only half-protected her from the downpour but she didn't care anyway. She simply pressed on, hoping for a sign of help.

Finally, cresting a small rock hill, she stopped and stared at the tiny, twinkling lights of a small town. She did not know its name and didn't care. With a growing sense of elation she plunged down the hillside. She knew she had to be careful. She had not forgotten the newspaper article. By now, she was sure, her story would be one of the hottest in the state. As she made her way down the hill she repeated several times, "Please, God, get me through this. Just let me live, that's all I ask." She wanted a white knight to appear on the horizon and gallop down to save her. She almost smiled at the picture because she knew no one would. Helen had tried and as a result she almost lost her life. Maybe she did die, for all Tava knew. That was a responsibility Tava did not want to have. "From now on," she vowed, "I help myself. I can't expect people to get me out of things. I've got to rely on myself, period."

That thought carried her into the tiny mountain village of Katy. There was one general store, a saloon, an old-time hotel, and several homes along the one street. "Well," she laughed at herself, "folks, now you can see a real fugitive." She had some idea of what she looked like but didn't care. Her body hurt too much and her mind was too dulled by the past events. Not knowing where she found the reserve, she picked the saloon and walked in the front door.

The place was busy with locals and tourists keeping dry until the storm passed. Tava ignored them. She thought a shot of whisky might clear her head.

She approached an older gentleman with a huge gray

beard and leathery skin. The man was six feet five and wearing the clothes of a local. On his head was a panama hat with a red bandana tied around it. He must have been in his sixties.

Tava was not even tentative. She was too tired to be. "Excuse me, sir. I've been through a hell of a lot in the last couple of hours and I need a drink. I don't have any money and I was hoping you would pay."

The bartender laughed out loud. "Well, Jake, can't ask for a more direct approach."

The older man named Jake turned slowly and looked down at Tava. He regarded her for several moments and finally said, "You look like a drowned rat, my dear."

"I feel like one, sir." Tava let him lead the conversation. It was all she could do to stay on her feet.

"Are those hands as bruised as they look?"

"I think so. I haven't had time to look. It's a long story if you really want to hear it." Her voice was not timid. She was willing to make up any story right now but was worried she was going to faint.

Jake turned to a gentleman on his right and said, "I have a lady in need of your chair, Max. You don't mind, do you?" Jake did not wait for an answer as he shoved the smaller man off the stool. Max rolled off without complaint and gave Tava a cursory glance.

Jake offered the stool with a little flourish. "My lady. A stool for your tired body." He took her elbow and helped her onto the tall stool. "Teddy, a double shot for my new friend."

The bartender poured the drink and put it down in front of Tava. She took it in her shaking hands and downed it. The warmth coursed through her quickly and spread throughout her body. The effect was just what she needed. Her senses returned to her, and the bustle of the busy saloon was comforting her. She was pleased to see she was not drawing too much attention.

"Thank you, Jake."

He did not smile but said instead, "Only my good friends call me Jake."

"So?" Tava was not in a mood to play. She was hoping to get a ride to Sultan Valley. If Helen wasn't going to get her there, then someone else would.

"All right, enough begging. You may call me Jake."

"Thanks, Jake. Can I get another one of these?" She returned her attention to him and smiled. "This is my last one, I promise."

"I am wondering to myself how much this pretty young thing has eaten during the course of the morning."

Tava shrugged. "What time is it, Jake?"

"My clock tells me noon."

"Is that all? It feels like midnight."

"It's the storm. Makes everything look black as night. Well?"

"What?"

"Have you eaten anything? If you haven't, I am more inclined to feed you than succor your wants with the almighty booze."

"No, I haven't eaten."

"Well . . . Teddy, a large burger and fries for my charge." Jake brushed aside Teddy's worries with a slight shake of his head. "I hope you like meat. It's all we roughnecks eat in here. Do you have a name?"

"Margie," Tava lied.

"Margie. Lovely. So. I have lived here in Katy for fifteen years and this small little town has grown to love me, and I it. I am a retired literature professor who spends too much of his time immersed in the ways of the past. That is me. And who are you?"

"Nobody, Jake. I'm just tired."

"Where's your husband?"

"Michael?" Tava laughed at herself. I wonder what Michael would say to that, she thought to herself. She missed him. She spoke to him inside her head. "I'm okay, Michael. I'm coming home."

"So, you're attached." Jake acted like he'd uncovered a deep secret. "I guess I won't be sweeping you off your feet?"

"Doubtful, Jake. But it's a nice thought anyway." She smiled and leaned on the counter. She realized she shouldn't be too complacent. Z could be anywhere. She was hopeful he was hurt but couldn't know for sure. Not knowing frustrated her the most.

"What are you thinking? You have the look of a frightened child."

"Don't let it fool you. Listen, Jake, have you got a car?"

"Margie, those things are the destruction of our society. I moved here to get away from that menace. And look." Here he pointed to the dark street outside. "Look at all those cars. Each one a little torment to my sanity. More dangerous than cigarettes in my opinion."

"I need to get to Sultan Valley." She was careful not to say home. She knew the paper was delivered here too.

"Why?"

"Friends."

"In high circles, I guess. I suppose we can find someone going that way. But certainly not in this weather. You may have to hole up here for a couple of days. They say it's going to be wretched. This storm is going to last for at least two days. Sorry."

"Me too."

Tava's food arrived and she devoured it in five minutes. Jake watched in obvious amazement. He was surprised to find her so ravenous. The girl could not be over twenty-five, he thought. She was scruffy, fairly bruised, in a torn dress with scraggly hair. She was a mess to put it mildly. There was something about her though. He could not put his finger on it but there was something about Tava. He suspected she was a few steps above what she appeared. There was a sense of breeding about the young woman. Jake could feel it about her. She might not have any money now, but somewhere she did. And where was the husband?

"Where's your husband?" Jake discovered early in life that being coy and evasive got him very little. This woman intrigued him. At the very least she was an amusement during the storm.

"Michael is away on a business trip. I was touring the countryside and had an accident. That's why I'm so shaken up. I'm hurt but I'm okay."

"We'll have one of the boys save your car when this weather clears."

Tava played along. "Sure." She had no intention of searching for the nonexistent car. As far as she could tell, Jake was harmless. He was snoopy but playful. He reminded her of a few professors she had had at William and Mary. She was not sure if she liked him. She was learning not to trust everyone she met. "Thank you for the food, Jake. That was very good."

"I'm surprised you remember what it tasted like."

Tava chuckled. "I've always been a fast eater. I don't suppose there's any place I can hole up until this thing passes over?"

"If you won't think unkindly of me, I will offer my extra bedroom."

"Jake, are you always so nice to tourists?"

"You seem much more interesting than these yokels. There's something about you that intrigues me and I want to find out what it is."

"I'm not a big mystery, Jake. You've been reading too many novels."

"Perhaps. Is there anything else we can feed that voracious appetite of yours?"

"I don't think so. I guess I just want to lie down. I think the crash banged up my side."

"Well then. With a lady in distress I must do without my customary third drink. Follow me and away we go. Teddy, I trust my credit is still good."

With a huge smile, Teddy said, "Always, Jake. See you tomorrow." And then under his breath, "Where does the guy get it?" He shook his small head as he turned his attention back to the bar.

Jake collected a tweed hat and forest-green umbrella. He limped slightly on his left leg but moved gracefully. He tapped his hat onto his head and then headed for the door. He only paused to make sure Tava was keeping up. He stepped outside, surveyed the swirling wind, the sheets of rain and the black clouds. "What a magnificent day! These afternoons, Margie my girl, are why I moved here. Too many people bake themselves all year-round in a blazing sun. They miss the invigoration of a day like today. Wonderful. Simply wonderful." He popped open his umbrella and urged Tava underneath. He moved across the street and down one block.

They stopped in front of a little gray cottage with white trim. It seemed like a cottage in New England, Tava thought. It was very neat with a tiny front garden and a patch of grass. A white picket fence stood around the little front lawn.

Jake moved them up the walkway and onto the porch. He shook the huge umbrella dry and collapsed it. Fumbling for some keys, he found what he was looking for with some difficulty. It was a matter of seconds before they were both standing in a tiny, wood-floored entry hall with the wind now muted behind the closed door.

Tava breathed in deeply, relieved that at least for now she was safe. No one, she hoped, would bother her here. She shrugged out of Z's huge leather jacket and handed it to Jake. He hung it up and removed his own tweed jacket and hat.

"All we have to do is warm up and then get you to bed. That is what you want?"

"Yes."

"Fine. Up the stairs and I'll show you your room. Can I get you anything to drink? A cup of warm milk? Something more spirited? Anything?"

"You're very nice, but I just want to sleep."

"All right then. Up we go."

It was a neat little home. Jake was a fastidious man. Everything was in its place. There was no dust around. The small rooms were not cluttered with knickknacks but piled high with books. He was an intellectual and his books proved it. He caught Tava staring at the collection.

"Don't let them worry you. They're harmless. It's only the things in them that you need to worry about." He chuckled. He enjoyed amusing himself.

He continued up the stairs. It was a steep climb and opened into a tiny hallway. He turned left and switched on the light. "Here you go. Just collapse there. If you want, leave your clothes by the door and I'll wash them for you. Homemaking is not my forte but I certainly know my way around a washing machine." He smiled warmly.

Tava gravitated to the bed. Although she was too tired to realize, the colorful quilt beckoned her to sleep. The little room was so inviting, she was too drained to resist. Her thoughts were dulled by the impending need for rest. She sat heavily on the bed. "Thank you, Jake. I'll just leave my clothes by the door. This means a lot to me."

"Good. Sleep tight. I'll pop in on you later." He closed the door quietly behind him.

Tava shrugged out of her sneakers and left the dress and underwear in a ball by the door. She fell asleep almost immediately. She barely pulled the bedspread over her before her heavy eyelids came down. She slept heavily and deeply, blocking the world from her senses. Her body was putting itself in automatic, trying to restore the energy it had lost over the last few days.

Jake padded down the stairs and into his kitchen. He was excited. He loved taking in stragglers. It was an old man's passion and he clapped his soft, pudgy hands together, running his fingers through the gray whiskers on his face. He was in the mood for tea and put some water on to boil.

36

It was midnight when Tava woke to the pounding of shutters against the side of a wall. It shook her awake with a start. At first she didn't know where she was and pulled the cover up around her for protection. As the grogginess cleared she remembered where she was and what she was doing. She wondered where Jake was.

"Hello?"

There was no answer. Tava was instantly alert. The little she knew of Jake told her he liked to talk. Tava expected an immediate answer. She found her clothes neatly folded on the chair beside the door and scrambled into them. The feeling of clean clothes was almost too much for her.

When she was ready, she inched the door open and crept down the little hall, peeking into what she thought was his bedroom.

"Jake?" she said softly. She kept her back to the wall. The dark crevices scared her now.

She inched her way back to the head of the stairs. "Jake?"

Again no answer. Tava did not know what to do. It was obvious there was no way out of the house from upstairs. She decided against staying put. If there was anything down there it needed to be met head-on.

She took the first two steps confidently and then stopped. She was overcome with a picture of Michael. She wanted him to know she was alive. If she could just for one moment hold him, brush her cheek against his and kiss his warm full lips. She needed him now and it hurt to be so far away. Does he know I'm still alive? She gathered up her courage and continued down the stairs.

Tava listened intently for any sound of Jake. The small house was silent. She tried one last call. "Jake, it's Margie. Are you there?" When no one answered she went white with fear.

It did not feel right.

Tava was learning to trust her instincts. And now they were blaring. She looked for the leather jacket and couldn't see it. She peeked into the living room and didn't find anyone; however, the lights were on. She moved in obvious pain and she was stiff from the long sleep.

Tava was only aware now of her beating heart and her breathing. No other sound existed. She felt the blood pumping at her temple and the sound filled her ears. It was almost deafening.

Finally she decided to run. The house was too dangerous. She listened one last time for Jake and sprinted across the living room into the hallway. She pulled open the closet door for the coat and screamed as Jake came tumbling down with a hideous thud.

He fell loudly onto the floor, bound and gagged. There was blood in his hair but he was alive. His eyes were terrified and he tried to scream. His eyes went wide with terror as he tried to motion behind Tava. He tried to shake her help away when they heard the voice.

"I take it, darling, you did not like the way I drove my motorcycle." Tava spun around and with a sinking terror locked eyes with Z. He was just as dirty as she, more so because of all the rain. He looked deadly calm. His white teeth gleamed through his crooked smile and he wagged his index finger at her. In his other hand he was holding his bomber jacket. "You were looking for this, I think."

Z threw the jacket at her and Tava let it drop at her feet. She was too stunned to do anything else.

"You better pick that up, darling. It's terribly cold outside and we are leaving now." His voice was sharp, clean, and direct. It impelled her to react. "You had me worried. I was trying to explain that to our good friend the professor.

"Are you okay, Jake?"

"You know, it's a funny thing about you. Usually I don't leave people behind. But I get such a warm feeling around you that I just get this . . . I don't know . . . magnanimous urge. He's all right. Just shook up. I think it's the first time he's been tied up and stuffed in a closet." Z laughed.

Tava knelt down to pick up the coat and whispered, "Call my parents. Tell them I'm all right."

Z laughed. "Little girl, your attempts at being secretive are comical. Of course he is going to call them. I want your lovely parents to know you're alive. It'll drive the price up." With that he lapsed into silence.

Tava reluctantly picked up the big jacket and shrugged it on. It was hopeless to run and she knew it. Jake struggled, trying to stop her but it was no use. He was too tired to continue and had to give up.

37

Buddy was intoxicated with rage. He felt like he was stumbling through a thick morass of unexplainable events. He was now convinced Sultan Valley was against him. Public support was still behind Tava. No one knew where she was and even with all the questions still needing to be answered, all eyes were on Buddy. The locals knew Tava and could not believe she had done what Buddy was accusing her of.

He assuaged his fears by thinking about Z. The man was not cheap but he had come highly recommended. He knew how to get rid of unwanted people. As soon as Tava Blackhurst showed up dead, that would finally put an end to this terrible affair.

Buddy tried to keep himself busy with the politics of Nicholls Development. There were already rumors of a management buyout. Blackhurst Industries was still in the market. Buddy expected Thomas to withdraw after his daughter's implication in the murder but he hadn't. Buddy expected sole ownership of Nicholls and he was willing to do anything to get it. These people were trying to take the company away from him and he couldn't stand that.

Stuck in the huge Victorian in Sultan Valley, Buddy was becoming paranoid. He was wandering the huge place like a ghost. He was talking to himself.

"Why does everybody want a piece of me, for Christ's sakes? I can't believe this." He was beginning to believe the elaborate lie he had created. Tava was becoming the arch enemy. He was so filled with hatred, he could not get her out of his mind. She was everything he hated. A murderess. A rich bitch. Buddy began to fall into a dream state of lies and half truths. At times he knew he had killed his father. He was convinced Tava had set him up to do it. It took on a life of its own and continued to haunt him, especially when he was drunk.

The pressure was becoming too much and he began to find solace in the bottle. Buddy desired proof of Tava's death. It was all he thought about. He was afraid to leave the phone for fear Z would call with the good news.

It was eleven at night and Buddy was nursing a second bottle of wine. He was watching the fireless fireplace and thought he saw his father's face in it. The booze was playing tricks on him. Suddenly he felt the need to write to the local paper. There were too many people writing in support of Tava and he felt the need to set the record straight.

With a drunk man's initiative he pulled himself out of the overstuffed chair and shuffled around the room to his father's huge desk. He sat down heavily and propped the bottle in front of him. The wine splashed against the inside walls of the green bottle. The movement made him sick.

He turned his attention to his letter. He wanted to tell Sultan Valley about all the hell he was going through. Buddy wanted them to know the pain he was suffering because of Tava. How dare they defend her!

"I told them she killed you, Daddy! Why don't they believe me?"

He found a pen and dug into the drawer for paper. He fished out a pile of paper and dropped it on the desk. He dumped the contents of a little packet on the table and fanned the contents across the top.

Buddy took another swig before he focused. Grace's face came into view. He blinked several times and could not believe his eyes. He was staring at sex photos of Hank and Grace.

He laughed out loud and felt the rush of excitement run through his tall, skinny body. His luck was still with him. It was too much for him to comprehend. His letter now forgotten, he pieced the photos into sequential order and whistled.

"Daddy, you old dog. I knew you were tricky but I didn't know how much." He grinned wildly. "This was part of your whole plan, wasn't it? Mr. Blackhurst was just too big for us so you had to do what you could to stop him. And look what you came up with. My, my. Mrs. Blackhurst almost seems to be enjoying it. You old goat. I didn't know you were so kinky."

With his discovery Buddy formulated his next step in his battle for Nicholls Development and in the investigation of his father's murder. These were too valuable and he realized he only had one or two chances to use them to his advantage. His choices seemed clear now and he couldn't wait for the morning.

He found the phone and dialed the operator. "Hello . . . yeah. Good evening, operator. My name is Buddy Nicholls." His voice slurred. "I want the number for the *Sultan Valley Tribune*."

38

"I miss my baby!" Grace wailed. She was outside by the pool. The stars were shining in the black sky. The pool lights were on and cast an eerie green glow against her. She was dressed in an evening gown for no apparent reason. She was continually drunk now. Her guilt was consuming her. As much as she tried to pass the blame for Hank's death on Tava, it kept coming back to her. Why did she bow to his blackmail? That was the question she kept asking herself. All of this could have been avoided if she had just been stronger.

Grace was sick of herself. She didn't like who she was and felt trapped in a used body. She was alone and hopeless. As much as she wanted to tell the truth, there was something stopping her. It was making her sick and feverish.

Thomas was slipping away. She could feel that and it hurt her. He was the only man she had ever really cared for. A long time ago they used to have fun. She remembered the days when they were frivolous, long before they had money.

"Goddamn money. Why do we have to have so much, Tommy? Why? All it brings us is torment. Look at me, Tommy. Look at what your fucking money has done to me." She swallowed another huge gulp and staggered to the edge of the pool. The gentle, rolling waves were hypnotizing her.

Grace was sinking further and further into her own world. Truth and fiction were blending now and she was finding it difficult to differentiate between the two. It unnerved her, and in her few moments of lucidity it terrified her. She needed something more. She needed solid ground to stand on. The rules of this game were constantly changing and she had no control over them.

She wondered briefly about Tava. She envisioned her daughter hiding somewhere, in a dark little room, frightened and too scared to find help. For that, Grace felt painfully ashamed. Up until now everybody was guessing Tava had gone to the Nicholls Estate to see Buddy. No one understood why Hank was dead but all the proof was pointing toward Tava. Her fingerprints were on the lamp. It seemed airtight and the only thing in Tava's favor was the town's sentiment.

By now the national papers had picked up on the story, and Tava was making headlines around the country. She was not known but her father was and that made her a perfect summertime story. Reporters were continually calling the house until Thomas had the phone number changed. TV crews and newspapers were trying to come on the property to record the family's pain and frustration. To all of them Grace came across as a haggard, unsympathetic woman, and the trade rags were beginning to paint her as a washed-up socialite.

Blackhurst Manor was completely off-limits to the media. At Thomas's insistence Kim hired several armed guards and stationed them around the perimeter of the estate. No one was allowed in or out without proper identification. A growing number of newspeople were camped outside the front entrance waiting to catch a glimpse of the Blackhursts. This was now the hottest story in the country and everybody wanted to be in on it.

"I told them I didn't want to do the damn party," she slurred. Grace lost her balance for a moment. "None of this would have happened if dumbo hadn't started the stupid takeover. Goddammit, Tom, why couldn't you leave Nicholls alone? Why did you have to get this one?"

Grace sat heavily and dangled her feet in the cool water. She was completely drunk and out of control. She did not know what she was doing. She felt hot, stifled, and closed in. She felt like she was living in a fishbowl. Every night new stories were appearing about the "Blackhurst Scandal" as they were beginning to call it. There were so many lies and half truths circulating, she was scared someone was going to find the real truth. It frightened her beyond belief.

She grabbed at her dress and unzipped it. She needed air. She stood long enough to completely strip. She felt better now. A gentle breeze blew around her skinny frame. Her breasts sagged but felt freer without the confines of her clothes. She dangled her feet again in the pool and it felt incredibly refreshing. She finally felt good. For this brief moment she didn't worry. All of it was closed behind a black curtain. It made her feel free. A silly little song filled her thoughts. The booze lulled her into a sense of security and she began to hum the tune about a drunken sailor. The lyrics were very suggestive and made her giggle with each refrain. She lost her train of thought halfway through the song and finished with a toss of her hands. She waved them hopelessly in front of her, floating now in an intoxicated sea.

Thomas watched Grace from the darkened kitchen window. It made him so sad to see her like this. His wife was totally out of control and very close to losing her mind. She needed an alcohol program desperately but he didn't have the time. Tava was consuming all of his thoughts and until she returned safely, Grace would have to wait. He observed Grace like a stranger. She did not elicit the kind of feeling she once had had from him. Thomas vaguely remembered the feeling of love. He missed it. He was beginning to feel it again with Kim.

He smiled at the thought of Kim. She was so cool. Her confidence was keeping him sane through this ordeal. He knew his family was being raked through the coals now. Their faces were being shown in every paper and on every television across the nation. Their lives were being dissected like dead animals, and there in the middle of the storm was his Kim. She was an incredible source of strength for him and he was learning to depend on her.

So much of his life was completely independent. Grace only clung to his money now. She didn't really want him. All of his employees treated him like God. There was no one for him to confide in, no one to share his fears and weaknesses with until Kim came into his life. He silently vowed to keep her happy. He wanted to isolate her from all of this. His private fear was losing her. He desperately needed her. Only in her presence did he feel like a man. To the world Thomas Blackhurst was a money machine and he was growing tired of it. He was beginning to discover there was more to life.

He watched as Grace removed her clothes. She was so skinny! A drunk was standing where a beautiful lady once had.

Thomas crossed outside and over to the pool. He almost did not know how to talk to her. "Grace?" he said softly.

"Oh, hello, Tommy. I missed you." She smiled at him. Her eyes were bloodshot and she was unsteady. "I want you to know, Tommy, I don't hate you. It's just all of this . . ." Grace did not finish and instead pointed around her. "We have too much, Tommy. It's not right."

"Why don't you come inside?"

"No. I like it out here." She grabbed his hand and held on to it desperately. "I love you, Thomas Blackhurst."

"You once did, honey."

Grace seemed to think about that for a moment and then nodded. "I guess that's right. We used to love each other."

"Yes, we did."

"Is it too much to ask you to hold me? Or is your little whore watching?" Grace finished her question softly.

"Sure, I can hold you." Thomas kneeled behind her and wrapped his arms around her naked body. She leaned into him and began to cry. Slowly at first and then stronger.

"I'm sorry, Thomas. For all of this."

"That's okay. It's not your fault."

High up in the wooded hills a high-powered video camera with a special night lens filmed Thomas and Grace by the pool. The camerawoman smoked incessantly and was smiling.

"They're going to love this," she said and kept on filming.

39

"He came out of nowhere. It scared the hell out of me and I'll tell you the guy was strong. Really strong. I've been around but I was no match for him." Helen was sitting in a small diner in Great Waters. She was sipping hot, black coffee and taking a drag from her cigarette. She was trying to remain calm.

It was midmorning and the sky was overcast and gray. Hans and Michael were looking concerned. Their search was not going as quickly as they hoped. And now with this new information from Helen their worst fears were confirmed. There was someone else who had Tava. Michael shook his head in despair while Hans sat still and contemplated. The Swede was analyzing the situation, looking for an answer. He was very displeased with this new development but it was something he could factor in now. The more answers he had, the less confusing the whole equation would be. This was not hopeless yet.

"So she was with you. How did she seem?"

"Scared. What do you expect with that creep after her?"

"Which creep?" Michael asked.

"That Buddy Nicholls guy. The one all over the paper."

Michael felt his heart beating faster. They had just met up with Helen and she was beginning to calm down. At first she was reticent to speak to them. She knew it was a delicate matter so after she recovered, she discreetly contacted Thomas. He was very appreciative and immediately contacted Hans and Michael to meet her.

Hans caught the same clue Michael did. "Why is Buddy the creep?"

"What do you mean?"

Michael rushed in. "Helen, we don't know what you're

talking about. All we know is that Hans dropped Tava off at the Nicholls estate, and several hours later Hank Nicholls is found bludgeoned to death and Tava has disappeared. Now we have Buddy Nicholls claiming that Tava killed his father, and the lamp that was used to kill him has her fingerprints on it. So we're flying blind here. Okay?"

"Michael, calm down. Helen is being very cooperative."

"This isn't a fucking game, Hans!"

"No one is suggesting it is. Relax."

Helen sipped her coffee. "No wonder the kid is scared. Nobody knows the truth. Maybe that's why she was trying to get home. I was all set to drive her back to Sultan Valley. To get the tape."

"What tape?" Hans asked.

"Jesus, you guys are in the dark! All right. This is the kid's story exactly like she told me." Helen leaned back in the booth and recounted exactly what Tava had told her. Michael grew quiet and Hans sat immutably silent, listening with all of his power. He did not want to miss anything. Finally the missing pieces were being filled in.

Helen spent the next fifteen minutes recounting Tava's experience with Hank and Buddy. "She was confused and scared. You would be, too, for Christ's sakes. With a raving maniac coming after you I think the natural thing to do is run. So she did and she's been trying to keep herself together since then. She's doing okay but she stands out like a sore thumb. She's like a little porcelain doll. All of this is the big, bad world and she's not prepared to deal with it. She's like a baby out here. She broke my heart."

"Now it makes sense," Hans muttered.

"That's why she wanted to get back. She needed the safety of home and realized that is the only place she's going to find peace of mind. This tape is her ticket. Without it she's dead. Provided this little asshole Buddy hasn't found it."

"What did that man look like?" Hans asked softly.

"I have no idea. I never got a chance to see him. I got in my truck and he grabbed me from behind.

"He scared the hell out of me. You know why?"

"Why?"

"Because he didn't sound scared. He was calm and sounded like he did this for a living. Normally I would expect a man to be nervous or apprehensive before he attacks someone but this guy was conversational. This was like going to the movies for him."

Hans was done. Helen had given them all she could and it was quite a lot. Hans now knew why Tava was running and if nothing else he could understand Buddy better. The man was terrified and justifiably so. "Thank you, Helen. We have to go. Mr. Blackhurst asked me to compensate you for anything you might need."

Helen waved him away. "No. I don't need any money. My needs are simple. You know what I want though? I want that asshole caught and I want Tava safe. She's a good kid. Let me know when you get her. I'm gonna be on the road but you can get a hold of me at this number." She handed Hans a business card. "See you, boys."

Hans slid out of the booth and Michael followed. Hans left and Michael paused to say, "Thank you, Helen. I'm sorry if I was rude. Tava and I are going to . . ." Michael fell silent.

"It's okay, kid. Just go save her."

Michael found Hans in the car. He got in on the passenger side and slammed the door closed. "Now what?"

"That was a good woman, Michael, and she did a tremendous amount for Tava."

"I know that, Hans."

"Don't be ungrateful. These are real people, boy, and they deserve more respect."

"I'm sorry."

"If you do that again, you're gone. I need a sane person with me, Michael."

"I'm sorry."

"Sorry might get you dead." Hans pushed the car key into the ignition and stopped. "All right. What do we have?"

This was a routine they went through with every new piece of the puzzle. It was integral to the process and Michael was learning quickly. This time Michael started. "We have Tava on the run from Buddy. Buddy killed his father after he found him trying to rape her."

"No, Michael. Tava went there willingly. I dropped her off that night. She was apprehensive but she was determined to do whatever she had to do by herself. She was there for a reason."

"I'm calling it rape."

"Call it what you want, but remember there's more to this."

"All right. Fine. Buddy barges in, sees it, and kills his father. He flips out and goes for Tava 'cause she saw the whole thing. Tava escapes and runs. She's scared out of her mind and ends up on a bus going north. From there she calls in, Grace scares her, and she flips out. She knows her only proof is a tape sitting in Buddy's house so maybe she decides to try and sneak back and get it. Helen helps and then this guy gets involved. Where did he come from?"

"Buddy," Hans answered.

"How do you know that?"

"Who would benefit from her death?"

"Buddy would."

"So we have a hired killer on Tava's trail, almost from the beginning. And now he has her."

"Right." Michael answered. "But he doesn't have the tape."

"Correct. And that is going to make him stop and ask questions. I know these minds. I'll bet you he was instructed to get the tape and then kill Tava. But with no tape, he's going to start questioning Buddy. He has several options, it seems, and none of them really includes killing Tava."

"We hope."

"It's an educated guess."

"I hate these guesses, Hans."

"I am afraid they're all we have." Hans dialed Thomas. "This is Hans."

It was Kim on the other end. "Hans, any word?"

"A little. We've met with the woman. She was helpful. Buddy killed Hank. Is Thomas there?"

"Let me put him on." She handed the phone to Thomas.

"Hans," his voice came on. It was strained and tired. "What have you got?"

"Tava was with this woman. Tava told her the entire story. Buddy killed Mr. Nicholls and tried to kill Tava. Apparently he walked in on them."

"What does that mean, Hans?"

"According to the story, Hank was trying to have sex with Tava."

"Oh my God . . ." Thomas's voice trailed off. It was several moments before he returned. "Where is she now?"

"We're still looking. We believe she has been abducted by a man working for Buddy. Beyond that, we don't know."

"Find them, Hans. Find them and let's get this over with. I want my daughter back."

"I understand, Mr. Blackhurst. One more thing."

"Yes."

"There is a tape that exists supposedly showing the whole event. Tava was trying to get back to Sultan Valley to get it and clear herself."

"Where is it?"

"In the Nicholls's house."

"My God. Where inside?"

"Only Tava knows that."

"I'll see what I can do on this end. In the meantime keep moving. Find her. The newspeople are swarming and I can't get them to leave us alone. This is growing into more than we can manage."

"We will do our best, sir. Plan to hear from us every twelve hours or so. My guess is this man is going to keep her on the run. You have our number in case anything comes up. Good-bye, sir."

"Good-bye, Hans."

The phone went dead and Hans turned to Michael. "I'm amazed the man is still functioning."

"We're all under strain. Where to next?"

"We need to check out the area around the warehouse where Helen was knocked unconscious. That will hopefully lead us on."

They pulled the car out of the restaurant parking lot and moved into traffic.

Michael was battling with his fear. He hoped Tava was all right. He needed to know she was surviving. All he wanted to do was hold her in his arms and protect her from all of this. He felt so helpless, it was maddening.

40

It was pitch-black out and Z had Tava's hands bound together in thumbcuffs. They chafed against her delicate skin and were drawing blood around the base. Tava did not cry out though. She had made Z very angry with her escape.

They were about three hundred miles north of Sultan Valley in Jake's truck, and Z had Tava pinioned on the floor of the cab. Her thumbcuffed hands were wrapped around the emergency brake and Tava was not able to sit up. As a result both her arms were numb and she was feeling claustrophobic. The dirty floor smelled and the carpet was harsh against her skin. Z was keeping the heat cranked and Tava was sweating uncontrollably.

She felt as if she were going to pass out and finally found the courage to tell him. "I can't stand it," she pleaded weakly.

Z ignored her. He was keeping his concentration on the road. The tail end of the storm was dumping water on them.

"Excuse me." Tava tried one more time. She was afraid he might kick her.

"What?" he asked angrily.

"I think I'm going to pass out."

"Good. Then you won't bother me."

"It's too hot. I'm going to throw up."

"If you complain any longer, I will chain you to the bed of the truck. I don't think you would like that. It is very wet out there."

"Please, let me sit up."

"Consider it punishment. You have already caused me considerable time and embarrassment. Your only saving grace is your father."

"My father isn't going to like this."

"I said be quiet." He took the heel of his boot and stomped it on her hands. Tava cried out in pain but held back her sobs. She swallowed her grief for fear he might kick her again. "You must learn, Tava, that when I say something I mean it. I do not want you to talk. If you follow the rules, there will be no problem. You women find it very difficult to follow orders."

Z lapsed into silence. He was formulating his plans. He had two problems to deal with. The first was with Buddy. The boy was going to panic when Z told him their contract was off. Still, Z reminded himself, Buddy seemed more interested with the videotape than with Tava. That might quiet the southern whelp. There was not much young Nicholls could do anyway. Tava was Z's now and he knew she was quite valuable.

His second problem was keeping Tava out of sight. The entire state was looking for her. He needed a safe, secluded place to hide her.

"Tava?"

"What?" she gritted between her teeth.

"I wouldn't take that tone with me. Do I make myself clear?"

"Yes."

"Yes what?"

"Yes, sir."

"Much better. What is your father like?"

"My father is a very nice man."

"That would make sense. Your mother?"

"My mother has got her problems like the rest of us."

"I don't have any problems."

"I guess you're lucky."

"It's not luck, my dear. What is his security like? Does he have people that protect him?"

"Yes."

"How many?"

Tava did not like answering these questions. She felt she was giving away secrets. But she had no choice. "One main one. He doubles as our chauffeur."

"How quaint. What is his name?"

"Hans."

"Doesn't sound American."

213

"He's Swedish."

"Interesting. I guess he's well trained?"

"I don't know. He seems to know what he's doing."

"Hmm." Z now had to consider the possibility of involving professionals. It made sense for Thomas to surround himself with good help. The nagging question for Z was how good. "This Hans. Do you know him?"

"Yes."

"Tell me about him."

Tava swayed. She was light-headed and sleepy. She wanted to throw up. "Can I please sit up? I promise to be good. You can cuff me to the door. Please. I can't stay down here."

Z smiled. He knew how far to push someone. He'd put her down there on purpose. He knew the heat would deprive her of her energy and quietly sap her independence. The poor girl was desperate now and frightened. In this state she was much more predictable and Z felt more comfortable with that.

He dug in his coat pocket for the keys. He tossed them down to her. "If you can undo yourself, you may sit up on the seat. When you're up redo them around the door handle. Please keep in mind that jumping from a truck at sixty miles an hour is much different than from a slow moving motorcycle." He smiled to himself. He was very self-satisfied. He enjoyed the power he wielded and it made him feel strong and in command.

Tava struggled with the thumbcuffs and finally undid them. She pulled herself off the floor and onto the seat. Her arms were practically useless to her. Finally being able to stretch them drew blood back into the arms and they began to tingle so much, they hurt. She handed the keys back to Z and quickly recuffed herself on the door handle. She knew she couldn't escape from the truck and she did not want another beating. Z pretended to be nice with his soft voice but Tava knew his heart was cold. The man had no emotions save for greed, and Tava was only alive because of it.

Her body was drained but her spirit raged with indignation. She hated being chained like an animal. She hated the cuffs and hated Z more for making her wear them. She couldn't stand the humiliation and vowed secretly to make him pay. Until then she knew she had to be careful. This man was deadly serious. As much as she wanted this to be a game or a bad dream, it was all too real and terrifying. But as long as she kept her mind active, she could stay in control.

"I'm sorry I ran from you."

"You won't do it again. If you are a good girl, you might get out of this."

"I just want to go home."

"All safe and sound?"

"I just want to be home." His voice was grating on her. It was deep and sultry but tinged with an unspeakable menace. It unnerved her. His voice was a constant reminder of the kind of danger she was really in. Once again she was in a situation completely out of her control and she despised it. She knew in her heart she would not let anyone run her life for her again. She was angry with herself.

Z noticed her silence. He watched her briefly and discovered how beautiful she was. Small-boned but perfectly proportioned. Her short, dusty blond hair was tangled and dirty now but he could see that it was once silken. Her strong, sharp features gave her the appearance of a model or an athlete. Mixed among these was a soft, warm glow. She radiated a confident beauty that aroused in him a bold, questioning interest. He had first taken her for a soft, spoiled rich girl; brainless and silly. Her escape attempt may have been more than stupid, he thought; it may have been a brave, desperate try for freedom. Z could respect that in her. He found himself reevaluating his captive. She was young, but surprisingly mature.

"You are quiet."

Tava shook her head yes. She was lost in thought.

"What are you thinking about so hard?"

"Why Buddy would do this to me."

"He is a petulant boy. He has his affairs to take care of."

"Like killing?"

"That is what he hoped for. But he was a bad boy and did not share the whole story. You are much too valuable and for that he loses you."

"What are you going to do?"

"It's simple, my child. You and I are going to ask your poppa for a little money."

"I won't do it."

Z grinned broadly. He liked her spirit. "Oh?"

"I won't." Tava stuck to her conviction. She wasn't going to help him.

"Of course you're going to help because you want to stay alive." It was a simple statement and very true. "You can be as brave as you want but the reality is you will do exactly as I say because you must. Your need for life is far greater than your father's is for money. My guess is he will pay a tremendous amount for you. Wouldn't you think?"

"I have no idea."

"Don't be ridiculous. Of course you do. I think you have a good idea. I think you are much smarter than you let on."

Tava shrugged her shoulders. She didn't trust this man and did not enjoy talking to him. She did allow one question. "When are you going to call?"

"Soon."

In the distance a motel sign blinked on and off. The pouring rain made it appear blurry through the foggy window. Z maneuvered the truck off the road and into the gravel parking lot. He parked in front of the office and cut the engine. In the window they both saw an old woman tottering behind the counter.

"You see that woman?" Z asked.

"Yes."

"She's dead if you try to run or yell."

"I understand." Tava believed him.

Z left the car and Tava watched him enter the office. It all seemed like slow motion. The whole scene was surreal and Tava shook her head to clear the sleepiness. The heat inside the cab was making her fall asleep. She forced herself to stay awake. Every moment counted. She needed to keep her senses clear and knew if the chance came again, she would run. She wondered what it was like for prisoners of war. She knew now why they felt impelled to escape.

This man went against all decency, and the will to run from him overpowered anything else. Tava did not fight the urge. Instead she embraced it and let her understanding grow inside her like a hidden power. He was not going to suspect it. Tava was going to make sure of that. He was going to believe she was the most docile lamb. She noticed him looking at her and decided to use it to her advantage. If her looks were good for anything they might as well help save her.

Z finished his transaction and returned to the truck. "What a nice old woman. She sends her best."

"What are we?"

"Married. Young lovers bedding down for the night. Sort of romantic, isn't it?"

Tava did her best to ignore him.

Z pulled the truck down the line of rooms and parked in front of Number 12.

They moved inside and Tava remained standing until she was told to sit. She collapsed on the twin bed. Z dug in his coat for the keys and undid her left thumb and attached the open cuff to the bedpost.

"That should make it easier to sleep." Z shrugged out of his coat and left it on the chair. A huge gun hung ominously under his arm. He caught Tava staring at it. "Surprised? All of us bad guys have them." He laughed at himself. "I'm going to clean myself." He moved over to the bathroom. "I will be five minutes. I expect you to have your dress off by the time I come out."

Tava caught her breath. What did he mean? What was he going to do?

She heard the shower go on. Her breathing was very hard and she desperately wanted to be free. She tried the thumbcuffs one more time but couldn't break free. Her thumbs were too sore and she just couldn't get it over the knuckle. She used her left hand to reach for the phone. She pulled the receiver to her and listened for the dial tone. There was none! Then she noticed the key lock on the phone.

She searched in vain for a way to slip the cuff off the bedpost and could not find one. It was a strong metal rod running from top to bottom and was welded on both sides. She was completely trapped.

"Dammit!" she hissed through her teeth. "There's got to be a way. There has to be."

The shower cut off.

Tava lay still and tried to stifle the sound of her own breathing. He said he wanted her dress off before he came out. She couldn't let him touch her. Not this man. It was too horrifying. Michael, she yelled inside her head, please come get me!

She didn't want to make him mad again. She knew what that was like. It was an effort but she finally pulled the short red dress off her body and dropped it to the floor. Her cotton underwear was soaked but she left it on, praying he would leave her alone. Her mind was filled with terrifying pictures of what he might do.

Tava tried to get underneath the covers but froze when she heard the door open. She forced herself to stay calm. It was tremendously difficult for her to keep her emotions under control.

Z was toweling off and to Tava's discomfort he was completely naked. His body was muscled and she could tell he was as hard as rock. This was a man who cared for his body. She could appreciate the effort, if not the man. His stomach was chiseled and well-defined. His arms were thick and muscled. His legs were those of a runner. He looked like the Greek statue of David.

Tava tried to avoid his private area but couldn't. The man was big but not aroused. She hoped that was a good sign.

"You look lovely," he remarked. "I thought you would." He dropped the towel on the floor and walked over to her. "You have beautiful skin." He sat on his bed across from her. "Your breasts are pleasing." He stared at her for a long time. She was petrified.

Z finally broke his trance and grabbed for the key to the phone. He unclicked the lock and picked up the receiver. "What is your home number?"

Tava gave it to him. She realized he was toying with her. She watched him dial and wait for someone to pick up.

"It's still ringing. What number did you give?"

"It's a private line to his study."

"Ah, here we go. Hello. I would like to speak with the gentleman of the house." Z muffled the phone and asked Tava, "Who is the woman?"

"Probably his assistant." Tava did not take her eyes off him.

"Hello?"

"Yes?" Thomas answered. "This is Thomas Blackhurst."

"Good. I go by the name of Z. Mr. Blackhurst, I have a little story to tell you."

"Who is this?"

"If you'll just hold all questions, sir, I will get to that. I was hired by a lovely little boy named Buddy Nicholls to kill your daughter."

Thomas could not keep the fear from his voice. "Is she all right?"

"Yes. She is for now. I have decided to break my contract with Mr. Nicholls and deal directly with you. You are a businessman, Mr. Blackhurst, and can appreciate a good bargain. I am willing to sell your daughter back to you."

"What have you done to her?"

Z sounded surprised. "Nothing. But I could if I wanted to. Couldn't I, Tava?"

"Is she there?"

"Of course."

"Let me speak to her."

"Tava? Your poppa would like to speak to you." Z handed the receiver to her. He continued smiling. He was in a very good mood.

"Daddy?" Tava was calm but frightened.

"Tava baby. Are you all right?"

"I'm fine. I didn't kill Hank, Daddy."

"We know that, honey. Your driver-friend told Hans about it."

"Helen? She's all right?"

"She's fine."

"Thank God." Tava relaxed a little, realizing Hans was looking for her. "Daddy, Buddy is dangerous."

"We know, sweetie. We're working on it. Your friend told us about the tape but Buddy's in the house and we can't get to it. Don't tell anyone else where it is."

"All right." Her voice was shaky but strong. There was so much she wanted to say but didn't know how. She missed him with all her heart.

"Honey, put the man back on. Stay calm and know we love you."

Tava reluctantly handed the receiver back to Z.

"Yes?"

"How much do you want?"

"I want a tremendous amount of money. You are rich and I am greedy. As long as we respect that about one another, there will be no problem. Now, what I would like you to do is get a good night's sleep. I know we will. We'll call you tomorrow. God speed." With that he hung up, cutting Thomas off in midsentence. "That should keep him up all night. Well, I think it's time for bed." He pulled back his sheets and then turned back to Tava. "Surprisingly I have some respect for you. And while I would love to indulge, it weakens the mind and I cannot afford that. So, with that impressed rudely upon me, let me have your free hand."

Tava gave it to him warily. He took it and kissed it and then brushed it against his penis. "For good luck." He released her and crawled into his own bed, switching off the light. "You may want to get inside the bed. Sleeping comes so much easier when you are comfortable. Good night. Ah, I almost forgot. One last call." He turned on the light and dialed. Buddy picked up on the other end.

"Mr. Nicholls, always a pleasure."

"Goddammit, where have you been! Are you fucking crazy! Have you done it? Do you have my tape?"

"So many questions, Mr. Nicholls. Why don't you slow down? Now, am I fucking crazy? No. Where have I been? Looking for the Blackhurst woman. Did I find her? Yes. Does she have your tape? No."

"No? What do you mean, no? She's got to have it."

"She doesn't. And I have no idea where it is."

"So what're you saying?"

"Exactly that. She does not have it. She may have at one point but I cannot tell."

"Fuck! It could be anywhere!"

"I suppose."

"Have you taken care of her?"

"The Blackhurst girl is all tucked away. I don't think anyone is going to be bothering her anymore."

"Thank God. One less thing to worry about. Did she say anything about the tape?"

"She did not. I tried to get it out of her but I applied too much pressure. It was unfortunate but necessary."

"Jackass. I told you I wanted the tape."

"I wouldn't call me a jackass, my friend. That is not a safe thing to do. Our agreement is over. Forget me, Mr. Nicholls. Good luck."

"Thanks a lot." Buddy slammed the phone down.

Z hung up and switched the light off. He settled himself in and began to drift to sleep.

Tava couldn't hold back her anger. "What if he finds the tape?"

"Children have so many questions," he sighed. "He will leave me alone now. If he finds the tape, that is your concern. If he doesn't, so much the better. The twit gets what he deserves. I don't care. I would love to see his face when he finds out you're still alive. Good night." Z rolled over and went to sleep.

Tava threw her head back against the pillow. She was petrified now. The one hope she was clinging to was to get away from Z, rescue the tape, and clear her name. Now even that was being taken from her. She suddenly realized that if she did not get that tape before Buddy did, she still might be blamed for Hank's death, even if Z surrendered her to Thomas. Tava tried to hold back the cold fear of defeat. She could not let herself fall apart. This was not over until the very end, and until that came, she was going to fight it every step of the way.

41

A small car appeared in the distance. It was a beat-up Chevy and the car made its way slowly toward the street entrance. The news trucks lined both sides of the road in a tight line. The little car moved slowly through the area and made its way tentatively toward the Blackhurst entrance. Normally driving in would have been no problem but now with all the notoriety the police stopped the car at the gate.

"What do you want?"

"Hi, Arnie," Jason said. He was one of Sultan Valley's paperboys. He was a bright seventeen-year-old with horn-rimmed glasses and bright eyes. The policeman recognized him immediately.

"Jason. How can you do this so early?"

"Six isn't early, Arnie. Everybody needs their paper. Including the Blackhursts, although they may not like this one."

"How come?"

"Check out the headlines."

The policeman unfolded the *Sultan Valley Tribune* and read the morning's lead story. SUSPECTED KILLER'S MOTHER SLEEPS WITH DECEASED!

"Jeez." He whistled. "Where do they get this stuff?"

"There's pictures in the back. You're not gonna believe them. So, can I take it in to them?"

"No. Mr. Blackhurst's orders. I've got to do it. Beat it, Jason. Hey, you got any extras?"

"A couple."

"Why don't you feed 'em to the news guys? They look a little hungry. They're going to be pissed off they missed this one."

Jason shrugged his shoulders. "Why not? They're gonna find out sooner or later." He backed the car out of the driveway and pulled off in the direction of town. Passing the TV vans, he tossed two rolled papers at them and yelled, "Wake up, boys. This story is burning!"

Arnie laughed. He tramped down the stone driveway reading the story. He kept shaking his head. He liked Thomas but couldn't understand Grace. She was so pushy. And now this. "Everybody's got a secret, don't they?" He whistled.

He knocked on the door and Annie answered. "Hello, officer."

"Hi, Annie. The paper's here. How's everybody?"

"It was a quiet night. You make sure those newspeople stay away."

"That's my job."

"You know Mr. Blackhurst appreciates it."

"We all like Mr. Blackhurst. I don't know how much he's gonna appreciate this though." Arnie handed her the paper. "This just gets weirder and weirder, doesn't it?"

Annie took the paper and smiled. "The man's been through a lot. It can't get much worse."

"If you say so." Arnie gave a friendly salute and backed off. "If you need anything, just let us know."

"Thank you." Annie closed the door and looked at the front page. "Oh my God."

Kim passed through the entrance hall and overheard Annie. "What is it?"

"I don't believe this." She dropped the paper to the ground and instantly knelt and riffled through the pages to the pictures. The paper had only printed the last explicit ones but it was unmistakable: Grace Blackhurst and Hank Nicholls making love. "I don't understand."

Kim knelt beside her, scanning the story and pictures. She sat back heavily and shook her head. "How could she do this? This has got to be somehow connected."

"That woman has been trouble since the day I knew her. There's so much hate locked up inside her, it makes me sick. The whore." Annie's voice was hard and cold. She never spoke her mind but was safe with Kim.

"I've got to show this to him." Kim scooped up the paper and tucked it under her arm. "Not a word of this to Grace. We're going to let Thomas deal with this in his own way. Agreed?"

"I've got nothing to say to that woman. She's death to me."

Kim recognized the sadness in Annie's eyes and thought she understood the older woman's pain. She knew Annie loved Tava and realized she was blaming Grace for what was happening. Kim did not know how it all fit together but she knew Annie was not wrong. She touched Annie's hand gently. "We're going to get her back soon, Annie. Keep believing that."

"I pray for it every second." Annie disappeared into the house.

Kim knew she would find Thomas in the kitchen. She had left him there with explicit orders to eat. The man was not keeping his strength up and she was struggling to get some food into him. He looked terrible. He was unshaven and distant. He was consumed with finding Tava. Nothing seemed to concern him expect her safety, not even his own health. Kim admired that in him. She realized it was his undying commitment to his daughter that embodied his entire reason for success. She was concerned that one day he might burn out. It was a real worry for Kim and she vowed not to let it happen. She hated having to add to his strain but she knew Grace's story was going to fan the ugly flames. She wondered how much worse it was going to get.

He was picking at a bowl of cereal, intently glued to the morning news. His body seemed frozen like a statue. Kim immediately recognized the tension in his thin body. His refined muscles were straining under enormous tension. There was something terribly wrong.

"What is it?"

Thomas said nothing but pointed at the screen. He was looking at himself holding Grace by the pool the night before. The announcer's voice intoned deeply, "The strain of the Blackhurst family is beginning to pull them apart. Their seclusion is abnormal. Our sources are saying that they refuse any help from the police and are now living in a semistate of delirium. Their deep fear for their missing daughter Tava and the death of Hank Nicholls is pushing one of the country's premiere families over the edge."

The television picture cut back to the studio and the face of Jessie Hiller. She was wearing her concerned face and staring into the camera. She paused for a moment and touched her finger to her ear. "This just in. In a bizarre twist to one of the most baffling murders in the country, we have just received conclusive evidence that Grace Blackhurst, wife to financier Thomas Blackhurst, was having an affair with the deceased, Hank Nicholls. What this means to the investigation and the plight of the young Tava Blackhurst remains a mystery. We understand confirming pictures have been disclosed. Parents, we are about to show sensitive material we do not believe should be viewed by your children. While we have blacked out the sensitive areas of the bodies, the nature of the photos is both violent and sexual."

The television screen filled with Grace's face in ecstasy. Her breasts were blurred but the bedroom was very clear. Hovering over her was Hank Nicholls. They were both naked and caught in the intimate act of passion. Thomas's eyes grew larger. He couldn't believe this. It went beyond the bounds of understanding. The television continued to flash the pictures at him. They kept slapping him in the face. Each picture was like twisting the knife in a little farther. He felt like dying. His world was crashing down and now he realized how frighteningly unpredictable this entire event was becoming. He was not in control. Grace was even working against him. Poor, innocent Tava, what are they doing to you? You don't deserve to suffer this.

His thoughts were only eased by knowing Hans was out there on Tava's trail. Just after his call with Z, Thomas tracked Hans down and told him to stay on alert. At this point everybody was waiting for the mysterious Z to call again.

Just as suddenly Buddy's face filled the screen. It appeared to be live. Jessie's voice broke in. "Mr. Nicholls. You are the son of Hank Nicholls, is that correct?"

"Yes, I am." Buddy was cleaned up now. He was shaven and in a suit and tie. His eyes were still tired and ringed in black circles but the effect was more of a grieving son than a killer.

"You are the one pressing charges against Tava Blackhurst for the killing of your father, is that correct?"

"Absolutely. The police have the proof."

"And of course until she is found we must all live with the questions of why," Jessie said. "Where did you find these pictures?"

"In my father's belongings."

"Did you know your father and Grace Blackhurst were having an affair?"

"No. These come as a terrible shock to me."

"Do you think there is any connection to these photos and your father's death?"

Buddy calculated his answer and delivered it brilliantly. "Well, I don't understand women, Ms. Miller, but I guess I can see why Tava would be angry. She must have known. Why else would she have killed my father?"

"If there was one thing you wanted to say to the Blackhurst family right now, what would it be?"

Buddy faltered on purpose. His voice caught in his throat and tears began to stream down his cheeks. "I would like them to know I am not a hateful man and I don't hold them responsible for their daughter's actions. But I do want justice for my dead father. That's why I went public with these photos. I don't feel the police are doing their best to find Tava."

"Why is that?"

"Well, Mr. Blackhurst is a powerful man . . ." Buddy left his statement hanging there. He knew everybody would understand his intent. He was doing his best to win public opinion and sway sympathy over to his side.

"Thomas," Kim spoke quietly. "Turn the TV off."

Thomas's hands automatically switched the offensive set off. "I am going to crush that boy. Kills his own father and then blames it on my daughter. He does not know what he's playing with."

"Don't let it eat you up, Thomas."

"He can't do this."

"He already has."

Thomas was quiet and then said, "I wonder if we're going to survive this, my dear?"

"Yes, we are."

Thomas sounded battle weary. He'd been up since four, pacing the halls waiting for Z's next call, and now this was adding to his misery. He was too overwhelmed to begin to put the pieces together. He willed himself to stay strong for Tava. "Get Grace up and meet me in front of the house."

"Why?"

"I know what that little shit is trying to do and I don't like it. There are more cameras in front of my house than there are in front of his. Move."

Kim hurried away, knowing there was no stopping him. Thomas reached for the phone and called the *Sultan Valley Tribune.* "Hello, who is this?"

"Sara Knowles."

"Put John on the line."

"I'm sorry, sir, he's not in yet."

"This is Thomas Blackhurst."

"Yes, sir. I'll get him right away."

The phone was silent for five seconds and then John Henderson answered. He was a big man with a friendly personality. He was one of Thomas's favorite people in Sultan Valley. "I suppose you've heard," John said.

"I just saw it on the TV."

"I'm sorry about the article, Thomas."

"What article?"

226

John paused. "Haven't you seen your paper?" He sounded more worried now.

"What do you mean?" Thomas reached for the paper and read the headline. He didn't have to finish. "Christ, you too?"

"I'm sorry, Thomas. I couldn't let this one go."

Thomas was about to explode and then submerged it. As much as it hurt him to admit it, John was only doing his job and the man had been objectively quiet up until now. "I know, John. I'm giving a press conference in five minutes out front. I wanted you to know."

"I've already got a reporter there."

"Of course you do." Thomas was suddenly at a loss for words.

"Thomas? Are you there?"

"Yes."

"I just want you to know, we don't like writing this stuff. All of us down here still believe Tava is innocent."

"Thank you, John. I appreciate that. I'll see you later." He hung up the phone. He rubbed the sleep from his face and tried to clear his head. He did not know what he was going to say but knew it had to be good.

He crossed through the house to the front door. He opened it and stepped out.

"You!" he called to one of the security guards down the driveway. "Let the newspeople in!"

"Yes, sir!" The man ran off.

Thomas tried to tame his unruly hair and then gave up. He wanted America to see the pain he was going through. No little slick conniver from Houston was going to do this to his family.

The horde descended like flies. They pushed each other to reach the great Thomas Blackhurst first. The vans sped down the road and screeched to a halt. The dust kicked up and blew across the flower beds. The throng quickly formed a packed semicircle in front of Thomas. He stood there silently and waited.

A few of the reporters tried to ask questions immediately but received no answer. Thomas waited patiently for the TV people to get their equipment set up. He only said, "I am waiting for my wife. Please bear with me."

The newspaper people were writing furiously in their

pads. The TV people were briefing their headquarters. Finally the equipment was in place and the hurried rush of excitement was replaced with eager expectation.

Kim found Grace asleep in bed. She rushed over and threw open the drapes.

"Grace, get up!"

"Who is that?" came the sleepy reply. "Get the hell out of here."

"It's Kim, Grace. Thomas asked me to get you up. There are reporters outside. Something very important has happened."

Grace licked her dry lips. "What the hell are you talking about?"

"Just get up, Grace. Thomas wants you out front."

"You don't tell me what to do. This is my house, honey."

"Fine, Grace. I'm not here to fight." Kim found Grace's robe on the floor and threw it on the bed. Kim wanted her to look passable for the cameras. If Kim was right, every station in the country was going to carry this interview and she wanted Thomas to look as good as possible. Buddy just planted a huge doubt in people's minds and it was going to take a very convincing appearance to heal the wounds.

"What'd you say about reporters?"

"Thomas has invited them in for an interview."

Grace was coming awake now. "Why?"

"There's been a new wrinkle to the story."

"My God, they haven't found my baby have they? Is she all right?"

"It's not Tava, Grace." Kim was doing her best to avoid the subject.

"Listen, you little bitch, get out of my room."

"Stop calling me that, Grace. I'm not the one with the dirty little secrets." Kim approached the bed now. "I know your type, Grace, and they make me sick. So drop it." Kim's voice was very firm.

"Who do you think you're talking to?"

"Grace, please. Thomas wants you out front. You're going to be on television."

"I thought he didn't want to talk to those people."

"Someone's forced his hand." Kim had her arms crossed over her chest impatiently.

Grace threw the covers back, sat up, and pulled the robe over her gray silk nightgown. She brushed her silver hair back. She was very angry with Kim. She was unimpressed with the black woman's confidence and felt she could break her in a second. "I said get out of my room."

Kim did not appreciate Grace's tone and decided to bring her down. She was tired of seeing Thomas hurt by her. "Buddy Nicholls found the photos, Grace. He's given them to the press."

Grace went dizzy. Her head spun and she immediately reached for a drink. The glass on her night stand was empty. She did not want to appear caught off balance and she was not sure she was hiding her surprise. "What photos?"

"The ones of you and Hank Nicholls."

Grace became haughty. "What're you talking about?"

"You know exactly what I'm talking about. Makes you kind of nervous, doesn't it? Now that the whole world knows what the real Grace Blackhurst is like."

"What am I like, Kim?"

"A conniving tramp."

Grace breathed in sharply. "That goddamn Nicholls boy."

"Thomas didn't need this right now, Grace. How can you be so selfish?"

"Listen, Miss High and Mighty . . ."

"Nobody cares about you, Grace." Kim began to leave and Grace was on her feet, blocking the door.

"What do you know about me? You know what you are? An opportunist. All you're doing is spreading your legs for my husband, so what does that make you?"

Kim was not going to be sucked into a fight with Grace. "We're not talking about me, Grace. We're talking about you, and right about now so is the rest of the country. So your husband is going out there and try to salvage what decency he has left. Your little escapade was very short-sighted, Grace. Do you have any idea what this is going to do to you? To your husband? And God knows what this is going to do to your daughter. Don't you care? There's only so much goodwill in people, Grace. The evidence is all pointing to Tava and this only helps it. What is wrong with you? What kind of mother are you?"

"A damn good one."

"Save it, honey."

Grace lashed out and slapped Kim. She did it as hard as she could, the way she did with Tava a few short weeks ago. This time, however, Kim saw it coming and moved with the blow. Grace's hand glanced off her right cheek and flew wildly into thin air. Kim spun once and before Grace realized what was happening, found herself shoved up against the wall. Kim pinioned her with her left hand firmly around Grace's neck. The other hand came down once into the older woman's stomach. The air flew from Grace's body and she sank to the carpeted floor. Kim knelt only long enough to say, "I missed your pretty face on purpose. You've got to look good for the cameras." She left Grace there on the floor and slammed the door behind her.

Grace gasped loudly for breath. Her body buckled and convulsed. She needed oxygen, and her body spasmed without it. She gulped for air and it was five minutes before she began to calm down. Her hatred for Kim grew a hundredfold. It wasn't the cold hate she held for Buddy. This was a burning revulsion that enraged her entire system. She knew she would seek revenge. Kim would have to watch her every step now because Grace was out for her. "I hope you enjoyed yourself, Kimmy dear. 'Cause that's the last time you're ever going to do that to me."

She pulled herself to her feet and readjusted her robe. She cinched it tight around her thin waist and opened her ornate bedroom door. She found a mirror in the hall and did her best to press her silver hair into some semblance of shape. She even grinned at herself. "They may have me down, but they do not have me out. They can be sure of that."

"Here she is now," Thomas said with unusual confidence. He looked magnificent. From deep inside him he was exuding the kind of magnetism that made people listen. He was putting on a show and no one knew it. He was in complete control. This was his affair and he was going to run it the way it benefited him. He was going to do anything to help Tava. In the past few minutes he only had enough time to guess the damage this was doing to Tava's case. Right now it only made it worse and for that he finally despised his wife. How, he wondered, could she go to such lengths to ruin their happiness? He wondered for the first time if she was really worried about Tava or was this just a silly little game to her. But now, in front of the cameras, there were no worries. Not for these people.

"Mrs. Blackhurst," one of the reporters from the back yelled out, "is it true you slept with Hank Nicholls on the night of the murder?"

Grace stepped up to her husband's side and linked her arm through his. She smiled and shook her head. "Don't be ridiculous."

Thomas covered her hand with his and patted it. He knew they were being scrutinized by thirty million people this morning. "My wife takes offense to that. I only have a few things to say to you folks and then I'm going to have to cut this short. Firstly, these bizarre accounts of impropriety are grossly exaggerated and unsubstantiated. It does not surprise me that a bereaved boy would grapple with his father's death, but it does concern me when he seems to be grabbing at straws. I am concerned for young Buddy Nicholls's sanity."

"You saying he's crazy?"

"I'm saying the boy is confused and should seek some help."

"So you two are denying that the pictures are of Hank Nicholls and your wife?"

"Completely. Darling?" Thomas turned to his wife. Only Grace could see the hardness in his eyes.

"I have been completely faithful to my husband and he to me. We love each other unequivocally." She leaned farther into him.

"Come on. We've all seen the pictures, Mrs. Blackhurst."

"I don't know what you're talking about. I have heard that funny things can be done with photography. I think you may all want to keep in mind that Buddy Nicholls is a young man who has been put under a tremendous amount of stress. With the passing of his father he has had to assume a tremendous amount of responsibility. Responsibility that would break a much stronger man. The boy is confused."

"We believe he is attacking us out of some misguided attempt to save his father's company," Thomas added. "Some of you may have heard that I was in the process of trying to buy Hank Nicholls's company. All I can guess is that Buddy Nicholls is trying to stop that at all cost."

A young woman piped up, "There are those saying that your daughter killed Hank Nicholls out of some blind anger after seeing these pictures."

"Completely false," Thomas said. "My daughter did not kill Hank Nicholls and that will be proven soon."

"Where is your daughter, Mr. Blackhurst?"

"I don't know. We're very concerned for her safety."

"What are you saying?"

"My daughter is not a killer. My wife is not an adulteress. We are simply concerned parents and if Tava is out there and she can hear us, I want her to know that we love her and we want her home. And one last word of caution. We know who killed Buddy's father. We will stop at nothing to make sure that person comes to justice."

Thomas cut off all other questions, grabbed his wife by the hand, and swept back inside the front door. The performance was impeccable and everybody knew it. The newspeople ate it up and were busy broadcasting it all over the country.

As soon as the door closed, Thomas threw Grace's hand aside and turned on her. "What the hell are those pictures?"

"I don't know."

"That's not good enough, Grace. Maybe the newspeople bought my line but we both know the truth. That is you."

"Believe what you want. It's not me." Grace felt the heat of blame pressing itself against her. She felt she was blushing.

"What did you do to Tava?"

"I didn't do anything." With that she turned to leave. Thomas grabbed her by the arm and flung her around. "What're you going to do, Thomas? Hit me? For what? Practicing what you do with little Kimmy? Screw you, Thomas, and all of this." She pulled away from him and walked back down the hall.

Thomas was left shaking. Grace's pictures were too much. He knew she was linked to this but still could not prove anything. He was walking a very delicate line now. If he pushed Grace too far, he might never get the truth. Better to back off now, for Tava, than to ruin the whole thing. This was his only choice and he seethed with the anger that came from impotence. He spotted a vase near the door and with the rage of several men, grabbed it and threw it as hard as he could against the wall. It shattered with a terrific noise that made the windows shake but did not relieve the emotions racing inside him.

42

Michael slammed the television off. He was fuming at the rerun of the news conference. He knew Grace was lying. The pictures were obviously her. The only thing he didn't know was how it all fit together.

"I can't believe her! Did you see that, Hans? It looked like she was selling Girl Scout cookies!"

"She gives a believable performance."

"Oh come on. You don't believe it, do you?"

"No."

"Well?"

"What do you want me to say, Michael? The woman is a liar. She was cheating on her husband. It does not come as a great surprise. This really is not our biggest problem although it adds to it. This is not going to make Tava's time any easier."

Michael sulked. He was angry with himself. He was not acting professionally and it reflected on him. The one thing he had learned from Hans up to this point was to keep a clear head. Passion had no place in this kind of hunt. All it did was muddle the thoughts and dull the fighting instincts. Michael was being pushed now, beyond where he'd ever been before. Hans was giving him a lesson in life and Michael kept reminding himself he needed to learn quickly. He was well aware of the responsibility being thrust upon him. He cared too much for Tava to screw things up.

"I'm not angry at you, Hans. I'm sorry. I need to keep myself under control. How does this affect us?"

"Buddy is throwing up a smoke screen. He may be sick but he is doing the right thing. I would do the same."

"I want to snap his little neck."

"That doesn't do us much good. Unfortunately we are stuck waiting. So just sit back, be quiet, and wait."

They were holed up in a squalid motel after tracking Tava to Jake's home. By that time Jake had already spoken to the police and was eagerly waiting for the television crews to descend. Hans and Michael left him quickly. He was able to give them a description of Z that at least gave Hans a better idea of what he was up against.

Now they sat in their small, wood-paneled room waiting for Thomas's call. At this point Tava could be anywhere. Waiting was the hardest. Watching the clock tick by was most painful.

The only clue they had was Jake's old truck, but searching for it now seemed fruitless. All they could do was sit and wait. Hans knew Thomas would call as soon as he heard something.

One hundred miles south Z was watching Tava sleep. He had to shake himself to clear his head. He was becoming enchanted by her. He berated himself for being less than professional. He told himself he should be calling Thomas to set up the exchange. Money was what drove him. The pursuit of riches saw him through many wars and more than one assassination. He was a soldier of fortune and his services always went to the highest bidder. In Tava's case that was now her father. He was more than able to double or triple Buddy's measly half million. To his pleasure he realized he was going to make more money from this simple kidnapping than he'd made over the last three years.

But here she was, the object of all this. He never asked himself why he was doing it but he did question the feelings deep inside himself. They were small, queasy sensations and they bothered him. They grew in intensity when he watched her. She was such an innocent child. She was trying to be so brave. He found Tava endearing, if not a little stupid. He was convinced she did not realize the kind of danger she was really in. Nothing of this could seem real to her. His threats, he realized, only mattered because he backed them up with physical abuse. He wondered if she'd ever been hit before.

234

He was his own man and did not let women intrude into his own private male world. Women were objects to Z. They were there to please him when he needed it. They were never to be confided in. Women equaled treachery to Z. The only good woman was the kind he paid for sex and left early in the morning. He found comfort in those energetic explosions. For those brief moments he forgot the pressures of the world and allowed himself to be someone he was not: a kind man. He chose this life because he was good at it. Killing was easy and he felt absolutely no remorse in practicing his art. He was in complete control of his own destiny and would not have it any other way. This was his world and it was just the way he created it. Z was happy but hollow. He was never completely relaxed and always had to watch his back. After twenty-five years of this sort of living, Z had many enemies. It was a pressure he always lived with and he incorporated it into his lifeblood. It was always there and in a sick way Z thrived on it.

And yet he watched Tava.

Just by lying there, she was reaching into him and softening the hard parts of his soul. Z did not fight it but he did not like it. It made him nervous and he wondered if these feelings were a teenager's infatuation.

"Oh, Z." He smiled at himself, half-embarrassed. "Why are you letting this girl in? She is nothing." He rebuked himself for caring. It did not seem right but he could not stop watching her.

Her full red lips blew softly in and out with the gentle, flowing currents of air. Her hair, tangled around her head, softened her features and made her seem vulnerable. Z followed her frame down underneath the blankets. He wanted to crawl in with her and shut the world out for an hour or two.

"Z, my God, what are you doing?" he admonished himself. "Put this female out of your mind. She is only flesh." He paused, still watching. "But what flesh she is!"

Tava felt his eyes on her. She refused to open her own. She knew if she did he would be watching her and she couldn't stand to see him. If she saw his eyes she knew she would have to believe all of this. She was praying she was going to wake up in her own bed.

She thought of Michael. "Where are you?" she whispered

to herself. "I need you now so badly." She wanted to cry. Then her father flashed in her mind. He'd told her secretly over the phone that Hans was looking for her. Someone was out there trying to help!

She missed her father. She wanted to be alone with him and just talk. She missed the safe, quiet moments they used to share. As a small child she used to follow him into his office and stand in front of the desk, head barely above the edge. She used to wait quietly until Thomas pretended to discover her.

"Who's that?" he would say.

"You know who it is."

"I don't think I know that voice."

"It's me, Daddy!"

"Who's me?"

"Tava!" she would squeal with pleasure.

"Aren't you my daughter?"

"Yep!"

"Well, I guess you'll have to sit on my lap and help me work." He would then push away from the desk and slap his huge legs and lift her onto his enormous lap.

They would spend the rest of the afternoon playing. Sometimes he would read to her. Other times they would draw together or make calls. It was perfect, she realized, absolutely perfect.

Her eyes opened and Z was there, his cold gray eyes piercing her, caressing her body. She felt dirty and wanted to vomit. It was obvious what he wanted but Tava was not going to give in. She'd almost let it happen with Hank and would not let it happen again. Even if she had to die, she would not let him come near her. No one was going to touch her body without her consent ever again.

She curled up into a ball and pushed herself away to the other side of the bed. Her voice was soft but unmistakably strong willed.

"Don't even think about it. You can kill me if you want but you're never going to touch me."

Z did not break eye contact with her. He crossed his legs and rested an elbow there. "I have an eye for beauty. I find yours shocking."

"My beauty is my own."

"Not if I say so."

"You can kick me and slap me and beat me up but you're not going to fuck me."

Z winced mockingly. "Such language. Where do you girls pick these things up? They are so offensive."

"I mean it."

"I can see that."

"Stay away from me."

Z took a deep breath and let it out slowly. "For now," was his only reply.

He reached for the phone and dialed Thomas's private number from memory. "Hello, Mr. Blackhurst. I hope you've been having a pleasant morning. It has been an exceptionally nice one for me. I have given this much thought over the evening and have come to a price. Your daughter is worth quite a lot to you. That is painfully obvious. Equally obvious is your wealth. Naturally I see a connection."

"Get on with it."

"Don't get short with me, Mr. Blackhurst. You can't afford that."

"I want my daughter back."

"And you can have her for one million dollars." Z was testing the waters. He was confident Thomas would pay a tremendous amount for Tava but did not know how high he was willing to go. Even in this business there was give-and-take.

Thomas did not hesitate. "Fine."

Z did not believe him. "This is not a joke, Mr. Blackhurst."

"I agree to your terms. I said I wanted my daughter back."

Z felt like a teenager again. A million dollars would put him over the top. He could retire. Z smiled to himself. This was more than he had hoped for. To think he had almost killed this girl for pennies. It was too incredible. "I want this in cash. You can imagine I am not interested in many people being there when we make the exchange. I have rented a cabin and we will meet there."

"Where is it?"

"I am not going to tell you just yet. How long to get the money?"

"I can have it in two days."

"You are an amazing man, Mr. Blackhurst. Hold one

moment, please." He covered the receiver. "What do you want?"

"I want to take a shower."

Z was too preoccupied with Thomas to think. He nodded his head quickly and released Tava from the thumbcuffs. Before he spoke he watched her cross into the bathroom. "Leave the door open."

Z returned to the call and in the background registered the shower's noise.

Tava moved quickly. She was holding her ratty red dress and quickly slipped into it. She did not have any shoes but that didn't worry her. Even Z's jacket was left on the floor near the bed. None of that mattered now. Tava watched Z's face and realized she had just been given her chance. The look he gave when her father accepted his one-million-dollar demand proved to Tava that money was the main weakness in men. Perhaps it was sex, but money drove people to murder. Greed was what it was all about.

Her opportunity handed to her, she took it without thinking. She was sure Z would not be this distracted again. Z was too volatile to trust and she was not about to wait for him to make all the moves.

It was self-preservation that propelled her. She turned on the shower and let the hot water kick up a healthy steam. She left the door partially open and heard Z talking to her father. They were working out the details of the transfer. As she hoped, there was a window above the toilet. She did not care about the noise. She trusted the water to cover her moves. She stood on the seat and wedged the window open. It was an old building and the windows simply slid sideways. There was barely enough room to slip out but Tava squeezed through without too much pain.

She rolled on the ground and scanned the area quickly. This time she was determined not to get caught. Without looking back she plunged into the woods driven with a blinding fear of Z.

Z realized the steam from Tava's shower was making the room damp. It was bothering him and he broke in on Thomas. "One moment, Mr. Blackhurst. I will be back shortly." He dropped the phone on the bed and moved into the bathroom. "Why do you have that damn thing on so hot?" He pulled the curtain back and found the stall empty. His eyes went instantly to the window. He slammed it open and searched for Tava. He cursed himself for letting her out of his sight. She was more spirited than he realized. "Goddamn women!" Then he remembered Thomas and the one million dollars.

Tava could not be far but he needed to move quickly. He found the phone and said, "I will be calling you back with the details. Please remember, Mr. Blackhurst, Tava is only alive because I say so. If you make one misstep, she is dead. I want your money but I do not want your hassles. Understood?"

"Understood. Just keep her safe."

"You do not have to worry, Mr. Blackhurst." Z hung up the phone, threw a towel around his waist, and ran for the front door. The morning was turning hot and cars drove by quickly on the two-lane highway in front of the motel. He scanned up and down the road and did not find Tava. Z was sure there was not enough time for her to catch a ride. He ran around behind the motel. He knew she would be scared. He knew she only had a few minutes and that meant she was desperate.

He searched the trees quickly and found a piece of her torn dress. "Tava, my dear, you are so predictable. I think that is why I am so infatuated with you." He knew she would not get far. He had enough time to get dressed and then go after her. He was so sure of himself, he started laughing. One million dollars was within his reach and he was not going to let it slip away.

Tava waited just long enough to watch Z follow her fake trail into the woods. With no time to think, she decided on a course of action. Avoiding the police, she planned on working her way back to Sultan Valley as soon as possible. It was now critical to get home. She needed to sneak into Buddy's house, recover the video, and turn herself in. She just couldn't allow this travesty to go any further.

For a brief moment she wavered. She desperately wanted to call her father. She wondered if she could find a place to hide long enough for Hans to come get her. As much as she wanted to call Thomas, she knew it was not a good plan. She did not know how long her ruse was going to work. She only had a few minutes and time was too precious to rely on her father. She had to solve the situation herself. Z already proved he was very good at tracking her down and Tava felt she could not take the chance.

Sitting there, with the birds chirping and the cars driving by, she realized she was running away from the problem, hoping blindly that it would just disappear. She was instinctively responding to her need for safety first. She was now doubly determined to take control of the situation and bring it to a close. Even if she had to turn herself in without the tape, she was going to do it. But first she was going to try to get it.

Tava watched a delivery truck swing in and circle in front of a café across the street. A bundle of papers were thrown on the door stoop and caused a cloud of dust to swirl up around the window. Tava felt drawn to the dirty pile. She needed information and felt cut off.

She quickly ducked inside the motel room and grabbed her shoes. She pulled them on and hurried out to the road. Watching for trucks, she moved across the burning asphalt and hurried up to the café door. A young boy was struggling with the pile of papers.

"Can I get one of those?"

"Sure," the boy smiled. He dropped the bundle and cut the binding string.

Tava realized she had no change. "I don't have any money."

The little boy squinted his eyes and looked behind him. "Well," he said, drawing out the word, "don't tell." He handed her the paper and disappeared inside.

"Thanks." She moved behind the café and leaned against the back wall. The front page jumped at her like a knife. Her eyes were riveted to her college graduation picture, again spread across the front page. It pictured her smiling without a care in the world. The photograph was only three months old and now seemed so faraway. Tava read the headline with trepidation: TAVA'S MOM SLEEPS WITH MURDERED MAN. Her eyes went wide.

Until now this had all seemed like a murky dream. Tava was living through the past hours half-believing that Hank's murder had never happened. It was a game she was playing with herself and now the truth was undeniable. She scanned the story and saw the pictures. "Well, Mother, now your fucking secret is out. This is so unfair," she said. It was disgusting and the news-hungry press was having a field day with it.

"I can't believe this," she breathed. She felt exposed. "All of this is for nothing. I hope you're happy, Mother."

It began to dawn on her that she was too vulnerable. With a press like this she was going to be spotted quickly. She had to get out of this little town. The press was making her and the Blackhurst family infamous in every small town in the state.

She threw the paper in a rusty can and scanned the parking lot for a ride. She couldn't be sure Z was going to believe her ruse for very long.

As much as she hated to do it, she was going to have to take a chance on a stranger again. She spotted a clean-cut, good-looking man topping off his tank and paying for the gas. She tried to make her cropped hair look as pleasing as possible and ran over to him.

"Excuse me."

"Yes?"

"I wonder if you could give me a ride?"

"Where are you heading?" The look on his face was mixed with pleasure and surprise. His face was rugged and handsome. His hair was short and well-groomed. He was wearing a white polo shirt and khaki shorts. Tava thought he looked about twenty-nine.

"I'm trying to get to Sultan Valley."

"Sounds like everybody's in Sultan Valley right now."

Tava hoped she wasn't blushing. "Really? Why?"

"Haven't you heard? There was this big murder. Everybody is talking about it."

"I just heard the mountains are pretty there."

"That's true. Well, I'll tell you, I'm not going straight there. I'm heading a little east. I could drop you close to there and you could catch a ride over the mountains."

"That'd be great."

"Let's go then." He slapped the gas flap closed and crossed around to the driver's seat. He noticed Tava's body. He liked the look of it. She had all the right curves and it piqued his interest. He didn't normally pick up poor girls but this one seemed all right. He hopped in behind the wheel and gunned the engine. "Come on. Get in. I don't bite."

"Great." Tava got in the passenger side, keeping an eye out for Z. She was ready to duck if she saw him.

"You look worried. Everything okay?"

"I didn't sleep well."

43

"Thank you all for coming. I know this was short notice." Buddy was dressed in an expensive Italian suit and he undid the jacket button. He was standing at the end of a long dark mahogany table. It was lined with the directors of Nicholls Development. "I don't have much time so we need to make this as brief as possible. As you all know, the unimaginable happened a short time ago. My father was murdered." He paused here to let the words sink in. "I know his greatest wish would be to keep this great company afloat through these turbulent times. That is why, after great thought, I am assuming the controls."

The five other men around the table shuffled. One, a gray-haired, sixty-year-old named Harrington, pounded his fist on the table. "That is outrageous, son. What do you know about running a company? My God, the impudence! First you boot Larry out of his office and now you come up with this hare-brained scheme."

Buddy turned to Larry. "That was my father's office and it stays in the family. I'm sure you don't have a problem with that, do you, Larry?"

Larry squirmed in his chair. He was a meek man, more an accountant than a leader, and he acquiesced. "I don't have a problem with that, Buddy. I would ask that you listen to the board though. That is why we are here. To keep Nicholls

Development alive. Thomas Blackhurst is continuing to make a play for us. Even after all of this!"

"I know."

Another older gentleman spoke up. "It hits me kind of funny that your father isn't even cold and you're making your own play for his job."

Buddy glared. He was absolutely still and smoldering inside. He knew these men would cause resistance. He glanced at his watch and realized he needed to be on his plane back to Sultan Valley in one hour. It was time. "All right. Let's make this quick." He picked up the phone and asked the secretary to let his lawyer in.

The wide doors swung open and a little bald man with an enormous mustache waddled in. He smiled at the group and took his place next to Buddy. He wore a rumpled white suit and his tie was askew. He opened his ancient leather briefcase and pulled out a stack of papers. He took some time in finding the one he desired. Once in hand he found the page he needed and cleared his throat. He glanced at Buddy for permission to speak. Buddy nodded. "Good morning, gentlemen. You all know me but, for the record, let me say my name is George Cove and I am Hank's lawyer. And as a result also Buddy's. Buddy asked me to come in to read you this. It's Hank's will." Again he cleared his throat. "To my son, I leave all my shares in Nicholls Development in the hopes that with it he will grow and with guidance, lead my company to greater heights."

The board shook their heads.

"I don't believe it," one of them said.

George piped in. "Hush up. There's more. 'My entire shares of Nicholls, while not widely known, consist of over forty percent. The man who controls my shares controls Nicholls'."

Buddy stopped George. "There it is, men. I control Nicholls. My father, in his quiet way, bought up as much of the outstanding shares in this company as he could. It was his baby and he wanted to see it run his way. Well, his way is my way and it gives me great pleasure to relieve all of you of your duties. George is helping round up a new, younger board to drive this company to greatness. You guys are just deadweight."

"You can't do this," a voice protested.

"Yes, I can, can't I, George?"

"Sorry, gentlemen. Buddy can do whatever he wants. He controls Nicholls. Hank called just before he died and asked me to purchase as many shares as possible. I did that. I believe it was his defense against Blackhurst. In any case, Buddy has the legal right to fire all of you and that is what he is doing. Sorry." George packed up his suitcase and left.

Buddy smiled at all of them. "My father appreciated all you did for him and you will all be treated fairly. Thank you for your years of service. Now, if you'll excuse me, I have a plane to catch. I should be back in a couple of weeks. As soon as they catch this Tava bitch. Have your offices cleared out by the end of the month." With that he buttoned up his jacket, collected his folder, and left.

On his way out he stopped at his secretary's desk. "Keep me posted. Those bastards will probably try something."

"Yes, sir, Buddy."

"No, Gloria. Not Buddy. *Mr.* Nicholls. You have my number."

44

The sun was beginning to drop below the trees. The sky was still deep blue but the sun was starting to allow the trees to cast long shadows across the road.

They were going eighty-five miles an hour through the curvy mountain passes. Tava gripped her door handle until her knuckles were white.

"My name is Aaron." When he spoke, he turned his head to look at her. His teeth were sparkling white. "How come a pretty girl like you is traveling all by herself?"

Tava fought for control of her stomach. "I like it alone. I don't have to worry about anyone that way."

"So you don't have any family?" He grinned widely as he

took the car into a sharp bend. The car swayed and tried to hold the road. It barely made it around as the car's tires squealed for traction. "I hope this doesn't bother you. I know what I'm doing."

"No. My folks are dead and I was an only child."

"Well, that's okay. So no one knows you're traveling out here, huh?"

"Not really."

"You don't mind my driving, do you? I like putting this to the test."

"It's fine by me." She tried to loosen her grip on the handle.

"I like to get where I'm going. You're not from around here, right?"

"Uh-huh."

"You don't mind if I take the scenic route, do you? You'll get to see some beautiful country."

Tava's senses sprang to life. "I don't know. I've got to get to Sultan Valley."

"It won't add any more time. It's just a more interesting way." He raised his eyebrows as if to suggest something, and Tava did not like it.

"Well, I don't know . . ."

Before she could finish, he jammed on the brakes and threw them into a controlled spin. White smoke spewed from underneath the tires and made a horrible screeching sound. It was like a high-pitched scream. The car jackknifed and before Tava realized what was happening Aaron was shooting the car over a narrow wooden bridge and into a clump of trees. A dirt road snaked its way through the towering stand of trees as the car hurtled dangerously between them. Aaron was laughing.

"What is this all about?!" Tava demanded.

He continued to laugh in a high, raspy sound. It seemed very guttural and Tava cringed. "I told you. This is the pretty way. Pretty ways for pretty girls. Hold tight. It tends to get a little bumpy." He had to yell over the whine of the engine.

The car bumped and thrashed over roots and gravel. The road was an old logging trail. Tava closed her eyes and prayed, not for the first time. Her sense of God was an emotional one. She felt the presence all around her, in the trees, the people. She prayed now to that energy to get her through this. This ordeal was beyond a nightmare and she had no idea when it was going to end. She prayed for peace. She prayed for a quiet place where she could hide, with Michael, and shut out the world. She fantasized about being the only person left on the earth, far away from danger and vicious people. She wanted all of this to be over!

Aaron was pushing the car beyond its limits. It sounded like it was going to explode. It was a sound that pushed its way into Tava's head. She tried to block it out but found she couldn't. He kept the pace up for an eternity. The setting sun was completely lost in the dense forest. As they sped on Tava could see the small patches of blue sky turn to crimson and then to black. The car lights were on and its two beams lit the road ahead of them.

Tava was losing her sense of time. It seemed late. Aaron hadn't said anything for a long time. He had also stopped staring at her. For the first two hours he had kept sneaking glimpses of her. She decided to ignore him and stare out the window. At one point she thought of jumping from the car but it was too dangerous. The trees were so close and the road so rocky that she would surely die if she tried it. She wondered when the hypnotic whine of the engine was going to end. They were now very deep into the forest. Lost, for all Tava knew, and driving in the direction of the moon. It shone brightly and hung low, bobbing in the distance every time the car crested a small hill.

Finally, the motor wound down. Tava was aware of her teeth gnashing and felt the pain of her aching jaw. It was a dull ache that matched the rest of her body. Tava's limbs felt drugged. Her body was giving out on her. She was too run-down.

Aaron brought the car to a slow crawl. He seemed to be looking for something. His eyes were scanning the tree line. He finally found what he was looking for after ten minutes. "There it is," he murmured to himself, "right on track." He turned the engine off and let the car glide to a halt. "Everybody out." His voice was still bubbly. He appeared driven by inner voices. He hopped out and popped open the trunk. He reached inside and pulled out a duffel bag. Leaving the trunk open, he moved around to Tava's door and tugged it open. "Come on, honey. Everybody out."

Tava tried to stay calm. She had no energy and that scared her. If she had to run, it would be impossible. She had no idea what he was doing but knew it couldn't be good. "What are we doing, Aaron? I've got to get to Sultan Valley."

"Little detour is all. I wanted to show you this." Using his thumb, he motioned to the trees. "In there. Come on." He started moving toward a dark clump.

Tava stood her ground. "What's in there?"

"A surprise."

"I'm not in the mood for surprises. Please. I'd just like to go."

Aaron was puzzled. He shook his head and finally in a huff unzipped his bag. He pulled out a gun and pointed it at her. "Look," he said matter-of-factly, "this is a gun. I don't want to use it but if you don't come with me, I'm going to have to. It's your choice."

Tava breathed in despair. "Not you too."

Aaron was taken over by his inner voices and pushed Tava into the trees. He kept saying, "It's right up here. Keep going."

Her last step brought her through the trees and onto a rocky precipice. She lost her breath and reached behind her for something sturdy to hold onto. Her hand found a branch and only then could she take in the nighttime magnificence. She was overlooking a water-filled gorge, stretching the length of two football fields. Its dark, mysterious waters lay two hundred feet below her. Tava was standing on a cliff with a commanding view of the entire lake. The height made her uneasy. The sheer enormity of what lay beneath her was overwhelming. The moon shone brightly and lit up the surface like glimmering ice. The moon's white reflection was mirrored perfectly in the still, calm waters of the lake.

"So? What do you think? It's beautiful, huh?"

His voice made her wary again. "It's amazing," she whispered.

"I love it here." And then without a pause, "Take your clothes off." He was standing to Tava's left. His voice was shaking from the excitement he felt. The gun was still in his hand and now pointing at her.

Tava knew screams would do nothing. Survival was the key. She knew she had to comply if she wanted to get out of this. Doing this now was better than bleeding to death from a bullet wound. Tava did not want to die and she was going to do whatever it took to survive.

She stepped out of her shoes and reached behind to unzip the red dress. She pulled it off and dropped the bundle at her feet. Tava kept her eyes on Aaron. He was grinning. The smile on his face was indescribable. His eyes told her what to do and she removed her bra. Standing now in her panties, she felt a stillness. Everything seemed superreal and moved in slow motion. She brushed the hair from her face and even managed a smile. "What do you think?"

"You're really pretty. You like my lake?"

"Yes, I do."

"Take the rest of it off."

She did as she was told.

"Now, throw your clothes over the side."

Tava kept her voice low and nonthreatening. "Can't I keep them?"

"Nope."

She gathered her clothes and moved over to the edge of the cliff. She threw them over and her bra caught on a root sticking out of the face of the cliff. The rest of the clothes tumbled down and hit the water far below.

"Now, come over here." Tava walked over to him. "That's far enough." With his free hand he dug into his pocket and pulled out an army knife. He held it out for her. "Take it."

She did.

"Now, open the tiny blade. Slowly."

She did.

"All right. Now, cut your finger."

Tava hesitated only for a moment. She was playing for her life. The gun reminded her of that. She slit her middle finger at the head. The thin line immediately turned red and blood began to flow. It burned terribly and Tava dropped the knife as she struggled with the stabbing, hot pain.

"Get on your knees and hold your finger out."

Tava knelt on the crackling, dry needles on the forest floor. Aaron moved slowly over, keeping the gun trained on her. He bent down, steadied her upheld hand with his, and licked the blood. His hot tongue slid around her bleeding finger and he finished by sucking on it. He finally straightened and backed away.

"Spread your legs."

Tava sat back and did as she was told.

"Lie down and turn your head toward the water." His voice was harsh and cold. Tava acquiesced. Aaron knelt down close to her. With his smooth, long fingers he touched her. "How's that feel?"

Tava couldn't speak.

"I asked you a question." He dug the gun into her neck.

"Feels good," she said quietly. There were no tears now, just blind anger. She wanted him dead.

"You girls never say anything different, for Christ's sake! What's wrong with you?"

"Just tell me what you want me to do."

"Stand up!" Tava did not move fast enough and he hauled her up by her short hair. "Walk to the edge over there and close your eyes."

This was it. Her moment never came. She was expecting him to falter, give her some moment to either attack or get away. But now, it was over. He was going to push her over. His twisted mind got off on young women's blood and then he killed them. God knows how many women lay at the bottom of the lake.

"Please, Aaron. You don't want to do this."

"Don't ruin it." His face was now angry. "Stand up and get over to the edge. You're goin' to love this, baby. We're goin' to do it up against that tree." He pointed at a large tree very near the edge of the cliff.

"No."

He brought the gun down across her face and knocked her over. The pain was immense and she immediately felt the swelling. She could feel a small chip from her cheekbone sliding underneath the skin.

"You're all alike! I didn't want to do that. Why do you always make this difficult? Walk over there or I'll shoot you."

It was with a terrified step that Tava moved closer to the rocky edge. There must be some way of getting out! How?

A small tuft of rock loosed underneath her feet and tumbled down the cliff wall.

"Close your eyes. And put your back against the tree."

She did. Her mind was racing. The voice inside her head was screaming, "Run! Get away!"

Aaron inched up toward her. "Keep those eyes closed!" His right hand touched her breasts and moved to her neck and held her there. He undid his pants with his free hand and dropped them around his ankles.

Tava recoiled from his touch. This was it! "No!" she yelled. "No!" With a sudden burst of desperation she spun violently and knocked the gun from his hand. She struck out violently at him and caught him in the stomach. He was too surprised to compensate and stumbled backward. With one quick step she kicked him in the crotch and he yelled out in excruciating pain.

"Fuck you!" she yelled. "Die, you motherfucker!" She kicked him again and he spit up blood. "How does it feel? How does this feel, Aaron?" She continued to kick him until he stopped moving. She collapsed near the edge and buried her face in her hands. She was sobbing and could not stop the flow of tears.

A loud explosion filled her ears. She saw Aaron's body jerk once and fall silent. She looked around wildly and found Z. He had his gun trained on her.

"Is this what you want? Guns and killing?" He was seething with anger. "I will not be made a fool! Stand up!"

Tava dragged herself to her feet and stood there silently. She was beyond fear now and simply a wasted, empty shell. She waited for his next command.

"Drag the body to the edge there. Now." He emptied another shot into Aaron's dead body. It jerked and fell back again.

Tava grabbed the body by the foot and dragged it over to the cliff. She knew he was dead and liked it. She was sick to discover so much hate in her soul but was truly happy to have Aaron gone.

"Dump it over the side."

Tava pushed Aaron to the edge and with a kick of her foot sent the body tumbling down the cliff. She watched it bounce against the rocky sides and hit the water with a huge splash. She turned back to Z. She knew in her heart she couldn't go on. She had done her best to get away from this man but he was just too good for her. She shook her head silently. She was giving up. She had no energy left to fight him.

"I can't take this anymore, Z. I'm lost." In her heart she

felt nothing but coldness. She started to see stars. She was growing dizzy and swayed dangerously close to the edge.

"Come away from the cliff."

"I'm too tired, Z. I can't stand this anymore," she murmured and lost her balance. In that fleeting moment her eyes flew open and the moon blinded her. Life was at a standstill. She was falling backward and could not stop herself. She was terrified but gave into the sensation. She lost her footing and went over only to be caught by Z. She slammed against the cliff wall directly below the edge. The water lay below her, lapping against the rock wall.

She was dangling by one arm. The grip on her wrist was an unflinching vise grip. The impact knocked the air out of her and she was losing consciousness. She was gasping for air. She felt like her lungs were going to explode. The last thing she remembered was being hauled up and the scraping sound her naked body made against the cold, sharp rocks.

45

Hans and Michael were continuing to search for Tava at Thomas's insistence. Z was being too evasive and Thomas wanted to cover all of his bases. The two younger men were getting closer. They tracked Jake's old truck to the motel and confirmed Z's description with the old woman. It matched the one Jake gave them. They both smelled the scent and it was making them anxious to find her. At least she was still alive.

Their search led them to the newspaper boy who said he'd seen Tava but by herself. Hans believed Tava had escaped and that realization finally led them to the gas station.

"Excuse me. We're trying to find a young woman. We were told you might have seen her."

The attendant was a stodgy old goat with bright eyes. "I ain't seen no one."

Michael showed him a photograph of Tava. "You sure? She would have looked something like this. Probably a little dirtier."

"You deaf? I told you, I ain't seen no one." He walked away from them into the office.

They followed.

Michael waited for the man to turn around, grabbing him by the throat. He shoved him against the wall and held him there. The pressure was just enough to scare the hell out of the little guy.

"I'm choking!"

"No, but you will be if you don't help," Michael said. "I want to know where she is."

"Michael, maybe he's telling the truth."

"Look at his eyes. They tell everything. He knows something." Michael squeezed a little harder. "What do you know?"

"Nothin'! Leave me alone!" The man tried to squirm free but Michael was too much for him.

Hans pulled a wad of money from his back pocket. "Maybe you'll remember for five hundred dollars."

His eyes went wide, "Get the goon offa me."

Michael threw him into the corner. The little guy stumbled into the brooms and landed on his butt. Hans stuffed the money in the man's breast pocket. "That's for your trouble. Where did she go?" He kept his voice low.

The scrawny fingers riffled through the cash. His eyes kept darting from Michael to Hans to the money. "All right. She left with a local guy named Aaron. He's kinda creepy. She said something about wanting to get to Sultan Valley. Aaron said he'd give her a ride."

Michael grew excited. "She might be home."

Hans cut him off. "What else, little man?"

"Nothing. That's it."

Hans moved to punch him and he cowered. "All right! Jesus. There's a lake he takes his ladies to. He showed it to me once. About three hours from here. Way out in the woods. He takes 'em there, you know, to play." The man offered a dirty smile. "I guess that's what he had in mind."

"How do we get there?"

* * *

252

Hans and Michael found the cutoff with some difficulty. The drive through the trees was maddening. The tire marks were like an arrow pointing them in the right direction.

The bumpy road seemed to last forever and then the car came into sight. It was empty and the trunk was open. It did not take long to find the path that led them to the lake. With Hans's gun drawn they entered the clearing and found it empty.

The sun was blazing. The heat on the lake shimmered like heat waves against the sand. Michael watched Hans drop to his knees and run his long, strong fingers through the needles of the forest floor. He was silent except for his breathing and was concentrating intently on the search.

"Blood."

"What does that mean?" Michael asked. The thought of blood made him cringe. He was very near to losing his composure. He had to know Tava was alive. Without Tava he was nothing. So much lay ahead for them. So many unspoken dreams that he wanted to share with her. Tava was his life and without her he was lost.

"Control yourself." Hans heard the tone in Michael's voice. The last thing he wanted was hysterics. "There is not much. That must be a good sign."

"Tava, please be all right." He turned away and sat down, dangling his feet over the precipice. His attention was caught by Tava's bra hanging off the root. "Look at this!" His voice grew excited.

Hans joined him at the cliff. "It must be hers." He reached down and snagged it between the tips of his fingers. He examined it. "Smell it."

Michael did as he was told and breathed in deeply. It was very faint, but he smelled her. "It's there. That's Tava's scent." He searched the water two hundred feet below. As much as he prayed not to find her, he had to keep looking. Suddenly his eyes caught the body and he pulled back with a gasp. "Oh my God. Look."

It took them an hour to find a way down the rocky walls. Once they reached the body, they found Aaron facedown, pasty white and bloated. Hans checked the body for any telltale signs and found two bullet holes. They searched for Tava and found no more signs of her.

"She's still alive." It was the only logical conclusion Hans could come to. "She must be. They struggled and must have gone over, and Tava pulled herself back up."

"Now what?" Michael asked.

"Continue the search. If she is alive, then she can be found. There is always a clue. At least we know we are close."

46

It was like a groggy dream from which she could not wake. She fought for consciousness but her body was denying it to her. The pictures she saw were blurry and gray. She tried to make shapes out of them but couldn't. She finally gave up and drifted back into sleep.

Six hours later it was the sound of a door closing quietly that woke her from her reverie. As she regained consciousness she became aware of her sore body. Her entire right side was scraped and bruised. She touched her swollen cheek and recoiled from the sharp sting. She was facing a stone wall. She slowly rolled over and found herself in a one-room shack. The windows were covered but sun sneaked through. A table and two chairs were to her left in front of a makeshift kitchen. A bucket of water acted as the sink and a small Coleman gas stove stood on its spindly wire legs. The walls were thin and wooden.

With great difficulty she pushed herself into a sitting position and the blanket rolled down around her waist. She felt the harsh canvas against her sensitive breasts and realized she had been sleeping on an army surplus cot. It was hard and unyielding. She shook the sleep from her head and tried to get her bearings. She was still unsteady. She remembered hearing a door close but found no one inside.

She sat there. There was nothing else she could do. She had no energy. The long sleep had sapped it from her. She kneaded her sore arm and ran her hand lightly over the red scratches along her side. She was still naked.

Ten minutes passed and Tava finally heard footsteps approaching. She thought about pretending to sleep and then decided not to. She felt her body tense as the door slid open. Her hands used the blanket to cover her bare skin. A gloved hand appeared and was followed by a man dressed in black leather. It was Z.

His voice was barely above a whisper but she caught every word. "You're awake." Tava nodded her head yes. "Good. You slept a very long time. Do you know how angry you made me?" He dug in a brown bag and pulled out a newspaper. "You're a star. I had no idea you were becoming so famous. You should see the papers. You are all over them."

"Where are we?"

"Do you realize how many people are looking for you? I should ask for two million from your father."

"How did I get here?"

"I brought you here."

"Where are my clothes?"

"You weren't wearing any when I saved you. You won't be needing them anyway." He drew up a chair opposite Tava and sat down. "I am glad to see you are all right. I consider you my prized little cow. I want you all fattened for auction."

"No." Her memory came back and she remembered Aaron. "Where is . . ."

"You pushed him over the cliff. Remember? He almost took you with him if it hadn't been for me. But you're safe now."

"My God."

"God doesn't have much to do with this." Tava shrank back. "You are quite beautiful." She did not say anything. "Surely you must be hungry." He reached behind him and pulled out an apple. "For you."

"How can you just kill people?"

"It comes quite easily after a time. The money is very good." He paused for a moment to watch her. "You have a wonderful, wild quality. Has anyone ever told you that?"

"Fuck you." Tava was at the end of her rope. Now she did not care. If all of this was going to work out for her, fine. If she was going to die, that was all right too. She was through being the wilting flower. It did not pay to be meek. If she was going to die, it was going to be with courage. "Did you hear me? Fuck you, slime."

"Surprisingly spirited. I wouldn't have thought. With all of that blue blood. I had you pegged for someone far more docile." Z was wearing a satisfied smile. "I appreciate that in a woman. You had me going, back at the motel. The fabric on the branch was a nice touch. I probably spent an hour or so tromping around the backwoods looking for you. I do appreciate your amateur attempts."

"Well, appreciate this." She flipped him off. He only laughed and then, with an uncanny quickness, grabbed the finger and pulled Tava onto the floor at his feet. He kept his smile on the entire time. "You are a little kitten. I eat kittens. Don't forget that." He let her go and she hurried back to her cot, the fire of independence still burning in her belly.

"Fuck you anyway."

With that he let out a belly laugh. "You are a joy," he roared.

"Real funny."

"Hysterical as a matter of fact." He contemplated her for several moments. "Your body is perfect. When I tucked you in, I marveled that such a thing of beauty could be caught up in something so ugly as this. How did you get into Buddy Nicholls's affairs?"

"I was doing someone a favor. I don't want to talk about it."

"Fine. Then make love to me."

"You too? Just spread my legs and let you in? You guys are all alike, aren't you? One right after the other. I can't believe it."

"Is that a yes or a no?" He crossed his arms across his thick chest.

"What if I say no?"

"Let's find out."

Tava considered her options. The man was crazier than Aaron in his own way. "How'd you find me?"

"You're a novice. Novices leave all sorts of juicy clues.

There was a very helpful gas station man who saw you leave. It's amazing how a few dollars can get people talking. Your friend apparently was known for his eccentricities."

"You probably would love it if I said no. You'd like the fight, wouldn't you?"

"Don't bait me, child. My temper rarely boils but when it does, I am not pleasant to be around."

"Oh, so you're gonna screw me and then give me back to my family, is that it? Huh? Is that all you want?" Tava was looking for survival now. Her fight for independence was clearing her head and helping her make rational decisions. "If that's all you want, fine. You can have it." She lay back on the cot and threw her blanket off. Her bruised body lay on display. "Come and get it." Her voice was bland. "What are you waiting for, big man? It's what you want, isn't it?"

Z was surprised to find Tava so cool. The few short days on the road were doing something to this girl and he had to be careful. He had traveled all over the world and been with many women but this one was something different. Barely an adult and yet so confident. Not the spoiled little debutante he was expecting. "Child . . ."

"Stop calling me that. You either want it or you don't. I'm too tired to play your stupid little games. Here," she pointed to her body, "it's all yours. Wake me up when it's over, fucker."

He desired her. He found her body so perfect. Her skin was smooth and milky white. Her muscles taut and sinewy. He found her breasts round, lovely and firm. He wanted to touch her. "I have wondered to myself over these past few days what it would be like to touch you." He was craving a taste of her. She was a frightened innocent in a deadly game and that excited him. "In different circumstances I would ask you to be my lover."

Tava closed her eyes. This was more than she could bear. For all of her bravado she was terrified. She had only ever been with Michael and Hans and they had both been so tender. Hank was an animal and had thankfully never fulfilled his twisted desires. She couldn't imagine having this man inside her. But, he was volatile. She could sense his desire and to antagonize him would be stupid and meaningless. She had to survive. However she could.

He stroked her hair and held it in his tight fists. He kissed

Tava's neck. He tried to deny himself. And still his desire fought him. Her neck was so soft and warm, he could not hold back. "I thought I could deny myself but apparently I can't."

He was on top of her quickly. He left his clothes on and only undid his fly. His shirt became untucked. Tava shut her eyes tight and closed her mind. With each thrust Tava cringed silently. He was harsh against her. She was dry and the friction was uncomfortable. Tears of anger squeezed out between her closed eyelids. Her teeth were clenched and she refused to accept this man. He was dead to her. He meant nothing. What he was doing meant nothing. Tava was fighting him with her will. He was too much for her physically, but mentally she was the victor. There was nothing he could do to her that was going to touch the real Tava. Deep down, her soul was still clean.

Her arms touched against his sweaty sides. She was revolted by his rhythm. He was pushing farther and deeper. His frequency increased and he was going wild. He seemed possessed. She held her breath for the inevitable. Her hands were closed tight. Her entire body was a defense against this man. He was close now and she just wanted it to be over.

Finally he erupted inside her and collapsed. His wet body was like a deadweight. He climbed off her and did his fly up. Tava kept her eyes closed, pretending it had never happened. She was not going to let this affect her. It was simply what needed to be done. She shut her mind down and pretended to sleep.

Later, she opened her eyes to find him emptying his grocery bag onto the table.

"I bought these," he said, "at a little store." Tava could see his satisfied smile. "You must be hungry."

"I would like to wear something, please." Her voice was subdued.

"No. There is nothing. You will stay that way."

"Fine. Then I want to clean myself."

"Just like a woman. You will find the necessities around back."

She stood up. She felt stiff and in deep pain. Her sores ran deep. She pulled the blanket around her and moved for the door.

"Leave the blanket."

"I'm going outside."

"Leave the blanket."

She dropped the blanket where she stood and opened the small door. The light streamed in around her. Its warmth felt good against her skin. Her eyes were momentarily blinded by the sun's intensity. It took a moment for them to clear and for her to gain her balance.

They were on a hill. The land swept down in front of her and lost itself amongst trees. The woods were dense around the cabin. She tried to get a bearing on where they were but it was impossible. She scanned the trees for more shacks but could not find any. She listened for any sign of life and was only greeted by the tweeting sounds of a bird at play. She saw a Chevy parked near the cabin. It was a huge cruiser with fat tires and an enormous engine. She wondered where the keys were.

"Hurry up," he called behind her.

She moved behind the wood shack. The needles on the ground stung her feet. She felt exposed out in the open. Z was clever in keeping her naked.

Tava found the outhouse. It was a dingy, rotting little shack with a hole in the ground. A roll of toilet paper hung from a rusty hook. She closed the flimsy door and relieved herself. As she pulled on the roll of paper the hook pulled from its loose base and landed at her feet. She went to put it back and realized it looked something like an ice pick. A thought came to her.

"I can't," she whispered to herself. She wanted to talk herself out of what she knew she had to do. Time was too short. She knew it. Her father would pay anything to get her back but Tava could not wait. She needed to escape now or he might want to do it again.

"Tava, how can you?" she asked herself. She was running on automatic now. The little spike was thin and rusty. Its bottom was bent and Tava fit it between her index and middle finger. It stood three inches above her knuckles.

"Just do it." That's all she had to say to herself. She did not question the voices inside her. They were guiding her now and she trusted them. Life was too short to be a slave. He deserved this for violating her.

Tava wiped the perspiration from her brow. She called out

to him. Her heart was pounding in her ear. "Hey! There's something in here!" she screamed, knowing it would draw him out. She listened for him.

"What's the problem?"

She heard him running toward the outhouse. "Something in here. I think it's a snake or something!"

"Come out."

"I can't move!"

She heard him laugh. "Why are all women scared of little bugs?" He threw the door open. Tava missed her timing and lunged too soon. The tiny spike embedded in his left shoulder. He staggered as she pushed out past him. He fell backward, clutching his bleeding shoulder and yelling like a wounded tiger.

"Come back here, you little bitch!"

Everything seemed unreal to her. Like tunnel vision the road down the hill was the only thing she saw. She ran as fast as she could without looking back. It wound down in a twisty path between the trees. The sun flashed its long arms around her as she went. She began to feel an exhilaration. She ran faster. As soon as she hit the road, she could flag down the nearest car and get to a police station. She would give herself over to them.

Tava couldn't feel the rough ground beneath her. It was as if she had lost all sensitivity. The only thing she heard was her own reassuring voice telling her she was making it. The wind whipped around her body and urged her on.

Her eyes caught a paved road in the distance. She saw a car speed by. She was safe! She doubled her efforts.

She was gaining now. The road was within fifty feet. Just a few more seconds and she would be home free. Just a few more moments! Sound was returning to her. She could hear cars passing by and the sound of birds again. Also the sound of her panting breath. She never moved so fast. Her body was beginning to scream from the pain.

And then he caught her.

They landed in an agonizing ball. She struggled against him, trying to break free but he only slapped her down. With one vicious blow to her head, he knocked her unconscious. He collapsed on top of her, still struggling to pull the spike from his shoulder.

47

Thomas was in the police station. He was livid. "Why can't you find my daughter? Everybody's having a field day!"

"I know. I'm sorry. We are looking everywhere for her. We think maybe she's left the state. Have you heard from her?"

"Nothing. If she's seen the paper, she's probably too terrified to come in."

"Every police person in this state is looking for her and I'll be serious. They're going on the assumption that she's dangerous."

"This is ludicrous."

"Ludicrous or not, it is real. The best thing to do is get her in here where we can protect her. No telling what's going on out there."

Jack's attention was drawn to the front lobby. Someone was kicking up a huge commotion. "Excuse me a sec." He hurried out front.

Buddy was yelling at the sergeant on duty. "What kind of little shit hole is this? I want some justice, for Christ's sake. My father's murderer is running around free and now you people don't give a damn. You're like the Keystone Kops!"

"What's the problem here, gentlemen?"

The sergeant spoke up. "Captain, Mr. Nicholls seems to think we're not doing our job very well."

"Is that right, young man?"

"Young man? Shove that shit . . ."

"You're going to have to lower your voice, son. I don't like to yell." Jack was not impressed with this skinny southern loudmouth. His personality was growing more severe. Jack couldn't quite put his finger on it but there was something about him, something that didn't quite fit. "You just calm yourself down. My people are the best and if you have a complaint, fill out the paperwork and we'll get on it."

"I can't believe this. You people are a joke."

"Hold on there now." Jack was getting angry. This boy was pushing just a little too far. "I don't appreciate your tone of voice. Your money doesn't buy you any special favors, my boy. You keep that in mind. You're just a little snot-nosed kid in my book."

"I'm going to sue your ass for negligence! This all has to do with favoritism. Little Tava Blackhurst kills my father and you all sit around here protecting her!" Buddy was riding a wave of indignation and anger. This was not going to get him anywhere. It might even ruin his tenuous advantage. He had to control himself. "I'm sorry." He lowered his voice. "I'm sorry. You and your men are doing a good job. I appreciate that."

"I understand the pressure. Now, what're you yelling about?"

"Someone threw a rock through my front window. I think someone's out to get me."

"We'll send someone around. It might just be kids. There's some resentment with all of this. The Blackhurst girl is popular around here."

"Popular or not, the little bitch killed my father."

Thomas came out of the office just in time to hear Buddy slur Tava. His rage overcame him. Like a madman he lunged for Buddy. He had the young man by the collar before Buddy could duck. Thomas grabbed him by the hair and drove his fist into Buddy's face. Buddy screamed for help.

Jack let Thomas hit Buddy two more times before pulling him off. It took two of them to drag him off. Buddy's nose was bleeding.

"What? Are you fucking crazy?" Buddy yelled. "I'm going to sue your ass off."

Thomas was fuming. "You ever call my daughter that again and I'll kill you."

Jack tried to hush him, "Thomas! Stop that!" His voice was a warning and Thomas backed off.

"Don't threaten me, old man." Buddy warned. "You don't know what you're dealing with."

"I know exactly what I'm dealing with, you little fucker.

You killed your old man and you know it. As far as I can tell, you greedy little son of a bitch, you're having one hell of a good time since he's gone."

"I don't have to take this." Buddy stood up. "Don't push me, Thomas."

"I'm going to sink you! I was considering withdrawing my offer but not now. I'm going to run you into the fucking ground!"

"Never happen. I took control of the board! You don't have a chance."

"You want to see? Fine. You want to see how good I am? Watch this." Thomas's eyes were flaring. Each word was like a knife into Buddy. "Eight hours ago you were in Houston and you fired the entire board. George Cove read the will and it turns out old Hank left you with forty percent of his company. That was stupid. He had his faults but at least he had a passion for his company. God knows what you have a passion for.

"You got forty percent of the company. That makes you a very rich man. But guess what? That means there's sixty percent of your company just sitting out there for me. And it's mine. Just stand back and watch, little boy, because by this time tomorrow I am going to own that company, and the first thing I'm going to do is throw you out on your ass!"

"Try it!"

"Consider it done." Thomas's voice was low now and threatening. "Makes you kind of nervous, doesn't it? You know I can do it."

"Screw yourself!" Buddy turned and fled from the station. He doubted Thomas could move that quickly but it made him nervous. Buddy needed to mount a defense, and he would have to get his people moving on it tonight.

Jack urged Thomas into a seat. "Calm yourself, Tom. It's not worth it."

"You're thinking the same thing I am, aren't you?"

Jack thought for a moment and nodded yes. "Thinking it and proving it are two totally different things, my friend. Everything points to Tava and you know it. I know she didn't do it and I think I know who did, but how do we show it?"

"So what can we do? I swear to God, Jack, I'm near my

end. My baby's out there. God knows what's happening to her. It's tearing me apart. I swear to God I want to kill that son of a bitch but I can't!" Thomas did not plan on breaking down and he was fighting it very hard. Tava needed him to be strong but the pressure was mounting.

Jack could see the anguish in the man's face. It broke his heart to see such a good man dragged through the media pit. He was convinced now that Buddy had done the killing, but he needed the proof. And until Tava was found, nothing could be done. He made a mental note to watch Buddy from here on out. The boy was becoming irrational and could become dangerous.

Jack felt impelled to do something for Thomas. He was a friend for many years and to see him broken like this was too much. "We're going to watch him. You don't have to worry about that. And we're going to find Tava. It's just a matter of time."

"Time is not something I have, Jack." Thomas rose to his feet. "Just do what you can and make sure to keep that kid away from me." Thomas left the station quickly.

Jack watched him go and prayed that Tava was found soon. His little town was already a mess and the longer this dragged on, the more painful it was going to get.

48

The grocery store owner, a small man with a paunch and a beard, was speaking with the town deputy.

"I'm telling you I saw this man tackle a naked woman out on Highway Twenty-two. And it didn't look like they were having much fun."

"You've got a suspicious mind, Homer." The younger man laughed. He was clean shaven.

"I think you should check 'em out, Tim."

"Come on, Uncle Homer, it's almost midnight. I'm off duty in a few minutes."

"Now, you'd kick yourself if you found out this was something big. What if it's drugs or something? Ever think about that? Maybe it's coming in from Canada, or the Colombians are setting up a headquarters here. Come on, Tim."

"Homer, we get tourists here all the time."

"Not suspicious-looking ones. I'm gonna call the sheriff if you don't."

Tim laughed. "Don't do that. All right. My God. I'll drive by. Happy?"

"I'd feel better if you did. Thank you, boy."

Outside it was pitch-black and the crickets were chirping loudly. The forest was swaying gently in a warm breeze. It was night and a wolf was howling in the distance. It had been a long and grueling hunt and finally Hans was sure he was near the end. Hans signaled Michael to keep quiet and stay put. Hans was going to investigate.

Inside the cabin Z asked Tava, "How's your face?"

Tava was sitting on the cot again. Her head was still spinning from a few hours ago. The majority of the right side of her face was swollen and parts of it were blue. "Hurts like hell."

While Tava lay unconscious, Z had cleaned the wound in his shoulder and bandaged it tight with strips of the blanket Tava was using. He also took the time to bind her hands and feet behind her. She was positioned on her side, and every time she tried to move the knots pulled tighter.

Tava noticed Z moving stiffly. His shoulder obviously still hurt him. He caught her looking at him. "I'm sorry I missed your face," she spat.

"Fuck you too," he replied. Z was impatient but stopped himself from hitting her again. It was beneath him to let this girl get to him so much. "You cannot goad me anymore."

"When are you going to talk to my father?"

"Tomorrow, if I have anything to say about it."

A noise caught his attention. He turned down the kerosene lamp. It was casting an eerie glow in the small enclosure. He crept over to the curtained window and crouched down. He turned his trained ears to listen. He detected the sound of shoes against leaves and then nothing. The silence seemed to go on forever.

Hans watched the cabin lights dim. He froze and silently berated himself. He breathed calmly through his nose, careful to let the steam of oxygen escape slowly. He was absolutely still. If Tava was in there, her life might depend on his silence.

He stood there for ten minutes. It seemed like an eternity. Hans gained a respect for the stranger. He could sense a fellow professional. The patient wait was the sign of a master. Anybody else would have barged outside, brandishing a gun and yelling. This person was waiting. He was a patient man and patience was the number one skill in this profession. Hans knew Tava was in there. This proved it. He was now worried more than ever. Getting her out might be tougher than he expected.

Hans crept back into the forest. "She's in there."

"How do you know?"

"I know. And we are dealing with someone who knows his business. Get prepared. Listen very closely. It is now or never."

Tava watched Z move quickly. He turned the light up and dug into his duffel bag. He withdrew an enormous gun and checked the bullets inside. He had a full clip.

"It looks like we have company. You keep your head down and shut up."

"I don't hear anything."

"You wouldn't. Now, be quiet." He kept the light on but moved away from the door. He checked Tava's knots, made sure they were tight, and dragged a chair into the corner. He sat down and waited. His senses were alive. Everything in him told him there was someone out there. He did not have to see to know. Z was too experienced for that.

Tava closed her eyes. From where she lay, Z was almost out of her field of vision. If bullets really were going to start flying, she wanted to be as far down as possible. The idea made her sick. She had seen what they could do to a person and they terrified her.

Hans and Michael inched toward the house. A hundred

feet from the cabin they split. Hans maneuvered around the back. Michael crept closer, his body trembling from the anticipation. His palms were sweaty and he had trouble keeping his grip on the butt of the pistol. It felt foreign to him and ugly. He hated its weight and what it stood for. Yet it might be the only thing to save Tava.

Michael was frightened but he did not flinch from his duty. Getting Tava out safely was his only objective. He waited for Hans's sign. Finally it came. A quick gleam of a flashlight and then darkness again. Now came the count.

One.

Hans gauged the strength of the wood wall. He determined that with enough force he could push through. He needed enough speed though and that was worrying him.

Two.

Michael concentrated on his energy. He was going to need total control. This maneuver was going to require extreme agility and strength.

Three.

Michael took a deep breath and whispered to himself, "Whatever happens, Tava, I love you."

Go!

They converged on the house together; Michael in front and Hans in back.

With the speed of a sprinter Hans aimed for what he thought was the weakest part of the wall. He launched himself into the air, feetfirst, and kicked with all of his strength. The wood splintered under his force and gave way. He crashed through the flimsy wall and rolled.

At the same moment Michael started yelling and shooting in front.

When Hans entered, Z was shooting at the front door. That is what Hans was hoping for.

In one deft motion he scanned the room and found Z. In the split second Z was looking at the door, Hans sighted him and clipped off two shots.

They rang out loudly like cannon fire.

The first of the two bullets missed. The second caught Z directly between the eyes. His body quivered in spasms. The gun dropped from his hand. The extreme look of shock was a memory Hans would always carry with him. It was a look he would never forget. In a strange way he respected the man for his intelligence and it was with mercy that Hans pumped another bullet into Z, putting him out of his misery.

Michael stood frozen outside. His mind was racing too quickly to realize there was no sound coming from inside.

"Michael!" Hans called out. "Michael! It's all right. I'm going to open the door. Do you hear me?"

The tears in Michael's eyes were ones of terrified fear. He was flooded with the horrifying thought of Tava's death. He was too scared to look.

"Michael!"

"What?" he managed.

"I'm going to open the door. It's okay." Hans knew what the boy was going through. He knew it was the first time Michael had fired a weapon and he had to be very cautious. He eased the door open. "Put the gun down, Michael. It's all over."

"Is . . . is she dead?"

"No. She's alive."

Those were the words that broke the spell. Michael dropped the gun and ran for the door. He pushed past Hans into the cabin. When saw Tava, his elation turned to extreme concern. "My God, what did he do to you?" Michael rushed over to her. Hans handed him a knife and he cut the knots. He wanted to hug her but was afraid it would hurt her too much. "Honey, my God." He wept. His tears streamed down his face. He quickly cut Tava's ropes. After freeing her, he held her gently.

Tava was still in shock. The gunfire was deafening and it took her several minutes to dare open her eyes. When she found Michael and Hans looking at her, she was overcome. Like Michael she was overwhelmed with tears. All she could do was touch his face.

"Oh, Michael," she cried, "I thought I was going to die."

"It's okay. You're all right now." He kissed her lightly and helped her up. He draped his jacket over her shoulders. "Take it easy. You're safe now."

Her eyes found Hans. The Swede crossed over to her and held her chin delicately. "I am glad to see you."

She smiled wearily.

"We must go. Time is of the essence. The entire state is looking for you and they are getting a little anxious."

Hans holstered his gun and with Michael's help walked

Tava toward the door. Before they were out, she stopped them. She turned to face Z's body.

"Is he dead?"

"Yes."

Tava crossed over to the body. She only felt hate. She tapped his lifeless foot and spat on him. "I hope you're burning in hell." She turned and walked out the front door.

"Hold it right there!" Tim was petrified and thought he saw a gun in Hans's hand. "Drop it!"

All three stopped in their places immediately. Hans spoke calmly, "Everybody relax. Officer, my name . . ."

"I don't care what your name is! Don't move."

"I am just trying to explain . . ."

"Shut up!" Tim wavered. His backup was at least ten minutes away and this was the first time in his short career with the police force he had faced anyone with a gun. "Drop your gun. I'm not going to say it twice!"

Hans slowly opened his jacket and pulled the gun from its holster. He dangled it between his fingers and let it drop on the ground in front of him. He reassured the officer that they had every intention of turning themselves in. "We do not want any trouble, officer."

"Shut up." In the dark Tava looked like a wild woman with her hair frizzed and her face hidden in the dark shadows. Michael was supporting her. He looked desperate. "Throw 'em all down!"

Hans spoke softly, knowing the man was nervous. "We want to turn ourselves in."

Tim didn't hear him. He was sweating profusely. He needed his backups. "All right, everybody sit!"

Hans made the mistake of moving first. Tim thought Hans was going for the gun and fired.

Hans fell like a rock, letting out an audible grunt as he was hit. His body crumpled to the ground, completely still and awkwardly bent. Michael was stunned for a few short seconds and then he knew he had to get Tava out of there. Without a second thought, knowing that Hans would have wanted it this way, he locked his hand around Tava's and pulled her down the slope.

Tim stood there, petrified, watching Hans's body. The Swede did not move. Tim could not see any sign of life in the man and he was too scared to approach it as the sirens echoed in the distance. It was the first time he had ever shot someone and the effect left him sick. His own gun dropped from his hand and all he could do was watch, tongue-tied as Michael and Tava disappeared into the darkness of the thick woods.

The sirens spurred Michael on faster. The branches whipped at his face. He moved as if he were hunted. He never let go of Tava's hand. She was strangely quiet. He knew the quick movement must be killing her. Her body was one big sore. It hurt him to push her on but it was their only chance. They needed to get to safety. He had a vague idea of running for Sultan Valley. At least there he could get to Thomas.

As the moon reached its apex and shone its white light over the dense forest, the crackling sounds of two desperate lovers echoed softly as they pushed themselves farther into the backwoods.

49

"I don't want to hear your advice! This is personal and if you're not able to do it for me, then get out!" Thomas was screaming at Kim. She was furiously trying to convince him to give up the takeover of Nicholls Development.

"Thomas, you don't need this one. Jesus, Wall Street has already caught wind of it. They don't want to touch it with a ten-foot pole. Let it go, Thomas." She was calm and doing her best to keep Thomas from this silly move. He was breaking his number one rule: never get emotionally involved. "Please. My God, you can go after anything you want, why this one? You don't need it."

"I know I don't need it. But I'll tell you something. That little shit is in it up to his neck. I can feel that and it's driving me crazy. I think he's done this to keep the company. I know it! I can sense the greed coursing through the little weasel's veins and it's killing me! I'm taking this kid down, and I'm going to do it now." He checked his watch. The morning bell had already rung on the New York Stock Exchange. It was ten o'clock on the East Coast.

Thomas knew the investment community was upset about all this. It was turning into a war between the two parties but Thomas did not care. He dropped the last bomb. "This is all coming out of personal liability. I'm going to borrow against all of my holdings. I've already talked to the bankers. They're ready to go. Are you going to make the call or am I?" He glared at Kim. Even now she seemed so beautiful and competent. He thanked God she was with him through this. Tava was out there somewhere, frightened and alone. There was no word from Hans, and Grace was wandering the house like a ghost. Kim was the only island of sanity in the entire place. "Are you going to make the call or not?"

Kim crossed her arms. She'd never seen Thomas like this before. He was a madman. This was the most ridiculous proposal she'd ever heard. "I won't let you use your own money."

"I'm going to split it up. I am going to break that little company apart and scatter the pieces across the country. By the end of today Nicholls Development is going to be mine. I want Buddy Nicholls screaming! I'm going to squash the little shit like a bug. I'm not going to say it again, Kim. Make the call or I will."

She knew there was no going against his wishes. He was too determined. "All right. You win. I still think it's the stupidest thing you've ever done."

"I know it is. I told you, this is personal."

"That's a lot of money to be throwing around for a grudge." She dialed the Blackhurst offices in New York. Harry answered.

"Kim? What's the boss say?"

"The boss says we're going to go for it. Offer whatever it takes. He wants all sixty percent. Money is no object."

"My God. Are you sure? We've been getting calls all day. No one believes it."

Thomas picked up the other line. "Harry, if you still want

271

your job, make the call and let's get this going. I want controlling interest in three hours. Do it now."

"Yes, sir." Harry did not need to be told twice. He picked up his hot line and it was answered on the other end by a buyer on the floor of the New York Stock Exchange. The sound was deafening and Harry had to yell to make himself understood.

"Buy! Get it all. Mr. Blackhurst wants this done today!"

50

Buddy was pacing his huge house. The police had just finished grilling him about his father's death. They spent two hours going over the details again and again. It was exhausting but he did not break. He felt completely depleted of energy but giddy. Tava was still going to burn. The case against her was airtight. Her fingerprints were on the lamp, not his. He was sure they were never going to find Tava because Z had killed her. The only thing that bothered him was the videotape. It was the last shred of evidence against him and he wanted it destroyed. But he did not know where it was.

Buddy had not left the house since his altercation with Thomas at the police station. He was unable to sleep and stubble clung to his face. His hair was uncombed and his eyes bloodshot. He had found his father's liquor cabinet during the night and emptied a bottle of bourbon. He felt relieved now but agitated. Something was in the air. He didn't know what, but it was there like an intangible premonition. It clung to him like a bad dream. It was a strange sense of foreboding.

In frustration he picked up a book from the desk and threw it across the room. It shattered a full-length mirror, and the splinters came crashing down. Finally the house was plunged into silence. The emptiness was too much for

Buddy and he cranked the music. The sound of the telephone was barely discernible.

"What do you want?" Buddy yelled

It was his secretary from Houston. "Mr. Nicholls? I thought you should know . . ."

"Hang on, I can't hear you." He turned the music off. "What do you want?"

"Mr. Nicholls, I thought you should know. The entire board of directors walked out this morning. They've cleaned out all of their desks. Secondly, and I just heard this from New York, Mr. Blackhurst is buying up our stock like crazy."

"He's what?"

"Buying up Nicholls stock, sir. And the price is amazing. Honestly, sir, I'm thinking of selling my own shares. It's too good to pass up."

Buddy felt he'd been hit with a sledgehammer. "Oh my God. I didn't think he'd move that quickly."

"What?"

"Nothing. Have George call me."

"I don't think so."

"What?"

"I quit, sir. And if you don't mind me saying, I think you're an asshole." She hung up on him.

Buddy stared at the receiver and slammed it down. "I don't believe this! What the hell is going on?" He groped for the phone and stabbed at the numbers. George answered at the other end of the line.

"Buddy?"

"What's going on, George?"

"Not good, kiddo. I just came from the office. All the executives have left. Your little stunt with the board made them all a little angry. It looks bad."

"Can we stop Blackhurst?"

"I don't see how."

"What do you mean? There's got to be something!"

"He's doing it all by the book, son. My people are even telling me he's using his own money. I don't know what's going on out there in sleepy Sultan Valley, but you're pissing off a lot of people."

"I need you to stall. I've got to think."

"I'll do what I can."

"Get down to the office. Watch things for me. Make sure those assholes don't take anything. I'll call you back later. How much of the company does Blackhurst have?"

"Last count, he's up to twenty-five percent and climbing fast. It's all gonna be done in a couple of hours. He's got you by the balls, my boy. Come this afternoon, Thomas Blackhurst is gonna own the majority share of Nicholls Development and there isn't a damn thing you can do about it." George sounded almost happy.

"Well, dammit, George! How am I protected?"

"You're all right, I guess. Your stock is worth a lot right now. You're not going to like this but you may want to think about selling your shares to Thomas Blackhurst. You will not get a chance this good again."

"Never! He can choke on my shares!"

51

Tava woke in Michael's arms. It was a feeling she'd forgotten and it seemed strange to her. He was warm and had the smell of a man. She breathed it in like a rare perfume. Finally, she thought, it's over.

They were in the forest, her body aching terribly. She could see the ugly bruises along the side of her body. She tried to sit up painfully. "Michael," she whispered, "get up."

Michael shot awake. "What is it?" He was on his feet pacing the small clearing. "Who's out there?"

"No one. No one. Shhh."

He was still uneasy but sank down in front of her. "How are you?" The look of concern on his face touched her.

"I'll live. I hurt but I'll live. I can't believe you're here." It was as if all her pain and anguish erupted all at once. She broke down in a crying fit that shook her body like a rag doll. Michael held her in his arms, like he did before Hank's death. He let her cry herself out, stroking her hair gently. His strong hands comforted her. She finally regained her composure. "Oh, Michael, I missed you so much." The memories hit her. The shots.

Z dead.

Hans shot and crumpling to the ground.

Michael dragging her through the trees with the sound of sirens in their ears.

They must have run for an hour before collapsing in exhaustion. All she could remember was Michael's tight grip on her hand. It was the only thing keeping her moving.

"What about Hans?" Her voice was weak, scared to hear the awful truth.

Michael shook his head, "I don't know. He might have been breathing. It all happened too quickly to be sure." The memory was too much for him. He had grown to respect the Swede for his cool composure and lightning-quick mind. Tava would not be here if it had not been for him. "The policeman panicked. I don't know. It was too dark."

All Tava could do was shake her head. "I can't believe it. Hans dead? It's just too much." The tears left her and were replaced with steel. "I've got to tell you what happened."

"We should get out of here, honey."

"No. Now. You have to hear it all. In case this gets any worse, I want someone else to be able to tell them." The only thing she couldn't tell Michael about was Z. She was too embarrassed and it made her feel too dirty.

The sun was hot. It was midday and the heat was overwhelming. Even in the shade of the trees it was eighty-five degrees.

Tava and Michael were skirting Highway 287. They were keeping to the trees. They found the road about an hour ago and since eleven had seen at least ten police cars speed by. Now that there were two more bodies to this nightmare, the hunt was intensifying. Michael thought the only reason helicopters weren't being used was because of the trees. At least they were covered from above.

Tava was still naked. Her only covering was Michael's windbreaker. Her feet were raw and bloody. She winced with every step but her resolve pushed her on.

Both she and Michael knew what they had to do. The police could not be trusted. Not after what had happened to Hans. So the only thing left was to clear Tava's name themselves. They were going to get the videotape and then go to the police. That was the only sure way to clear the whole thing up. It was imperative, they decided, to get to Sultan Valley as soon as possible. Once there, they would figure out how to get the tape. Michael felt sure he could take Buddy out. They planned to be in and out just long enough to get the tape. The only thing standing between them was eighty miles of highway and the police.

Tava saw the rest area first. They approached it carefully. The place was full of people. Some were picnicking and others were stretching their stiff limbs. Tava and Michael were hoping to find a car.

They worked their way up to the rest area. Tava was too conspicuous so Michael scurried across the road by himself. Tava waited for him just out of sight in the trees. He first went to the bathroom and splashed cold water on his face. He felt drowsy and needed to be alert. He did his best to tame his wild hair and tucked his shirt in. Leaving the rest room, he scanned the area and found a likely target.

He waited for five minutes. The seconds seemed to take an eternity until finally he was sure. He watched the last of a large family exit an enormous motor home. He checked for onlookers and disappeared inside the RV.

His heart was pounding in his ears. He did not have much time. Michael turned his attention to the rear. Moving quickly down the hallway, he entered the master bedroom. He scanned the small space and found what he was looking for. He hopped across the bed and ripped a drawer open. He dug through several pieces of clothing until he found a pair of gray sweatpants. He threw them on the bed. He tore open a second drawer and pulled out the first shirt he could find. It was a yellow pullover jersey. He found socks in a third drawer and sneakers in the closet. Piling all of this into his arms, he made his way back up front. The family was just finishing their meal.

He let himself out quietly and closed the door.

"What're you doing in there?"

Michael turned quickly to find a little boy staring at him. He breathed a sigh of relief and tried to cover. "Your dad asked me to make sure everything's okay. Are you a big boy?"

"Sure."

"All right, you go tell your dad everything's safe and sound. Okay?"

"Sure." The boy seemed satisfied and ran off. Michael thanked his luck and hurried away. Watching for cars, he ran across the road and found Tava.

"Here. These were the best I could do. Hurry up. A little kid almost caught me."

Tava was into her outfit quickly and the two of them were crossing the road in less than five minutes. They walked hand in hand as if nothing was wrong. They were scanning the cars for keys. They prayed for someone to be careless. The parking lot was filled with fifty different cars and RV's. One of them was bound to work.

It took them two passes before they found one. It was a tiny two seat green MGB. The owner, a young woman in tank top and shorts, hopped out and hurried over to the bathroom. Michael and Tava grabbed at their chance.

They jumped into the car, Michael behind the wheel and Tava in the passenger seat. The engine shook to life with a high roar and Michael threw it into reverse.

"Get us out of here!" Tava yelled.

"Hang on," Michael said over the roar of the squealing tires. He found first, the gears grinding, and roared out of the rest stop.

52

Buddy was pacing his home like a man out of control. He had a gun and he was talking to himself.

"They can't do this to me. I've got too much riding on this. Nicholls is my company! My company! They're not going to take it from me." His speech was in a dull monotone. He kept repeating it over and over. His hand kept loosening and tightening on the grip of the gun. He didn't seem to know he was carrying it. It was an extra part of his hand. It made him feel strong.

The hours were limping by. Since this morning every financial paper in the country called, wanting the scoop on the "Blackhurst Bloodbath" as they were calling it. Thomas's takeover was unprecedented in the history of Wall Street and the newspeople wanted the inside scoop. Buddy answered everyone of them with the same statement. "Nicholls is not for sale. The company is mine."

The phones stopped ringing an hour ago. Buddy missed their noisy intrusions. In Houston, George was manning the sinking ship. He wasn't able to do much. Buddy kept seeing Hank at the steps, trying to come down. He seemed to be calling to his son.

"Buddy! How could you?"

Buddy ran from the image and steered clear of the stairs. The only thing he'd eaten since returning from Texas was booze. He was white and sallow. His eyes were withdrawn and carried dark circles. He was like a ghost. The pressure was mounting and becoming too much for him.

The phone rang. He was on it like a crazed beast. "Hello?" His voice was weak and strangely pathetic.

"Buddy, I'm going to make this short. This is Thomas Blackhurst. I have just finished buying sixty percent of your company. It's mine, you little shit. You are fired. I'm putting my own people in, effective immediately. You are not welcome on the premises. If you try, I will have you arrested. I may not be able to prove that you killed your father, but this is at least some consolation. You are finished. Good-bye." The phone went dead and Buddy was quaking in desperation.

53

The little car was speeding quickly along at seventy-five. Tava kept checking behind her for police. She was sure they would discover the missing car and pursue them. It was just a matter of time. She was still sore but was feeling more in control. The horror of the deaths still haunted her.

"Michael?" she yelled over the whine of the engine.

"What?" Michael was sweating profusely. Unlike Hans he did not trust his ability to escape. This was out of his league and he was very scared. "What, Tava?"

"Michael, I just want you to know if we don't get through this, I love you."

"We are going to get through it."

"I feel like I'm drowning."

"Hang in there."

Tava started to break. It started in her voice and then as her body started to shake, it took her over completely. "I can't hold it, Michael. I can't do this!"

"Tava! Fight it, honey! We're almost there. It's okay. We're almost there! All we need is the tape! Tava? Listen to me!"

"I can't do it. I can't do it. This is all too much for me. You don't know what I've been through."

"You're going to be okay, honey! Get control! Get control!" He was helpless and only had his voice to ease her pain. It was too important. "Tava, listen to me. You are going to be all right. We are going to get the tape! Honey! Listen to me!"

Finally his voice pierced her confused, turbulent cloud of doubt. He said it loud enough for her to understand. She slowly pulled herself together with an extreme effort of will. She straightened in her seat and dried her eyes. "We've got to burn him, Michael. Buddy Nicholls can't go on like this. I can't have this over my head for the rest of my life."

"You're not going to." He continued to soothe her. She was under a tremendous strain. She was too near the edge and Michael could not allow her to go over.

Something flashed in his eyes. He checked the rearview mirror and his heart sank. He saw the flashing lights of a police car gaining on them quickly. The final showdown was about to begin.

There was no way they were going to listen to Michael and Tava. Michael knew that. Timing was everything and getting the tape was what was most important. Without the evidence they were nothing. His foot stepped firmly down on the accelerator. The speedometer began to rise past eighty. The tiny two-lane highway flashed by. The trees became a constant blur.

"What is it?" Tava answered her own question. She saw the police gaining on them. "They can't catch us, Michael. Don't let that happen!"

"Hang on." He floored the little car and the needle pushed itself against the top of the gauge. The little engine was straining under the pressure. The car was small enough to hug the corners but still the tires squealed and coughed up white puffs of smoke. They could at any moment lose control and shoot off into a tree. Michael was doing his best to wrestle the car under control. He was pushing himself and the machinery beyond the limits of endurance.

The police car, bigger and stronger, pulled up just behind them. Its engine was rumbling too. It made attempts to pull alongside the MGB but Michael swerved in front of them. If he kept them behind him, he was hoping he might finally outrun them. It was the only thing he could think of.

The little car barely made a sharp corner and shot across the center divider into the oncoming lane. Its left front fender banged against the rocky wall and ricocheted back into the correct lane. Both Michael and Tava were knocked violently around the little cabin.

A deep voice boomed out of a loudspeaker from the car behind them. "This is the police! Pull over now!"

"What do you want to do?" Michael asked her.

"Keep going," she yelled over the noise. "Keep going!"

Michael prayed luck was with them and threw the car around another corner. This time it felt as if the car were fighting to stay on all four wheels. Michael watched with amazed fright as the car behind them lost control and flew into a violent spin. The car slammed against a line of trees and finally came to rest with the engine steaming and the horn blowing at full volume.

"They know it's us, don't they?" Tava yelled.

"They must!" was his only reply. He checked the fuel guage and was relieved to find half a tank. There was enough gas to get them to Sultan Valley. He checked for a sign, hoping for some marker. He guessed they were still forty miles from the village. He also knew with a sinking feeling that there were more police cars to come.

54

Grace was clapping her hands. Her glass of whisky was tucked underneath one arm and staining the side of her dress. She was standing at the kitchen door overlooking the pool and the back lawn. Thomas was deep in conversation with Kim.

"Well, look at my Romeo."

Thomas's fuse was short. He had just hung up with Buddy and was riding a whirlwind of mixed emotions; elation at his success, and fear for his lost daughter. He could tell in Buddy's silence there was a dangerous undercurrent. The young man was running near the brink and this might just be the thing to push him over.

"Grace, go back inside."

"I understand there are congratulations in order," she slurred. She halfheartedly clapped her hands again and retrieved her drink. "I hear you got the little twerp."

"Grace, go inside. You're drunk."

"I am not." She sounded like a petulant little child. "Where's Tava?"

"We don't know. We're still looking." Thomas was growing redder with anger. Grace was pushing him.

Kim was embarrassed. It was sad to see Thomas moved to so much hate. How could he have ever loved Grace, she asked herself. It seemed so inconceivable.

"I am not going anywhere. This is just as much my house as it is yours. So shove it."

That was the final push. Thomas flew out of his chair, yelling all the way. "What's the matter with you! Don't you care about anything, Grace? Our daughter is out there somewhere running from a murder she didn't commit and you're sitting there getting drunk and laughing!"

Grace found her screaming husband to be amusing. She couldn't stop herself from laughing. In her drunken state she couldn't imagine a funnier sight: Thomas, beet-red and yelling. It was almost like she couldn't hear his voice. She tried to stop laughing but couldn't.

This stoked Thomas's rage. This woman was nothing like the girl he had married so long ago. She was a mockery of the Grace he knew. This bitter old drunk was an embarrassment. He had had enough. He grabbed the drink from her hand and threw it in the pool.

"Hey, that's my little drinky-poo, Tommy. Give it back."

"No! No more drinking!"

She laughed again. "Now you tell me." She started to move inside for another but Thomas stopped her. He whipped her around by the arm and slapped her across the face. "Wake up, Grace! You're killing yourself! No more drinking!"

She slugged him back, hard. He took the blow directly in the face. "What do you know about me?" Her words were so garbled, they streamed out in a jumble. "I used to love you! And now look at us. Look at me, Thomas! Look what I've become!"

Kim stopped him before he could get to Grace. She

literally had to push him away. "Thomas, this is not what you are. Don't let her do this to you!"

"I can't stand it! She doesn't care about anything! Look at her. It's disgusting. Christ, she needs a little sense knocked into her!"

"No one needs violence. That is not the way to handle this."

"What do you know, tar baby!" Grace taunted. She was trying to provoke a fight with Kim and in her drunken stupor saw nothing wrong with throwing out racial slurs. She had hoped to do something terrible to Kim the moment she saw her. Finally the opportunity had presented itself. "Come on, darkie. Isn't that what they used to call you in the South? Darkie? I kind of like that," Grace sneered.

Kim audibly took a deep breath. She released her grip on Thomas and fought for her composure. It was very rare that she was taunted about the color of her skin and she found it repulsive. Thomas reacted first.

"I swear to God, Grace, you are so near to losing everything you ever dreamed about. Look at yourself. You're reduced to being a bigot now? I'm not going to stand for it. If you want to fight, fine. I don't care anymore." He advanced on her.

Grace almost lost her smile. "Tommy, I haven't seen you this mad in years. It's nice to see a little life back in you." She backed up a few steps. "But just because you've reduced yourself to sleeping with that black bitch, don't start blaming me."

"Grace . . ."

"Leave her alone, Thomas!" This time it was Kim's voice ringing out loud and clear. It was strong and filled with an anger that stopped Thomas in his tracks. "Grace, you are a drunk and drunks say very bad things sometimes. Usually I can forgive them, but not this time. I have worked too hard, for too many years to sit here and take your kind of abuse. If you think throwing words at me is going to hurt, you've got another thing coming. You see, the difference between you and me is that I'm comfortable with who I am, and I'm happy."

"I was happy once!" Grace's spirits were plunging now into anger. This young woman standing in front of her embodied everything about Thomas and Tava that she hated. In her mind she was being shoved out of the inner circle. She hated Kim because the young woman was happy. It galled her even more because Kim was right and that made her angrier. "Don't think I've forgotten how to fight, honey. I may look like a wreck but you don't want to mess with me."

"You really want to fight me, Grace?"

"Screw you. Who do you think you are coming into my house and stealing my husband away?"

"This man stopped being your husband years ago, Grace. You chose the bottle over him and that's where you made your mistake."

"I can't stand you!" Grace yelled. She threw herself at Kim with as much force as she could summon. She was quick enough to get the young woman in a bear hug and tackle her to the ground. They struggled there until Kim found the energy to push Grace off of her. Immediately they were on their feet again and circling.

Thomas stood back and watched. This was as important for Kim as it was for him. He could not protect Grace forever. She had made choices in her life and would have to live by them. By letting Kim take Grace on he was finally admitting to himself that there was no future left for them. It was sad but it was the right decision. Kim made him happy. With that definitive understanding Thomas watched and waited.

"Getting nervous, Grace?" Kim said, brushing the hair from her face.

"Why don't you shut up!" With that Grace rushed Kim again but this time Kim was prepared. Using Grace's momentum against her, Kim tripped her and sent her flying headlong onto the stone patio around the pool. Grace recovered slowly and found the palms of her hands bleeding. Small pebbles stuck to her skin as she tried to brush them away. The pain was dull but the embarrassment was not. She searched wildly for a stone and found it with her left hand. Before Kim could react, Grace threw it. It caught her on the head above her left eye.

Kim stumbled back. The blow took her by surprise and before she could recover, Grace was on her again. She punched her in the stomach and brought Kim to her knees, gasping for breath. Next, with all of her weight, she fell on the thin woman, punching and gouging like a madwoman.

It was all Kim could do to protect her face. She felt her hair being pulled out at the roots. Her breasts were being pounded and she could feel Grace's fake nails digging into her skin and scratching with extreme pain. With the heightened strength of indignation Kim roused her energy and hit back.

Kim found Grace's face and grabbed her cheek with so much force that the older woman started screaming. Nothing Grace did could stop her. Her grip was like a vise and quickly Grace stopped fighting back. She was trying to protect herself by pulling away from Kim. Grace could not escape and it was terrifying. Finally, after what seemed like hours, her cheek was released.

"You're crazy!" Grace yelled. "Get away from me!" Grace tried to run for the door but Kim stopped her by grabbing her dress and pulling her to a stop. With a final pull she practically ripped the whole thing off of Grace. Standing there half-naked, pathetic, and shaking from the experience, Grace realized she'd met her match. Finally there was someone she could not intimidate. It was too much for her and she broke down in tears. She crumpled to the ground and Kim backed away.

She was a little frightened that she'd gone too far. She was younger and stronger and felt like she'd taken advantage of Grace. She was angry with herself for letting Grace get to her this way.

The sobbing was so powerful that Grace's body shook with the heaving convulsions of a pathetic, beaten woman. It was too much. She shook her head back and forth erratically and half-cried and screamed. Her yells turned into wailing and then she turned her full attention on Thomas.

"This is what you've done to me!" Her voice echoed around the house. She was frightening in her intensity. "This is what you've done to me! Are you happy? Are you?" She was not thinking, she was exploding. Her face was beet-red and the veins in her neck were straining and pumping with the full force of blood traveling through them. "I will never forgive you for this, Thomas Blackhurst! I will die before I let you come back to me! You can fuck whoever you want but you will never come back to my bed! Never!" She gathered her torn dress around herself and struggled to her feet. She took one step toward her husband and pointed her index finger at him. "I wish you were dead!"

Thomas was shaken. He chose his words carefully and spat them out between clenched teeth, "I wish you were too."

"Go to bed, Grace, and sleep it off," Kim said.

"Go to hell!"

Thomas yelled back, "You already have!"

55

The roadblock was four-police-cars-deep. They were blocking both sides of the road. The sun was sitting on the uppermost peak in the Grand Teton range. Michael and Tava were driving directly toward them, and the orange glow of the sun was muted in fiery silence. It was their beacon calling them home.

They saw the roadblock at the same time. They were ten miles outside of Sultan Valley now. The last fifteen minutes had been silent but filled with impending danger.

"How many police cars?" Tava asked now, her voice completely calm. It was if she had wrapped herself in a blanket of confidence. Her head was clear and she was in complete control. She knew exactly what lay ahead of her and she was not afraid anymore of meeting the challenge. Whatever the outcome, she was going to see this ordeal through to its end.

"Four, I think." Michael's voice was shaky. It was only through brute concentration that he kept them on course. "I don't see any way around, do you?" They were approaching the roadblock at eighty miles an hour. Michael had the headlights turned on. This strip of road was a long, flat stretch that gave them enough time to assess the situation.

"Maybe go around?"

"I don't know. Maybe." It looked tight. On this stretch of road there was a river on their right, fifty feet below them, and a jagged rock wall on their left. The police had picked this spot carefully. It was a natural bottleneck designed to force them to stop.

"It's gonna have to be the left. The river is too close on this side."

The engine whined. Michael wondered how the motor could be withstanding all the abuse. Still he pushed it harder.

"It looks like they're pretty close to the left. I don't know, Tava. What do you want to do?" He was sounding panicky.

"It's got to be the left. We've got to go around."

"Maybe we should stop."

"No!" She said it simply and defiantly. "We go through, now. If you want to stop and get out, that's okay, but I'm going through them. This is personal now, Michael. I've been through too much to let it end like this. It's got to be on my terms or none at all. That is the only thing I care about." She didn't have to yell. The conviction in her voice said all it had to.

"All right. I'm with you." Michael did his best to gauge the distance between the police car and the wall. It was going to be a tight fit, if they made it at all. He thought he saw the policemen kneeling and taking aim at them. He saw the reflection of the burning sun against the stalks of their rifles. "They think we're going to stop."

"Good."

The car was bearing down on the blockade now. Tava and Michael were moving with great speed and aiming for the center. They were following the divider line directly toward the cars.

Michael punched the car up to eighty five. The distance between them was dangerously short. They were now past the point of stopping. Any change and they would crash.

Tava was in Michael's rhythm. "Ready . . . Now!"

Michael wrenched the wheel hard to the left and straightened it again as fast as possible. The policemen opened fire. The MGB shot through the narrow space between the car and the wall, scraping through on both sides. The yellow sparks sprayed out like a million fire flies. The sound of the car and the gunfire were deafening.

"We made it!" Tava yelled. "I can't believe it!"

"Neither can I." A huge feeling of relief washed over him as he maneuvered the car through a series of snake curves.

Tava looked back in time to watch the police scrambling for their cars. "They're coming."

"Good. I've got a plan."

The policemen were stunned. The little car had done the impossible and broken past them.

Tava was making a fool out of them and they were forced to double their effort. The first car led the way through the snake curves and pushed on toward Sultan Valley. They were within seven miles of the town limits and wanted Tava stopped by then. A high-speed chase through the little valley was too dangerous.

It was growing progressively darker. The sun sneaked below the Tetons now and cast the sky into a purple-blue twilight. The sky danced with electric mountain clouds. It was a crystal clear sky and some stars were beginning to appear.

Out of nowhere the lead car slammed on its brakes. There was someone lying in the road! It was all the policeman could do to miss the body. The other three cars did their best to avoid each other. They barely avoided a pileup.

The first man out of his car withdrew his gun. He was steaming, "What the hell is this?" He slammed the driver's door closed and rounded the front of the car. His three companions followed him.

They approached the body cautiously. It was a young male and apparently unconscious. Maybe dead. He appeared to be unarmed. They moved up to him slowly and did not see the body breathing. The first driver knelt down and reached for a pulse.

Only then did Michael open his eyes and smile.

56

Tava pulled the car off the side of the road and into a clump of trees, just inside the town limits. She cut the motor and left the keys in it. Jumping out, she closed the door and watched for the chasing police cars. She hoped Michael was all right. His stunt was dangerous, she knew that, but realized it was the only thing that was going to buy her time.

The street lamps in Sultan Valley were on. The tiny square was alive with tourists and locals. It was a warm night and couples were window-shopping and eating in the outdoor cafés. The flowers were in bloom just as Tava remembered them. It seemed so long ago now. She felt she was returning from a long, long trip. She pulled her collar up and did her best to blend in. Her mission still lay before her and she was as determined as ever to complete it. It was tempting to pick up a phone and call Blackhurst Manor. She felt so compelled to do it, it hurt to push the sensation away. But she knew inherently this was her problem and she was going to finish it.

Keeping her head down, she moved quickly into the square. The roaring of an engine caught her attention. She turned just in time to see a Greyhound bus pulling away from the station.

Tava moved through the crowds, cut across the small park behind the grandstand, and crossed over the far road. She disappeared between a restaurant and gift shop. The brick alley was cool and comforting. Tava found the darkness safe. She focused on her objective; the videotape was her salvation.

She spotted the Victorian. The living room lights were blazing and she thought she saw someone walk by inside. Tava took a deep breath. Watching for onlookers, she made her way across the street and into the dark protection of a huge fir. In the darkness she got a better view of the house. Her heart froze when she recognized Buddy. He was pacing back and forth and holding something in his hand. She followed his frenetic movements, trying to get a better idea of who he was talking to. He was flailing his arms and shouting. His voice was muffled but the high pitch sparked memories of his screaming when she first ran for her life.

Tava faltered. She wondered if she had the strength to carry on. Although it was a silly dream, she was hoping to find the house empty. She wanted to sneak in, get the tape, and run to the police station. But that was not going to be.

"Please, Tava, please, just go do it," she whispered to herself. She got as far as the large bay window and the curtains were drawn. Still, peeking through the lace, she got a clear view of the interior. To her shock she found Buddy alone. He was yelling at an empty room.

And then she saw the gun. Buddy was waving it indiscriminately. Tava only caught the tail end of his sentence when he paced in front of the window. ". . . I'm gonna kill him, Daddy. That's the only thing to do. I've got to kill him to make it all okay. Just drive over there and do it. Pop him one in the head." With that Tava saw him take aim and fire at a flower vase. It shattered violently. The noise was deafening but Buddy didn't seem to care. She saw him empty his glass and disappear toward the kitchen.

"Now," she urged herself. "Do it!"

Tava crept around the house and up to the front door. She peeked inside and saw Buddy's shadow playing across the hallway. He was rummaging in the kitchen for more booze. Tava tried the door and it unlatched. She was short of breath and half-paralyzed. Her pain was forgotten. With a will that surprised her, she pushed the door open and moved silently inside. The air duct was to her right just inside the door.

All she had to do was reach down the hole, grab the tape, and run!

She heard Buddy now. He yelled and she froze. His shadow seemed to grow bigger, almost as if he were about to emerge, and then subsided. Tava heard drawers being pulled open and things being shuffled around. He kept up a continual conversation with himself.

She tore her attention away from the kitchen and back to

the air duct. To her surprise a covering had been placed over it. She knelt as quietly as possible and tried to pry the metal fitting up. It was stuck. Only panic gave her the strength to pry it loose. Her fingers bled from the effort but it finally gave. She lifted the heavy piece from its place and rested it next to the hole. In her excitement she thrust her hand inside. She almost yelled when her fingers touched the plastic casing. Her heart beat faster from the relief she felt holding the tape safe in her hand.

"Now just grab it and get out," she told herself. The tape was in her fingers!

"Well, well, well. I'm seeing a ghost."

Tava froze. She was so close!

"Welcome home, honey." Buddy's voice was even higher than Tava remembered. The alcohol played with his throat. He was grinning wildly and held a tall glass of vodka in his right hand and the gun in his left.

Tava ran for the door but Buddy beat her to it. With one kick he slammed it shut. The glass fell from his hand and spilled all over him. He didn't seem to notice and used the gun to quiet her. "Move and I'll blow your fucking head off."

Tava was absolutely still.

"I take it Z didn't kill you. Shame. All that money." He seemed to sway. "I always thought he was a liar. Aren't you gonna say anything?"

"Let me go."

Buddy laughed. "Are you kidding? What've you got in your hand?"

Tava tried to keep it from him but he grabbed it from her. He started laughing. "I can't believe this! I feel like such a dick. This was here the whole time, wasn't it? I didn't have to send Z after you. I could've saved all that money." He sighed. "Oh, well. You're gonna fry, baby, 'cause this tape is goin' bye-bye."

He moved her into the living room. "Turn around. I missed those cute little lips of yours. Oh. There. You see? You are beautiful." He touched her face. "This is why I fell in love with you. Shame you're gonna go to jail."

"It's not going to happen."

"Wanna make a bet? No tape. No evidence. Everybody thinks you killed Daddy and everything points to you. This is my way out, Tava baby. And, lucky me, the great Buddy Nicholls is goin' to take all the credit for bringin' in the desperado Tava Blackhurst."

He moved over to the fireplace. Turning a key in the fireplace, the dark cavity leapt to life with a huge gas flame. The fire shot up into the chimney and Buddy did not bother to turn it down.

"I'm gonna be a hero for catching you. Buddy Nicholls catches Blackhurst heiress. Sounds pretty good, doesn't it? Let's watch this together." With the gun trained on her he flipped the tape in his hand.

Tava watched him the entire way. Her fate was about to burn in flames. She waited. Her thoughts were clear. Every sense was honed in. He was going to give her an opportunity. It was going to happen . . . There it was!

For a fleeting instant his eyes left her for the fireplace. At that moment Tava sprang. Her left arm knocked the gun from his hand and the right moved in for the tape. They struggled and the tape was knocked free. It skidded across the floor and landed in the middle of the room.

With an enormous surge of energy Tava broke free of Buddy's desperate grip and shoved him away. He stumbled backward and fell into the flames.

Tava lunged for the video. It was in her hands and she was out the door before she heard the screams. She was forced to look back.

Buddy was on fire!

He managed to pull himself from the fireplace but his sleeves were in flames. He was disoriented and running around the room, trying desperately to extinguish himself. The sinister fire spread faster than he could move.

Tava watched Buddy ignite in a column of fire. His frantic attempts to put himself out only spread the flames, and now the room was beginning to burn.

"Help me! Help me!"

He was screaming for help. Tava was torn. With the tape in her hand and the door open, she could just run away. The police station was five minutes from there and she would be free. But she was riveted in place.

The flames were horrific and Tava realized no one deserved this kind of death. Buddy deserved the worst she could imagine, but not this.

Tava moved into action. She felt no pain. She moved as if in a silent movie. She had to put out the fire and get the two of them out of there now. The room was engulfed in flames and there was not much time.

Buddy was flailing helplessly and about to fall down. His whole body was now aflame and Tava realized if he fell, there was no way she could save him.

She ran to the dining room and tore down one of the drapes. With the heavy fabric bunched in her hands she stuffed the video down her front. Spreading the curtain out between her hands, she ran back into the living room. Buddy was flailing in front of the huge bay window.

Tava didn't think. She just aimed for Buddy and in one fluid movement rushed him straight on. She wrapped him in the curtain and with the force of her body pushed the two of them crashing through the enormous pane of glass. They landed as one, and the blow of the fall knocked Buddy unconscious. Tava began to black out as the glass poured down around them. As her eyes dimmed they were filled with the sight of the living room engulfed in fire. The red flames were taking over the entire house. Tava knew she had to get farther away but couldn't move. She was passing out.

Her last memory was of the moon highlighted against the black sky, stars twinkling in a sea around it, and in her young body, the overwhelming sense of peace, at last.

57

Tava woke slowly. It was like coming out of the deepest sleep in her life. Her body was bruised from head to toe and any movement shot bolts of pain through her. It took her several moments to adjust to the darkened room. She managed a small smile, realizing she was still alive.

The hospital room was private. Her eyes began to focus and she slowly noticed the flowers. They filled her room like a nursery, and the sweet scents filled her senses and relieved the pain.

She searched for people. She wanted to see a friendly face but did not have the strength to call out. Finally a nurse peeked her head in.

"You're awake."

Tava nodded her head. She tried to speak but only a low, guttural sound came out.

The nurse came over to the bed. She was gentle and friendly. "Don't try to talk. You've been through a lot." She could see the questions racing across Tava's eyes. She patted her hand. "You're okay, Tava."

The words filled her ears. She wanted to cry with relief. "Where? . . ."

"Your father's been checking in on you. He'll be back soon. Can I get you anything?"

Tava shook her head no. She held the nurse's hand, squeezed it, and then let her go. Watching the nurse leave, she let herself drift back to sleep.

"Tava?" Thomas's voice was soothing. He was whispering to her. "Tava?"

She opened her eyes. They felt heavy and she was groggy. He father's face came into view. She felt a rush run through her. It was a feeling she had never felt before. It was a mixture of relief and excitement. The emotion was more than she could bear without speaking or yelling. "Daddy!" The grin on her face told him everything.

"Don't try and talk, sweetie. He brushed her face with his strong fingers. He bent down close to her. "I love you." Tears were in his eyes.

Tears were also streaming down Tava's face. "I love you too." She tried to put her arms around him but the pain pulled her back.

"Take it easy. Take it easy. There's time for that later. Let me hug you." He leaned down and pressed his lips to her forehead and cheek. "I'll be here with you. If you need anything, let me know. Everybody's going to come down and see you when you're feeling a little stronger. Michael can't wait." He winked at her.

"Is he okay?"

He calmed her down. "He's fine. He told everything to the police. You're cleared of everything and so is he."

"Thank God." She was embarrassed now. "And the tape?"

"They've seen it. They had to pry it out of your hands at the house. You were very lucky. The firemen said the house was close to collapsing on you."

"Have you seen it?"

Thomas was quiet for a moment. "Yes. I'm sorry you had to go through that. You should have told me."

"Did Mom tell you."

"No. She's still denying she slept with him. I've pieced the whole thing together. Hank Nicholls was a very sick man. I don't know what your mother told you but never let her convince you to do that kind of thing again. It's stupid and you should have trusted me."

"Sorry."

"My God, don't be sorry! I can't believe you sacrificed yourself for me. Thank you for trying to help me, honey. You are a very brave girl . . . woman." He kissed her again. "Rest. The doctor says you have to take your recovery very slowly. I'll just sit here with you. Go back to sleep."

"Thank you, Dad. I love you."

He smiled and brushed her hand with his.

The doctors treated Tava's dark welts and wrapped her cuts and then left her quietly to mend. Tava's body had taken so much abuse, it was going to take weeks of patience for her body to heal.

Tava did not know what day it was and still grimaced from the quick movements. The doctors were trying to keep her drugged until she finally refused. She did not want to forget the pain. The horrible adventure taught her many things and while she wished it had not happened, she accepted it. It was her first step toward mental recovery and was one of her most important decisions.

Three weeks after she entered the hospital she was strong enough to start counseling. Z's rape was beginning to cause her nightmares and the hospital psychologist began to help her through the ordeal. Like the healing of her body it was a slow process and the two met daily. The psychologist was very careful to help Tava recreate the event in her mind and to ultimately accept it and then move on. Once Tava believed she had not brought the terrible act upon herself, she could see it for what it was: an act of violence she could not have prevented. She was a victim and that knowledge helped her accept it. She was glad Z was dead. She did not know if those feelings were right and she did not care. It helped her to know that he could never touch her again. Slowly her nightmares began to fade.

After six weeks the doctors decided she could handle the surprise they had been keeping from her. It was a sunny day near the end of summer and she watched the birds playing outside her hospital-room window. She was nearing the end of her stay and could not wait to get out. She missed the open air and was eager to move on and put this episode behind her.

Michael came in first. Besides Thomas he was her most constant companion through the recovery. His calm, helpful support eased her pain and she relied on him for his humor and his love.

"Hi, honey. How are you?"

"Michael! When are they going to let me out of this damn place? I want to get out of here!" She was playful this morning and determined to speed up her discharge.

"Couple more days. You look great. Listen, I've got a little surprise for you. Ready?"

"Not more flowers. Please."

"No more flowers, I promise. The flower shops are empty anyway. I think we've cleaned them all out. You're going to like this a little more." He backed up to the door and motioned for someone to come in.

There was a few seconds of mounting expectation and then Hans walked in. He wore a white bandage around his neck and seemed skinnier, but he was alive and Tava yelled with disbelief.

"Hans! You're alive! Why didn't they tell me?"

"I would guess from your reaction they thought you might have a heart attack." His eyes crinkled with humor, and a handsome smile grew on his face. "How are you?"

"Much better now that I know you're okay," Tava answered quickly. "I thought you were dead."

"So did I."

They stared at each other for a long time until Tava broke the silence. "I owe so much to you."

"You don't owe me anything. Besides, this fellow was my able partner. I could not have done it without him." He clapped Michael on the back. There was a genuine feeling of affection between the two men. Clearly the experience had brought them closer together.

"Thank you for everything," Tava said as she broke into uncontrollable tears. "I'm so happy you're alive."

He touched her lips to quiet her. "Your courage astounds me. You are not a little girl anymore."

Tava blushed at his words. He was so gentle and kind. She knew she owed him a huge debt. "Michael, Daddy has to know what Hans went through."

Hans allowed a smile. "He does. I'm afraid I could not get your boyfriend here to keep quiet. He kept going on and on about me. I really found it quite embarrassing. In any case I have been rewarded with a promotion. I am officially head of Blackhurst security worldwide."

"That's wonderful. You deserve it. You mean so much to me, Hans."

"And you to me, Tava."

Suddenly Annie was pushing her way in. "And I suppose I don't get a hug. I don't know why I had to stay away. No one knows this child better than I. It's criminal. And look at you. All those bandages." Annie covered her mouth in horror. "My God, child, look at you! Does it hurt?" The love in her voice was evident.

Tava let out a huge sigh of relief. "Annie."

Her old nanny scowled. "I would hope next time you run off you tell someone where you're going."

Tava was so happy. She was comforted knowing all these people loved her. The outpouring of support was more than she ever dreamed and it humbled her. She was caught with a thought.

"Michael, has anyone checked on Helen and Jake, the people that helped me? Are they okay?"

"They're fine. They're going to see you when you're out of here. Your father already has shown his appreciation."

"What's he done?"

"Well, he went a little overboard. He gave Helen a new rig."

"He gave her a new truck? That's great! Did she like it?"

"At first she didn't take it, but your father convinced her. You know him. She loves it and she's going to drive it down to show you."

"That's wonderful. And Jake?"

"Jake didn't want anything either. So your dad's buying him a new car to replace his old pickup, and a set of historical manuscripts. Something to do with Europe. Jake said they were the only things he 'lusted after since I was a babe in my mother's arms.'"

Everything seemed complete now. The people Tava cared most about were happy and taken care of. She could rest easier and she knew this good news was going to help her recover even faster. She was so excited, she wanted to yell with delight.

58

One Month Later

Charlotte was making a bed in one of the east bungalows at the Sultan Valley Resort. She was angry and upset because she was supposed to have the day off. At the last minute she was called in to sub, ruining her plans with her latest fling. She was pouting now and angrily throwing the pillowcases against the headboard.

She was still recovering from the emotional drama of the Blackhurst affair after following it with delight. Charlotte found the whole thing deliciously lurid and laughed when she thought of "poor little Michael's" girlfriend on the run for murder. She even started a pool to see how long Tava could stay on the run.

The summer day was glowing but nothing softened Charlotte's hardened heart. She pulled at the sheets, hoping to tear them. She heard the door open in the other room.

"This room isn't ready yet," she yelled angrily.

"Charlotte? It's Larry. Come out here."

Charlotte wondered what her boss was going to make her do now. She was getting very tired of his attitude and stomped into the living room to tell him so. "Look, Larry, I don't have time for this."

"Yes, you do."

Charlotte froze in her tracks. Standing next to the ex-marine were Michael and Tava. Charlotte recognized Tava immediately from the television. Michael looked stronger and was smiling. He held Tava's hand.

"Hi, Charlotte."

"Well, Michael. Long time no see. Aren't you going to introduce me?"

"I'd like you to meet Tava Blackhurst."

Charlotte nodded. "Pleasure."

Tava was quiet. Her demeanor was cool and confident. The bruises were healed although scars around her chin remained. "So you're the bitch that framed Michael."

Charlotte was speechless. "I don't know what you're talking about."

Michael broke in. "I feel terrible about this, Charlotte, I really do." The tone in his voice was not lost on anyone.

"About what?"

"Tell her, Larry."

Larry rolled his eyes. He clearly felt uncomfortable. "Charlotte, you are fired. The security guards are waiting to escort you off the premises."

"What is this? Some kind of joke?"

Tava answered first. "Hardly. You have fifteen minutes to get off the grounds."

"You can't do this."

"Yes, I can." Tava smiled now but only slightly. "My father owns the controlling interest in this operation and has given me full power to bounce your ass out of here. We don't need spoiled brats working here. Give her the check, Larry."

The older man did as he was told. Charlotte did not take it well. "I don't know who you think you are but you can't do this."

"I just did." Tava let go of Michael's hand and moved across the floor. She stopped inches from Charlotte. "Do you have a problem with this?"

"You're goddamn right I do!" Charlotte screamed. She threw a punch and Tava dodged it. Charlotte stumbled and fell on the carpet at Tava's feet.

"Good-bye, Charlotte. Next time, pick your fights a little better. Larry, if she's not gone in fifteen minutes, you're fired." Tava disappeared through the front door.

Michael paused and smiled, staring directly at Charlotte. "Boy, she's tough, huh? It's been nice knowing you, honey."

Tava waited for Michael in the limousine. She had a lot to do today and was eager to get moving. She was feeling very good. Her mind was clear and she felt directed. It was a new sensation and she gave into it with abandon. She was in control of her life and it felt very good.

She and Michael were scheduled to fly out in the evening. It could not come soon enough. Although she loved Sultan Valley and Blackhurst Manor, she was feeling closed in. She needed to spread her newfound wings. This was her first day out of the hospital and she had been planning for it as soon as she had regained consciousness.

The last month had been hell. The national media continued to hound her although now it was more paparazzi than investigative. The murder had made her famous. She was now known across the country and she was receiving all kinds of letters. People wanted money, influence with her father, and her time. People from Hollywood wanted her life story. Some of the letters were threatening and Tava found the whole thing tiring and scary. "Why would all these people care about me?" she asked herself.

She was tasting fame for the first time in her life and she did not like it. She was a private person but once the whole story came out, some people saw her as a hero. She was a figure of independence; a young woman fighting the odds and winning. Tava was not comfortable with the adulation and she was retreating. Inside she knew she was not all right. It was going to take a long time to confront and heal her deep wounds. Charlotte was her first stop, the second was going to be Blackhurst Manor.

Michael was her greatest supporter. He was always there for her. He comforted and stayed with her while she recovered in the hospital. He fended off the reporters and did his best to shield her from the legal proceedings. She only had to make one appearance in court to verify the legitimacy of the videotape and formally accuse Buddy of the murder. She had dreaded the event and although it was only a week ago, she still remembered it vividly.

"Ms. Blackhurst, we understand you have been through a tremendous amount. We have all seen the tape and are horrified by what we see. Today we are here to put a period on this sour event in your life. Buddy Nicholls stands accused of murdering his father."

"I understand." Tava was shaking softly on the stand. She did not want to look at Buddy's face but she was drawn to it. He was sitting stiffly in his seat, in a suit that didn't fit him and with a look of complete hatred on his face. He kept his eyes firmly on Tava and did not let her forget he was in the room.

"The defense recognizes your bravery in saving this young man. It was a tremendous show of courage. But you have saved a boy from a fiery death only to give him what? Life in prison. Please tell the jury what happened that night."

She started quietly. "I went there to see Mr. Nicholls. He had been drinking and was uncontrollable. He led me into his bedroom and began to . . . do . . . what he did. That is when Buddy came in. The tape shows it but it doesn't show Buddy's determination. People may not believe me when they see the tape, but Buddy initially acted to help me and something just snapped in his head. I don't know what it was but it was not a sane action. He eventually hired a killer to track me down and kill me. This hired killer double-crossed Buddy and tried to blackmail my father for my return. I think that must have driven him even farther into insanity. I don't believe Buddy Nicholls is sane."

"What do you know about me, bitch?" Buddy yelled out. He pounded on the desk. "You killed my Daddy! I didn't do it. That tape is a fucking lie! Why was she there in the first place? That's what I want to know! Why was she there?"

The judge had Buddy restrained. "Keep your seat, young man."

The courtroom calmed down and Buddy's lawyer proceeded on, "Why were you there?"

The state's lawyer broke in. "Objection, Your Honor. That has nothing to do with this case. It is completely irrelevant."

Tava spoke up. "No, that's all right. I don't mind. I know everybody is wondering. So if it's all right with you, Judge, I'd like to tell."

"I don't see any problem. I'll allow it."

She began haltingly. "Well, it all got out of hand. I . . . was . . . there to please Hank Nicholls. He was blackmailing my mother with those photographs and said if I didn't sleep with him, he would publish them. I did not want my father to have to go through that embarrassment so I said I would. The rest you can see for yourself on the tape."

"You went there voluntarily?"

"Yes, to protect my father." Tava could see now what a mistake she had made. She realized now her father would have preferred the truth, but at the time Grace had made it all seem so convincing. She saw through her mother now. She knew Grace had been acting out of selfishness, and it made Tava feel cold inside.

She knew the reporters were going to have a field day with this last piece of information but she did not care. It was too important to get the truth out. Lies had started all this, and truth was going to end it.

"You see! She loves me! The bitch loves me like a dog loves its master! It makes me sick. Sick!" Buddy bellowed.

Buddy was committed to an asylum back in Texas. His lawyer made the arrangements. With the great Victorian burnt to the ground there was nothing left in Sultan Valley for Buddy, and the land was sold off.

Tava tried to imagine a mind that could conceive of such brutality. Buddy had pushed her so far, she was in some ways indebted to him. Tava was discovering things about herself now and they were all for the good. Her biggest lesson was learning to trust herself. Buddy had forced that in her and she silently thanked him for it.

Michael checked his watch. "Okay, this is your show. Where to next?"

"Home. I've got a few things to take care of."

"You sure you're up to it?"

"I have to, Michael. My mother is not going away."

A new man was driving the car today. Tava smiled, remembering her joy when she had first discovered Hans was still alive.

The ride to the house was silent. Michael left her to her thoughts. She was recovering and he knew she would always be changed. But the new Tava was a more confident one, and Michael liked that. At times she still seemed disoriented or unsteady but that would pass.

Tava watched the August day flash by. The trees seemed to glow with warmth. Tava knew she could never stay away forever, but for a while she would have to. She was compelled to distance herself from this place to reconcile herself and the experience she had gone through. Still, she thought, this is where I belong. This is my home.

The car glided up the entrance. The flowers were gorgeous. They filled her heart with happiness. The drive up the long entrance worked its magic on her. The pretty trees, the flowers, and all the memories filled her with gentle reassurances that life was starting over again.

Her first sight of the house filled her with a passionate sense of solidity. This was her fortress against all that was bad; finally she was home. All those weeks of lying in the hospital had only built up her unflinching desire to return. Blackhurst Manor was just as she hoped it would be. It was sparkling in the afternoon light. It was overwhelmingly emotional for her.

"Are you all right?" Michael asked softly.

Tava nodded her head and waited for the car to glide to a stop.

Kim was waiting for them. Tava stepped out first.

"Welcome home, Tava." Kim gave her a big hug. "Your father is finishing up a few things in his office. He's got a surprise for you."

Tava laughed. "Not another gift! I wouldn't know where to put it." She held Kim's hand tight. "I haven't had the chance to say this, but I want to thank you for standing by him. He needed you to get him through this. I know there wasn't a lot of support."

"We were all worried about you."

"Some, more than others, I think."

"Tava, I don't . . ."

"It's okay, Kim. I understand what went on here."

They went in search of Thomas. "The two of you are leaving tonight?"

"Yes," Michael answered.

"Have you decided where you're going?"

"No. We're going to let the winds guide us." He squeezed Tava's hand.

Kim grinned. "I'm jealous. Your father and I are going to be back at work tomorrow."

"Sounds like Dad."

They found him in his office. He threw down his papers and hurried around the desk. "Welcome home. I wish you would have let me pick you up."

"We had some work to do. It's okay. I hear you have some news." Tava stayed close to him. She wasn't going to see him for a couple of months and was missing him already.

Thomas turned to Kim. "You do have a big mouth, don't you?"

"But of course."

They all sat. Thomas leaned against his huge desk and folded his arms. "Well, I have to say I feel like a little kid. This is sort of embarrassing."

"It can't be that bad," Tava chided.

"Out with it, Thomas," Kim said smilingly.

"Well, Tava, my darling daughter, so much has happened that I don't know where to begin. But I want to keep this short. So, I have decided that . . ." Thomas could not get the words out of his mouth.

Kim came to his rescue. "Tava, your father and I are moving in together."

Thomas breathed a huge sigh of relief. "Thank God it's out." He watched Tava for her reaction and was relieved to find a satisfied smile.

Tava stood up and kissed her father on the cheek. She did the same for Kim. "Isn't this great, Michael? I think you two are going to make a great couple."

"Thank you. So do we."

"Does Mother know?"

"I told her last night." Thomas answered. "I don't think she took it very well. I'll let you decide that."

"Where is she?"

"I think in her room. I hope this doesn't hurt you."
Thomas did not want to upset Tava.

"Daddy, it's been a long time coming."

Tava left them to find Grace. It was the one thing she had
kept putting off, but there were finally no more excuses. This
had to happen before she left.

She knocked once on the door.

"What do you want!" Grace cried out from the bedroom.
"Go away!"

"Mother? It's me."

There was a long silence as the door swung open. "Well,
look who's home." Grace allowed Tava to enter. She sat
herself on the divan and poured a large glass of scotch. "You
know I am always telling your father martinis are my drink,
but he keeps bringing this shit into the house." She downed
the tall glass. "You should think about drinking a little
more. It makes things a little prettier."

Tava sat on the bed and faced Grace. Her mother was
almost shrunken in her nightgown. She was wearing a satin
robe, undone and wrinkled. "I don't drink. And you should
stop."

Grace coughed. "Thanks for the advice. I'll keep it in
mind."

"Why didn't you come see me at the hospital?"

Grace refused to answer. She just poured herself another
drink.

"I asked you a question."

"I heard you. I'm not deaf."

"Well, if you heard me, say something." The tone in
Tava's voice was cold and serious.

"I don't know what to say. I missed you, if that's any
help."

"It isn't."

Grace tossed her head slowly from side to side. "Well,
kiddo, I did."

"Did you see the trial?"

"I was there."

This surprised Tava. "I didn't see you."

"That's because I didn't want to be seen. I can still do
some things right."

"You're going to make me do all of this, aren't you?"

"I don't know what you're talking about."

"What did you think of my testimony?"

"Not bad. You could've been a little more dramatic. Everybody's seen my exciting pictures anyway. Not much I can do about that."

"Aren't you sorry?" Tava pleaded.

A long silence ensued. Grace nibbled at her drink. "I haven't decided."

"Why do you have to be so cold?"

"It comes naturally, sweetie. I tell you one thing I'm sorry about. Marrying your father. You know he's dumping me?"

"Yes."

"That's his style."

"No, it isn't! How can you say that? He's tried to do what's best for everybody!"

"That's good, honey. Stick up for Daddy. You know what I'm getting out of all this mess? Nothing. A lousy house. Cash. And that's it. I've lost my friends, my husband, my daughter, everything. I'm the laughing stock of the fucking country."

Tava was on her feet, slapping the drink from Grace's hand. "You're pathetic. You lost all of us a long time ago."

Grace just sat there, defeated.

"Why do you hate me so much, Mother? What have I ever done to you?"

"Well, to start with, you ruined a perfectly good glass of scotch. Get me another one. I hate drinking from the bottle."

Tava grabbed the bottle from Grace's hands and threw it against the wall. "There's your fucking booze, Mother!"

"Temper, temper, little Tava. I know you want me to feel bad and say I did something wrong. But I'm too tired. I don't have the strength. So you better wise up. This is not a pretty world and you've got to do whatever gets you ahead. You've got to watch your ass, honey, or they're going to take it all away."

Tava was so angry, she couldn't talk. She was fuming and had nowhere to direct her energy. Her mother was right. She wanted Grace to feel remorse, show some sign of repentance. "Do you have any idea what you did to me?"

"Some."

"Doesn't that mean anything to you?"

"Yes, it does. I didn't know what was going to happen. I didn't want any of that happening to you. It didn't make me feel good. I worried about you, for Christ's sake."

For the first time in her life, Tava hit her mother. It was only one slap across the face but in that one move Tava expunged all of her pent-up hatred. With one focused blow to Grace's face, Tava's yearning for her mother's approval ended. It left her quickly and totally. "The sad thing is I know you're lying. Even after all of this you don't care."

She watched the older woman recoil from the blow. Instead of fighting back, Grace sat there while her cheek turned crimson-red. "Not bad, baby. Lesson number one. If someone pushes you, you push back." Instead of laughing this time, the look on her face changed to one of despair. A sadness filled her eyes and she became a pathetically lonely creature. "I'm," she said chokingly, "sorry." The word was said in a hushed tone, barely above a whisper.

Tava stepped away in disgust. "You owe me so much more than that. But I'm learning. I'm learning about you and relationships and life and a lot more. I've learned independence. And the saddest things I've had to learn are hate and distrust. You have wasted your life, Mother, so please stop trying to waste mine." Tava turned and walked to the door. Before leaving, though, she looked back one more time. "I am going to miss the relationship we could have had, Mother. You blew a good chance. I really wanted to love you but you never let me in, and now you've lost me."

Grace was sitting there, a husk of what she used to be, lost and out of words now. She saw a new Tava and felt sad that she would not get to know her. Her eyes welled with glistening tears that slowly dropped down her cheek. She did not bother to brush them away. She sat there, a beaten woman now, alone, tired, and unhappy, and the only thing she could choke out was, "I wish I had loved you. I'm very, very sorry."

Tava considered those words for a moment and felt her own eyes fill. She was taken over with a huge sense of pity, and it was with tears and an enormous sense of loss that she said, "Good-bye, Grace."

59

It was his gentle touch that electrified her. It was more than touching though. She quivered from his gentle stroking. How, Tava wondered to herself, did she deserve all of this happiness?

The plane banked gently to the left and headed south. It was dark outside. The corporate jet was theirs, to wander anywhere in the world they wanted to go. Thomas had it specially outfitted for the young lovers. The expanse was sumptuously appointed. In the rear of the plane a suite was constructed for them. A small kitchen was installed and stocked with their favorite foods. Farther up, a couch and two seats finished off the ensemble. A wet bar and bathroom lay in the front. It was like a flying hotel suite, and the two of them were a little in awe, knowing it was all theirs for the next two months.

The interior of the corporate jet was coordinated in deep, rich roses and burgundies. It radiated the classic, muted stillness of exclusive hotels. It was extravagant and conformed to Thomas's strict wishes. It was meant to be opulent, in a playful way, so that Tava and Michael could enjoy themselves wrapped in the safety of luxury.

Tava was on the bed, in the back of the cabin. Michael, his long, muscular body weaving its spell over her, hovered just next to her. He leaned over and whispered, "I love you."

"That tickles," Tava giggled.

"Good." He said it again. She filled him with so much joy, he wanted to laugh and cry at the same time.

Tava grabbed him around the neck and pulled his lips to hers. She kissed him deeply, trying to press into him, craving his touch, his strength, and his love. She was overwhelmed by the sparkling effects of infatuation. His attention and his support were so important for her. She

him again, this time with tears welling in her pretty
. "I can't get enough of you," she laughed.

They touched hands. Each finger pressed against the
ther. They were silent as they watched their fingers slowly
intertwine, enjoying the intimate warmth of sharing.

"Where do you want to go after Jamaica?" Michael asked.

"I don't care, as long as I'm with you."

"Yeah, but . . ."

"Shhh," she whispered. "Just hold me."

Michael wrapped his arms around her and she closed her
eyes, welcoming his weight. She breathed him in, wanting
the sensation to last forever.

"Tava?" he asked quietly.

"Yes?"

"Will you marry me?"

She nestled farther into him. She looked into his eyes,
kissed him deeply, and answered in a hushed, intimate
breath, "Yes, I'll marry you. I love you Michael, with all my
heart."

They were suspended twenty thousand feet in the air,
utterly, blissfully alone and completely immersed in each
other. And when they cried together, their tears were gentle
and filled with the passion of young love.

About the Author

Valerie Grey is the second oldest of four children. She has lived in Nigeria, Ethiopia, Canada, Brazil and the United States. She graduated from Lewis and Clark College in Portland, Oregon, with degrees in English Literature and Theater. She is happily married and now makes her home in Seattle, Washington.